Secret History

"Long John Pulaski was the first man to die here. Way back when Number Five first opened, in the 1800s."

This was news to Tom, but he had never been one for the local legends.

"One night there was a storm and the next day the river was running really fast. The other men were afraid of the current. But Long John laughed at them and stripped and jumped in. And in no time he was caught in the current and drowned while all his friends stood and watched. They couldn't do anything to help him.

"And he began to take them with him. One by one for days afterward, as the men swam out to Washington Island, Long John would pull them under until they drowned.

"I made a sketch of Long John once. Do you want to see it?"

"Sure."

Alex headed up to his room. In a moment he was back, holding the sketch out to Tom.

He recognized the man in the picture at once. It was the steelworker he had met and talked to in the mill when he was a boy. The one who had vanished. Tom froze. It was the man, down to the last detail. For an instant his mind flashed back to that day, the fire, the blackness around it, talking with the man, seeing his father's death . . .

STEEL GHOSTS

Michael Paine

BERKLEY BOOKS, NEW YORK

THE BERKLEY PUBLISHING GROUP
Published by the Penguin Group
Penguin Group (USA) Inc.
375 Hudson Street, New York, New York 10014, USA
Penguin Group (Canada), 10 Alcorn Avenue, Toronto, Ontario M4V 3B2, Canada
(a division of Pearson Penguin Canada Inc.)
Penguin Books Ltd., 80 Strand, London WC2R 0RL, England
Penguin Group Ireland, 25 St. Stephen's Green, Dublin 2, Ireland (a division of Penguin Books Ltd.)
Penguin Group (Australia), 250 Camberwell Road, Camberwell, Victoria 3124, Australia
(a division of Pearson Australia Group Pty. Ltd.)
Penguin Books India Pvt. Ltd., 11 Community Centre, Panchsheel Park, New Delhi—110 017, India
Penguin Group (NZ), Cnr. Airborne and Rosedale Roads, Albany, Auckland 1310, New Zealand
(a division of Pearson New Zealand Ltd.)
Penguin Books (South Africa) (Pty.) Ltd., 24 Sturdee Avenue, Rosebank, Johannesburg 2196, South
Africa

Penguin Books Ltd., Registered Offices: 80 Strand, London WC2R 0RL, England

This is a work of fiction. Names, characters, places, and incidents either are the product of the author's imagination or are used fictitiously, and any resemblance to actual persons, living or dead, business establishments, events, or locales is entirely coincidental.

STEEL GHOSTS

A Berkley Book / published by arrangement with the author

PRINTING HISTORY
Berkley mass-market edition / January 2005

Copyright © 2005 by John Curlovich.
Cover design by Steven Ferlauto.
Text Design by Stacy Irwin.

ISBN: 0-425-20070-1

BERKLEY®
Berkley Books are published by The Berkley Publishing Group,
a division of Penguin Group (USA) Inc.,
375 Hudson Street, New York, New York 10014.
BERKLEY is a registered trademark of Penguin Group (USA) Inc.
The "B" design is a trademark belonging to Penguin Group (USA) Inc.

PRINTED IN THE UNITED STATES OF AMERICA

10 9 8 7 6 5 4 3 2 1

for Sharon Davis

Prologue

THE NOISE WAS DEAFENING, AT LEAST TO TOMMY Kruvener's ears. All around him were the roar of machinery and the ungodly hiss of molten metal. It seemed to him that the only light came from the furnaces, spewing out rivers of white-hot steel. Steelworkers were everywhere, naked to the waist, their bodies lit in sharp outline by glowing molten metal. The air was unbearably hot, breathing was hard, and all he wanted was to get out.

The tour guide was droning on and on, bored with himself and his job, not even trying to be heard above the din. "This is a Bessemer converter, and it works by . . ." But none of the children in the group seemed to be paying attention. They stared around the huge mill, quite wide-eyed. A few of them seemed frightened, especially the girls; others were simply mesmerized by all the light, sound, and movement. Men worked high on scaffolds and ladders; it looked too precarious.

Mr. Kilbride, the teacher, let his attention drift idly

around the facility. He had seen this too many times before, with too many groups of kids, to find it interesting. But he was not too bored to keep an eye on his students. Billy Vicosz and a boy from another class were passing something back and forth between them and giggling. He slapped them both lightly on the back of the head. "Behave yourselves."

"Yes, sir."

Tommy had not wanted to go. He begged his mother not to sign the permission slip. "Please. I'm afraid."

"Now, Tommy," Mrs. Kruvener had explained patiently, "this is a steel town. Someday you'll be working in the mill yourself."

"No. Not after what happened to dad. Not after the way he died."

"That was four years ago." She was trying to be patient, but it wasn't easy for her. "I've let you skip the class trips to the mill every year because of what happened to your father. But you're ten now. It's time. Steadbridge is a steel town and it's time for you to learn. All the other boys love going there."

"None of them had their dads die there."

"Well, some of them did. Yes."

"Mom, I'm afraid of that place."

But she wasn't to be moved. Tommy went along with his fifth-grade class, toured the mill, and was on edge the whole time. At the entrance gate, under a large red and white sign that read UNITED AMERICAN STEELWORKS NUMBER FIVE, he paused and thought about pretending to be sick. But of course he could not let himself be seen to be weak by the other kids; that would be fatal. And so he went inside.

There seemed to be fires everywhere, and awful noise. It was like a picture of hell in his mother's Bible.

"Now, boys and girls," the guide suddenly shouted, "follow me over here. We're just in time."

Not much caring in time for what, the group of kids followed him obediently. Then, just beside the most enormous blast furnace, they stopped.

"Now watch. Careful not to get too close, though."

Slowly the door of the huge furnace opened. The gigantic crucible began to tilt, and a river of fire poured out before them. Blinding yellow-white-orange-red, so hot and so close they could barely stand it, but they stood there staring in awe. More and more flowed; it seemed an endless stream.

The kids loved it, all but Tommy. They were saying things about how cool it was, man that's great, and on and on.

Tommy, without realizing it, began to back away. Ruth Vinerelli, the girl who lived two doors down from him, saw him and stuck out her tongue at him. "You're such a sissy. Why don't you act like a man?"

He barely heard her. His could not take his eyes off the stream of terrible liquid fire.

A steelworker was standing not too far away. He was a large, muscular man, old enough for Tommy to think him ancient, and dressed in old work clothes, but he looked friendly. His jeans and denim shirt were dirty, his face streaked with grime. Tommy inched back and stood beside him. Looking up at the man, he smiled timidly, hoping this person wouldn't think him a sissy, too. "Hello, sir."

"My name's John." The man frowned at him, but not in an unfriendly way. "Shouldn't be here. You're only a kid."

"They didn't give us any choice." Tommy shrugged and pointed at the teacher.

The steelworker bent down beside him. "Look at that. Look into that liquid fire. It could melt your flesh, it could vaporize you and there'd be nothing left of you but a ghost." Despite the frightening words his voice was deep and calm. "That's what hell looks like. Do you know that? Look at it, boy. That's what it looks like in hell."

Tommy shifted uneasily, not sure what to make of this.

The steelworker moved even nearer. "This plant's been here since before anyone alive now was born. A lot of men have died here. Burned to vapor in the melt, crushed by machinery, suffocated by chemical fumes. Hundreds of men have died here, hundreds and hundreds. And if you look into that moving, burning hell, you can see them. They're there in the metal. If you get close enough, they might even reach out and pull you in with them. Into hell!" He laughed.

Tommy stared into the man's face. He was teasing, playing on what he took to be Tommy's gullibility. Trying to put up a brave front, Tommy said, "That's silly."

"Is it?" The steelworker laughed.

"Yeah. This is just a factory."

"Then what about that?"

There was a sudden rush of steam as if from nowhere.

Suddenly the air was filled with the manic barking of dogs. The man shouted "There!" and pointed. In a flash, without thinking, Tommy looked where he was pointing.

A man stood on a tall shaky ladder. Without warning the ladder tipped over and the man fell headlong into the steaming molten steel. At the last possible instant Tommy caught a glimpse of his horrified face: It was his father. The unseen dogs barked even more loudly.

"Remember!" he cried. His voice was something like a whisper, a hiss, and a cry.

Into the metal he fell, screaming. The molten mass sputtered and spat. Then where the man had been there were only a few faint puffs of smoke, which quickly dissipated in the hot air. The sound of barking faded, then stopped.

"No! No! No! Dad!" Tommy screamed.

Everyone in the tour group turned and looked at him, startled. They seemed not to have seen what happened, and they gaped at him as if he'd made the biggest fool in the world of himself. All the other steelworkers carried on as usual.

Mr. Kilbride rushed over to him. "What are you doing so far away from everyone else? You know we're supposed to stay together."

"That man—he—he—looked like my—"

"What man?"

"The one who fell in the fire. In the melted steel."

"Don't talk nonsense, Tommy. Come on."

In desperation Tommy turned to the steelworker. But the man was gone.

Mr. Kilbride took him forcibly by the hand and led him back to the group. The molten stream was finally tapering off. Tommy watched it, half expecting he would find the faces of dead men there. Bright yellow, white, red, orange ... In the shifting colors he thought he could see ... he thought ...

"What's wrong, Tom?" Ruth Vinerelli had moved beside him.

The sound of her voice helped him shake off the hypnotic effect of the molten steel and horror of the death he had seen. "Nothing."

"You look funny. Why were you talking to yourself?"

"I wasn't. There was a man."

"No there wasn't. You were talking to yourself." She made it clear this made him a fair target for ridicule.

"Never mind. Leave me alone."

Ruth looked around as if she was in the middle of a conspiracy. The group was beginning to move on to the tour's next stop. No one was looking. She quickly threw her arms around Tommy and kissed him, very hard, on the lips.

He pushed her away. "Stop it."

Ruth laughed at him, then went off to Mr. Kilbride and whispered something to him. The teacher looked at Tommy, a bit puzzled, then barked, "Tommy! Get over here with everybody else! I don't want to have to tell you again."

Tommy did so. Mr. Kilbride immediately went back to daydreaming.

The other kids had watched the melt with obvious fascination, as if it were a wonderful, magical toy they couldn't wait to play with. As the group moved away, the last trickle of it flowed out of the furnace, then it stopped. To Tommy's ears, for that last moment, its nightmarish hiss had seemed to conceal whispers and cries.

No. That old steelworker had been playing with his head, that's all. And the pictures in his mother's Bible . . . Hell? Tommy didn't think he believed in any such thing. What did the guy think Tommy was, a kid?

TIME WAS KIND TO TOMMY. TIME, OR THE URGENT needs of his own well-being, made the memory of that trip and what he saw in the mill—what he thought he saw— fade from his memory.

But as his mother had said, Steadbridge was a steel town. The mill loomed over it, huge and ominous, lit with fires like hell, visible from everyplace, quite inescapable. Even after the vision of his father plunging into the fiery metal had faded from his memory, the mill made him uneasy.

As soon as he was old enough, he left. There was a scholarship; then there was the world. All of the things he thought of as boyish, the sexual experiments, the drugs, the religion, were left safely and carefully behind.

His mother died halfway through his freshman year of college. One night he had a nightmare of her falling into white-hot flowing steel too, but when he woke, all he could remember was that his dream had been bad; the details were mercifully gone.

1

"**YEAH, IT'S STILL HERE. BARELY STANDING, I** think, but here." Without thinking about it, he spoke softly, confidentially, into his cell phone.

The shell of United American Steelworks Number Five loomed around him. All the machinery, furnaces, crucibles had long since been hauled away for use elsewhere or to be sold as scrap, but the vast building still stood. The windows, rows of small panes set high in the walls, were cracked and in some cases missing. And they barely served to let in any light. A few cracks and holes in the walls—some big enough to admit a man—allowed more, but not nearly enough to illuminate the place properly.

"Nah, not since I was a kid. The town was dying even then. Why would I have come back?" Tom Kruvener vaguely remembered his schoolboy visit and the impression he had then that most of the light in the place came from glowing steel. But only vaguely.

"No, I think it should be usable. I guess. But it'd be a

good idea to have an engineer check the place out before we buy. I'm not sure how solid it might be."

As he talked, he ambled through the ruin. The place was shrouded in gloom and shadow. Piles of junk and litter covered the floor, though the original concrete was still visible in a lot of places; but most of it was lost in shadow. Those high windows gave some light to the ceiling, but the lower part of the building was quite dark. It seemed . . . not right. From overhead hung cables, chains, ropes, pulleys, plunging down into near-darkness, their ends not quite discernible.

A few birds cheeped and flew around inside; it was too dark and they were too far up for him to get a good look at them. Tom wondered if they were trapped there, unable to find their way out. There were probably rats, too, and snakes, and God knew what else.

"But if it's structurally sound, it should work fine for what we have in mind." His voice echoed faintly in the cavernous space. "No, I can't imagine there'll be any trouble. Whoever owns it now will be glad to get rid of it. There's probably a hundred thousand bucks in back taxes."

In the darkness there was someone whispering. He paused to listen for a moment and was quite sure of it. And faintly, distantly, he thought he could hear the yelping and barking of a pack of dogs.

Then something came swiftly out of the darkness and brushed past his head. He dropped to the filthy floor and covered his eyes. It was one of the birds. Just as it disappeared into the overhead shadows, he saw that it was an owl. Their damned chittering must be what he was hearing. He picked up a pebble and flung it up at the roof, wishing he could see the bird that had swooped at him. A moment later the pebble clattered to the shadowed floor.

He stumbled over a piece of rubble, nearly fell, and dropped his phone. It took him a moment to find it among the litter. When he reached to pick it up, something scuttled away among the rubble.

Brushing off his suit, he went on, "Sorry 'bout that. No, Mike, I can't think why the taxes should be a problem. Once they find out what we want to do here, they'll offer us every tax incentive in the world. Listen, I have to get going. That hotel that used to be here is gone, so I'll have to find a place in another town or out on the main highway. I'll give you a call later or tomorrow. I want to check out the town and see what I can find out."

He put his phone in his breast pocket. Without warning it rang again. "Hello? Oh, no Michael, I don't think they'll have video conferencing. We're talking about a hotel in East Kneecap, Pennsylvania. I'll be damned lucky if they have a bar. Talk to you tomorrow."

In the darkness again he heard someone whispering. This time he was quite sure of it. "Who's there?"

Nothing, no answer, perfect stillness.

"You might as well show yourself. I know you're here."

Nothing. Absolute silence. Well, it would be surprising if tramps didn't hole up in this ruin. Or kids eating drugs, or . . . Then the owls started cheeping and flapping about again. Tom decided he'd had enough for one day. Rather than walk all the way back to the entrance, he pushed his way though a large crack in one of the walls.

Outside it was a blindingly bright late spring afternoon. He emerged on the back side of the building and gave his eyes a moment to adjust. It was more badly rusted than the front; it must face the wind and elements more directly. Idly curious, he pounded the wall with his fist, half expecting to knock a hole in it. It held solid. *Good, the place would be more than usable,* he thought.

A few feet beyond the back of the mill were two pairs of railroad tracks. Ties were missing; some of the rails were gone. Beyond them ran the Monongahela River, deep, turbulent, and dark, swollen with heavy spring rains. A small wrought-iron footbridge led out to what was always called Washington Island, though no one seriously believed George Washington had ever stopped there. Before the plant had closed and the island turned into a jungle of weeds, the steelmen used to take their lunch breaks there. Tom had a distant memory that the bridge was called the Polonski Bridge, or the Pulaski Bridge, or some such. He really couldn't recall.

He circled around to the front. Weeds grew everywhere, half of them dead and brown. The soil had to be unhealthy. More railroad tracks wound through the mill grounds, rusted, ties rotten, unused in years. Where the main gate had stood, there were two metal poles that had once held the sign identifying the place; the sign itself now lay decaying in the weeds. The sight of it, for no obvious reason, made Tom grin.

Dominating everything was a huge brick smokestack, a hundred and twenty feet tall, rising from the back corner of the mill. It was made of yellow brick, but a century or more of use had made it a dull, unattractive brown. A rusted metal staircase spiraled up the outside of it. Tom remembered it from when he was a kid. At night, an enormous tongue of fire leaped from it into the sky, an unnatural beacon announcing the town's presence to . . . to whomever had the misfortune to be in the area, he guessed.

It was cold and dead now, like everything else here. But it was intact, not one brick missing or fallen. He could even see the lightning rod at the top. Tom wondered how it could have stayed up so long while the rest of the mill crumbled.

The factory, vast as it seemed inside, looked even more so from the exterior. To Tom's eyes, it was colossal; not in Rome or Egypt had he seen anything more imposing.

Yet it was somehow all new to him. He had spent his first eighteen years in this town, and the mill had always dominated everything. But all he seemed able to remember was the fiery river inside, mixed somehow with the memory of a girl, and the fire dancing at the top of the smokestack—and that only faintly. Strange realization, that the place where he grew up was lost to him; he forced it out of his mind, not knowing if he found it comfortable or not.

From behind him came a sound, and he turned to see

what it was. A boy came out of the mill, stood, and stared at him. The kid was ten, maybe twelve or so. Thin, pale, freckled, with long black hair and large eyes. Too young for drugs, Tom imagined, or hoped. Except for the shoulder-length hair, he could have been a choirboy off a Christmas card. He had been inside; Tom had known there was someone in there with him.

The kid stared at him for a moment, then laughed at him. "You sh-shouldn't be here." His voice was lower than Tom expected. The stutter was only slight.

"I know." Tom, annoyed at the boy, made himself smile. "We're both trespassers."

"They won't be p-put aside," the boy said.

"Uh, no, I guess they won't."

The boy, like the mill, seemed not right. Tom found himself wishing the building had collapsed years ago, or that it had never occurred to him that it might be a good buy for Overbrook Media. There was something about this boy, not just the stammer, that made Tom think he might have some sort of mental or emotional handicap, something in his manner that . . . He made himself smile again, a tight professional smile. "I'm Mr. Kruvener."

"You shouldn't be here. They won't be p-p-put aside."

Smile. "You already told me that."

"I'm Alex. Grandma Kibben told me to come and tell you."

"Who's that? Tell me what?"

"What I said." There was a sudden gust of wind and the kid's hair blew into his face. He made no move to brush it aside. "Grandma Kibben says you're a damned chump." He laughed.

"She does." Tom kept his voice carefully neutral.

"Don't come back here. A lot of men have died."

Was the boy threatening him? It seemed so completely unlikely. For an instant, Tom flashed back to a long-ago school trip, though he couldn't quite recall why the exchange was triggering a sense of unease.

The boy fell oddly silent. Tom found himself feeling foolish. "Wait a minute. You don't mean Mrs. McKibben, do you? That crazy old woman who used to teach history and civics in the high school?" Everyone had hated her.

"Grandma Kibben."

Uh, right. He had had enough of this. "Well, it was nice meeting you, Alex. But I have to be going now."

"Good. Go. You shouldn't be here."

"Um . . . look . . . um . . . just so you know, I'm not doing anything bad here. I want to make sure . . . I want to make sure there's no more dying around the old place. Okay?"

"It won't work out like that. Grandma Kibben says so. You're b-bringing death with you." He started laughing as if this was the funniest thought in the world. "You're a chump."

"Look, I—" He caught himself. No use trying to reason with this boy. "I have to go. Take it easy."

He turned and headed toward his car. Fumbling in a pocket for his keys he turned around to see what the boy was up to. The kid picked up a piece of concrete and quickly, accurately flung it at Tom's head. Tom ducked to one side.

The boy, laughing quite heartily, ran off, back into the mill.

"You little shit!" The place had to be dangerous, especially for a kid who didn't seem quite right in the head. Tom made a mental note to hire some security as soon as he could. Kids shouldn't be playing here.

There was no one in sight. He found the spot in the chain-link fence where he had pushed his way inside. His BMW was waiting. He had thought there was no need to lock it, not in an area as dead as this. Not in a town as dead as Steadbridge. But that was before Alex showed up. Little shit.

THE TOWN WAS HARDLY MORE THAN A MINUTE'S drive from Number Five. Tom found himself thinking he

should have walked it. Then he came to the intersection of
Columbus Avenue and Laurel Street. The rear of the Parish
of St. Dympna stood tall and ominous, its yellow brick
filthy with years of pollution or soot or just plain dirt. It,
and most of the town, was built from the same yellow brick
as Number Five's smokestack. And it was now the same
unpleasant brown.

He stepped on the brake for a moment. Laurel Street—
his mother's house was there, not far from the church. No,
he couldn't face that quite yet. Just as well he hadn't
decided to walk.

The heart of the town was—or had been—McKinley
Square. The main entrance of St. Dympna's was there. And
it was once the center of a lively little business district—
food shops and bakeries, a hardware store; everything people in a small town like Steadbridge might need, you could
get there. Only a small handful of the stores still seemed to
be open. The ones that weren't boarded up had broken or
missing windows; empty storefronts gaped like death's
heads. At one corner stood the Hippodrome, the town's single movie theater, closed and boarded up like nearly everything else. A few large black letters still hung up on the
marquee, not enough to tell what the last movie had been.

Halfway along the far side of the square, a neon sign
announced Hank's Bar & Grill. More neon in the window,
advertising Stroh's, looked inviting. But Tom decided he
wasn't ready for the smell of stale beer and generations of
cigarettes. Hell, there was probably sawdust on the floor.

There had been a tidy little park planted with seasonal
flowers, always tended by a retired cop with nothing else to
do. In the center of it, where six paved pathways crossed,
was a statue of the plump president, now stained green and
grey with pigeon droppings. The paving on the pathways
was cracked, and chunks were missing; weeds grew up
through cracks. There were no pigeons. Even they had had
the sense to move elsewhere.

For that matter, where were all the people? In the town's

prime, McKinley Square had always been busy and, by Steadbridge standards, crowded. Now . . . there weren't half a dozen people to be seen.

He took it all in and tried not to think about how deeply he hated it. Why had he spoken up at that meeting? "I know the perfect place—an old steel mill in the town where I grew up. It's more than big enough for a couple of sound stages, with room left over for offices, storage, whatever we need. And even if it's not usable, the town's pretty much dead. We could get the land for a song, and it's already developed." Why hadn't it occurred to him that they'd send him to check the place out? "You know the place, Tom, you're the logical guy." Never speak up at meetings.

He ambled around the square. One of the shops still open was McCarthy's McKinley Bakery. They used to have the best jelly donuts. He could always work off the extra calories at the gym. Hell, he'd have to hope the hotel had a gym. But a McCarthy McKinley jelly donut . . . the prospect was simply too good to pass up. One good memory of Steadbridge, at least.

The place was empty, the display cases nearly so. When he came in, a bell rang on the door. Exactly as it had been. Glum thought.

"Be out in a minute," came a woman's voice from the back room.

"No hurry."

There were a few cupcakes, yellow with chocolate icing, a few Danish, a few assorted other pastries. But there was a whole tray of jelly donuts. Tom remembered the place smelling wonderful; today it didn't smell of much anything, which was probably just as well.

A woman who looked ten years older than Tom came out of the back. She had dark hair and was wearing a little baker-shop uniform. "Help you?"

"A jelly donut, please."

"Sixty cents." She reached into the case and got one. "Need a bag?"

"No thanks. I'm going to eat it right away. I haven't had one of these in years."

She handed it to him with a little paper napkin. "You live someplace where they don't make jelly donuts?"

"Not McCarthy McKinley ones, they don't."

"I have news for you, mister, they don't make them here either. These are from a chain."

He bit into it. "I see what you mean. How long has it been . . . ?"

"We bake the bread for the local schools, the old folks' home, and sometimes church events. That's the only real business we do. This place hasn't been a real bakery since the last Ice Age. You want your money back?"

"No, it's okay."

She looked at him like he was crazy.

"Expense account."

"Oh." Her expression didn't change. She started stacking some empty trays. "So somebody's paying you to visit Steadbridge? Nice work if you can get it. I guess. Personally, I'm holding out for Paris."

Tom smiled at her. "Well, Steadbridge has Paris beat in one way, anyhow." He lowered his voice to a mock whisper. "No Parisians."

"You look familiar."

"You probably saw my wanted poster at the post office."

"Probably." She frowned. Then her face lit up. "Tom? Tom Kruvener?"

He had no idea who she was. "Uh . . . yes."

"How can you not recognize me? It's Ruth."

"Ruth Vinerelli?"

"The same. How on earth have you been? And what on earth brought you back here to this dead burg? I remember when you left, you swore—"

"Never say never." He looked her up and down and grinned. "Ruth. It's so good to see you. I figured anybody with any brains would have gotten out of here."

"They did. And it's Ruth Fawcett now."

"Married?" He dropped what was left of his donut into the trash.

"Widowed. It's been ten years. Single mom with a kid. So how could I afford to live anyplace but here?"

"There are always plenty of opportunities for a smart woman."

"Like I said, why do you think I'm here?"

For a moment they stood staring at one another, neither quite knowing what to say next.

"What about you? You have a wife?"

"An ex."

"You always were a coward. Like a cupcake?"

"No thanks. There's no reason for yellow cake to exist."

Another awkward moment of silence.

"So, who else is still here?"

"Oh, not many. When the mill shut down ten years ago, the whole town shut down with it. The population's way less than a quarter of what it was. The biggest thing that's happened here in years was the party Old Man Harvey threw the last night before he closed the Hip. You should have been there. Three drunks fell out of the balcony. It was news for weeks."

"God, I remember going there with you and Bill Vicosz. Sneaking up into that balcony every Saturday for those kids' matinees. Cartoons, crummy horror movies, cheap science fiction . . . Christ, I didn't think I'd feel nostalgia for anything here."

"I don't know why. We all talk about you nonstop."

This caught him off guard. "Uh . . . you are kidding, right?"

"Of course, stupid. Here, try a slice of this cheese bread. It's the best thing we bake. At least it'll get the taste of that donut out of your mouth. Boy, you look great."

"You too, Ruth." He hoped his lie wasn't too transparent.

"I look like hell and you know it. Try raising a kid on your own. On the income from McCarthy's McKinley Bakery."

"Honestly, Ruth, I could never have imagined you working in a place like this."

"It's part-time. I work for the local police department too. Secretary. Part-time."

"Why not get a full-time job?"

"Aren't any. This is an 'economically depressed area.' Places can't afford to pay benefits. There's only one full-time cop."

She looked away.

"Listen, Ruth, why don't you have dinner with me tonight? We can catch up. It looks like I've missed a lot here."

"How can you miss a vacuum?"

"I'm serious. Eight o'clock?"

"There's no one to watch the kid. I leave him with a neighbor lady during the day. She's old. Nights, she goes to the senior citizen center in the next town. She's too old to be driving, but no one can stop her."

"Bring him along, then."

"Not a good idea. He's restless. He'd fidget. Especially with the food you can get here."

"That bad?" He wasn't surprised.

"The best place in town is Walchek's Diner, and you could use their coffee in your transmission."

"Oh." He wanted to get as much information about the local scene as he could, and Ruth seemed like she enjoyed talking. "Tell you what, then. Why don't I bring something? I'll order dinner for three from the hotel."

"Tom, you don't have to."

"I want to. You still live on Laurel?"

"Heavens no. That was my parents' place. Steve and I bought a place over on Regina. Two-thirty-eight."

"I'll be there promptly at eight." He reached for the door.

"Tom?"

He glanced back at her.

"It really is good to see you again."

"You too."

Ruth Vinerelli. Who'd have thought?

Outside, the sky was beginning to cloud up; it was turning dark already, and there'd be rain that night. The evening chill was beginning to touch the air. Off in the far corner of McKinley Square, Tom noticed the tall bronze crucifix on the spire of St. Dympna's. It was brightly polished, just as it had always been. It didn't seem possible the old church was still in use.

Heading back to his car, he passed a storefront with a prominent sign:

GRANDMA MCKIBBEN

PSYCHIC

CLAIRVOYANT

MEDIUM

TAROT READINGS

PALM READINGS

TEA LEAVES READ

SEES ALL, KNOWS ALL

COME IN AND ASK

I KNOW MORE THAN YOU DO

Then underneath was another sign, a hand-lettered one, that said CLOSED—IN CONFERENCE.

On the sign was a drawing of a beautiful young woman dressed as a gypsy. Tom shaded his eyes and peered in through the window but couldn't see anything. Then he tried the door. Locked. Too bad. He wanted to know if this was really the old bat who'd creeped him out so in high-school. She'd be ninety, if not nine hundred. He glanced at the pretty woman in the drawing again. If Pennsylvania enforced its truth-in-advertising laws, this couldn't possibly be her.

He knocked.

No answer.

Again.

From inside came the voice of an old woman. "Go way. Can't you read?"

"Please. I'm looking for someone." He rattled the door-knob. Locked.

"Go home and get drunk. I am."

Oh. Not quite certain what to make of it, he headed for where he'd left the car. He'd have plenty of time to find out about her. If there was anything worth finding out.

Just as he got to his car he felt the first scattered rain-drops. The clouds were ominous; he hoped the storm wouldn't get too bad.

JUST A FEW MOMENTS AFTER TOM LEFT THE square, the boy Alex came around a corner. The wind was kicking up and the sprinkles of rain were a bit heavier. He went straight to the psychic parlor.

"Grandma K-Kibben?" He knocked at the shop door. "Grandma Kibben?"

After a long moment the door opened and Alex put on a bright smile.

Grandma McKibben was indeed ancient. Plump but not pleasingly so, hair unkempt, wearing a housecoat and bed-room slippers. She smelled of what she always told Alex was her "medicine."

"Alex, darling. Come in."

"He's here, Grandma. Just the way you said."

"I know, Alex. He was just here." She closed the door and gestured him through the parlor to the back room.

The boy skipped ahead of her. "Did you talk to him?"

"No. He's one I couldn't face. Not today." She shuffled, unsteady on her feet.

They went through her fortune-telling parlor to the back room. It was furnished sparsely, just a table and chairs, a battered old comfy chair. In one corner stood a corroded bronze floor lamp, its paper shade torn and skewed at an unattractive angle. A TV set rested on a metal stand, and there was a cot in one corner. The TV was on; a game show played noisily. Grandma McKibben turned the volume down but kept one eye on the screen. "Do you want mint tea?"

"Yes, please."

She lit a gas burner and put on the kettle.

Alex fidgeted. "Is there going to be a storm?"

"Not a bad one, Alex." She shuffled to the table and sat down.

"Are they coming out tonight?"

"No, they'll stay in the mill."

"Good. Grandma?"

On the table was a gin bottle; the glass beside it was nearly empty. She poured a tumblerful and drank. "Hm?"

"Will you tell me about Long John Pulaski?"

"Again? Alex, I've told you the story a hundred times."

"Once more, please? I'll never ask again, I promise."

"That's what you said last time. I'm not in the mood." The kettle whistled; she poured water for the boy's tea. Then her eyes narrowed. "What are you doing here? You know you're not supposed to be."

"I ran away from Mrs. O'Donegal again."

"Nobody loves a brat, Alex."

"Tell me again how he died and became the first ghost here."

"Your mother will be getting off work soon. Go over to the bakery and meet her." She dropped an ice cube into the teacup and handed it to Alex.

He sipped it quickly. "Can I drink some gin?"

She drank. "You're being a nuisance today."

"That man who came here. Somebody's going to die, right?"

Long swallow. Nod. "Maybe a lot of people."

Alex smiled. "Good. Maybe I'll see my dad."

From the pocket of her housecoat, she pulled a deck of tarot cards. She fumbled them and dropped more than a few but seemed not to notice. "Watch." She spread them out on the table, then picked one out after another. "These are the Lovers, Alex. And do you know what this one is?"

"Death."

"Right. And this?"

"The Castle." He inspected the card. "The windows are all lit up with fire, like Number Five."

"Now it's time for you to go home to your mother."

"You sure they won't come out tonight?"

"I'm never sure, any more. This stuff doesn't work for me the way it used to." Her fingers caressed the gin bottle.

"Mom says nothing's the same."

"Everything's the same, Alex. The past is never dead. It's not even past."

"I don't know what you mean."

"Good. That's just as well. Go home now."

The boy kissed her on the cheek, holding his breath so as not to smell her "medicine," and left quickly.

"Alex, here! Take an umbrella!"

But he was gone.

It was a relief to the old woman. She took another drink, a long slow one. She had lied to the boy. They were restless tonight. That man. It was his doing.

TOM STARTED THE CAR, SWITCHED ON THE HEAD-lights and wipers, and headed for the Interstate. On the way in, he had passed a Sheraton Motor Lodge that was probably the closest place to stay. It was six miles out of town, along the river road, but what could he do?

Ahead of him, inescapably, loomed Number Five. And there were lights inside. Glowing reddish, yellowish lights. His guess had been right: there were tramps camping in the place, building fires against the already chilly night. He made a mental note: we'll really have to hire security, first thing.

It didn't occur to him to wonder why tramps would need enough campfires to light the place so brightly, or why campfires would pulse and glow so, like the fires of hell. In the distance, he thought he heard a pack of dogs barking, barely audible above the rain.

2

THE HOTEL BAR—YES, THERE WAS ONE—LOOKED
like every bar in every inexpensive hotel in America.
Faux wood paneling, chrome, a TV set tuned to ESPN, and
ferns. Lots of ferns. Tom wondered what would happen to
an alcoholic with a fern allergy.

"Bourbon."

The bartender, a young blond-haired man, nodded ac-
knowledgment and smiled.

"Do they teach you that in bartender school?"

"Teach what?"

"That smile. I swear, every bartender I've ever seen has
that exact same ingratiating-but-neutral smile. They must
teach it to you, in between the fuzzy navels and the zom-
bies."

He poured Tom's drink. "I'm a failed lawyer."

"Oh."

"Three fifty."

Tom put a ten on the bar. "You want to hear something

funny? My colleague back in Manhattan thought this place might have video conferencing."

"We do." He was offhand.

"Oh."

"The owner thought it might attract more business travelers. Funny, huh?"

"A scream. How do I make arrangements for it?"

"At the front desk."

Tom got out his cell phone and dialed Mike's home number. "Hey, it's me. Just checking in."

The bartender switched to the Game Show Network.

"No, things are on track, I guess. Labor here will be dirt-cheap. The town's practically a desert. Somebody told me they've lost three quarters of the population since the mill closed." Wrong thing to say.

A rerun of *Joker's Wild* blared. Tom waved a hand to get the bartender's eye. "Can you turn that down, please?"

The man scowled at him but lowered the volume.

"I'll get some pictures tomorrow if this damned rain stops. No, I'll send them right away. They have the Internet here in the hotel at least. But I'm six miles away from the town here. Would you believe there's no Internet access in Steadbridge itself? Mike, this really is the middle of nowhere. I mean, there's nothing. Anything we'll need, we'll have to have brought in. It could cost a—"

Mike wanted photos. Mike wanted a video conference tomorrow at 4 P.M. Mike was Tom's boss but was five years younger. "No, they don't have video conferencing. I told you."

The bartender shot him a shame-on-you glance.

Tom stuck his tongue out at him. "Sure, Mike, anything you want. Now I have to go. Believe it or not I have a dinner date. With a very talkative native. We were even—well, let's just say we dated when we were kids. Later."

Then, putting on a smile he hoped was a reflection of the bartender's, he said, "Keep the change. Expense account."

He downed his bourbon in one swallow and walked out of the bar.

THE RAIN WAS COMING DOWN HEAVILY AND steadily as he passed Number Five on his way to Ruth's. The fires seemed even brighter. The place must turn into a regular hobo jungle after dark. Well, with all the unemployment, it wasn't surprising.

It took him a while to find Regina St. The fact that he didn't remember pleased him considerably. There had to be some way he could persuade Overbrook not to buy the mill and convert it, but so far nothing he'd come up with had worked. Why had he been so damned persuasive at that first meeting? But then, it wasn't till he actually got back that he realized fully how much he despised the town and everything it represented.

Mental note: Stop talking about the things that might make the place attractive. The labor here isn't cheap, it's unskilled. The factory isn't just old, it's falling down. There had to be all kinds of things he could say.

The problem was, his early pitch had been true. The site really would work for them. If only he could keep anyone else from coming down here. . . .

238 Regina. A dingy little row house in a solid block of them. The rain was even heavier now. At least Ruth's house looked warm. He saw her at the window; then the door opened.

"Tom?" she shouted.

He rolled down his window. "I don't have an umbrella."

"Hold on. I'll be right out."

In a moment they were under the umbrella together, making for the door. Tom carried an extra large pizza. The wind blew, and they both got wet anyway.

"I hope you both like pepperoni."

"We may be poor, but we're not backward enough for

vegetarianism." She shook the umbrella, then put it in the corner behind the door.

Tom put the pizza on an end table. "Sorry, this is all I could find. I wanted to bring something from the hotel but the chef's off sick. Food poisoning."

"It's okay. We both love it."

He looked around the room. It was, as they say, simple and homey. "Where's your boy?"

"Taking his bath. He'll be down in a few minutes. You want a drink?"

"Bourbon if you have it."

"On the rocks?"

He nodded.

"Be right back."

Tom checked out the room. A big overstuffed couch, showing its age. A TV with an antenna, no cable. Lots of bric-a-brac. On the wall beside the door hung a framed photograph of a very pregnant Ruth holding hands with a young man with a goatee and buzz cut. The dead husband.

On another wall hung a portrait of Ruth, not as she was but as she had been when Tom knew her, young, fresh, pretty. And opposite was a painting of the interior of Number Five, midnight dark but with fires glowing, steel flowing. Something about it—he decided it might be the way the artist used color—unsettled him.

"Here." She was back with two tumblers.

"Thanks. Cheers. I wanted to bring some wine, but I forgot Pennsylvania's damned silly liquor laws. I couldn't find a state liquor store."

"It's okay. Everyone in Steadbridge keeps a lot of alcohol in stock. My kitchen could pass for a chemical refinery."

"Is that as ominous as it sounds?"

"There's a state store just north of McKinley Square. It's the only business in town that's still thriving. Well, the only legal business."

Tom laughed. "It used to be mighty easy to score weed here."

"Still is. Problem is, no matter how big a supply comes into town, the price never goes down. Shows you what economists know. Want to see the rest of the place?"

"Later, okay?"

From upstairs came the sound of a door opening and, faintly, the sound of water flowing down the bathtub drain.

"Alex will be down any minute."

"Alex?"

"My kid. He's been wild today. Skipped out on his babysitter. The old lady next door. She needs one of those aluminum walkers. He's way too much for her to handle, but there's really nobody else."

"How old is he?"

"Ten. He's nothing but trouble, but I love him."

Yeah, Tom thought, and he thinks I'm a chump and has a great throwing arm. "Shouldn't he have been in school?"

"Special Ed., two school districts away. The van picks him up in the morning and drops him off at two. He's . . . well, I'll tell you all about it sometime."

Alex came bounding down the steps, pulling a t-shirt over his head. "I smell p-pizza!"

"Alex, your hair's wringing wet. You get back up there and use the dryer."

"But I'm hungry."

"No pizza till you dry your hair. Hear me?"

"But M-mom, I—" Then Alex noticed Tom. For a moment he stood stock still. Something like fear crept into his face. He looked from his mother to Tom and back again.

His mood change seemed not to register with Ruth. "Alex, this is Mr. Kruvener."

"I know." The kid was frozen.

"We've already met," Tom explained to her. "This afternoon. After he ran out on his babysitter, I imagine."

Alex took a step back and away from him. "I'll dry my hair, mom."

"Thank you. And put on a clean t-shirt while you're at it. That one reeks of Mrs. McKibben's 'medicine.' "

"Okay." He went slowly back up the steps, not taking his eyes off Tom.

Ruth took a long drink. "I'm sorry, Tom. Alex is—I'm never certain how he'll react to new people and situations. Let's sit down."

"It's okay." He moved behind her. "You still smell the same, do you know that?" Lightly he stroked the back of her hair.

"I smell of flour and powdered sugar, and you know it."

"No, I mean it."

"Don't be foolish. I look like somebody's spinster sister. Hell, that's just about the way I live, anymore. The lady of a certain age who drinks too much."

"No." He made the lie sound tender.

"Alex was a difficult birth. Actually, he has . . . he was born dead. The medical team managed to resuscitate him, but there was brain damage. He's always had perceptual problems. He can't read. He's a wild boy."

"Ruth." He put his hands on her shoulders and turned her around so she faced him.

Alex came bounding down the stairs, drying his hair with a towel. Tom and Ruth pulled quickly apart.

"Let's eat now, okay?"

Quite unexpectedly he crossed the room to Tom and held out his hand. "Pleased to meet you, Mr. Kruvener." There was no smile.

They shook. "Likewise, Alex. Your mom and I are old friends."

"I know. Grandma Kibben read my cards today. The first one she picked out was the Lovers."

"Alex!" Ruth avoided looking at Tom. "We were *not*—"

"And the second one was Death."

WHILE THEY ATE, RUTH BROUGHT TOM UP TO DATE on all the gossip—who was still here, who was gone, who was in jail, who had died—mostly about people he had happily forgotten, some of whom he couldn't remember at all, no matter how much she prompted him. Alex was mostly silent, eating more pizza than either of the adults, occasionally correcting some detail in Ruth's account. Once or twice Tom caught him staring.

Ruth refreshed their drinks and gave Alex a caffeine-free Coke. Half an hour later, the pizza was eaten and the rain ended.

When he had downed his last slice, Alex jumped up and ran to the window. "It stopped. Let's go for a walk."

Ruth stood up and collected the paper plates and napkins. "That's up to Mr. Kruvener. He's our guest."

Alex turned to him. "Please?"

He did not much want to see any more of the town.

"Mom and I take a walk every night after dinner if the weather's okay."

"Oh. Well, all right then. I can't interrupt your routine."

Ruth carried the trash out to the kitchen. When she came back Alex was holding the front door open. "Let's go."

"Take your pill first."

"When we get back."

"No pill, no walk."

Alex ran upstairs and came back in an instant with a glass of water and a white pill.

"Let me see you take it."

Obediently he made a show of putting it in his mouth and drinking.

"Good. Let's go." To Tom she mouthed the word *Ritalin.*

The streets were still wet, and there was an uncomfortably cool, damp breeze blowing. Puddles filled the cracks and potholes. There were lights in a few houses, not many. Their footsteps echoed. Alex ran ahead, and when Ruth told him to come back, there was another little test of wills. Tom liked her patience and firmness; he could never handle a boy like Alex. For a few moments, they walked without talking.

Now and then Tom glimpsed someone else, always at the edge of his vision, always fleetingly. When he looked again they were gone. One even seemed to glow, maybe in the light from a window; but when Tom tried to get a good look, the person had left. Eerie feeling, that they were alone and yet not alone at all.

"So, how long are you going to be here, Tom?"

"I don't know, a few days, maybe a bit more. My company's looking for an old factory, so I'm checking out Number Five."

"So there might actually be jobs coming here again?"

"It's too early to know." Christ, he hoped not.

"What kind of company?" The kid started running off again. "Alex!"

"Overbrook Media. We do video and TV production. Gearing up to make our first movie."

"That's exciting. I've always seen myself as a new Ava Gardner."

"You'd have to be Linda Blair for this one."

"A horror movie?"

"A cheap, crummy one, with one of the dumbest scripts ever written. But you can make a lot of money off them if you market them right. There's practically no one else in the street. We haven't met anyone face-to-face."

"Not after dark. I'd count my blessings if I were you. But Alex likes it."

Alex jumped into a large puddle, splashing them. She took hold of him firmly by his t-shirt and pulled him out of it. "Those are new shoes."

Tom laughed. "Do you have any idea how much you sound like your mother?"

"Be quiet or I'll give you a pill, too."

"Yes'm."

"It's probably true." She looked faintly abashed. "The past never lets go of us, does it?"

"I wish it would."

"Sometimes I do, too. But then the past is the only thing we actually own, too, the only thing we can really be sure of."

"How morbid."

"Alex, get out of that mud!"

They had walked several blocks and come to St. Dympna's. Light shone faintly through the stained-glass windows. Brighter ones lit the parish house.

"Let's go see Father Bill." Alex ran toward the church.

"Alex! If I have to tell you one more time to—"

"Sorry." He ran back and rejoined them.

Tom looked up at the polished crucifix on the roof. "I'm amazed the place is still in business. Are there enough Catholics left here to make it pay?"

"What a way to talk. But it's true. The Protestants all had sense enough to clear out of here, but Bill manages to keep the place going somehow. The diocese keeps planning to shut it down once and for all, but something always makes them change their minds. So I guess poor St. Dympna's stuck here like the rest of us. Nobody leaves, any more."

"What do you mean? The town's empty."

"I know. But nobody leaves any more. Ten years ago when word leaked out they were closing the mill, there was this huge exodus. People couldn't leave fast enough. But once it actually happened, once the furnaces went cold—I don't know, something changed, somehow. People keep talking about leaving but no one ever does. Some of the older ones even talk about the town being haunted or cursed or something." She looked at Tom and grinned. "Maybe it is. Maybe your company would be crazy to come here. Imagine being trapped here for all eternity, like hell."

Alex had been listening to this and behaving himself. Suddenly he blurted out, "They won't let you take Number Five."

"Who, Alex?" He stooped to get down on one knee, then remembered the street was wet.

"Let's go see Grandma Kibben."

"Absolutely not! You know I don't want you hanging around her." She turned to Tom. "You remember her, don't you? Used to teach history? She was half crazy back then. When her husband and two sons were killed in an accident, she went completely round the bend. She runs a psychic parlor over on the square now. And she's drunk all the time, too. Eighty-two years old and drunk all the time."

"I saw the place today. I didn't think it could be the same woman, but . . . Three members of the same family killed in one accident? Wow, I didn't think the roads here were that dangerous."

"It was an accident at the mill. Electrocuted by a loose power cable. That's when Pat died, too. They were the last ones to die, just before the place closed."

"Your husband?"

She nodded. "Bill used to say it was more a death mill than a steel mill." She made herself smile. "And look what it's done to the town. When the mill died, we all died with it. Well, there are worse curses. I guess."

"Bill Vicosz? God, all these memories crowding back into my poor little brain. When did he get out of here?"

"You don't know? He's still here. Bill's the pastor at St. Dympna's."

He laughed out loud. "You're kidding. He used to sell weed. He used to have sex with everyone in the school, male, female, and indeterminate. He used to listen to metal and steal homework."

This was the first thing they'd said that really caught Alex's attention. "Father Bill was a wild kid, too?"

Ruth bent down and kissed the top of his head. "Maybe

his mother didn't love him enough to make sure he took his Ritalin."

Tom liked the way they looked together. "Your mom's kidding you, Alex. They didn't have Ritalin back then. It was the Old Stone Age. Let's head back, okay? I'm walked out."

"You want to stop in and see Bill?'

"Not tonight. I don't think I could take the piety. Even if it's phony."

"Not from this priest. But you really should stop in and say hi before you leave. You used to be such good friends."

"I will. Promise. Is there someplace we can get dessert?"

"Not unless you want a slice of Walchek's pie. If you don't like it, you can always use it as a paperweight."

"Never mind."

BACK AT THE HOUSE, TOM SETTLED INTO THE couch. It was Alex's bedtime; Ruth sent him upstairs to get ready.

"Well, then. How's it feel to be back in Steadbridge?"

"I'm not sure. I'm feeling a lot of conflicting things."

"Been back to see your parents' place?"

"No." He said the word emphatically.

"You'll have to resolve all that if you move back here."

His voice went cold. "This isn't the only place we're scouting. There are a lot of options, right now."

"Good. I'm still not clear about you're planning, though. To turn the mill into a studio, or what?"

"That's a good possibility, if the engineers and architects say it's feasible. If not, we may demolish the place and put up something new. That would be a great tax write-off for us. The key to the whole thing is doing everything as cheaply as we can."

Alex was standing on the stairs in his pajamas, listening.

"You shouldn't tear it down. They wouldn't like that."

Ruth ignored this, quite pointedly. "Come over here and say good night to me and Mr. Kruvener."

He did so, kissed Ruth, shook Tom's hand. Then he headed upstairs.

"He's a good boy, Tom. He's just got a bit of hell in him. The doctors say he'll calm down when he gets older."

"Listen, I have to get back to my hotel. It's been a long day."

She lowered her eyes. "Spend the night here, maybe?"

"Oh, thanks, Ruth, but I've got a video conference first thing in the morning." He hoped the lie wasn't too obvious. He gestured at the portrait on the wall. "You were a pretty girl. You still are."

"Don't be funny."

"Don't be hard on yourself. You're so good with Alex. Not everyone would be." He stood up. "Who's the artist, anyway?"

"Oh, he did them."

"Alex? That's incredible. He's good."

"Can't read or write a word, but the visual parts of his brain make up for it. He sees the world in a way the rest of us don't, somehow. I guess that's what talent is." She sounded tentative. "I hope he didn't cause any trouble for you today. He really is a good boy."

"Seeing him with you, I can tell. Mind if I use the bathroom before I go?"

"Upstairs, on the left."

The door to Alex's bedroom was open. It was small, and it was exactly the kind of mess boys' bedrooms always are. There was a desk covered with art supplies, sketchbooks, and canvases. He was in bed, reading a comic book. Tom knocked lightly. "Your mom said you don't read."

"I like the pictures. Someday I want to be an artist."

"You already are one. A good one. I saw the painting of

your mom downstairs. It's just what she used to look like."

"I know."

Odd response; Tom wasn't sure what the boy meant. "Listen, I don't think we got off on the right foot today. I'd like us to be friends."

"Okay." His voice was neutral.

"I'll—I'll see you again."

"Okay."

"Good night, Alex." He turned to go. A charcoal sketch on the desk caught his eye. A steelworker on a ladder, tumbling, about to plunge into a flow of molten metal. Tom recognized the face: it was his father. And suddenly his own boyhood vision came back to him. For a moment he turned to stone. There were things he wanted to ask the boy, but there was no way he could think of to do it without feeling foolish. Then, slowly, watching Alex who was watching him, he left Alex's bedroom.

A few moments later he was downstairs, saying good night to Ruth. In the doorway he kissed her lightly on the cheek, and she walked him to his car. A few scattered drops of rain came down, then stopped.

"Tom? Don't let them build your studio here. Don't move back here. It's already making you unhappy. I can see it."

"I've been unhappy since I became an adult."

"No, I mean it. It's doing that to you. It must. Everyone here is unhappy. And none of us can do a thing about it."

It was the last thing he wanted to hear. "Ruth, what's wrong here? Something's happened to this town, something worse—or more—than just having the mill close."

"Nothing, Tom. It's just a dying steel town. You don't belong here. It's so wonderful seeing you again, and I feel terrible saying it, but you should go. Now, and while you can."

"You're not making any sense."

"No. Believe me, Tom, I know it." She kissed him impulsively, very hard, then rushed back into the house.

He called good night after her and got into his car. Driving back, he took a long route that kept the mill out of sight.

When he got to his hotel he made straight for the bar. A woman bartender was on duty. He put a fifty on the bar and told her to keep the bourbon coming.

3

"**T**OM!"
     A dark swirl of fire and smoke, driven by the throb
of machinery and the barking of dogs, drifted gradually
into the plywood furniture and kitschy paintings of his
hotel room. Someone pounded relentlessly at the door.

"Tom! Get up!"

He groaned and rolled over. "Go away. Can't you see
the DO NOT DISTURB sign on the door?"

"That's how we know you're in there."

"Go away!"

Brief pause. More pounding. "Open up."

"All right, all right, just a minute." Slowly he pulled
himself out of bed and looked around for his shorts. They
were nowhere in sight. He wrapped the bedspread around
himself and shuffled lethargically to the door. Throwing
the bolt he muttered, "That sign means you're not supposed to make up the room now."

Standing there were his boss, Mike Cavendish, and a colleague, Melissa Fortenski. They were both dressed in business clothes and were grinning artificially, like bartenders.

"What the hell are you doing here? And on a Saturday?"

"Same as you, Tommy." Mike was the picture of blond jock heartiness. "Checking out Number Five."

"It isn't in here. Go away."

"Dear, dear." Melissa pushed her way past Tom and into the room. She was in her late twenties, immaculately coiffed and made up, blue suit, always efficient. "I think our Tom's been drinking." She looked around the room and wrinkled her nose. "Probably on his expense account."

Tom pulled the bedspread more tightly around himself. "It doesn't take Nancy Drew to figure that out. You might have let me know you were coming."

Melissa looked him up and down and grinned. "You should spend more time at the gym."

"Didn't know ourselves till the last moment." Mike got between them, pulled a chair to himself and sat down. "None of the other prospects seems to be panning out. We thought we'd come down here and see what the place is like."

Swell. "Even so." He said pointedly to Melissa, "There is such a thing as professional courtesy. This is my project."

"Overbrook's project." She smiled to show she meant it seriously.

"My assignment, then." He sat on edge of the bed. "This really isn't working out either. It'd be a big mistake to locate here."

"If you say so, Tom. We're not trying to undercut your authority, believe me." Mike noticed a near-empty bottle on the desk. He reached over and sniffed. "If this is the best liquor you can get here, you're right."

"Wait till you try to get a jelly donut."

"I beg your pardon?" Melissa crossed to Mike and took

the bottle. She inspected the label and laughed. "This is Siberia with cheap bourbon."

"It's not even that cheap. The state has a liquor monopoly. Left over from when they repealed Prohibition."

"You're kidding."

He sat on the bed. "No one this hung over ever kids, Melissa. You ever hear the classic description of Pennsylvania? 'Two cities separated by Alabama.' Why don't you both get checked in while I shower and dress. I'll meet you for breakfast."

Melissa grinned. "Shoofly pie and apple pandowdy?"

"We'd be lucky to get that."

"Actually," Mike yawned and scratched himself, "we've already checked in. We were supposed to be here last night but we got lost on the way out here from Pittsburgh. All these damned back-country roads. Ended up in a place called Mill Creek or something."

"Christ, that's sixty miles from here."

"Eighty five, but who's counting? Anyway, we drove most of the night. We both need some sleep. But breakfast first sounds good."

"It was a fascinating drive, though. We saw three deer, four raccoons, and a skunk." Melissa's voice sloshed over with irony. "Ah sho does envy whoever ends up having to live in these here parts, bub." She looked pointedly at Tom; the message was unmistakable, and his hung-over heart sank even more.

Mike jumped energetically to his feet. "We'll meet you in the lobby in fifteen minutes, then you can give us a full report."

He eyed his bed longingly. "Make it half an hour. Or better yet, how about breakfast tomorrow?"

"Nine o'clock, then." Mike was all heartiness as he set his little watch alarm; Tom despised him. "How's the food in the hotel?"

"It's pretty much our only choice. Unless you want to sample the haute cuisine at that Denny's down the road."

"You always did have a sick sense of humor. It's good to see you, Tom." Melissa gave Tom a quick peck on the cheek, which he didn't believe for a moment and which she didn't expect him to.

Grandly, as if they were doing him a favor, which they were, they swept out of his room and closed the door behind them. Tom looked through the peephole and they were kissing in the hallway, with Mike fondling Melissa's breasts. He found himself wondering if it would be possible to use the video conferencing cameras to get pictures of what they were really up to, the real purpose of their trip, for her husband and his wife.

AN HOUR LATER, AFTER A LONG HOT SHOWER AND three Alka Seltzers, Tom stumbled into the lobby. He was in shorts, sneakers, and a t-shirt. Mike and Melissa were still in their business clothes, sitting on a couch reading newspapers. They looked unhappy, which pleased him.

He made his entrance parodying Mike's energy. "Morning, cruisers. Everyone on deck now! Time for shuffleboard!"

"Shut up, Tom." Mike got to his feet and straightened his tie. "You might have dressed."

"I'm going to be rooting around in the ruins of a steel mill. Armani didn't seem right."

"Just look at this news item." Melissa handed Mike her paper. "Farmer Hartman's brood sow is with pig again." She frowned at Tom. "And you told us this place was dull."

They were the last people in the world Tom wanted to be with. "Let's get some breakfast."

Mike yawned. "Yeah. Then we're heading to bed."

"To each his own." He couldn't resist. Melissa shot him a dirty glance; Mike seemed not to catch it.

The waiter, apparently a highschool kid, hovered. The breakfast menus were printed in bright red on bright yellow stock. Tom lost his appetite the minute he saw it. "Just coffee for me."

"Same here." Mike yawned even more deeply.

Melissa ordered eggs sunny side down and glared at Tom to warn him not to make any wisecracks.

"So." Suddenly Mike was all business. "Tell us all about Steadbridge."

The waiter poured coffee. Tom sipped his; it was awful. "Not much to tell. The mill's a shambles. It'll cost a fortune to renovate it. I'd say pulling it down and rebuilding would be cheaper."

Melissa tasted her coffee. "This isn't bad. Not Starbucks, but . . ."

"Local secret. They grind up boll weevils and add them to the grounds."

She froze. "You are joking. Aren't you?"

"Yes, Melissa. This is Pennsylvania, not Texas."

"So far I haven't noticed much difference."

"Wait till you meet the locals." He took a long gulp.

Mike tasted his coffee and made a sour face. "What about them?"

"That'll be a problem. There doesn't seem to be anybody left in Steadbridge but old people and kids too young to leave. I don't know where we'd find any labor."

"They'll come when we post the jobs." Mike sounded quite confident. "We were thinking if we implode the mill, we could film it. Make a spectacular finale for *The Colors of Hell*." He got out his PDA and made a note for himself. "Very cost effective."

"Is that what we're calling it now?"

Melissa smiled sheepishly. "Dumb titles sell. Or so all the pros tell us."

"Some pros."

She had the waiter refill her cup. "Those pros aren't half as dumb as the prose in the screenplay. Have you seen the latest draft?"

"No. I'll offer a prayer of thanks to St. Dympna."

"Saint who?!?"

"St. Dympna. The local Catholic church is named for her. She's the patron saint of the nervous and emotionally disturbed."

"We've come to the right place." Her eggs came. She dug in.

Mike drained his cup. "She'd make a killing in Manhattan."

"Anyway, look, both of you. You've seen how remote this place is. There aren't even marked roads to get you here. This is no place for Overbrook."

"We'll get proper signage when we butter up the local politicians."

The waiter was back. "You guys opening some kind of business here?"

Mike sat back in his chair. "A movie studio. What do you think of the idea?"

"That's great! Will we get to meet Tom Cruise?"

"Not on our first project, no. But you think people around here would like the idea? Would people want to work there?" Mike smiled at the kid, as if his nosiness was welcome for some reason.

"Sure! You'd have guys coming down from Johnstown and Altoona and everything!" The boy was beaming. "When do we start?"

Tom decided to interrupt the euphoria. "Nothing's definite yet. We're just here looking around."

"Oh." The kid's high spirits dropped like a rock. Then, "Hey! Maybe you could make video games too!"

"We'll have to think about it."

"Great!" The kid refilled their cups and bounced away.

Melissa grinned. "And while we're at it, why don't we make Pokémon cards, too?" Her hand was under the table; it was fairly obvious she was rubbing Mike's thigh.

Still again Mike yawned. "Look, I'm spent. Melissa and

I are going to get some sleep. Why don't you meet us for dinner, then we can go into Steadbridge and look around."

"That sounds good." He'd be away from them for the day, then. "Six o'clock?"

"Sounds perfect. We'll see you then."

"What are your room numbers?" They hesitated. "I might need to talk to you."

They told him. "But we'll be sleeping all day."

"Be sure to hang your DO NOT DISTURB signs on your doors."

Abruptly the little business breakfast ended. Tom tried not to picture them in bed together. Not even he had a sense of humor that dark.

AFTER A FEW HOURS MORE SLEEP, TOM DROVE slowly into town, looking for unattractive things to show his colleagues. Steadbridge in bright sunlight was every bit as ugly as Steadbridge on an overcast day. The rust was redder and the soot blacker, that was all. He hoped the town's stark emptiness would speak for itself, that it would look like a ruin instead of an opportunity.

He parked outside Number Five and tried to imagine it all cleaned up and renovated with a big Overbrook Media sign in front. He couldn't. After a moment, he was inside. He paused. "Alex?" No sign of the kid. No surprise, he guessed; he must go to school sometime.

The sunlight pouring in through cracks and windows only made the shadows seem darker. There was no one in sight. Where did the tramps go in the daytime? Why didn't at least a few of them stay longer? How could so many men camp here and leave no trace of themselves?

He walked quickly to the far end of the building, where the offices had been. Shaky stairs and a catwalk led up to and connected them. He started to climb, but the structure was too shaky and he scrambled quickly back to the floor.

It didn't stop swaying and creaking for more than a minute.
The offices seemed ready to collapse. He pictured Melissa
in the worst of them, tried to conjure an image of her face
as it crumbled around her. No use. Too hung over for his
brain to work that creatively.

One of the damned owls swooped at him, not as closely
as the one yesterday. He shouted at it: "Hey!" and in an
instant a swarm of them filled the air, circling him. Why
couldn't they be cardinals or jays, anything to give the
place a touch of color?

With his toe he turned over a loose piece of concrete. A
garter snake slithered rapidly away.

There was no point being here. The engineers would see
things he never could. He decided to walk into town.

THE BRONZE CROSS ATOP ST. DYMPNA'S BLAZED
brilliantly in the noonday sun. McKinley Square needed
flowers. The bright day made it all so dreary. A few very
old people walked around the square, some with canes or
walkers. Children accompanied some of them. These people couldn't be the parents. He thought of Ruth, leaving
Alex with an elderly babysitter while she worked. Worked
for a pittance. She deserved a better life than that.

Ruth.

He had enjoyed her company the previous night more
than he wanted to admit. Without thinking about it, he
headed toward the bakery.

Ruth wasn't there. Another woman in a uniform, a
woman in late middle age, stared at him as he stood in the
doorway.

"Is Ruth here?"

"Why?"

"I wanted to see her, that's all."

"Why? Who are you?"

No sense going in. "Nobody." Maybe Ruth was at her
other job.

Grandma McKibben's shop was still closed. He knocked and there was no answer.

So: There was McKinley Square, there was the rest of Steadbridge, there was Number Five, and all of it seemed to add up to nothing. The first time he ever got drunk, when he was fourteen, with Billy Vicosz, they had vomited on the base of the statue. Shocking disrespect for such a weighty president. He remembered seeing pigeons peck at the bits of food in it. Why, of all the memories, had that one come back?

Bill. For a moment Tom stared at the facade of St. Dympna's. Yellow brick, covered with grime. Sections of two stained glass windows replaced by squares of cardboard. There was no way he could face Bill. *Father* Bill. Not possible. The things they used to do together . . .

Maybe he should have a jelly donut. Maybe this one would be better. Maybe there was something good left in Steadbridge. The thought was foolish and he forced it out of his mind.

The Hippodrome. The one place in town Tom remembered fondly. He ambled over to it. The marquee seemed ready to fall; like everything else in town, it was covered with rust. He tried to figure out, from the remaining letters, what the last movie had been. E—NA—T—. *Terminator 2*? He stood staring up at it, as if somehow more letters might appear.

"Why don't you buy a vowel?"

Tom turned to see who it was. A man about his own age. Thick black hair, thick black horn-rimmed glasses. Goofy smile. It was Bill Vicosz. Shorts, polo shirt, sandals, nothing remotely priestly about him.

"Bill!" Impulsively Tom ran and put his arms around him. "You drugged-out son of a bitch! It's great to see you!" He wasn't sure he meant it. But at least Bill wasn't rusted and rotting. Not to appearances, anyway.

"Tom." They hugged and patted each other's backs. "Ruth called me this morning and told me you were here."

"She would."

"Why, is it a state secret or something? That's Number Five up the road, not Fort Knox."

"You look good, Bill. For a priest, that is. Ruth said so." Bill was tall, thin and pale, unshaven, and his black hair seemed not to have been combed; he did not look good, not at all.

"There aren't many of us left from our old crowd. And we all talk too much." He laughed. "But we never seem to say much. Steadbridge. Let me buy you a jelly donut."

"They're from a chain."

"Believe me, I know it. But they're the best we can get. How 'bout a sandwich at Walchek's?"

"No thanks. I had to take a close-up look at the old Hip. I swear, it's the only thing in this sinkhole I have any fond memories of."

"Me, too. I try not to think about it too much."

In one of the display cases there was still most of a hand-lettered poster. Tom crossed to it and read:

KIDS' MATINEE SATURDAY

LON CHANEY IN

THE INDESTRUCTIBLE MAN

17 CARTOONS

"Jesus," Tom laughed, "Did he keep showing *The Indestructible Man* right up to the end? It must have been the kids' feature every other Saturday since the Depression. The first one, I mean. Whole generations of Steadbridge kids must know that turkey by heart."

"I can't imagine there was a cheaper movie he could rent."

The original ticket booth was still there, standing under the marquee instead of inside the lobby. Tom pried the door open and stepped inside. The brass fittings were all corroded to a vivid green. There was a smell of stale urine.

"I always wondered what it would feel like to be inside this thing. It was a position of power." He punched a few of the buttons, which were of course unresponsive. "You can't go home again. Not that I want to."

"It's even worse when you can't leave."

"Ruth said something like that last night. Why don't people just . . . just leave, and let this place die for real. I did."

"I still remember us sneaking up to the balcony to smoke dope."

Tom broke out in a grin. "It was the only way to watch *The Indestructible Man.*"

"Or any of the other movies we got. Remember those Sunday night revivals? Watching the dead perform up there in front of us. W.C. Fields, Bette Davis, Clark Gable. How I loved them all. Still do. But they're not the same on video. Did you know *The Indestructible Man* was directed by a phantom?"

"I didn't think anyone directed it. It just kind of happened, by accident, in front of a camera."

"No, really, it was credited to a guy named Jack Pollexfen. I did some research once, tried to find out about him. He's not listed in any existing reference book. A phantom, a wraith."

Tom wasn't sure whether this was idle nostalgia or whether Bill was trying to tell him something. Bill's face, priestlike, was giving away nothing. "You want to go inside?"

"In there?" Tom glanced at the doors, which were chained and padlocked.

"There's a side door. The one we used to sneak in through, back when. I like to go in and sit in the dark and remember." He pulled a pint of whiskey out of his back pocket. "And forget."

"Does it still smell of stale gum inside?"

"You remember too. Steadbridge has more of a hold on you than you thought, doesn't it? The past never lets us go." He took a drink and handed the bottle to Tom.

Tom sipped. It was too early to get drunk. "I detect a certain monotony in the conversation here. You and Ruth sound so much alike."

"We have the same things on our minds."

There was an awkward pause.

Bill seemed to want to hold onto him, as if he didn't get enough company. "I swear, there are times I can see ghosts inside this old dump. Bogart, Bacall, Hepburn . . . The screen's torn, there's a huge gash across it, but the images, they're still there, somehow."

Tom took a drink and handed the bottle back to him. "I'm not sure I like the sound of that. What happened here, Bill? Why is this place so . . . so . . ."

"Come on."

Tom followed him around to the side of the building. There was a fire door hanging just slightly open. Bill pried it open wider and grinned. "The exact same one we used to sneak in through. Remember?" The interior was black.

He remembered. "Let's not go in."

"Don't be silly. Bogey's waiting for us." He stepped inside.

Reluctantly Tom followed. The darkness inside wasn't quite total. Cracks in the roof and walls let in sunlight. Shafts of light pierced the darkness, as at Number Five. "It looks like a Spielberg movie." Seats were torn up. Garbage littered the floor. There was indeed a diagonal gash in the screen, from the top corner nearly to the bottom.

Bill shouted, "Frankly, my dear, I don't give a damn." His voice echoed, and there was the sound of a great many wings. He smiled lopsidedly at Tom. And took another drink. "Bats. I like to scare them. They're in my theater."

Tom sniffed the air. "This place still smells the same. There's a layer of dust or dirt over top of it, but I'd know the smell anywhere."

"See. The town's got a grip on you, more than you want to admit. You'll never leave, now. You'll never get it out of your blood." He passed the bottle back.

Tom took it. It was nearly empty—no chance of getting really drunk. He drained it. "Let's get out of here."

"I want to show you the balcony."

"No thanks."

From somewhere behind them Tom heard a voice. He was certain of it. He turned to face it. There was no one. Annoyed, he went to take another drink, then realized the bottle was empty. At the edge of his vision he saw someone standing, watching them. He turned quickly to face whoever it was. There was no one there.

"Do tramps hang out in here, too?"

"What do you mean?"

"Like they do in the mill."

"You've got it wrong, Tom. There's nobody living in the mill. Do you understand that?"

"I've seen them. Well, I've seen their lights."

"No, Tom. Just stay away from the place. Will you do that?"

"I can't. Duty calls."

"You have a duty to stay alive."

"Like you? Is this living?" He gestured around them, then realized what he'd said. "Sorry, Bill. I didn't mean that. Can we please get out of here?"

"Come on over to my place. We can talk some more. Catch up. There's a fully stocked liquor cabinet."

"Does everybody here drink?"

"Well, you know, heroin's too expensive."

Tom wasn't sure if he was joking.

Back outside the sunlight blinded them for a moment.

"Come on. Right across the square. How long has it been since you've been in a church?"

"Frankly, my dear, I don't give a damn."

"Sure you won't have a donut?"

"No thanks."

"Go on, spoil all my fun."

In a moment they reached the church, and Bill pulled open the heavy front door. Tom stepped inside, hoping there would be no more unhappy memories. He was pleased to realize that seeing the place left him feeling nothing.

The church had been designed to suggest the interior of a stable, very Christmasy. Exposed beams in the ceiling; rough-hewn, rustic pews. There was a smell of incense, long years or even decades of it; it reminded him of the aroma in the Hip. Same business, one way or the other, he figured. Selling the long-dead to the hungry living. A small group of very old women sat in the last pew, praying the rosary. Tom wondered if they were the same ones who'd always been there when he was a kid.

"Widows," Bill whispered. "Steadbridge has a lot of those."

At one corner a flight of steps ascended to the steeple. Tom found himself smiling. "I always wanted to go up there when I was a kid. Like sneaking into the balcony at the Hip. Can we take a look now?"

"It's not safe. Sooner or later, when we have the money, we'll have to have it pulled down."

"Who rings those god-awful discordant bells?"

"Why, Quasimodo, of course."

They ambled up the central aisle. Tom remembered more of the place than he wanted to. "You actually say Mass and all that?"

"Yep."

"That's got to be a sight to behold."

"Come and behold it, then."

Tom kept silent.

In a moment they were at the altar. Bill made straight for a door to one side. "Come on. This way to the rectory."

"Aren't you supposed to genuflect or something?"

"Don't be primitive."

A long, narrow passage connected the church to the priest-house. Small stained-glass windows lined its walls. In a moment, they were there.

Bill put on an overly hearty manner. "Morning, Mrs. Charnocki."

The housekeeper glanced at them and said nothing. She was washing dishes. Plump, elderly, hair in a bun. She looked as if she hadn't approved of anything for decades.

"You remember Tom Kruvener, don't you? He used to be a member of our parish."

She glared at Tom. "He used to talk during Mass. He used to laugh at us saying out rosaries in the last pew."

"He probably still does."

Tom put on a smile; he hoped she could see how insincere it was. "I promise you, Mrs. Charnocki, I don't talk in church any more."

She snorted and went back to her dishes.

"Come on." Bill held open a door. "Come into my parlor."

"How many innocent boys have heard that one?"

Mrs. Charnocki slammed down a platter and stared daggers at Tom. Bill laughed at her, or at both of them. "When I meet an innocent boy, I'll let you know."

The parlor smelled old, which it was. A huge mahogany desk, heavy brocade drapes, books lining the walls. Tom glanced at a few titles. They were in Latin. "You can read these?"

"Of course not. I'm a priest, not a scholar. Here." He opened a cabinet and took out a bottle of bourbon.

"No, Bill, really, it's way too early."

Bill filled two glasses and held one out to him. "Get drunk with me. Once, for old times's sake."

"I have a job to do."

"All the more reason."

"I really shouldn't."

"Ruth said something about a movie studio coming here."

"Not if I can help it. We're just scouting possible sites. I—I don't want to live back here."

"You might not have any choice."

"Are we going to debate the existence of free will?"

Bill laughed and pushed the glass into his hand. "You're still a handsome guy, Tom. Drink. For auld lang syne."

Tom stared at the glass in his hand, then took a quick swallow. Bill gestured at a pair of overstuffed leather chairs, and they sat.

"What's going on here, Bill? What's wrong in this town?"

Bill smiled. "Pretty much what you see. The place is dead, but there's still life in it. Or maybe it's the other way around. You want to get high?"

"In St. Dympna's rectory? My conscience couldn't bear it."

"You're a movie executive. You're not supposed to have a conscience."

He laughed. "My memory then. I keep seeing things—people—phantoms or something, out of the corner of my eye. Last night in the street, just now in the Hip. When I try to look at them, they're gone."

"Gone but not forgotten."

Tom took another drink, a longer one. "I keep expecting to see my father. And he'll still be drunk, and he'll still be beating my mother. And me, for that matter."

"You were such a sad kid. I loved you, you know. Really loved you."

"I know. You and Ruth. You were the only ones who ever—Jesus, listen to me. I haven't had that much to drink but I'm getting maudlin."

"Well, you've come to the right place." Bill crossed to the liquor cabinet and opened it so Tom could see. "Fully stocked. 'Sufficient unto the day is the evil thereof.' "

"Does the bishop know?"

"He's my supplier. Besides, bishops are good at keeping secrets. Get out of Steadbridge, Tom. Now. While you can. Your father really is waiting for you. Maybe not literally, but . . ." He let his voice trail off, smiled, drank.

And Tom drank, too. Bill had been such a strange kid, always aware what Tom was thinking and feeling.

"Come on. Let me show you the rest of the house before we come back here and get serious."

"No. One more glare from Mrs. Charnocki and I'll turn into stone."

"Leave the old bat to me."

Unsteady, and fully meaning to get unsteadier, they lurched off to see the rest of the rectory, arms around each other's waists.

"You know," Tom stage-whispered, "I don't think I've ever been inside a church when there weren't old women in the back. Do they come with the place? Do they pay rent? Do they get mail here?"

"Steadbridge doesn't forget its dead, Tom." Very softly he added, "And they don't forget us."

SIX O'CLOCK. MIKE AND MELISSA WERE STILL IN bed. Melissa sat up and looked at her watch. "Mike, get up. It's six. He'll be here any time."

Mike pulled her down and kissed her left breast.

"Stop it. We have to shower and dress. Kruvener's probably waiting for us down in the lobby."

"Let him wait. I want to lick something."

"Don't be cute. Get up."

Sullenly they showered together. Their coupling had not been exactly successful for either.

It was quarter to seven when they got to the lobby looking, they hoped, fresh and innocent. There was no sign of Tom.

They asked at the desk. "Not in."

"The jerk wouldn't stand us up, would he?" Melissa's dignity was affronted.

"Yeah, he would. I've worked with him a lot longer than you have. But it's probably something dumb, like a flat tire or something."

"I'm starved. Let's eat."

The chef was still off. The waiter microwaved a pair of frozen dinners for them. They ate without talking much. Melissa's only comment was, "Maybe he's right. Even by hotel food standards this is awful. Would you want to live in a place where Swanson's passes for cuisine?"

"We don't have to live here. Do you really care what we feed actors and screenwriters?"

"They'll demand catering. With good food."

"This is a goddamned B horror movie. None of them will have that kind of clout."

She speared a piece of chicken with her fork. "There has to be someplace to eat better than this."

"Are you kidding? We're lucky the hotel doesn't have a Mail Pouch Tobacco sign on the side."

At seven thirty they were finished, and there was still no sign of Tom. They stood in the lobby for a moment, feigning shock at his unprofessional behavior.

"Maybe he's found himself a little girlfriend, Mike."

"Or a boyfriend. I've always wondered about him."

"He's not that imaginative."

They decided to drive into Steadbridge themselves. Being careful to get accurate directions from the desk clerk, they headed east along the Monongahela. There were no road signs. Melissa thought the river was pretty, even though it was still running high, swift, and muddy.

When the mill finally rose up in front of them it came as a relief. It was twilight; night would fall soon enough. Mike cruised to a stop at almost the same spot where Tom had parked. His car was still there. "At least we found our way here."

"Now if can only find our way back. I've never been to a place like this."

"I have, once or twice. Believe me, you haven't learned enough to hate it yet. Besides, we can follow Kruvener. He'll know the way."

There before them was Number Five, enormous and

decaying. They got out of the car and gaped at the smoke-stack like tourists.

"I shouldn't have worn heels."

"Kruvener was right about something, for once." He shouted "Tom!" as loud as he could, then waited for a response. There was none.

"The future home of Overbrook Pictures. What a dump." Melissa picked a wildflower from among the weeds, sniffed it and threw it away.

"We're calling it something else. The board doesn't want it known that Overbrook Media produces schlock tits-and-gore movies. But Kruvener's right, we should just pull the damned thing down. Anything we build would be better."

They walked around the outside of the mill.

"Tom! Tom Kruvener!"

Nothing.

An orange-and-white cat sat on the spiral staircase a few feet above them cleaning itself. Melissa tried to get it to come to her but instead it climbed higher up the smoke-stack.

Mike craned his neck to look up at the top of it. "That'll look damned impressive when we knock it down. Down-right spectacular."

Melissa stepped onto Pulaski Bridge, to walk out to the island. It shuddered under her step and she pulled aback. "This goes too."

She stared down into the swiftly running river. "Mike! Oh, my God, Mike!

"What's wrong?"

"Someone's drowned. There's a man's body down there."

She forced herself to look again. He was a huge man, muscular, middle-aged, and dressed in work clothes. His jeans and denim shirt were dirty, his face streaked with grime.

"God, Mike, get on your cell phone and call 911!"

Mike moved beside her and looked down into the water. There was nothing. "Where? I don't see a thing."

"He was there, Mike. I swear I saw him."

"Of course you did. Let's go inside."

She moved closer to the bank. "I am telling you, Michael, there was a drowned man there, right under the bridge."

"Well, he's not there now, is he? Even if you really saw something, it'll be miles downriver by the time the police get here. We don't want to begin Overbrook's involvement here that way."

She stepped back and took hold of his arm, as if she was afraid the riverbank might collapse under them. "I guess you're right." She pretended to dust off her blouse.

"Now come on, Melissa. Let's check the place out."

"Are you serious? We've done our duty. We know what to recommend. Now let's go back to that alleged hotel and fuck our brains out. We can book a return flight for the morning."

"No, I want to see the inside. The more detailed our report, the better."

"I'm not dressed for it."

"It's a steel mill, not an Alp. You'll be fine. Besides, Kruvener's around here someplace. I want to see what he's up to. Come on."

He pried open a door, and held it for her. In an instant they were inside, staring at what Tom had seen before them. Owls chittered in the darkness. For a long moment they stood still, gaping at the monstrous space around them. Nearly everything was in shadow. Neither of them seemed to want to break the silence.

Finally Mike shouted, "Kruvener!"

More silence.

"Where can the dumb bastard be?"

Melissa took a step away from Mike. "Well, I suppose I can see this place redone as a sound stage. It could be usable."

"I want my implosion."

"I think you'll get it." She picked up a small piece of cement, inspected it briefly and tossed it aside. "If you work fast, that is. This place seems to be falling down already."

"Or would it be more fun to demolish it piece by piece, and film that?" He didn't give her time to answer. "No. An implosion will be the thing. That thundering cloud of dust, the incredible sight of all this collapsing to rubble."

"What do you think it's doing now?"

He grinned like a schoolboy. "So we'll just help it along. When we're done, no one will ever know this place was here. Let's check out the rest. Maybe we can find our wayward colleague. You head back there." He pointed. "That looks like where our offices—excuse me, Kruvener's office—would be."

From somewhere came the sound of a loud hiss. The looked at each other. Mike shrugged. "Probably the river."

"Rivers don't make that kind of sound."

"Whatever."

He ambled off in the direction of the main entrance. Melissa headed toward the back of the mill.

When she reached the offices she had sense enough not to try the stairs. She stood stock still, looking around at it all. The only thing to do was tear it down. She shouted over her shoulder, "This is worse than the front. Down it comes!"

There was no response.

"Tom?"

Nothing.

Then, softly, came the sound of barking dogs. It faded. A light flared in one of the offices above her. It caught her off guard for an instant, then she regained her composure. "Who's up there?"

The light went out.

"I know you're up there. You're trespassing." So was she, but she had to project an authoritative image. "Uh . . . Tom?"

Whoever it was didn't move, didn't show himself. It was much darker now, and she was feeling uneasy. Time to get out of this place. She turned to go back and rejoin Mike. Behind her was a man with half a face. His one remaining eye seemed to be glowing, or reflecting some light from someplace. He reached out a hand to grasp her. Melissa screamed. "Mike! Mike, there's someone here."

She pushed past the man and ran. When after ten yards she looked back he was gone.

"Mike!"

Mike didn't answer. Off in a corner of the mill, the light of a fire appeared. It grew enormous, licked the walls, then vanished. "Mike!" Nothing. "Tom!" Nothing. She pulled out her phone and dialed Mike's number. No answer. From behind her she heard voices. There was a group of men, some scarred, some burned, some missing limbs, some tall and strong and whole. From someplace came the red-orange light of a fire and it lit them in sharp outline. Their arms reached out for her.

She screamed and ran though the mill. Barking filled the air, deafeningly loud. On all sides men appeared, then faded. Fires flared, then went out. Then there was silence. "Mike, for God's sake!"

Then she was back at the spot where they'd separated, not far from the entrance. Through the entrance she could see the crescent moon in the sky, not far above the horizon. Something sat at the center of the entrance. When she was close enough she could see what it was: the head of Michael Cavendish. Eyes opened wide in terror, mouth twisted. It sat in a pool of molten metal, which reflected the moon's light. Trails of smoke rose from it and dissipated in the night air.

A thin trickle of molten metal dripped from midair, striking the head and dripping down the face. The flesh steamed.

She let out another scream, louder and louder. As she ran for the door she stumbled over a stone and fell, scratching her face. A pillar of fire erupted at the entrance, light-ing Mike's severed head starkly; she had no way out. Again there was the roar of dogs. She screamed. Above her another phantom firelight appeared. She looked up just in time to see the ghostly outline of a blast furnace, door opening slowly, molten steel beginning to pour. When the glowing melt hit her it vaporized her instantly, so fast her nerves didn't have time to register the pain.

Slowly Mike's severed head sank lower and lower, as the molten metal turned it to vapor, bottom to top. The men surrounded the spot. For a time they did a ghostly slow-motion dance around it. Then, like the fire, like the fur-nace, they vanished.

4

SOMETHING WOKE TOM. GROGGILY HE WONDERED if he'd ever get a full rest in Steadbridge. His neck was stiff; he had fallen asleep at an odd angle on the couch in Bill's study. Someone was shaking him.

"It's time for you to get up. Father Bill's saying Saturday night Mass."

He rubbed his eyes and stared into the disapproving face of Mrs. Charnocki. "What time is it?"

"What's your wrist watch for?"

She pretended to straighten up the room, but it was plain she was there for the sole purpose of annoying Tom. He tried to ignore her but she made more and more noise as she fussed about the room. He yawned, sat up, looked at his watch. Eight thirty. It was nearly dark outside.

"Are there enough Catholics left here for a Saturday night Mass to be worthwhile?"

"It's part of Father Bill's duties. Some people take their jobs seriously."

"Why," he asked with heavy emphasis, "are you being so disagreeable to me, Mrs. Charnocki?"

"You're a troublemaker. You always were."

"I'm a media executive who may bring a lot of jobs to this dead burg." He felt embarrassed to be hiding behind that.

"You broke the rectory windows."

He gaped at the windows, which were quite intact. "What are you talking about?"

"Twice. Years ago."

"I was a kid then. You can't possibly still blame me—"

"Did you ever confess?"

"No, but—"

"Then you still carry the guilt."

He let out a brief sigh. "Father Bill was with me when I did that. As I recall it, he threw more rocks than I did."

"That's different. He's my priest now."

"Yeah. Look, why don't you get out of here and leave me alone? Your priest wouldn't want you being so rude to his guests."

"He's a priest. At least he *knows* what he did was wrong."

"I—" There was no point bickering with her. "I have to go to the bathroom. Do you want to come with me and criticize?"

She stomped out of the room.

Tom looked at his watch again, as if it might tell him something different. Eight thirty. Then he remembered Mike and Melissa.

There was a phone on Bill's desk. He quickly dialed the hotel's number. They weren't in. No one had seen them since they had dinner in the restaurant. They'd be furious with him, but in the morning he'd give them a story about his rental car blowing a gasket or something. Why couldn't they have carried on their damned affair in New York, like decent people?

He spent a few minutes freshening up in the bathroom

then decided to face the gorgon again. She was in the kitchen, making what looked to be Bill's breakfast. She glared at Tom. "I only work until eight. Unless something keeps me here longer."

So Tom was that something. It pleased him. "I made a phone call to my hotel. Should I leave a dime on the table?"

"Which hotel?"

He told her.

"That's a toll call." Her eyes widened as if this was the worst transgression she could imagine, worse than breaking windows.

He flipped her a quarter. "Keep the change."

It took him a moment to find that passageway to the church. In the sanctuary Bill, dressed in bright pink vestments, was just finishing Mass. The altar was spotlit, but only one in four of the overhead spotlights was on. Except for the bright pink priest, the church was filled with gloom. Was it for mood, for drama, or for economy? Tom watched it all from a spot behind the altar.

A few dozen people sat in the pews, scattered through the church that was much too big for such a tiny crowd. They muttered their responses to Bill's prayers dully, mechanically. None of them seemed the least bit involved. But then, as he remembered it, no one ever had.

Bill moved to the foot of the altar, raised his arms in a rather dramatic gesture of blessing, and intoned, "Go in peace."

"Peace be to you," muttered his flock. Then they got up and shambled slowly out. All except two old women in the last pew who sat saying their beads. Maybe they were riveted, figuratively if not literally.

Bill turned to Tom. "I knew you were watching. Do I look too absurd?"

"Pink's your color. You should wear it more."

"I'm serious, Tom. Come and talk to me while I get out of this stuff."

"I'm still a bit drunk."

"Who isn't?"

Tom followed him to the sacristy and watched as he climbed out of his pink. "What is it, some kind of holy day for Communist sympathizers?"

"Tomorrow's Laetare Sunday. Surely you remember."

Tom smiled and shook his head. "I remember as little as possible."

"I sometimes think these brightly colored dresses are the only reason I became a priest in the first place."

"You're not the first. If that's any comfort."

"I feel like such a damned fool, wishing these people peace. If there's one thing they have, it's that."

"There's a difference between peace and stagnation."

Bill hung his robes neatly on hooks. "Not as much as you might think."

"Look, I have to get back. I was supposed to have dinner with a couple of colleagues. They'll be pissed."

"Oh. I was thinking we might—never mind. Will I see you again before you leave?"

"I imagine. The way things are shaping up, though, I may end up back here permanently. Or at least till I can find another job. I'll be sending out résumés as soon as I get back to New York."

Impulsively Bill threw his arm around his shoulder. "It is good to see you again, Tom."

"You too." He only half meant it.

"Someone I can actually talk to. Be honest with."

"There's always Mrs. Charnocki."

"Bastard."

THE NIGHT WAS CLEAR AND BRILLIANT. A MILLION stars seemed to shimmer in the sky. He remembered the old days, when fire danced on the smokestack and the mill belched out smoke and sulfur, obscuring the sky. There were times when even the moon had to struggle to be seen.

Seeing the stars liked this seemed . . . he could not make himself finish the thought. It felt colder than it ought to be. The street was empty. Where was his car?

It took him a few moments of hung-over thought to remember he had left it at the mill. "Damn."

He decided not to walk along the main road to the mill. There was more of Steadbridge to see. Unfortunately. His footsteps echoed as he walked through the streets of the town, more loudly than seemed quite natural.

1618 Laurel Street: home. He tried to conjure an image of his father but couldn't remember him clearly. His mother . . . her death when he was nineteen had devastated him. A poor kid from a backward town, alone in the world, forced to make his own life before he was ready to.

Like Ruth's, it was a row house in a long block of them, all identical. Small porch, small windows, low doorway, tiny home. Cheap housing, built by the United American Steel Company for its workers and their families. He realized he'd been looking at the wrong house, 1616 not 1618, and he walked slowly onto his parents' porch.

The door was hanging open. He took a few steps toward it, then made himself stop. The inside was perfectly black. He visualized it. Even in darkness he could have found his way around, he thought. But he had no desire to go in.

Why was the door open? Could there be tramps, still more of them, squatting in his family's home? He pushed the door open a few more inches. There was no sound inside. He stepped in.

Uselessly, knowing it was a futile gesture, he flipped the light switch on, then off. Out of the darkness of memory came an image of the living room as it had been when he was a boy. Television, photos on the walls, his father's highschool sports trophies . . .

From his pocket he got his lighter and flicked it. A dump, as he expected. Trash littering the floor and the stairs. There were still a few pieces of battered living room furniture, still two framed photos hanging crookedly on one wall. His parents' wedding picture and, next to it, a family portrait, mother seated, Tom on her lap, father standing behind her with his hand on her shoulder.

From upstairs came a loud voice. "Tommy!"

It was his father's voice. He knew it instantly. There was no way he could mistake it. He dashed frantically into the street and stood panting, staring at the house's empty door and windows.

He had had too much to drink and was still feeling it. Dead fathers instead of pink elephants. He had gone cold; he was freezing. A light flickered on in the house.

He ran.

Three blocks later he was winded. He realized his face was streaked with tears. Trying to get control of himself, thinking mad frantic things, he stumbled and fell. He buried his face in his arms and let himself weep.

"Slow down there, buddy. What are you doing here?"

Tom looked up. At the next corner, thirty feet ahead of him, in the light of a streetlamp, stood a cop. Overweight, middle-aged. Tom gaped.

"It looks like you've had one too many."

He walked quickly to Tom and helped him to his feet.

"You want to take it easy on that stuff."

"A priest got me drunk."

The cop helped him dust himself off. "You're a friend of Father Bill?"

"An old friend, yeah."

"Father Bill has evening Mass. He can't have been drinking."

"That's what you think."

"All right, that's enough, pal. Come on. You can sleep it off at the station."

"But—"

"You're not going to resist arrest, are you?"

For a moment he considered it. It would get him fired

from Overbook, which would get him out of Steadbridge. "No, I guess not."

"That's a good boy. Come on, now, the station house is just around the corner. Who are you, anyway?"

Tom told him his name.

"And what are you doing in our fair town?"

"Getting drunk."

The cop pushed him. "Don't be a smart-ass."

"I can't help it. It's the only thing I've ever been good at."

The police station turned out to be an old storefront just off McKinley Square. Unlike everything else in town, it was lit brightly. In the front window at a small desk sat Ruth, working on a small old Macintosh. The cop hustled him in the front door and pushed him into a wooden chair. To Ruth he muttered "Drunk and disorderly."

"Tom?!"

"You know this guy?"

"Yeah, Hank, he's an old friend."

"Well, you ought to tell him not to get falling-down drunk and then try to blame it on our parish priest. There's such a thing as respect."

"He's an old friend of Father Bill too. It's probably true."

This seemed to catch him off guard. "We can't have strangers coming into town, acting this way and slandering our decent citizens."

"Why don't you just try and chill a bit, Hank? The only 'decent citizens' we have are too old to be anything else, and you know it."

"Really, Ruth, I—"

"Tom grew up here. On Laurel, not far from where I lived."

For some reason this struck him as unexpected. "Oh."

"And he's back here on business. His company may open a branch here. It would bring a lot of jobs."

"Well, he still shouldn't say things like that about our priest."

"They were friends. Great and good friends." She said it emphatically, so he couldn't miss her meaning. "And so were Tom and I."

Hank scowled. "Oh."

Through this exchange Tom had stayed quiet, looking from one of them to the other. Ruth was in charge, that was clear. And she was standing up for him. When was the last time anyone had done that?

"Look, officer, I—"

"Call him Hank." There was a twinkle in Ruth's eye.

"Well, Hank, I left my car parked out at Number Five. I was walking out to get it when you saw me stumble. That's all there is to it."

"I should give you a breathalyzer test."

"Why bother? I was drinking. With Father Bill. I admit it, and he'll tell the magistrate the same thing."

Ruth laughed. "Hank's the magistrate. And the mayor. Package deal."

Hank sat down next to him. "About these jobs you're going to bring here . . ."

"It's not certain yet. I'm just looking around, trying to see if Steadbridge would be a suitable location for us. To see if we'd get a friendly welcome." He leaned on the last sentence so Hank couldn't misunderstand his meaning.

"But there would be a lot of jobs?"

"A lot."

"Why haven't you come and talked to me about this? You can't do anything here without my say-so."

"I just got here. I've been reacquainting myself with the town. Looking up my old friends, like Ruth and Bill."

"You still should have . . . I mean, if it's business . . ."

Ruth got to her feet. "My shift's over, Hank. If you're going to book Tom, you'll have to do the paperwork yourself."

This seemed to throw Hank into a minor panic. "Well . . . well, I guess it'll be all right. Just don't do it again." He frowned at Tom in what was supposed to be a threatening, authoritative way. "And watch what you say about Father Bill."

"Thank you, officer."

"I told you, call him Hank. Everybody does."

"Hank, then."

"You come and talk to me about this business thing tomorrow, understand? I'm the law here."

Ruth pulled on a sweater. "Judge Hank Roznowski, the Law West of the Alleghenies. Tomorrow's Sunday, remember? He'll be in on Monday. Come on, Tom, I'll walk you to your car. Let's get Alex."

"He's here?"

"I told you how hard it is to get a sitter at night."

Hank put his feet up on the desk. "Did you tell him how many people are afraid of the kid?" It was clear he enjoyed being one up on her, for a change.

But she ignored this. "Let's get him. The cell's back there."

"You lock him up?" Tom couldn't help laughing.

"No, idiot. He likes to play at being a convict, that's all. And since there's not usually anyone else around, he works at his art."

She led Tom to the rear of the building. There was a single cell, eight feet by eight. Alex was sitting on the cot, pressed into the corner, sketching. Pages from his sketchbook, pencils, pastels littered the cell.

"Time to go, Alex."

The boy shook his head as if he was coming out of a trance. "Mom. Mr. Kruvener."

"You can call me Tom, Alex, if you like."

"Tom." There was no expression in his voice.

"Come on, we're going to walk Tom out to Number Five, then head home. He left his car parked out there."

The kid walked to the bars and stared at Tom through them. "You know what happened out there?"

He could have been referring to any of a million things. Tom didn't know what to say. He felt a bit foolish, being thrown off balance by a boy Alex's age.

"I'll be right out, mom. I just have to get all my stuff." He started gathering up his sketch pads and pencils.

He left one sketch behind, on the floor. It was a portrait of Melissa Fortenski, screaming in terror.

MOONLIGHT WASHED MCKINLEY SQUARE; THE statue of the plump president looked like a frozen specter. Tom tried to avoid thinking it resembled Hank.

"Thanks for getting me out of that. Not that I know how I got into it."

The three of them crossed the square, heading north to the mill.

"Hank tends to be, ah, jealous of his town. He gets a bit enthusiastic. I have to bring him down a lot."

"Well, even so, thanks."

"He came here just before Number Five closed. He was supposed to be a mid-level manager of some kind, I think. And he never left."

"I'm not sure 'mid-level manager' qualifies him to be mayor."

"No one else wanted it. You want to stop at my place for a pick-me-up?"

"No thanks. I was supposed to have dinner with a couple of colleagues tonight. I need to get back to the hotel and make nice with them."

"So Bill's better company than a couple of sophisticated New Yorkers?"

"Believe me."

Alex dropped a handful of his pencils. With no fuss Ruth helped him pick them up. Alex was being even more quiet than usual.

The river seemed to be going down, or at least not flowing as turbulently as it had. The moon, broken into a million fragments, was reflected in its surface. Tom and Ruth chatted idly about more old friends, old teachers. A streetlight on one corner was flickering. "Should we report that to Mayor Hank?"

"You think he ever does anything?"

The mill was dark, for once, no lights, no smoke, no glow at all. Moonlight played tricks, made it seem impossibly tall. Tom decided it all looked better when the hoboes were there with fires.

Just behind his car was a second one. Ruth and Tom looked at one another, puzzled. Whose could it be? Alex stepped back away from it.

There was an Avis sticker. Tom tried the door. It was unlocked. In the driver's-side visor was the rental slip. The car had been rented to Michael Cavendish.

Everything was quite silent. Tom turned to the mill and shouted. "Mike!?" His voice echoed.

There was nothing.

"Melissa!?"

Perfect silence. Unbroken blackness.

"I should go in and look for them."

"Tom, you don't know they're in there. They could have walked into town. Found a bar. Lord knows we have enough of them."

"I'm not sure I can see them in a corner saloon in Steadbridge."

For the first time Alex spoke. "Don't go in. You won't find them."

"How do you know that?" Tom got down on a knee. "What do you know about this place, Alex?"

"I only know what I can see. You won't find them in there. You know it, too."

Smiling, Tom looked at Ruth. But she was taking Alex quite seriously, as if he might know. Uncertainly he got back to his feet and let out a much louder shout. "Mike! Melissa!"

Echoes, then deathly quiet. The mill seemed deliberately still to him.

He forced himself to smile. "Well, I guess you're right, Alex. They would have answered."

"Come back and have a drink."

"Thanks, Ruthie. But I'm really spent."

He kissed her goodnight, then made a show of shaking hands with Alex. Then he sat in his car and watched them as they walked back to town. For a moment, he considered going inside Number Five anyway. Mike and Melissa could have tripped on a cable or hurt themselves some other way. But he wasn't sure he could face it.

There was no way around it; he had to try.

He went round to the back of the mill. It seemed to him that the bridge to Washington Island was swaying slightly. Because of the swift river current? The damned thing was probably going to come down sometime soon.

The interior of the mill was hidden, except for a few spots where moonlight got in. For a long time, for what seemed eternity, Tom stood silently just outside and listened. Everything was perfectly still. The owls and other birds must be off hunting, or asleep, or . . .

"Mike? Melissa?" This time he didn't shout; his voice was almost a whisper.

He took a step inside and stumbled.

"Mike?"

He moved still further inside the mill. And tripped again.

"Melissa?"

Dead silence.

There was no point to his being here. Even if they were in the mill, even if they'd had an accident there, or were making love there—which didn't strike him as quite unlikely—he'd never find them in the Stygian blackness.

Outside: moonlight, swollen river, Number Five looming over him. He could not go back to the hotel. He needed . . . he wasn't sure what. This was accomplishing nothing. It was time to get back to the hotel.

He got in his car and turned the key. Nothing. The engine was dead. He tried again; it didn't respond. The battery was dead, or the starter, or . . . "Goddamn it." He glanced at Number Five and forced himself not to think it was holding him there.

Five minutes later he was at Ruth's door. Only the upstairs lights were on. He knocked, and she came down and opened the front door. He smiled at her, a bit shamefaced. "I think I'm more drunk than I thought."

"Come on in."

"My car won't start."

"It's all right."

Before either of them quite realized what was happening he had her in his arms and they were kissing, deeply and passionately.

"Do you want a drink?"

"No. The only thing I want in the world is to make love to you again."

Neither of them noticed Alex standing on the stairs in his pajamas, watching them. He closed his eyes, not because he didn't want to see them but because he was seeing something else. Very softly, at the bottom of his breath, he whispered, "Steadbridge finds lovers. Steadbridge makes people love it, whether they want to or not, even if they hate it." By the time they interrupted their kiss to go up to her bedroom, he had gone.

SLEEP, SOUND SLEEP. IN RUTH'S ARMS.

Middle of the night. There was a bright, almost blinding light, like a flash of lightning, or a fireball in the sky. It woke Tom. For a moment he was disoriented. Then, remembering where he was, realizing that the light must have come from the mill, he rolled over and went back to his comforting sleep.

BRIGHT MORNING. SUNLIGHT FLOODED THE BED-room. The telephone rang insistently.

Groggily Ruth got out of bed to get it. Her body was better than Tom realized; her body was younger than her face.

"Yeah?" Pause. "Hank? For Christ's sake, it's seven o'clock in the morning."

"It's Sunday. You should be getting up for Mass."

"Why don't you let me worry about that?"

"I just thought you'd want to know your friend Tom's missing, along with his colleagues. I called their hotel, and no one's seen them."

"Tom spent the night here. On the couch." She smiled at Tom as she told the lie. "You were right, he was too drunk to drive."

"Well, what about the other two, then?"

"How should I know? Maybe they're on someone else's couch. Their car's parked out by Number Five."

"I know. That's where I am. Ruth, they're missing. You get your pal down to the station first thing after Mass, you understand?"

"Sure, Hank." She hung up.

Tom rubbed his eyes. "What did he want?"

"He thinks you and your friends are missing."

"We are. I mean, they are. They'll turn up."

"The law's on it. We'll have to go to the station after Mass."

"I saw Bill say Mass last night. It was a pretty creepy sight. I'm not going again."

"Well, you're going to the station. Alex and I will meet you back here after church, then."

"You'll have fun. It's Laetare Sunday. Bill looks pretty in pink."

ALONE IN RUTH'S HOUSE TOM FOUND HIMSELF
restless, and anxious. Where could Melissa and Mike have
gone? Why was he feeling more and more trapped in a
place he hated? He had to get outside, burn off some of the
nervous energy that was building up in him.

He showered quickly, dressed, and went out to walk.

The stores on the square were all closed; not surprising.
A few people straggled toward St. Dympna's. Maybe he
could find a coffee shop somewhere.

He kept walking. A few blocks beyond the square was
Steadbridge High. Battered, spray-painted with graffiti,
boarded up. Even when it was open and full of students it
had always seemed too small to be called a proper high
school. Now it hardly looked large enough to have been a
decent neighborhood elementary school.

One entrance was open, the door off its hinges and rest-
ing against the wall. He had to see inside. The halls were
familiar, unpleasantly so. There were people who seemed
to remember their adolescent years happily; Tom thought
they were mad. He ambled though the building, principal's
office, biology lab, auditorium; nothing he saw had warm
associations.

Then he reached the gym. He had never been an athlete.
Slacker was more his line. He mimicked a jock, shooting a
basket, though there was no basket, only a backboard with
half a hoop.

"What are you doing here?" From nowhere Hank
appeared.

Tom felt foolish. "Is that the way you start every conversation?"

"Ruth said you were at her place."

"I was."

"You're trespassing."

"The door was wide open. I spent enough miserable

hours in this place to have a right to enjoy it in ruins, don't you think?"

Hank ignored this. "A couple of kids were sighted here, runaways from Somerset County. An eighteen-year-old girl and a sixteen-year-old boy. Have you seen them?"

"Nope. Just you."

"If you do, let me know."

"I will."

"Sometimes homeless types camp in here. Men, mostly. I don't like to think what they'd do to two kids."

Tom shot another imaginary basket. "I thought the tramps all slept in Number Five."

"Nobody sleeps there."

Tom looked at him as if he was crazy. Some detective.

"Now, what about these jobs you're bringing?"

"I told you, there's nothing definite. Should we really talk business on a Sunday?"

Hank fingered his badge. "You shouldn't be in here. You be at my office tomorrow morning at nine."

"You mean your storefront?" Tom couldn't resist needling him a bit.

"Be there."

"Yes, sir."

Hank gestured, official-like, at the door, and Tom left.

He decided to sit in the square and wait for Ruth and Alex to get out of church. There was one bench there that wasn't too dirty. He sat and stretched out his legs. From the church, faintly across the square, came the sound of hymns. The bronze cross gleamed brightly. He wondered who polished it, and how.

His cell phone rang.

"Yeah?"

"Tom? It's Phil." Tom's heart sank a bit. Phil Morrissey was the head of production for Overbrook. The last thing Tom wanted was another one of them coming out here.

He forced himself to sound cordial. "Isn't it a bit early? And on a Sunday morning?"

"I've been trying Mike and he's not answering."

"He's missing."

"What!?"

"Mike and Melissa went out last night and didn't go back to the hotel. Their car's parked by the old steel mill here."

"That's not possible."

"If Overbrook thinks it can pump new life into this graveyard of a town, anything's possible."

"Very funny. Were they, uh, were they—?"

"Yes, they were. Isn't it amazing what can pass for a business trip?"

"Shit. If this gets around—this isn't the way we want to establish our presence there."

"I don't get the impression the local police are all that sharp."

"Good. Don't push them. Stay there till you hear from me." He hung up.

It sounded unpleasantly final.

AN HOUR LATER HE WAS AT THE MILL WITH RUTH, Hank, and Alex. Hank inspected both cars. The keys were still hanging in Tom's; when Hank turned the ignition it started at once. Tom swore it wouldn't start last night; Hank clearly didn't believe him. Ruth glanced at him with an expression that said, all you had to do was ask—why make up such a transparent story?

Inside the mill there was nothing, no sign Melissa and Mile might ever have been there.

"But they must have been." Tom was finding their disappearance more annoying than anything else. "Why else would they have parked here?"

Hank shrugged. "You tell me. Why would you pretend your car wouldn't start?"

"It wouldn't. I—" He stopped himself. There was no point trying to explain it. "Look, Mike and Melissa are having an affair. They just went off someplace together, that's all."

"Without their car?"

"Maybe they rented another one. Maybe they hitch-hiked. Maybe they had pogo sticks."

"Don't get smart with me."

"I'm sorry. But they are having an affair. They'll turn up. I can tell you, Overbrook Media wouldn't want any publicity about it. We're a family values company."

Hank stared at the floor. "Well . . . Normally I'd have to bring the state police in on something like this. But as a favor to Ruth and you and Overbrook, I'll hold off a bit. But I want to hear all about your company and what you're planning to do here. Now."

"Fine. Can we go to the station?"

"Sure. And you won't be able to leave town till I'm sure I've got everything you know. Understand?"

"All too well, yes."

5

AFTER A LONG MORNING BEING CROSS-EXAMINED by Hank, Tom needed escape, at least for a while. He suggested a country drive, maybe a picnic, and Ruth offered to pack a lunch for them. Before long he, Ruth, and Alex were in a state park twenty miles outside of town. It was just above a spot where a wide shallow stream emptied into the Monongahela.

It was spring, so the park was a riot of bright greens. Oaks, elms, maples were coming slowly, beautifully out of their winter death. Before they had been at the park ten minutes they saw cardinals, blue jays, finches. Young rabbits nibbled at vegetation and squirrels scrambled among the branches overhead. The air was cool and fresh.

Ruth spread a blanket on the ground and sat. "All these animals around. I feel like Snow White. If they could only sing."

Tom sat next to her. There was no sign Alex resented

their intimacy. "This is the first time in a week I haven't smelled rust."

"Be glad it's only a week."

"Why don't you come back to New York with me? The thought of you languishing in Steadbridge . . . you deserve a better life than that."

"Is cement better than rust, then? Besides, I'm not sure how Alex would feel about that. He's lived his whole life here."

"So had I, till I didn't any more. The schools in New York will be able to deal with him so much better. You should think about it."

She pretended to check for something in the picnic hamper. "Don't you think you're moving a bit fast?"

"In our business you learn to grab the brass ring while you can. Besides, we were always . . . I feel like I've picked up a novel that got interrupted."

"Well, I'd slow down, if I were you. There are a few chapters you're missing."

Impulsively Tom took off his shoes and socks and waded a few feet into the stream. "God, this is cold."

"What did you expect this time of year?"

Not far upstream there was a tiny cascade as the water tumbled over a line of rocks. Tom kicked some water playfully at her, and she backed off a few steps.

"Look, Ruth, there are tadpoles. Do you know how long it's been since I've seen tadpoles?"

"You're displaying an unattractive tendency to romanticize, Mr. Kruvener. Maybe you better come back to land."

Not far from them Alex had climbed a tree and shinnied onto a branch that hung out over the stream. He was scanning the landscape happily, not paying much attention to the adults. "There's smoke in Steadbridge."

"Good." Ruth walked to the edge of the water. "Maybe it'll burn down. You want to see New York City, Alex?"

"No."

Wading back to the bank Tom slipped, fell, got soaked, splashed Ruth.

"Tom!"

"Gotcha!"

"City slicker."

Giggling like kids, they went back to the blanket. Alex crossed to a branch on the other side of his tree, picked a few leaves and scattered them in the air above them. Tom swiped at one of them. "You'd like Manhattan, Alex. There's a million things to do. The Toys R Us has a real Ferris wheel inside."

"I don't like rides."

"Oh. And there are some really great art schools."

This seemed to catch the boy's attention. "Better than Mrs. Riccardi?"

"Yeah, I think probably so."

"I see so much I don't know how to draw. Could they teach me?"

"They sure could."

Alex fell silent and thoughtful.

Twenty feet down, the stream poured its waters into the river. Tom took Ruth's hand and they walked there. Fewer trees, more sun, he'd dry off more quickly. The river's current was a bit less swift now, the level a bit lower. If there were no more storms, it would return to its usual character soon.

"Let's go back and eat. I hate the river, Tom."

"Why on earth?"

"Whenever I see it I think of death."

He laughed. "Is it that polluted?"

"More than you'd think to look at it. Most kinds of fish have died out. But it's not that."

"What, then?"

"You've never read about the Johnstown flood? Up there." She pointed upriver. "It was man-made, you know. A group of millionaires built a dam on one of the tributaries and created an artificial lake so they could sail their yachts. They ignored all the warnings from the engineers that the thing wasn't safe. When it finally broke, during a terrible storm . . ."

"I've heard of all that, sure. I guess I was never curious enough to find out any more." He noticed she was keeping a careful eye on Alex, back in his tree.

"It was awful, Tom. Unimaginable. A wall of water, twenty, thirty feet high swept down this valley, drowning everything, bringing the town and the people with it. For weeks there were bodies floating in the river, more than anyone could deal with or even count. The water even tore the dead out of their graves."

She turned slowly back to where they'd left their things. "I can never see the river without envisioning it."

"I thought Alex was the one who saw things."

"Don't be funny, okay?"

Alex was hanging down from his branch, swinging. "I'm hungry."

"Then let's eat."

They passed another hour in idle conversation. Tom complained about too much mustard on the sandwiches. Alex found a baby robin that had fallen out of its nest, and Tom helped him put it back.

Just as they were going back to the car Ruth said, "I'm not sure Alex should get more art training. I've been thinking about pulling him out of the class he's in now. The things he sees . . . the ones he's able to sketch are unsettling enough. What else he sees . . . I'm not sure I'd want to know."

"If he has these demons inside him, it would be good for him to get them out."

She fell silent, obviously not sure she agreed with that.

AFTERNOON. CLOUDS STARTED BUILDING. TOM dropped Ruth and Alex off in Steadbridge claiming, more or less truthfully, that he had to get back to his hotel to check for messages. "I'll see you later, okay?" On the ride, Ruth kept watching the river. Part of him wished they'd never made their excursion.

There was no word from Mike or Melissa, but there was a voice mail message from Phil Morrissey. Two words: "Stay put." It simply wasn't possible that Number Five was the only option for Overbrook, but . . .

Still another bartender was on duty. Bland smile, bourbon, ESPN. Tom had two doubles and decided to take a nap. The previous night had been long and energetic, and he hadn't had anywhere near enough rest.

There were treacherous dreams, fire, phantoms, Mike and Melissa in torment. Tom smiled in his sleep.

EVENING. THE HOTEL BAR WAS EMPTY. THE DESK clerk stopped Tom as he went into the restaurant. "Mr. Kruvener?"

"Hm?"

"We're wondering about Mr. Cavendish and Ms. Fortenski. Officer Hank told us they're missing, and we're wondering about their bills. And what to do with their things." Like most of the other hotel employees, he seemed to be a teenager. Tom wondered if that's the way the world looks when you're middle aged.

"Just leave their things in their rooms for now, okay? Overbrook Media will cover their bills. Don't worry about that."

"Ms. Fortenski's things are all in Mr. Cavendish's room."

"Oh." He smiled sardonically. "Well, there must have been some kind of mix-up. Why don't you put them in her room, then wait till this gets resolved, okay?"

"Yes, sir. And you're sure about the bill?"

"Of course. Don't give it another thought."

A sandwich, another quick bourbon and he was off to town again. There were heavy clouds, wind, lightning, thunder, but no rain. It was already dark, thanks to the clouds. Tom decided to see a bit more of the town before heading to Ruth's.

McKinley Square: empty. St. Dympna's: dark. He knocked at Bill's door. Mrs. Charnocki opened it, and glared at him. "Father Bill's not here."

"When will he be back?"

"That's up to him, now, isn't it?"

"It's Sunday. Isn't he on duty or something?"

"Come back tomorrow."

"You're just the kind of public face the church needs, do you know that?"

She closed the door in his face.

Tom looked around and headed to McKinley Square. There was no one in sight. Nearly every building seemed to have its facade masked, boarded up. There had to be someone who could talk to him, tell him what he didn't understand about Steadbridge but needed to. Ruth wouldn't, that much was clear. For a few minutes he sat in the square trying to make sense of the weird confusion his life had suddenly become. How could he live here? He had to get back to Manhattan and send out some résumés.

There were a few heavy raindrops, then they stopped. He thought about heading to Ruth's. Suddenly from the corner of his eye he saw a light flicker on. It was at Grandma McKibben's storefront.

He stared at the sign in the window: I KNOW MORE THAN YOU DO.

What could possibly be the point of talking to her? A half-mad, drunken old bat.

He knocked.

No one answered.

Again. Rain started falling, not heavily but steadily.

He heard someone shuffling toward the door. Slowly she pulled it open. "You. Thomas Kruvener. What do you want?"

He made himself smile. "Mrs. McKibben. You remember me."

She was overweight and didn't carry it well. Her hair was thin and unkempt. The housedress she wore seemed not to have been washed for ages. Her breath smelled of cheap whiskey. "Whether I do or I don't, what of it?"

"I was in your tenth-grade class."

"I know it. I knew you'd show up here, sooner or later. I know a lot."

He wanted to tell her it didn't show, but he bit his tongue. "I don't have an umbrella."

She scowled at him. "You better come in, then."

He followed her into the front room.

Four Tiffany-style lamps made to resemble spider webs glowed dimly in the four corners, one red, one blue, one green, one pale golden. They gave the only light; the room was mostly filled with gloom and shadow. He wondered if it was deliberate, to impress the gullible; but somehow Grandma McKibben didn't strike him as that calculating.

At the center of the room was a séance table with four chairs arranged around it. On it sat a crystal ball on a tripod base of what looked like bronze; beside it, half spread out, was a pack of tarot cards. Astrological charts covered the walls. Everything in the room was faded and worn, like its owner.

She gestured and he sat down in one of the chairs.

Without looking at him she muttered, "Twenty-five dollars."

"I beg your pardon?"

"You always were a dull boy. I said twenty-five dollars." She pointed with a thumb at the wall behind her. There was another hand-lettered sign that read: READINGS $25.

"I didn't come here for a reading. I only thought we might talk."

"It's the same thing. I can't resist telling you the truth. I did it when you were a boy, but you were too dense to recognize it. Has adulthood made you any smarter?" She still had the unpleasant manner of a stern schoolteacher.

"I like to think so."

"You're the exception, then. Pay up or get out."

Feeling a complete fool, he got out his wallet and paid her. He started to reach out, to touch the surface of the crystal, but she caught his hand and pushed it away. Her own hand was cold and leathery. "It will be the cards for you, I think."

"Um . . . whatever you say, Grandma." He leaned on the final word to stress the irony.

She dealt out a card. He saw a human figure on it but the light was too dim to make out any detail. "You've been keeping company with Ruth Fawcett."

"Um . . . yes, I have. You don't need the tarot to tell you that."

"And Bill Vicosz."

"Father Bill." He chuckled. "Yes."

Another card. "When you were young you loved them. Both. Do you still?"

"That isn't what I came to discuss."

"No. It wouldn't be, even though it's what this is all about. Everyone holds onto what they love, one way or another. Talking to you, telling you too much, will be the end of me, I've been warned clearly enough, but that's all right. The only thing I've desired for more than a decade is to be dead. You want a drink." It was not a question. She stood heavily and shuffled off to the back room, which was no more brightly lit than the "reading room." Something was flickering there, he thought probably a television. Tom tried to make out what the back room was like but, again, not much was clear.

He drummed his fingers on the table. "I was sorry to hear about your husband and sons."

"I have Seagram's," she shouted. "Is that all right?"

"Yes. You should have a cat, a black one. It would add to the atmosphere."

"I hate cats."

"Oh." He wished rather desperately he hadn't come here. "How about an annoying, yippy little dog, then? I can see you with one of them."

She came back with two large tumblers full of whiskey and handed Tom one. "You should take this more seriously, little Tommy."

The glass was filthy. He put on a forced smile. "Well, here's to hepatitis."

"If you don't stop making fun of me, you won't learn a damned thing, and I'll have made an easy twenty-five dollars."

"Sorry."

"This isn't Steadbridge High. You're not the beautiful boy everyone adored, or wanted to, if you'd let us."

"I never was."

"You were. You were just too slow, or too stoned, to know it. More than a few people wanted you, lusted for you, silently and from a distance."

"Really?" No one reliable had ever thought to tell him. He wasn't at all sure he wanted to know.

"And I'm not the crazy old teacher you scored points for tormenting. You want something from me now. You slept with one of my colleagues, back then."

"Um, yes." He didn't think anyone knew.

"She's dead."

Not a comfortable thought. "You can't go home again, huh?"

"Wrong. You can never leave. Not really."

For a moment there was stone silence between them. Tom had expected to have the upper hand here. He shifted in his chair and took a drink.

Suddenly the front door flew open. Alex ran in, carrying his sketch pad. "Grandma, look!" Then when he saw Tom at the séance table with her, he stopped in his tracks, eyes wide. "Oh."

For the first time Mrs. McKibben smiled, positively beamed. "Alex."

"Sorry, grandma."

"No, come in. You know Mr. Kruvener." Her tone was affectionate, not at all the way she'd been talking to Tom.

"Yes." The boy's face was blank as a snowdrift. "Hello, Tom. It's starting to rain."

"Hi, Alex."

Alex folded his sketch carefully in half, so Tom could not see it.

"Mr. Kruvener wants to know the truth about Stead-bridge, Alex. Should I tell him?"

"He . . . he should know."

"Should I show him the ghosts? Should I let him shake hands with them?"

"No!"

Tom got up and crossed to the boy. "Alex, does your mom know you're out this late, in this weather? Does she know you're here?"

"No. Are you going to tell her?"

He got down on a knee. "I'll make you a bargain. Let me see what you've drawn, and I'll keep your secret."

"No. Grandma McKibben says you're not ready."

Tom looked around and smiled at her, an artificial, bartender kind of smile. "She does?"

Alex nodded. He was looking more and more uncomfortable.

"Tell you what. It looks like the rain's stopping already. Let me see the sketch, then wait for me over in the square. I'll borrow an umbrella from Mrs. McKibben, just in case, and walk you home and tell your mom you were with me."

Alex looked to Grandma McKibben, uncertain what to do or say. She took a long swallow of her whiskey.

"I left this at the station last night. I just went back for it. Here." He handed Tom the drawing. Tom took it as a sign Alex liked him, or trusted him, at least as much as he liked Mrs. McKibben.

Looking genuinely upset, perhaps even frightened, Alex ran off, leaving the door open behind him. Tom watched as he headed in the direction of his home and hoped that's where he was going. Just as he vanished from view, the rain started again.

Feeling on top of the situation for the first time, he walked to the door, closed it, walked casually back to his chair, and sat. And unfolded the sketch. It was a sketch of Melissa Fortenski, screaming in torment. He froze.

Mrs. McKibben tried to stand up, tottered, nearly fell, and caught herself on the edge of the table, rocking it. The crystal rolled off its base and Tom caught it and put it back. "Steady, teacher. You should drink a little less."

A bit shaken, she sat down again. "Thank you for your concern. I could tell you the same thing. Leaving Mr. Cavendish and Mrs. Fortenski alone the way you did. How will you live with it?"

He crumpled Alex's sketch in his hands. How did she know about that? "Believe me, that was what they wanted. They're not into threesomes. Wherever they are."

"Don't talk dirty, boy."

"Yes'm."

"They're dead and you know it. You have the evidence right there."

"Evidence? They're missing. That doesn't mean—"

"You've seen *The Third Man.* I know you have. It used to play the Hippodrome on revival nights all the time."

This threw him a bit. "What of it?"

"A story about a fool, charging around making trouble for everyone, refusing to see what's right in front of his eyes."

"My taste ran more to *Frankenstein Meets the Wolf Man.*"

Slowly, wearily, she turned another card. "Ruth doesn't love you, you know."

Unexpectedly, this hurt. He hadn't wanted to drink any more of her liquor, he didn't want to give her the satisfaction, but now he took a deep swallow.

"You should drink a little less." She mimicked him.

"What are you going to do? Give me detention?"

"You're already being detained. I thought at least that much would have dawned on you."

He stood up. "Look, this is not what I came here for."

"What did you come for, then?" She laughed at him.

"I don't know. Not this."

"Sit down."

He stayed on his feet. "I paid for a reading. When do I get it?"

"What do you think this is?" She laughed again, then shrugged. "All I can do is tell the truth. Sit down." She bellowed it.

Tom kept standing.

Her voice turned more gentle, even a little bit sad. "I would have thought it must have dawned on you by now. Your future is your past. You can't escape it."

"Who would believe that?" Every molecule of him turned schoolboy, and he sat. As if on cue, there was a bright flash of lightning followed by loud thunder. "Well, you've got the right setting for this."

Much more softly she repeated, "All I can do is tell the truth. That's the kind of place Steadbridge is. All Alex can do is draw the truth."

Tom was feeling more and more shaken, and he didn't quite understand why.

Mrs. McKibben turned another card. Tom watched her as she studied it. A light, like a bright flame, flared, reflected in the surface of the crystal. He turned to see what it was, but there was nothing. He wanted the old woman to tell him something, anything, as long as it would make sense.

"Mrs. McKibben."

She looked up.

"I've had enough of this 'reading.' Now I just want to talk. Is that possible? Will you just talk to me, no cards, no visions? Tell me the truth about Steadbridge, tell me whatever it is I seem to be missing?"

She stared at him. He had the impression she was trying to see inside him.

Slowly she stood up. "Come on."

Tom picked up their glasses and followed her to her parlor. She switched on the battered floor lamp. The television was on, the sound turned down, an old set left over from the 60s or 70s. The place smelled, not just of stale liquor. She plopped down in her chair. "Sit, then, and let's talk for a while."

Tom refilled their glasses. He had the impression, or the hope, that she was nearly drunk enough to let her guard down. Then he sat. It was not a comfortable situation for either of them, and it showed, though Tom felt a bit more relaxed, or a bit less on edge than he had in the séance room. He sipped his whiskey.

"What's happened to you, Mrs. McKibben?" He kept his voice neutral. "You used to be the most upright, respectable teacher in Steadbridge High."

"I always drank."

"Oh."

"None of you ever saw it. Adolescents never notice much of anything."

"I guess not."

"You think I drink to escape reality. It's the reverse. We used to talk about you in the teachers' lounge. You were so handsome. You could have taken any one of us to bed. We all hated the one you did, even though she thought we didn't know about it. And we all hated you. You should have heard the talk."

"Even you? Even you wanted me?" He laughed. "You sure kept it a secret."

"You were such a dull boy in so many ways."

"You were my teacher. You're supposed to tell me what potential I had and how you hope I've lived up to it."

"Fool."

This wasn't going at all they way he wanted it to. "Are you going to keep insulting me till I leave?"

"Why not?"

"Well, I'll just be going, then. This isn't going any-where good."

"It was your obtuseness that made you attractive to us, I think. At least to me."

"You have a perverse side. Stop this."

"Yes. The dead want you. Do you know that? Or they're angry at you. Or . . ."

"Or what?"

"Or I don't know."

He stood up. "This is absurd."

"They're here, you know. Everywhere in Steadbridge. My husband, my boys, your father. They have a link to us, to the living, and they won't let it be broken. God knows why. If I were one of them, I'd want nothing but rest, not traffic with the likes of you and me. There are more of them here than living, breathing people, I think. They tend their fires and their furnaces and they keep us all in their grasp. Steadbridge is its own little hell."

It was the sort of rubbish he should have expected from her. I know more than you do, indeed. "I'll be going now, Mrs. McKibben. You can keep the twenty-five. Why don't you buy some better liquor?"

"You know where they are. You know what they can do. You have to stop."

"Of course."

She had been drinking steadily, and she had had way too much; Tom could see it easily enough. He'd have felt guilty, as if his presence was what made her do it, but he knew better.

There was more lightning and thunder, not as bright or as loud as before. "Look, I mean it. I really ought to go now. Do you have an umbrella I can borrow?"

"No."

Long pause. "Oh. Well. It's . . . it's been nice talking with you, Mrs. McKibben."

"Liar."

"I'll be going. Good night."

He headed out into the rain. For a moment he thought about taking shelter under the Hippodrome's marquee, till it let up a bit. But if it was like all the other storms since he got to town, it would go on all night. He decided to make a run for Ruth's.

It took her a few moments to open the door. "Tom, you're soaked!"

"Well, it's raining."

"Come in and dry off."

Alex was sitting on the living room floor in front of the TV. But he was ignoring it, drawing. He smiled when he saw Tom. Ruth got a towel from the kitchen and dried his hair for him. Tom found himself wondering, is this what home feels like? His memory failed him.

GRANDMA MCKIBBEN DOWNED THE LAST OF HER whiskey in three long swallows. Then, abruptly, she fell asleep.

The storm raged over Steadbridge, ferocious lightning and thunder, wind so strong it blew the rain sideways. Electrical power went out. Through it all she slept.

Then after an hour, the storm passed, the rain stopped, and the town was dark and quiet. Outside her shop in McKinley Square, rainwater trickled through dark empty streets, finding its way to the river. Birds that had found shelter from the storm returned to their nests to find their young missing. The river itself swelled again, its waters nearly reaching their banks.

She woke in her parlor, groggy, addled, and stared in the darkness at the blank, black screen of her television. There was no way she could know the time, and it took her a long moment of concentrated thought even to remember the day. If only George was still alive, or the boys. The thought of her sons brought a familiar pang. She reached for the whiskey bottle on the table beside her. It was empty. Oblivion would have been so much better than this.

Suddenly the power came back on. Her floor lamp blinded her at first, and it took what seemed forever for her eyes to adjust. The television flickered to life, and she saw the image of a televangelist praying over a stack of letters. In the front room, the spiderweb lamps came on. She should switch them off.

Woozy, unsteady, she got to her feet, holding the edge of the table for balance. She switched the TV to another channel. Another preacher. The last thing she wanted to see. She knew more than they did.

Then she was in the front room. She made her bleary way around the perimeter, turning off the lamps one by one. Then she saw that there was one more light.

In the heart of her crystal a flame burned. It flickered high, then low, seeming to dance in an impossible breeze. There had to be another bottle around somewhere. Where had she left it?

There: on the floor beside the television. She plopped into her comfy chair and unscrewed the cap. She could see the séance table in the next room. The flame in the crystal was higher now, bright enough to light the whole room.

Then another one appeared, at the center of the table beside her. It jumped suddenly into being and burned higher and higher.

There were men around her, the figures of men, a dozen of them. Some were virile and handsome, some scarred, some terribly disfigured. She knew at once who they were and why they had come.

"It doesn't make any difference," she whispered to them. To herself she said, in a drunken singsong, "I had to tell him. All those long years ago I wanted to touch his young body, and I hated the woman who did, and I loathed Ruth Vinerelli and Bill Vicosz because they had him and I didn't. Now I have him too. He'll be back." She took a drink from the bottle.

The floor lamp exploded in flames. A fissure opened in the wall opposite and a thin stream of molten steel, glowing white hot, poured out of it. It set fire to the carpet.

In short moments, the entire room was engulfed in flames, licking at Mrs. McKibben's filthy dress, singeing her hair, forcing her to close her eyes. When she closed them she saw more fire.

One last drink.

When the fire finally took her she was quiet, no screams, no tears, no laughter, nothing, not even a flicker of lust for that handsome boy.

The fire might have spread to the adjoining shops, might even have consumed all of Steadbridge, but the rain began again and put it out.

6

RAIN AND WIND CONTINUED FOR NEARLY A WEEK, and what little activity normally occurred in Steadbridge came to a dead stop. By the fourth day, the town's antiquated drainage system backed up; water flowed through every street and alley; people trying to cross them were swept off their feet and had to struggle. Gusts of strong wind tore roofs off houses and stores. The river poured over its banks into the lowest-lying parts of town; fortunately no one lived there any more. The foundation of St. Dympna's, the largest building in town, shifted, and a diagonal crack appeared in the facade.

During that week, Officer Hank ruled the official cause of Grandma McKibben's death was falling asleep with a cigarette, even though no one had ever seen her smoke. The ground was soaked to the point that newly opened graves kept collapsing into mud pits; it was impossible to bury her remains.

Tom received two more voice-mail messages from Phil

Morrissey within two days. The first told him to stay in
Steadbridge and make sure the police investigation into the
disappearances didn't become too high profile. Then came
word that Overbrook had tracked down the owners of the
mill and were in negotiations for it. He felt as if he was
being buried alive.

Ruth's bedroom ceiling sprang a leak; Tom helped her
move her bedroom things into a tiny sewing room. He
made love to her often but with not much passion.

Alex stayed in his room and drew apocalyptic visions of
a drowned world. When Tom saw one he smiled and told
Alex, "It's not that bad. Really."

Alex kept sketching. "Not now. It will be."

AFTER FIVE DAYS THE CLOUDS BROKE AND THE
storms gave way to blistering heat. Water-soaked spring
turned to baking, humid, premature summer. Tom took to
wearing shorts and t-shirts. "I remember when spring here
used to be pleasant. And even summer. Or am I romanti-
cizing again?"

It was morning, the day of Grandma McKibben's
belated funeral. Eight AM, and it was already eighty-two
degrees. Ruth made pancakes. "You romanticize everything. Me, Steadbridge . . . the only thing I haven't heard
you moon over is the company you work for."

"Wait till you meet the people. Not an ounce of romance
in them."

"There was a time I would have said that about you."

"It's still not too far off the mark."

"Romantic." She smirked. "Come on, breakfast is ready.
Pancakes, bacon and hash browns."

"Good home cookin'. Yup."

She called Alex, and the three of them ate their breakfast, mostly in silence. When they were nearly finished,
Alex asked Tom if he was going to the funeral.

"No, I don't think so. I've got a lot to do."

"You were the last one to be with her."

"Even so."

"She would have gone to yours. She felt sorry for you."

Oh. This was not something Tom wanted to hear, especially not over breakfast. Fine way to start a day. "I think I felt sorry for her. But not much. She was never a nice woman."

Ruth poured more syrup on Tom's pancakes. "And you terrorized her."

"She was a teacher, I was a student. It's the natural order."

Alex dipped a finger in a pool of syrup and licked it. "I loved her. She was nice to me. She was the only one who really understood."

"Did you ever see her smoke, Alex?"

"No. She said one regular sin was enough for her. That's not how she died."

He resisted asking the obvious question. The boy couldn't know anything. "Maybe that old floor lamp started an electrical fire. Or that TV of hers. Nothing in that place looked safe."

"She was the only one who understood. I'm alone now. Please come to her funeral with us, Tom."

"Alex, I barely knew her."

"Please."

Tom looked to Ruth. She was impassive, eating and pretending not to pay attention. Which of them, he wondered, was she trying to support that way? "Okay, I'll come along. Let's just hope it's a short ceremony. It's too hot to stay in a suit."

"Yeah."

Half an hour later, he was changing into his best suit. It didn't look good. "Is there a dry cleaner left in town?"

"No. The nearest one's in a mall a few miles off."

"I'll have to get this cleaned. Have to look my best when the troops arrive."

"We can take a ride up there, sure. Tom?" She was picking out a dress to wear. "Why don't you move in here? Half your stuff's here anyway."

"How would that look to my colleagues?"

"Damned lucky."

"I have to find housing for them. I was wondering, do you think we could get some people to clean out all these row houses, fix them up and make them livable, maybe slap a coat of paint on them?"

"I think they'd be glad of the money. But a lot of the houses aren't habitable."

"The ones that are, then. Part of me wants to let them all commute from the hotel, It'd serve them right. But if the production goes smoothly and everyone's happy, it'll reflect well on Kruvener."

"I'll have to talk to Hank. The town owns most of them. Foreclosures for unpaid taxes. I imagine we'll be able to work out some kind of rental agreement. The town coffers can use the money too."

He tried a necktie, then decided he didn't like it. "Hank does pretty much what you tell him, doesn't he?"

"That's what secretaries are for. Haven't you ever noticed?"

"Well, that all sounds good. I'll take the one that's closest to you. For appearances sake."

"That's an odd attitude for someone from the New Gomorrah."

Another tie, red, "power." Nix. "There are times I think I'd like to live on top of a remote mountain. With a shotgun."

"There you go again, being a romantic."

"I don't know which I like less, cities or people. But I want to get away from both. From everything."

Ruth crossed to him and picked out a dull green tie for him. "Here. Muted enough for a funeral. Trust me, Tom, you're not cut out for rural living. The first garter snake would send you shrieking back to Manhattan."

"Not until after I killed it."

"You see?"

"I wish you weren't always one-up on me."

"When we were kids, you said that turned you on. Zip me up."

Tom checked the tie in the mirror and decided he didn't like it. "You must have the wrong man, Mrs. Fawcett. I was never a kid." Her zipper was stuck. He gave it a strong tug.

"Careful with that."

"Anyway, I really should have my own place. Aside from appearances, I'll have a lot of work to do. And equipment—computers, faxes . . . We ought to find a big place we can use as a headquarters, maybe someplace close to Number Five."

"I hope the Steadbridge Power Plant can handle the strain. Why don't you try going easy on that zipper?"

He zipped. "Jesus, I hadn't thought of that. I'll have them bring generators, just in case."

"All your ties are repulsive, do you know that? You want me to dig out some of Pat's?"

He scowled at himself in the mirror. "No, don't bother. You saved them?"

"A couple of them." She checked herself in the mirror and looked unhappy with what she saw. "I've always had trouble letting go of things. Most of the power company guys were laid off ages ago. They'll be delighted to get work."

"I'd like to get my hands on whoever invented neckties."

Alex was at the bedroom door. In a black suit and blue necktie, he looked like a different boy. "Come on. It's time to go. That's an ugly tie, Tom."

GARDELLO'S FUNERAL HOME WAS AT THE EASTERN edge of town, just next to the graveyard. It was a standard funeral parlor, but Steadbridge style, only one "viewing room," threadbare carpets, tarnished brass, frayed curtains.

A dozen or so people milled around, chatting in hushed voices. None of them seemed to want to be there. The air was thick with the scent of flowers, stale generations of them. Sam Gardello stood unobtrusively in a corner, looking professionally unhappy. He was two years younger than Tom and looked twenty years older.

The coffin was closed. An inexpensive one, pine wood and lead fittings. Around it were a few bouquets, not many. One had a banner that read, "Grandma, I love you and miss you, Alex."

Tom, Ruth and Alex arrived just as the service was about to begin. At first glance Tom had the impression the place was full of people, then he realized it was practically empty. Trick of the eye, he told himself. He recognized two very old former teachers and hoped they didn't recognize him. Officer Hank looked like a lawman hunting for suspects. There were maybe a dozen mourners in all.

Bill Vicosz was there, overseeing everything, trying to look hardy, dressed in black cassock, white surplice, purple silk stole. Tom smiled and shook his hand. "I still think pink is your color."

"This is a funeral. Don't be a bitch."

"For Grandma McKibben's burial, nothing could be more fitting."

"Stop it."

"Did she have any family left, Bill?"

"None. The town and St. Dympna's are paying for the burial. And hoping like hell she had some insurance. Hank's going mad trying to find a policy among the ashes."

Gardello crossed to them, trying, not quite successfully, to look sad. "Tom Kruvener. I heard you were back in town."

"Your basic bad penny. Hello, Sam." They shook hands.

"You look great, Tom."

"New York keeps a guy young. You too."

"You're a liar, but thanks." He lowered his voice. "I don't suppose you have any weed on you?"

"Uh . . . no, I don't."

Gardello looked around and lowered his voice. "I'd kill for some. These things get harder and harder to stand."

"I haven't done drugs in longer than I can remember, Sam."

"All right, who are you, and what have you done with the real Tom Kruvener?"

"Um . . . I . . ."

"Why, Tom." Bill simply beamed. "Someone's actually thrown you off balance." He reached under his vestments, into his pocket, and palmed a joint. "Come on," he whispered. "Let's light up."

The three of them sneaked off to a side room and closed the door carefully behind them. Bill lit and inhaled deeply. "I can't tell you how much I hate funerals."

Tom took the joint. "Look on the bright side. With the town this small, you won't have to do too many more."

"How many people is your company bringing here?"

Tom laughed but didn't find the thought especially funny. "Don't be morbid."

The door opened and Ruth came in, closing it behind her. "You should be ashamed of yourselves." She crossed to them quickly. "Give me some of that."

Tom was grateful she had interrupted the conversation. "Pretty soon the whole funeral party will be stoned out of their heads."

Sam took another drag. "It'd help."

Again the door opened. A short, elderly man stuck his head in and sniffed the air pointedly. Tom recognized him as Mr. Evans, who used to teach algebra. "Do I smell dope?"

"No, Mr. Evans." Bill held the joint behind his back. "We're just saying a private rosary for Mrs. McKibben's soul."

Evans came in. "You're Tommy Kruvener, aren't you?"

Tom hated him and algebra. "Yes."

"Now I know there's dope in here. Give me a drag."

"Why, Mr. Evans, I had no idea you were a pothead."

"A lifetime of students like you will do that to a man."

"Oh."

Bill shifted uneasily. "Why don't you finish it? It's getting too crowded in here. They way things are going, Hank will be in here looking for an easy bust. It's time we got started." He arranged his robes, strode back into the viewing room and began the public prayers for Mrs. McKibben's soul.

Tom watched him go, took one last puff, and noticed that the outer room had become quite crowded. But when he followed Bill out there, it was the same dozen people. He was grateful he didn't have to talk to any more of them. Algebra, for Christ's sake.

EVERYONE WALKED TO THE CEMETERY FROM THE funeral home nearby. Officer Hank, Sam Gardello and two men Tom didn't recognize carried the coffin. Bill Vicosz led the little procession.

At ten in the morning the heat was already blistering. The sun beat down without mercy through a layer of haze, of smog. Tom wanted to loosen his tie. Did social etiquette still matter in Steadbridge, he wondered?

There seemed to be more people waiting for them at the graveside. He squinted to try and see who they were, but there was no one there after all. He shouldn't have smoked.

The graveyard was overgrown with grass and weeds. A number of headstones were tilted at unattractive angles; others were cracked or broken. As the funeral party walked the dirt path to Grandma McKibben's open grave, they kicked up dust. But beneath the arid surface, the ground was still soaked from the recent storms; puddles of water were collecting in the bottom of the grave.

Tom whispered to Gardello, "Will she keep in that?"

"I'll let you in on a professional secret," Gardello told him in a confidential tone. "They don't keep, no matter what. The bugs inside us eat their way out."

"So nothing goes to waste, huh? That's nice to know."

"Mother Nature keeps her children well fed."

From the corner of his eye Tom saw more people arriving. When he looked, they were not there. "I smoked more than I should have."

"That doesn't sound like the Tom Kruvener we all looked up to in high school. Stoner Number One."

"Was I really that bad, Sam?"

"You mean you didn't know it? We always wondered how you kept your grades up. Was there anyone cute in the school you didn't get it on with?"

"Don't you have some official duties or something?" Tom moved to the side of the grave. Alex took his hand. The boy was crying, just slightly but noticeably. Tom squeezed his hand to let him know it was okay.

Bill began the prayers. "Remember man that thou art dust and unto dust thou shalt return . . ." Tom tuned out almost at once.

His cell phone rang. He moved away from the others. "Hello?"

"Tom, Phil Morrissey."

"Phil. Look, can I get back to you? I'm at a funeral." It felt nice to tell him the truth for once.

"You got my earlier messages?"

"Uh, yes."

"Good. I just wanted to let you know things are coming together on our end."

"Things?"

"Things. Did you know the county owns the mill? Foreclosed for unpaid taxes. They're letting us have it for a song. Tax incentives, everything we could want. A real sweetheart deal."

"Great." He started to amble about the cemetery as they talked. "But aren't you being a bit premature? I'm the only one who's seen the place."

"And Mike and Melissa. How's that investigation going?"

He looked back at the funeral party. Officer Hank was idly picking bits of lint off his shirt. "The police are hard at work on it."

"Good. Just make sure they keep it quiet. His wife and her husband both want it hushed up. We'll have enough economic clout down there to make sure it stays that way."

"Needless to say." A small brown snake sped across his path and down a hole at the base of a headstone. He thought it might be a young copperhead.

"Personally I still think they ran off somewhere, Tom, but that's just between us."

Tom wondered who he could tell, even if he wanted to.

"Now, we're sending a pair of engineers down there. They should be there next Monday. We won't clinch the deal till we get their report."

"When can I come back?"

"You stay right where you are. We're giving you Mike's title, temporarily. Head of Production. You're to stay in Steadbridge."

"But—"

"With a raise, of course. Now, what we do depends on the engineers. Whether we demolish the place or rebuild, I mean. Personally, I want to demolish. I love Mike's idea of using that as the climax of *The Colors of Hell*."

"I wish I could get used to that title." He had drifted to the far end of the graveyard. There was a wrought iron fence. He leaned on it, staring into the grey haze of the sky.

"Hey, it'll sell the movie. Guaranteed."

"I'm working on housing for the cast and crew. I was hoping I could get back to Manhattan after that."

"Overbrook needs you." Phil hung up.

"Oh." He muttered it to the empty air.

Turning to rejoin the others, Tom found himself face to face with a half dozen men. From the look of them, steel-workers. Denims, work boots. One of them was missing an eye. Another had a long scar down the side of his face. They stared at him quite fixedly.

"Uh, good morning."

None of them moved. Beyond them he could see that the crowd at graveside had swelled.

"Did you know Mrs. McKibben?"

One of them shifted his weight; the others were frozen.

"Look, I have to get back to the service."

No response. Tom shouldered his way past them. In the distance he could see some kind of commotion at the grave. What looked like a fight.

Three men were involved. Through the crowd he could just make out what was happening. Two of them were restraining a third. He fought them, pulled free . . . and jumped into the open grave. What the hell . . . ?

Instinctively Tom ran back. He put a hand on Ruth's shoulder. "Are you all right?"

"Yes, of course." She seemed a tad astonished. "Why shouldn't I be?"

There was no one in the grave; only the coffin. Everyone in the small crowd was calm; there was no sign anything had happened. Bill was going on with his eulogy.

"But—I saw—"

"Be quiet. You'll upset people."

He forced himself to calm down and stay quiet. More than mildly disoriented, he looked back to where he had been. There was no one.

What he had seen had been bright and clear under the hazy sun. And he had not seen a thing, it seemed. There must have been more than just weed in that damned joint of Bill's.

The service ended. Bill blessed the grave, blessed the mourners, said a brief prayer for the town of Steadbridge. People formed small groups and began drifting off.

Ruth looped her arm through Tom's. "I didn't have a chance to introduce you to everyone."

"That's all right. Let's go home."

Alex took his other hand. "You called our house home."

"I did. I meant—I mean—hell, let's get out of here."

"Thanks for coming, Tom." Alex smiled at him for the first time he could remember.

As they walked back, a slight breeze came up the valley. Not enough to cool them, exactly, but it helped. Alex's hair blew gently around his face.

THAT AFTERNOON THE TEMPERATURE TOPPED ninety-five degrees and the air was thick and humid. There was no wind, not the faintest breath of it, and the sun was blinding, even through a layer of haze. Tom went to the mill, he was not certain why. To find something, anything that might tell him what happened to Melissa and Mike. To see the hobos he was certain inhabited the ruin. To find fire, or youth, or . . .

He wore nothing but shorts, sandals and a t-shirt the color of rust. Why had he chosen it? The mill was still the same mill, yet it seemed to startle him, as if he'd thought something might have changed, or grown. On the ground was a piece of corroded sheet metal. Something made him pick it up. He stood there with it in his hands, feeling foolish, then let it drop again.

Just inside the mill he stood once again, regarding the huge empty place. Though he could not know it, he was at the spot where Melissa had died. He listened. There was no sound. No point inspecting the place any further. The engineers would be here soon enough.

The river was still high, still swift, though it was dropping to something like its normal level. Tom stood and watched the dark waters. Just under Pulaski Bridge, he thought he saw something, or someone, a human figure in the water. But it was nothing. All day long he had been seeing things, seeing people who weren't really there. Damn Bill and his dope.

It occurred to him he had never been on Washington Island, and he decided now was the time. But when he put a foot on the bridge it creaked and shuddered in an alarming way. It couldn't possibly be safe. It should have been pulled down, or at least warning signs should have been put up.

He thought briefly of climbing the smokestack staircase, if only to get a new viewpoint on Steadbridge. But why bother?

Unsatisfied, and not even knowing what might satisfy him, he walked into the town. McKinley Square: a few kids playing, no one else in sight. Not even any pigeons. He thought about stopping at the rectory and having a drink with Bill. Instead he walked toward a part of town he hadn't seen yet.

Closed-up houses, mostly; cracked streets, weeds, a few old people and a few kids, exactly like everyplace else in Steadbridge. An elderly man was struggling to get a bag of groceries up his front steps; Tom helped him. The man did not thank him. At least, thank heaven, he wasn't seeing phantoms anymore.

Ruth's house was not air conditioned. There were fans in nearly every room, and they helped, but the heat cut through. She was in the kitchen, eating ice cream. "Want some?"

He smiled and shook his head. "Ruth, I'm lost."

She started to make a wisecrack about this being Regina Street, but she could see there was something really bothering him. She got him a dish of ice cream anyway. "It's strawberry. You always used to like it."

"Thanks. This damned heat. Where's Alex?"

"Off playing somewhere. He likes the heat. When we were kids we used to sneak into the Hip on days like this, remember? It was practically refrigerated."

"Everyone in town did. The place made a killing in summer." He ate quickly.

"I used to hate it, though. The air conditioning made my popcorn get cold before I could eat it, and the butter turned all icky. You should take it easy. That'll do you more good if you eat it slowly."

"I guess I'm hungrier than I thought."

For a moment they sat and ate in silence. Then he took hold of her and kissed her.

They made love. Her bed was too soft for his taste, and the window fan barely made a difference in the bedroom, but . . .

In her body he found something, not what he was looking for in Steadbridge. In his mind they were sixteen again and she was smooth and warm, not hot, she was beautiful, not ruined, and the word love had never occurred to him. Within moments they were both covered in sweat. It was not satisfying, not the way he remembered it being once. Why had all the good things died while the ugly ones remained? Were there ever any good things?

When they finished, they showered. Ruth got towels for them. Then they lay side by side on the bed.

"Ruth, I wish I'd never come back here. I wish I hadn't been born here."

She wiped the sweat off his forehead. "Not very good at pillow talk, are you?"

"I mean it. I've never been what you'd call a happy man, not in the conventional way. The things that seem to make other people happy . . . they've always seemed outside me."

"Maybe they are. Maybe people kid themselves because it's unbearable otherwise."

He got up and pulled on his shorts.

"Maybe you should talk to your priest," she said. "Maybe he's what you need."

"No." He was emphatic. "That was years ago. We were kids."

"So were we. Just go talk to him. He really does understand a few things, even though he's a priest." He started to say something but she cut him off. "I know it sounds weird, but Bill's been here all his life, thinking about this place and what it means."

"What does it mean?"

"I'm damned if I know. Ask him." She stretched out on the bed, luxuriated as if she was Joan Crawford and the sheets were made of satin.

From the front window he saw Alex coming up the street. He was barefoot, wearing nothing but denim shorts, and he was running happily. No sign of a sweat, even. Tom bent down and kissed her. "Don't take my mood personally. It's wonderful to have found you again."

"You found me, Alex, Bill, and Steadbridge all together. Package deal." She kissed back, hard.

"I wish . . . I don't know what I wish."

He slipped out of his shorts again and they started to make love a second time when they heard Alex's footsteps downstairs. Ruth pulled away from him and got dressed.

Tom did not much mind. Their lovemaking had hardly satisfied him. "That's the problem with kids. They're so inconvenient."

"Alex is my life, and you know it. I love him desperately."

"Yes, I know it."

"He says he's not afraid of you any more."

"Why do I have this bizarre effect on children?"

"He likes you." She slapped him playfully on the backside. "God knows why. Come on, let's get some more ice cream."

TOM HADN'T SEEN THE DINING ROOM OF THE REC-tory before. Heavy wood paneling, heavy wooden furniture, stained glass windows, an atmosphere of genteel gloom. There was a lace tablecloth. It felt old, faded to him like everything else in Steadbridge. Part of him wanted to find the room's age and solidity comforting, but he couldn't feel that. He and Bill sat at opposite ends of the table, sipping wine, not saying much. An obviously resentful Mrs. Charnocki served dinner to her priest and his guest. The appetizers were canned cheese on crackers.

"This wine is awful." Tom sat his glass one the edge of the table, hoping Mrs. Charnocki would knock it off as she passed.

"You should taste the stuff we use for Communion." Bill wasn't drinking much either. "A devious way to keep the faithful from wanting too much of it."

"You should be grateful they come at all."

"I am, Tom, believe me. I keep trying to figure out what I do for them that makes them so appreciative of me. I'm damned if I can fathom it."

Mrs. Charnocki brought salads, not trying even slightly to hide what she thought about the company Bill was keeping. They both fell silent till she was back in the kitchen.

"It's a miracle what a clerical collar can do for you." Bill reached for his wine but seemed to think better of it. "If I left the priesthood tomorrow, she'd be back to feeling the same contempt for me she had when I was a kid."

"No one in Steadbridge seems happy."

"Is anyone happy, anywhere?"

"I heard there was a guy in Idaho once . . ." Tom shrugged.

"I've heard the same rumors but I don't believe them. Let me get us a couple of real drinks. Bourbon?"

Tom nodded and Bill headed off to the study. Mrs. Charnocki reappeared, glared for a moment at Bill's empty chair, then turned on Tom. "Where is Father Vicosz?"

"In the bathroom. Diarrhea."

"The fish is ready and you haven't finished your salads."

"Gluttony is one of the deadly sins, Mrs. C."

"I drove all the way to Somerset to get fresh greens, and this is the thanks I get." She stomped back to the kitchen.

A moment later Bill showed up with two large tumblers of whiskey. "There."

Tom couldn't shake off his mood. "Are you happy here, Bill?"

"In the service of the Lord, how could I not be?"

"I'm serious. Ruth always seems so . . . I don't know. I feel like I can never quite reach her."

"She may feel the same way about you. You're harder to read now than when we were kids."

"Am I? I thought I was an open book."

"Yeah, *Finnegan's Wake*."

Not liking the sound of that, Tom kept talking. "I keep thinking about poor old Grandma McKibben. Much as I disliked her, I wouldn't have wished that kind of death on her."

"Is one kind preferable to another?" Bill took a long drink.

"There's pain to be avoided, surely."

"Should I give you the church's take on that one?"

"No, please don't."

Bill pecked at his salad. "I keep asking her not to use eggs in these." He pushed the plate aside.

"Maybe it's to cover up the taste of the strychnine."

"Elizabeth McKibben wanted to die, Tom. It was the only thing she wanted in the world."

Tom decided he'd had enough salad too. "Surely she wasn't capable of suicide."

"Not directly, no." He looked to the kitchen, hoping for the main course. Mrs. Charnocki was taking her time now.

"Then . . . ?"

"I had just taken up my post here when her husband and sons got killed. She came to me and said she wanted to die too. I thought it was just her grief talking, but it was something deeper. She tried to drink herself to death. Again and again. I don't know how many times she drank herself into a coma, or worse. They'd pronounce her dead, and then she'd wake up again. I gave her the last rites time and again and there she'd be, still alive." He drank. "More or less."

Finally Mrs. Charnocki appeared with the main course. Tom decided he'd sparred with her enough. "Salmon. Thank you, Mrs. Charnocki. It's my favorite fish."

She went back to her domain without answering him.

"Tough cookie."

"She works here for free, you know. Volunteer, for the greater glory of the Church in Steadbridge. I wish I could afford to hire someone who'd leave her attitude someplace else."

"Well, she knows how to cook fish, all right." He took a big mouthful. "I'll have to stop goading her."

Bill drank. "Funny thing about Mrs. McKibben. Every time she'd revive after one of her, er, episodes, she'd always claim her husband and sons sent her back. She insisted on it. I tried to get her to confess, hoping she'd realize how wrong suicide is, but she never would. Said it was expected of her."

"I don't understand Steadbridge, Bill. I thought, when I first came back, that I knew what to expect here. But the place keeps surprising me again and again. And again. Not pleasantly." He eyed his glass, reached for it, drank. "Every time I'm with you I end up sloshed."

"That's what friends are for."

They finished their dinner without much more talk. Tom tried to be civil to Mrs. Charnocki, to no effect. When they were finished, they headed to the study. Tom sat on the couch where he'd slept; Bill ran his finger along a row of books, looking for one.

"About what I was saying, Bill. I feel like I don't know this town at all."

"Maybe you never did. Maybe you always saw it through a haze of teen hormones and drugs."

"Who sold me the drugs?"

"Don't change the subject."

"Until the funeral today, I hadn't done anything for . . . I don't know how long, Bill."

"And you thought you knew Steadbridge." He found the book he was looking for and opened it to a page he had marked with a purple silk ribbon. "Ever read Plotinus? A philosopher. Heretic, in fact. I always remember how he described human life: 'The flight of the alone to the Alone.' "

"That kind of thought doesn't mean much to an agnostic."

"Steadbridge is a city of the dead, Tom. The dead are here, with us. They won't let us forget them. There are too many links between their world and our tight little town. And to be honest, I'm afraid what would happen if those links were broken. Things might get even worse."

"You're telling me McKibben was one of those 'links'?"

Bill nodded, got the whiskey bottle and refilled their glasses. Then he sat beside Tom on the sofa. "I don't suppose you might . . ." He looked away. "Just once, just this one night? For old times' sake?"

"That was years ago, Bill. We were kids. I was high."

"Oh."

"Ruth's expecting me."

"The highest calling for a woman is virginity. All the popes have said so."

"Well, it's a bit late in the day for that, isn't it?" He got up.

"I guess so." Bill stretched out on the couch. "You were the most beautiful kid. You're still not bad."

"So people keep telling me." He drained his glass. "I wish I'd known it years ago."

Bill smiled. "It's never too late."

"It's nearly always too late. Just look around this town. Everything turns to ruins, including us. Where's that bottle?"

He refilled their glasses, pushed Bill's legs off the couch and sat down beside him again. "What kind of links can there be?"

Before Bill answered, Tom knew what he was going to say.

"Alex."

There was a long silence, a perfect stillness. Finally Tom took another drink. "This isn't possible. This town isn't possible. People don't become links to the dead, it doesn't happen, mediums and such, they're all frauds."

"No, people don't 'become' links to the dead. Some of them simply are. I think you probably ought to leave now, before I do something we'll both be embarrassed by. Go home to Ruth and Alex."

Tom picked up the volume of Plotinus and began to page through it. "You actually find anything useful in this?"

"Sometimes. Just because he's been dead sixteen hundred years doesn't mean he didn't understand anything."

"And just because we're alive doesn't mean we do. Is that what you're saying?"

"I'm not saying a damned thing."

There came a knock at the door. Mrs. Charnocki stuck her head in and announced she was leaving for the night. Tom offered to walk her home and she refused with obvious distaste. "Good night, Father Bill."

When she was gone Bill got to his feet, unsteadily. "I'm drunk already, after only two glasses. I'm getting old."

"You should get out of here, Bill. This place isn't good."

"I can't. Bishop's orders."

"Can't you transfer to a different diocese or something?"

"This one's different enough."

"Look, I'm serious. I knew you. Know you. You could have a life, a real life, I mean. You deserve better than this."

"What do I deserve?"

"A life, god damn it!" He hadn't meant to shout, but . . .

"My life is in the church."

"With a big crack across the facade."

"Don't be snide."

"How long till this place comes crashing down around you? Or on you? What will you do then?"

"That's up to the bishop."

"Bill, get out of this town. Seeing you turn into what

Mrs. McKibben did—I can't think of anything more horrible."

"You haven't been here very long."

This was too infuriating. "Then will you for Christ's sake tell me what's going on here? What's so close under my nose I can't see it?"

"Good God, Tom, you sound like my father, searching my bedroom for my stash."

This stopped him short. "Am I being that awful?"

Bill nodded. "For a moment or two, anyway."

Suddenly they both laughed, not hard. Tom impulsively threw an arm around him and hugged.

"Are you trying to squeeze me to death?"

"Don't give me any ideas."

"You're the one who should get out of here, Tom. I've told you so before. It's too late for me, but . . ."

"I can't. Work."

"Quit."

"Without another job?"

"You'll get one."

"I can't go. There are things I love here. People I love here."

"You want some more?" He held up the bottle and Tom shook his head. "You're getting sentimental in your old age." He filled his glass to the rim and some bourbon splashed over the lip. The bottle was nearly empty.

Tom took it, held it to his lips and drained it. "Waste not, want not, huh? I really should be going. I haven't checked for messages at the hotel for a couple of days. Maybe the governor's signed my reprieve."

"Go without it."

"I told you, I can't. I'd never sleep again."

"You may not, anyway. Remember when we were in fifth grade and made that field trip to Number Five? When we came out you said it was like hell. Well, that's not too far from the mark."

"That's me. Tom Kruvener, clairvoyant."

"I'll never get out of here, Tom." He sounded both resigned and unhappy. "I'll die here."

"Oh." Tom whispered it. They hugged again, Bill kissed Tom softly on the cheek, and he left.

The night seemed unusually dark. He couldn't go back to Ruth's. There was the hotel. He was too drunk to drive, but what the hell. There wouldn't be much other traffic on these back roads. He couldn't hurt anyone but himself and that, he told himself, would be okay.

He started the car, drove east along the river. Not far from Number Five a cat walked in front of his car and he swerved to avoid it. The car collided with a phone pole. He got out to check. Dented fender. Overbrook would pay. The fires inside the mill seemed especially bright. They lit the smokestack, making it seem a shaft of yellow light reaching into the sky.

There were no messages at the hotel. He thought about having another drink but then changed his mind for once.

7

LATE SPRING WAS STEAMING HOT, LIKE HIGH summer, like the dog days. The weather forecasters called it a temperature inversion and said it seemed to have settled in for a long spell. Over the days, a thick layer of dirty haze grew over Steadbridge.

"I can't figure where it's coming from." Tom was miserable in the sweltering heat and humidity, and his allergies were inflamed by the smog. "You'd almost think the mill was still up and running, belching out sulfur dioxide."

"This is the worst spring anyone can remember," Ruth told him. "Even Hank's miserable, and he's originally from Texas."

"We're far enough from Pittsburgh and the other cities that this shouldn't be happening here. Hell, we're in the middle of the countryside."

"It'll pass, Tom."

It had taken Phil Morrissey nearly a month to send a

pair of civil engineers to inspect Number Five. There was still no sign of anyone directly connected with the production. There seemed to be no hurry. Tom had a growing suspicion that *The Colors of Hell* was more a tax write-off than anything else.

He had dutifully overseen the refurbishing of several dozen row houses, including one for his office/headquarters and another one for him to live in, just next door to Ruth's. If more were needed, they could be readied fairly quickly. The power compnay called a pair of linemen back from layoff to give the places power. And he hired a security guard to keep an eye on the houses after dark. Security at the mill was a bigger problem and would have to wait.

Tom made shopping trips to Johnstown and Pittsburgh for furniture and office supplies and equipment. Overbrook's Steadbridge branch was ready for business. Sooner or later, there might actually be some.

Despite some prodding from Ruth, Tom resisted having his parents' house renovated. The mere suggestion upset him.

"You should fix it up and live in it," she told him. "Maybe you'd feel more comfortable. More at home."

"I feel too much at home already."

"Something you know, familiar surroundings . . ."

"No, Ruth, really, I just couldn't."

Then Phil sent him a package with all kinds of production information, schedules, budgets, personnel records, the latest draft of the script. There were nearly two hundred pages of it with, apparently, more to come. He spent evenings doing homework, memorizing details. Apparently the director–screenwriter was a film school hotshot named Eric Charles Benson.

"This is going to be more work than I figured," he complained to Ruth.

"Not like making home movies?"

"Like making complicated, expensive ones. You want to read the screenplay?"

"What's it about?"

"As near as I can tell, it's about a haunted shopping mall."

"What do you mean, as near as you can tell?"

"It's not what you'd call coherent."

"No thanks."

The engineers were from Pittsburgh. The older one was a woman named Maggie, your basic grizzled veteran, in her late fifties at least. She told them she had been the resident engineer at a steel mill farther down the river, till it closed. The other looked to be just out of college; he wore a button-down shirt and tie. His name was Bob or something.

They worked separately. Now and then they'd put their heads together and powwow. Neither of them looked happy. "To be honest with you," Maggie told Tom at one point, "we can't figure out what's holding the place up."

Tom, Ruth, and Officer Hank watched as they pounded on walls, measured angles, took core samples. There was supposed to be someone from the county too, but he never showed up. During the course of a long morning, their checklist of tests and measures gradually got completed. Over lunch at Walchek's Diner they gave some preliminary conclusions, all pessimistic.

Ruth spoke for the town. "The mill's only been closed for ten years. It can't be in that bad shape."

"We'd guess it should probably have been torn down at least twenty-five or thirty years ago. The company doesn't seem to have kept it up. Corporations." Maggie dug into a dish of beef stew. "We've done more than a dozen core samples, and it doesn't look like there's much of a foundation left, if any at all. It was probably built a bit too close to the river."

"Maybe the river has shifted," Hank said helpfully. They ignored him.

"Reinforcing it would cost a fortune," her younger colleague added. "And it defies the laws of statics more ways than I could keep track of. By everything we know, it should have collapsed decades ago. Like Maggie said, we can't figure out what's keeping it up at all."

Ruth was sanguine. "Will power."

"Whose will?"

"Never you mind. There are some things engineers can't fathom."

Maggie tasted her coffee. "This is awful."

"Try drinking it for a month." Tom was still not reconciled to staying in Steadbridge, though it was clear by now he had no choice.

"I guess I should have expected it." She looked around the diner with plain distaste. "Oilcloth on the tables. I didn't know they still made oilcloth."

Ruth found herself resenting the attitude. "That's nothing. All our lights are fueled by whale oil."

Maggie drank and made another face. "Anyway, we still have a few more things to check. Some more core samples and so on. There has to be some kind of foundation down there, but we're damned if we can find it. The only part of the mill that seems to be structurally sound is that smokestack. Normally, that'd be the first thing to crumble. Go figure." She turned to Tom. "I don't suppose Overbrook would consider keeping it up till we can figure out what's going on underground?"

"Are you suggesting that the needs of science might be more important than a cheap horror movie? God, this coffee's worse than usual."

"Never mind, then. One weird thing."

"Hm?"

"Well, we still have to send the core samples off to be analyzed. But I'd swear the ground at the mill is rich with sulfur. More so than I've ever seen. I can't imagine why it would be like that. Once you get off the mill grounds, the sulfur isn't there."

Ruth decided she'd had enough breakfast and pushed

her plate away. "Maybe it's from some old steelmaking process."

"None I know of."

"Some really old one. The first mill was built back in the eighteen hundreds."

"No, I don't think so."

Tom tried to get the discussion back on track. "Seriously, I think everyone at Overbrook is sold on demolishing the place. They want to film the implosion and cut it into the movie we're making."

"Don't." Hank was unusually emphatic.

"If we buy it, Hank, it's ours to do with as we please."

Ruth got between them. "Then there's no chance you might simply want to renovate it?"

"It doesn't look that way."

"Demolition might not be the best idea."

"Overbrook Media, I'll have you know, does not deal in bad ideas." *Except for sending me here*, he thought.

At the end of their meal the engineers, along with Ruth and Hank headed back to the mill. Tom decided he'd watched long enough; he'd be seeing their report soon enough. Before they got back to their digging and drilling, he asked if they'd be staying more than one day. "You can stay in one of the company houses."

"No, thank God we won't need to." Maggie rubbed her hands together. "Pittsburgh's bad enough. I'm going to figure out how they built this thing if it kills me."

He made an excuse about having to fax something to Overbrook and headed in the direction of his office, leaving Ruth and Sheriff Hank to inspect the inspectors. But actually going to his office was the farthest thing from his mind.

Not knowing quite what to do with himself he decided to head out to the hotel. He hadn't yet moved the last of his things. It didn't take him long to pack and settle his bill. The desk clerk told him the bartenders were all going to miss him.

Tom smiled a sardonic smile. "My home away from home."

THERE WAS A BAR CALLED HANK'S JUST OFF THE northern corner of McKinley Square. He decided it was time to start checking out the local watering holes, such as they were. A neon sign flickered in the front window, advertising Stroh's. The place was empty except for the bartender and a pair of elderly men who seemed to have been drinking for hours.

"Bourbon." The place smelled of beer that went stale in the last millennium.

The bartender was young, in his twenties. "Sure. You that movie guy?"

"More or less, yeah. So the police chief owns this bar?"

"Yep. He loses more money on the place than he makes, though. People here like to drink at home."

"That's what I like about Steadbridge, good traditional values. Do me a favor and don't tell Hank I was in here, okay?" He left a large tip on the bar.

"Sure thing. He won't be by till after nine anyway."

"Good. Then give me another one."

"You shouldn't drink so much this early in the day."

"I can handle it. I got the habit early. What's your name?"

"Tony. Tony Kowalski." He smiled and they shook hands.

"Is this the best bar in town?"

"Practically. Any chance I can get a job in your movie?"

"I can't say. They're still doing rewrites on the script. If we need extras . . ." He smiled and shrugged. "I'll do what I can for you. And I expect you to do the same for me. You're likely to see a lot of me in here."

"Good. This town needs new blood."

"What about you? What keeps you here?"

"Oh, I have to take care of my grandfather. He got hurt

at Number Five way back when. He doesn't have anyone
else."

"Steel mill, my ass. The place was a death mill."

Tony made a mock-thoughtful face. "Um . . . yeah."

AS THE AFTERNOON WORE ON RUTH FOUND HER-
self getting restless. Watching the engineers at work bored
her, and Hank wasn't exactly a font of conversation. She
finally made an excuse about having to work a shift at the
bakery and left.

Hank ambled about the mill, trying to stay out of the
way, looking for something to interest him. There was
nothing. When a police call finally came in, a cat in a tree,
he was only too happy to leave.

Maggie and her colleague worked their way methodically through the mill, sometimes separately, sometimes as
a team. Neither seemed happy with what they were finding,
or not finding. Maggie made notes on her laptop.

Just before sunset the earth began to tremble. Sulfur
fumes gagged them. Maggie thought she could hear dogs
barking. They steadied themselves against the walls. After
a moment it passed.

"Are you okay, Bob?"

"It's Ben. Yeah, I think so. The foundation must be
worse than we thought."

"That felt more like an earthquake."

"I've never heard of any earthquakes in this part of the
country. I had two semesters of geology, and—"

"We're in the Appalachians. There must be faults, even
if they're not very active."

Ben stepped warily away from the wall. "I think it was
the foundation. Listen, it's getting late. We can't see anything else in here tonight. Let's head back down to Pittsburgh."

"Aren't you at all curious about this place?"

"God, no."

"If that was the foundation, there might be something really interesting. . . ."

"I've got a date tonight."

"Oh."

They walked outside, to where their car was parked. "Listen, Bill, I—"

"Ben, remember?"

"Sorry. I think I want to stay here for at least another day. There's something really odd about this place, but I'm damned if I can put a finger on it."

"Well, I really need to get back to town tonight. I've been after a date with this chick for weeks."

"Go ahead, then. I'll be fine. I'll have Tom arrange another car for me."

"You sure?"

"Yeah. Don't worry about it. I hope she's worth the drive."

"She is."

They said polite, professional goodbyes and Ben drove off. Maggie stared at the mill for a moment. Was there a hint of fire coming from inside? Must be a trick of the light, a reflection of the setting sun off the river or something. But how could it be reflected to the inside of the building? One more puzzle to unravel.

She stared down the road to Steadbridge. Unedifying sight. Oh well, she could take it for a day or two. She ambled toward the town.

After a few minutes she found herself in McKinley Square, looking up at the bronze corpulence of the former president, then up at St. Dympna's crucifix. Curious, she walked about the square for a few minutes, then explored some of the adjacent parts of town. The light was dying. It wasn't long before she realized she was lost, or at least disoriented. If she made her way back to the square, she'd be able to find her way to the Overbrook office. Tom's offer to put her up in one of the company houses must still be good.

The street lights flickered on. She found it odd that only

every second or third one lit up. Half the town was dark. By design? Depressed economy, she imagined.

There was someone at the next corner. She couldn't make it out. "Excuse me!"

The figure didn't answer, didn't move. She walked toward it. "Excuse me, please?"

The figure stirred. Before she could get too close it began to glow, bright orange like fire. Then it vanished.

Maggie stood staring at the spot where it had been. The heat of the day, or the sulfur fumes, must have gotten to her. There was no other explanation.

She saw someone else in the distance, a good four blocks away. "Excuse me!" she shouted, "I'm afraid I'm lost. Can you help me?"

The figure erupted into bright light, faded and was gone.

Then from behind her came a voice. "I can help."

She turned. It was a boy. Thin, very pale, long dark hair. Still a bit off balance, she made herself smile. "Hi."

"Hi. I'm Alex."

"I'm Maggie. And I'm lost."

"What are you doing here?"

"As I said, I'm lost."

"You're one of the ones who are telling everyone to tear down the mill."

How could he know that? "I'm an engineer, Alex. They asked me to check the place out."

"You shouldn't."

"Well, it's my job. Do you know where Overbrook Media is?"

"Next door."

She looked around, puzzled.

"Next door to my house, I mean."

"Oh. Could you take me there, please?"

"Sure. It's not good to tear it down. People will die. People already have." He started walking.

"But it's so old. Don't you think a nice new building would—"

"They won't like it."

"Well, whoever they are, they don't really have a say in the matter. Overbrook's buying the mill. What do you know about all this, anyway?"

"More than you do."

"Oh."

He kept walking. Somewhat amused, she followed him. After a block and a half of walking in silence, he suddenly pointed at a door. "There."

Entertained by his odd demeanor, she smiled. "Thank you, Alex."

He quickly disappeared into his house. Maggie went to the door he had indicated. A hand-lettered sign read OVERBROOK PRODUCTIONS OR WHATEVER. She knocked.

Nothing.

Again, more loudly. She hoped there was still someone inside; there didn't seem to be much chance of finding a place to sleep without Overbrook's help.

The door of Alex's house opened and Tom came out. "Maggie. I thought I heard someone knocking. Shouldn't you be back in Pittsburgh?"

"Well, if I had any sense, yes. But this mill . . . there's something peculiar about it. I want to stay and check it out for another day or two. I can give you a better report then."

"Any chance you'll decide we should leave the place up?"

"Zilch. But I should be able to give you some solid ideas about how to rebuild once it's down."

"Hang on a sec. I'll get you the keys to one of these houses."

He ran into the Overbrook office and pulled a set of keys out of a desk drawer, then rejoined her. "It's just down the street, here. Let me show you."

They walked. It was nearly dark. A red glow in the sky came from the direction of the mill. Maggie seemed not to notice it, or not to think anything of it. Tom called the security man's cell phone to let him know one of the houses would be occupied.

"Do you have a change of clothes with you?"

"No. I didn't expect to be here overnight. I could use some towels and a bar of soap, though. And some dinner."

"Ruth and I were just about to go out. You're welcome to join us."

"Where are you going?"

"Walchek's."

"Swell."

BEN DROVE QUICKLY, KEEPING THE RIVER TO HIS right. The country roads were narrow, but there was no traffic. Ahead of him the sun set, and its last rays gave way to a deep grey night sky. There was some bright star showing, barely, through the smog, he didn't know which.

In the road ahead of him there was a light. As he drew closer he realized it was a fire blocking the road. He pulled to a stop twenty feet from it and tried to see what was burning—a car? brush?—but there was no way to tell. At moments it seemed to him there were figures in it, alive and moving. There was no one else in sight. He looked around for a way to get past it, but the riverbank was too close on one side, and the other was blocked by a stand of trees. If the flames grew much higher there would be a forest fire, at least a small one.

He got out his cell phone and started to dial a number, then realized it had gone dead. "Shit."

This wasn't possible. A fire in the middle of nowhere. Nothing fueling it, nothing he could see. No one around who could have lit it. Of all nights.

There was nothing for it but to head back to Steadbridge. He could call his date from there and make his apologies. She'd understand. He hoped.

He turned the car around and drove back east along the road. The car radio was dead too. One of his headlights flickered and died. A rabbit dashed in front of his car and caused him to swerve; he stopped just short of the riverbank.

This was too much. As he drove he mouthed a long string of invectives against small towns, the steel industry, rabbits . . .

At his rapid clip Steadbridge was only a five-minute drive. The town looked dead. Hell, he thought, it really is dead. Then he noticed the light in the mill.

As he got closer, it was clear there was a fire inside Number Five, or a number of fires. How . . . ? If that had really been an earthquake before, it might have opened up some fissures in the earth, and . . . No, that was crazy. A tongue of flame erupted from the smokestack; fire leaped a hundred feet into the sky.

Three blocks from the mill his car died. He let it coast to a stop, not bothering to pull to the side of the street. And he walked the rest of the way to Number Five. The whole place was lit brightly. This was how it must have looked when it was alive, when it was still a mill and not a ruined hulk.

He walked toward the entrance. Fire seemed to cascade from the walls. Despite himself, he found it quite beautiful. He had seen film of the old mills, back when this valley was still the center of the world's steel industry. The pictures always thrilled him, frightened and thrilled him.

There were men inside the mill. Working. Pouring steel, drawing cables . . . Some of them seemed to be on fire, quite engulfed in flames.

Knowing this wasn't possible, but quite hypnotized by the sight before him, he stepped inside. Everywhere the flames danced. He heard the yelping of dogs.

Then from out of the inferno a gigantic dog galloped. It was nearly as large as a horse. It had three heads. It sprang at him, knocked him to the ground. One of its heads tore open his abdomen. The second bit into his throat. The third sank its fangs into his eyes. He lived for nearly ten minutes, knowing he was being eaten.

AFTER DINNER TOM AND RUTH WALKED MAGGIE back to her place and said good night to her; she settled into her temporary house. But she was restless. She needed a drink. Even in a town as dead as this there had to be a bar. Against her own better judgment she went out into the street and headed in the direction of McKinley Square. There'd be a bar there, if anyplace.

A few blocks past the square she saw the glow of the neon sign in the window of Hank's. The sheriff himself was tending bar. She pulled up a stool.

"Evening, miss. I thought you'd be gone by now. You lost?"

"Not literally, no. Give me whatever you have on draft."

He filled a glass for her. A bartending sheriff. In a town this dead, it wasn't surprising.

"So, why aren't you back in Pittsburgh?"

She shrugged. "I find Steadbridge so stimulating. I just couldn't leave."

From a booth behind her came a man's voice. "That's our home town."

She turned to look. The man was in his late thirties. Around his neck was a clerical collar.

"I'm Bill Vicosz. Pastor at the church across the square."

"Maggie Rahway."

"Miss Rahway's one of the engineers checking out Number Five for Overbrook."

"Oh? Where's the other one?"

"Pittsburgh, bless him." She raised her glass in an unspoken toast.

"Well, it beats Steadbridge. Why don't you come over here and drink with me? We can tell each other the stories of our lives."

"Mine would be way too long."

"Mine too."

"A small-town priest? How exciting can things be here?"

"Lady, you have no idea."

Something in his manner made her wary. "Thanks, but I just stopped in for a quick drink. Nice meeting you, though."

He smiled and saluted her with his glass. "Here's to old loves unfulfilled."

"Here's to fires that should have died but still burn bright." She returned his salute.

Hank went over to Bill's table with another drink. They had a low, whispered conversation. She couldn't hear what they were saying, and she didn't care. She went quickly back out into the empty streets.

IN THE NIGHT TOM AND RUTH MADE LOVE.

When they were finished and moved apart in the bed, Tom noticed how bright the mill was. It hardly seemed worth mentioning.

"You remember when we were kids?" he asked her. "We both used to smoke afterward. I thought it made me look sophisticated."

"Oh?" He could tell she was smiling in the dark "I just did it so I'd have an excuse not to talk."

"I wish there was some way I could persuade you to get out of this place with me."

"We had a picnic, Tom"

"You know what I mean. This town is bad."

"Evil."

"Bill's the one who knows about evil. I just know this isn't a good place for you. Or Alex."

"We can't go, Tom. I've told you so many times. Things hold us here."

"I wish I knew what."

"No, you don't."

"I keep trying to reach you, but I can never really get inside. What are you holding back? And why?"

She said nothing.

"Ruth?"

"None of us ever knows anyone else, Tom. Not really. And it's not a matter of holding back. It's a matter of sanity. We all carry death around inside us. We're never without it. If you look deeply enough into someone else's face, you'll see a grinning skull. So we all keep our distance."

"I need a drink. You?"

"Mm-hmm."

He went downstairs and fixed two cocktails. Then he got back into bed beside her. "Cheers."

"Here's looking at you."

They drank without talking for a few minutes.

Then the liquor took hold, or started to. "Ruth, am I any good? Or am I the only one around here worth taking to bed?"

"Both. But you're not as good as you used to be. No one is."

"If that's supposed to make me feel any better . . ."

"It's not."

She rolled over on her side, turning her back to him. End of conversation.

In a short time they were both asleep.

In his own room, Alex was awake and restless.

VERY LATE, AFTER MIDNIGHT. TWO FIGURES, A BOY and a girl, each with a large backpack, moved through the empty streets of Steadbridge. Now and then they held hands; mostly they walked apart from each other.

"We can use any of these places," the boy said gesturing at the abandoned row houses around them.

"I'm tired of sleeping in ruins."

"When we get to Miami—"

"We've been living like this for weeks. I'm sick of it. We're never going to go to Miami."

He did not feel like arguing. They walked.

After a while they came to a row of Tom's newly renovated houses. Each had a sign in front: "Overbrook
Media." The boy smiled. "Let's break in."

"We're in enough shit already." She sat down on the
curb. "All we need is to get busted."

"There's no one around. Who could see us?"

"I don't know, God or the devil or someone. I want to
get some sleep."

The boy crept onto the porch of the nearest house and
looked in the window. It was empty. Carefully he tried the
doorknob. Locked.

From his pocket he took a folding knife and tried to
force the lock, but he didn't know how to do it. The girl
watched him. "Some survivor. Some street smarts."

"Look, Beth, I—"

She sprang to her feet, picked up a rock and threw it
through the window. "There. Now we can get in, okay?"

From up the street someone shouted "Hey!" and shined
a flashlight in their direction.

"Cops! Jesus!"

They ran. Behind them Tom's security guard laughed. It
was just a couple of kids looking for a place to make it.

In a few moments Beth and her boyfriend were at Number Five. It was quite dark, quite silent. For a moment they
were awed by its sheer ominous size.

"We can sleep in there. Nobody will find us."

"I told you, Josh, no more ruins. I'm sick to death of
stealing food and sleeping in dumps."

"We don't have much choice."

"We can go home."

"No. Maybe you can, but I can't. Not there. No."

It was another familiar argument. They both fell silent.
Josh gaped at the mill for a moment and then pushed his
way through the fence. "Come on."

She followed him. "Shit, I hate this."

He stumbled, fell and cut his hand on a shard of glass. "I'm bleeding."

"Here, wrap it in this." She got a handkerchief out of her pack and gave it to him.

The interior of the mill was completely black. Trying to staunch the flow of the blood from his hand, he went to the door and peered inside. Silence, blackness.

Beth walked to the foot of the smokestack. "Let's go up."

"I thought you were tired."

Without answering she began to climb the steps. Reluctantly, Josh followed.

"I want to see the river from up there." It seemed every third or fourth step was loose or shaky, but they climbed anyway.

Ten feet up, she stopped. Above her stood a man. His face was a mass of scar tissue, and he had no arms.

From somewhere, not far away but not very loud, came the barking of dogs.

IN HIS ROOM ALONE, IN THE DARK, ALEX WAS WIDE awake. There were people at the mill; he knew it, he could see them in his mind's eye. The mill was restless. This would not be a good night.

Wanting to distract himself he switched on the light on his nightstand and tried to concentrate on a comic book. The pictures were vivid but for once they could not hold his attention. The words, as they always were for him, were a jumble. He focused on one and tried to make the letters make sense, but it was no use.

He knew he wouldn't be able to sleep.

Not knowing what to do, he crept quietly downstairs. It wasn't possible to watch television; it would wake his mother and Tom. He knew from a hundred earlier nights what a light sleeper she was.

In the kitchen he looked for a snack. There was nothing

he wanted to eat. Then his eyes fell on his mother's store of liquor. One by one he opened several bottles full of clear liquids and smelled the contents. They all repulsed him. Then he tried the wine.

Red wine, deep red. The smell was not obnoxious like the others. He poured a few drops into a glass and gingerly tasted it. It was strong and bitter but he liked it. He poured more, switched off the light and carried the glass up to his room.

Lying in bed he drank. At first small sips, then longer ones. He didn't exactly like the taste, but he didn't exactly dislike it either. In a few moments he began to feel its effects. It was good. This was why people drank, he realized, and he liked it. The light-headedness, the way he forgot unpleasant things.

He took a long, deep swallow and it made him gag, but that was okay. He had learned to drink it slowly, no more swallowing, just sipping. His head began to spin. He closed his eyes and saw flame.

From his mother's room came a sound. It took him a moment to realize clearly that it was the sound of her bed creaking; she or Tom had shifted position, that was all.

The room was feeling stuffy. He got out of bed to open the window. And stumbled, caught himself on the edge of the bed. And smiled. This was fun.

At the window he saw that the mill was ablaze, engulfed in flames, brighter and more furious than he had ever seen it before. *They are more alive than ever,* he thought. He took another long sip of his wine, and the flames leaped higher into the sky.

IN THE RECTORY BILL VICOSZ WAS RESTLESS TOO. He had had too much to drink. Or not enough. He stood naked in his bedroom, looking out at the blank, sleeping town.

An impulse made him want to see more of it. He

climbed into a pair of shorts and walked the passageway to the church.

In the sanctuary he stopped. There was a small lamp burning on the altar, giving only the faintest light to the vast space. Everything was perfectly still. The place had never looked so empty to him. He wanted company. He found himself wishing Tom was there with him. *But that was a long time ago*, he thought. Nothing good lasts, everything good dies, especially that. The church had taught him as much, but it was so easy to forget and hope.

He wanted to see more of his town.

The bell tower. He had not had it inspected since that crack had opened in the church's facade; the inspectors had said the church itself was still usable, but they hadn't checked the tower.

He climbed. As he did every time he ascended the narrow stairs, he remembered seeing *Vertigo* at the Hip. With Tom. If only our memories died the way other things died. Paint flakes, metal rusts, flesh decays, but the things we remember stay fresh as spring moss, as mushrooms after rain. . . .

Only the mill's smokestack was taller than St. Dympna's bell tower. He stood and looked out over his town, wishing fervently it was not his. *If only*, he thought, *there was some actual point to praying.*

The mill was ablaze. It was not possible, it was built of steel not wood, but it was completely engulfed in bright hot fire. This was not the first time, not at all, but he had never seen it so fierce before.

The link was growing stronger. It had to be cut.

8

"**H**OLD ON A SEC, PHIL. I THINK THE SHERIFF HAS something." Tom was at the back of the mill the next morning with Ruth and Hank when his phone rang, uncharacteristically early by Overbrook standards.

Someone had found the charred bodies of two people and reported them anonymously. Burned, as Hank put it,. beyond recognition; he seemed pleased at his cliché. Yet there was no other sign of fire to be seen. These people had burned—from the expressions on their faces and the bodily contortions, burned alive—without touching anything around them.

It was another blindingly hot morning, yet Hank seemed cool and comfortable in his uniform. He was rooting around inside the building, looking for footprints or fingerprints or whatever. Suddenly he broke into a smile, bent down and picked something up. It was a quarter.

"No, I thought the police had found something. Go ahead."

"Like I was saying, he'll be there today or tomorrow." Phil was obviously annoyed at being interrupted.

"What's his name?"

"Eric Charles Benson."

"And you said he's a film school graduate?"

"Yeah."

"How recently?"

"Last month."

Splendid. "Look, we're going to have to get some security at this place, and soon. Two people dead here, two missing. It's more charnel house than steel mill. I've got a man keeping an eye on the houses after dark, but—"

"Take it out of your slush fund, for now. What did those engineers say?"

"One of them's still here, actually. Says she wants to be as thorough as possible."

"But what does she say about the building?" He was sounding more and more irritable.

"She says we ought to tear the damned thing down. If we don't, it's likely to fall down. On us."

"Well, we're going to use it for this shoot. Can't she find a way to buttress it or fortify it or something? If we have to, we'll get a variance in the safety codes somehow."

Ruth found something at the foot of the smokestack. Tom shaded his eyes to see. It was a backpack, or what had been one, badly singed.

"The actors might squawk."

"Let 'em. You know what Hitchcock said about actors. Just get this damned investigation closed quickly and covered up. We don't want publicity."

"Are you sure? Everyone here says the mill's haunted or something. It could help sell the movie."

"Overbrook Media does not want to draw attention to this. And we do not want to spend a dime we don't have to, till we're sure we can make money at this. Period."

"But Phil, if the place is dangerous—"

"Then it's dangerous. We'll implode it at the end of the

shoot. That's what'll sell the movie. Every news program in the country will carry it. You know how they love that stuff. In the meantime we'll make do." He hung up.

Tom crossed to Ruth. She yawned, then grinned. "Home office trouble?"

"I think they're blaming me for the kind of place Steadbridge is."

"That's as good an explanation as any."

He didn't want to talk about it. "What's Hank looking for?"

"I'm not sure he's sure. Anything to make some sense of this."

"Well, it'll be an easy investigation to close. He can just say they fell asleep with lit cigarettes, same as Mrs. McKibben."

Hank came out of the mill. "There are parts of another body in there, I think. Burned, too, but torn to bits before or afterward." He paused, looked around, took a deep breath. "This was obviously drug related."

"What?!" Tom couldn't hold his astonishment in.

"We all know how ruthless drug gangs can be."

"Uh, right." Case closed, apparently. At least Overbrook would be happy.

Ruth showed Hank the burned backpack. "It matches the description of one of those missing kids' pack. Doesn't it?"

"You're right, Ruth." He turned to Tom. "See? Kids. Drugs. Or Satan worship."

Neat logic. He didn't feel like arguing. "I'd stick with drugs. Is there a reliable security firm anywhere around here? I think we ought to start having the place patrolled, at least after dark. Whoever hangs out here could be trouble for us."

"Nobody hangs out here."

Tom gestured at the charred corpses without saying anything.

"Oh. You could hire some local men, couldn't you?"

"I'd rather have it done professionally."

Ruth and Hank both registered disappointment.

"But let me think about it. Maybe we can get a security firm to hire some Steadbridge people, okay?"

Maggie came around the corner and strode up to them, obviously in a good mood. "Morning, everyone."

Ruth gestured at the burned corpses.

"Oh. Good God."

"I doubt," Tom said sourly, "if He had anything to do with it."

"Cynic. There's another mystery."

They all looked at her.

"My little colleague Bill never got home last night."

"I thought it was Bob." Tom's phone rang again. He let it; voice mail would pick up.

"It was Ben," Ruth said firmly. "Did he tell you where he was going?"

"Said he had a hot date. I'm sure he's just shacked up someplace, probably at his girlfriend's house. But his family's worried."

The sound of a siren approached. Ruth went and looked around the corner of the mill. "It's the guys from the county coroner. I've never seen human remains like this before. It'll be interesting to see what the coroner makes of this."

The ambulance attendants quickly got their gear together, reported to Hank, then picked up the remains, including the body parts, and slid them carefully onto the stretchers. Hank supervised. "Not much left for Doc Peters to autopsy."

One of them, a man in his fifties, shrugged. "I've seen worse. You should have seen what we had to take out of here back when the mill was open."

Cheery thought. Tom looked at Maggie. "Look, I'm not sure how much longer it'll be before you can get any work done here. You want to get some breakfast?"

"No thanks. I just had a really awful jelly donut. I think I'll go back and work on my report for a while. Let me know when I can get back to it out here, okay?"

She walked off just behind the stretcher-bearers. As she got to the corner of the building she stopped. "Ruth, your boy's here."

Ruth and Tom went to the corner and looked. Alex was standing beside the ambulance, watching fascinated. He reached out as if he wanted to touch one of the bodies as it passed.

"Alex!"

Her face was a picture of maternal frustration. "My precocious little boy."

She ran over to him. "Come on, Alex, this is no place for you. You have enough morbid thoughts already."

Tom looked back at Hank, then decided to join Ruth.

Maybe he ought to check voice mail. That might have been Phil again, and he had sounded cranky enough the first time they talked.

He played the message. "Mr. Kruvener, this is Eric Charles Benson. The writer–director of *The Colors of Hell*? I'm, uh, I'm lost. Can you come and get me?" For a moment he fell silent, then he added, "I've got some camera equipment with me." His tone made it sound like he thought that was good news.

"Well, Ruth, it sounds like you're not the only one with a problem child to take care of."

"What on earth do you mean?"

"My little baby Eisenstein is here."

Alex looked thoughtful. "The relativity guy?"

"No," Ruth explained patiently, "that was Einstein. Eisenstein was a movie maker."

"Like Walt Disney?" His face lit up.

"From the sound of him, Alex," Tom said, "this guy's more like one of Disney's target audience."

"Huh?"

"Nothing. You want to come with me and meet him?"

"Sure!" It was as enthusiastic as Alex had sounded about anything since Tom met him.

Tom called Benson back.

"Eric Charles Benson."

"Hello, Eric Charles Benson. This is Thomas Martin Kruvener."

"Mr. Kruvener. Tom." He sounded pleased. "Where am I?"

"I don't know. I left my Ouija board at home."

"Huh?"

"You'll have to tell me where you are, Eric. I'm not a psychic."

"Oh." There was a puzzled pause. "Well, there's this little park or something."

"Yeah? And?"

"There's a statue of some fat guy."

"President McKinley."

Another pause. Then with exaggerated certainty, as if he was determined not to let anyone put anything over on him, he said, "There was never any President McKinley."

"This is just a guess, but you're not looking to make historical films, are you?"

"No. Why?"

"Never mind. I'll be there in a couple of minutes. Don't let the pigeons eat you till I get there."

"Like in Hitchcock!" Benson's voice was bright.

"Right." He hung up and turned to Ruth.

She had been eavesdropping. She was laughing. "If you could see the look on your face."

"While I'm hiring security guards, I probably ought to take on a babysitter. Want to come along?"

"No, I've got to help Hank with the paperwork. You two have fun."

"Come on, Alex."

The two of them walked along the river. For a few moments, they didn't say much.

"Tom?"

"Hm?"

"What's a movie director do, anyway?"

"Mostly he stands back and lets the cameraman do his job."

"I don't know what you mean."

"We'll be shooting the movie during the early part of the summer. Once school's out, if it's okay with your mom, maybe we can have you watch. Who knows, you might even learn something from Eric Charles Benson."

"That'd be great!"

"Maybe we can even let you work as a gopher. Just a little part-time job for you, a couple of hours a week. You could earn a little money."

"What's a gopher?"

"He's a guy who runs errands for people."

"I can do that."

"It'll be a real job, though. You'll have to behave yourself."

"And you're making this movie in the mill?"

"Yep."

"I can help then."

"Maybe we can even give you a title. Would you like to see your name on the screen? 'Assistant to Mr. Kruvener: Alex Fawcett.' "

"I c-can't read."

"I think you and this director will have a lot in common."

"Really?"

"Joke. I hope."

"Oh. Well, anyway, I'd like to do that."

In the river a pair of fish were jumping. Tom noticed it without commenting; but it seemed to him that must mean the Mon was back to normal. "We'll have to check with your mom and make sure it's okay with her. And you'll have to behave. No more throwing rocks at people."

"Oh. I'm s-sorry about that, Tom. Grandma McKibben told me about you and about what's going to happen here, and I was s-scared."

"What could she have told you?"

"Mom told me not to talk about it."

"Oh."

For a couple of minutes they walked without saying much.

"Tom, do you love my mom?"

"You do ask rough questions, don't you?"

"I want to know."

"So do I."

"Huh?"

"I don't know if I love her. And I sure don't know if she loves me. What do you think?"

"I think she doesn't know either. But Grandma Kibben saw the L-lovers in her cards when you first came here."

"She saw Death, too, remember?"

"I tried reading her cards once. Didn't understand anything I s-saw."

"That's probably just as well. There's enough around here to be afraid of."

McKinley Square. There was no one in sight. At one corner, a Hummer was parked, filled with cameras and other film and video gear. "Well, it looks like our director has disappeared. Most people usually seem to take a day or two."

"Maybe he's hiding."

"I should be so lucky." His eye drifted to the Hippodrome. "Maybe he's over there, checking out the theater."

They went and looked. No one.

When they turned and went back there was a young man sitting on a bench, eating a donut. Tom studied him. Loose khakis, white sneakers, collar-length hair, Steven Spielberg beard, thick eyeglasses. This simply had to be Eric Charles Benson.

He called across the square. "Eric?"

The guy looked around, not sure where the voice had come from.

Tom and Alex crossed to him.

"Eric?"

"Tom Kruvener?"

"That's me. This is Alex Fawcett."

Eric ignored the boy. "This jelly donut is terrific."

"It's from a chain."

"I know. It's great."

"Uh, fine. Why don't I take you to your place and get you settled in?"

He wiped his hands on his shirt. "I'd rather go and see the steel mill first, if you don't mind."

"That might not be the best idea. The police are out there. There's been some trouble."

"Well, I'd like to see it anyway."

"Eric, two maybe three, people died out there overnight. The police are investigating."

"Really?" He brightened up.

"Yes, really. Runaway kids, apparently. Somehow they managed to get themselves burned to death."

"Wow. I'd like to see that." He had more in common with Alex than Tom had actually expected.

"The coroner's men have already taken the bodies away."

"Oh." He was glum. Then he broke out into another smile. "Oh well, they probably don't look as cool as the burned bodies I've seen before."

"You've seen—?"

"In movies. Did you see *Final Destination 3*?"

"No, I missed that."

"It was so cool."

"I'm sure it was. Let me show you where you'll be staying, okay?" He started to go.

"I can't tell you how pissed I am that somebody else thought of making a *Mortal Kombat* movie first."

"Life is full of little disappointments. Can we get going?"

For the first time Alex joined the exchange. "Do you make cartoons?"

"No." Eric didn't try to hide his disdain for the boy.

"You should make cartoons."

"Animation's not my field, Alec."

"Alex."

He took a long look around the square. "This town is really crummy, isn't it?"

Tom sighed, he hoped loud enough for Eric to hear. But it was lost on him. "Come on, Eric."

"My Hummer's over here. I hate towns like this."

"Have you seen many?"

"Only in movies. But everybody always hates them."

"So you speak from experience."

"Sure."

Their film, Tom gathered, would not be long on irony. They got into the Hummer; it was so full of luggage and equipment that Alex had sit on his lap.

Tom cranked down his window. "You know, you just might find there's more to Steadbridge than is apparent at first glance."

"I can handle this place."

As they passed the church, Eric stopped and did an exaggerated double-take. "St. Who?! Who the hell is St. Dympna?"

Tom decided breezy nonchalance was the only attitude that would keep him sane. "She's the patron saint of the nervous and emotionally disturbed. Surely you've heard of her?"

"Who would have a saint for people like that?"

"Can you think of a group that needs one more? Is there a patron saint of director-screenwriters?"

"The Hippodrome?" He noticed the marquee across the square. "There was actually a movie house called the Hippodrome?"

Alex picked up a video camera and started fiddling with it.

"Put that down, kid!"

Alex looked at Tom.

"Why don't you hold off till later, okay Alex? By the way, Eric, Alex here is going to be your assistant director."

"Are you kidding me?" There was a note of minor outrage in his voice.

"Of course." Tom was pleased with himself. "But he's going to work as a gopher on the set, I think."

"Well, just keep him out of my hair."

"Yes, sir."

"When I tell Uncle Ph—Mister Morrissey about this place . . ."

"Yes?"

"He won't be happy. There has to be another location we can use."

"Mister Morrissey's the one who's insisting we shoot here."

"Shit."

"Watch your language, will you?"

Eric floored the gas pedal. "Stuck in this slimehole of a town for three months."

"I can't wait till you meet the sheriff."

"I can't wait till I meet the attendants on my flight home."

After a few minutes more of this they arrived at the Overbrook row houses. Tom installed Eric in the one farthest from his own. "Why don't you get settled in? I'll be back in an hour or so and we can have lunch."

"Hominy grits and corn pone?"

Tom hustled Eric inside the house where Alex couldn't hear them. "All right, now look. You're the director–screenwriter, but I'm the executive in charge of production. We're going to be here for a couple of months, maybe longer if we have trouble on the shoot. We have to get along with the people here if we're to get this film made. Do you understand that?"

"What kind of trouble could we have?"

"Nothing they taught you about in film school. Now I

expect you to behave professionally. Do you understand me?"

Eric sniffed. "I went to NYU."

"And you skipped Professional Behavior 101? When's the rest of the crew start arriving?"

"Not for a couple of weeks."

"Good. Their quarters will be ready then. If you need anything, let me know."

"I'm shooting the movie myself. On digital."

"Fine. I'll see you in an hour or so." He left without waiting for a reply.

LUNCH, WALCHEK'S.

Tom introduced Eric to Ruth and Maggie. "Ruth's going to be our liaison with the town. Maggie's the structural engineer who's been checking out Number Five to make sure it's safe."

Eric smiled and said hello to them. It was fairly clear he didn't want to be dealing with them, especially Ruth. He read his menu. Fortunately the menus at Walchek's were short, so he couldn't hide behind it very long. He ordered a burger, fries and coffee. Everyone else asked for pot roast.

"So." Tom tried to sound like someone used to presiding at meetings. "I thought Ruth might show you around town this afternoon."

"Why?"

"Well, you're revising the script, right?"

"Yeah." He sounded dubious.

"Then you must be looking for locations. There's some interesting old architecture you might want to use."

"Can't we just build what we need?"

"Have you seen the budget? You're to shoot this as quickly and cheaply as possible. We have to wrap by the Fourth of July."

"But sets must be in the budget."

"We can build a few small interiors. That's what we'll be using the mill for, a studio. But even they will have to be basic."

Ruth sensed the tension and decided to get between them. "I haven't read the script, Eric. What's the story?"

"It's about a haunted mall."

Maggie giggled but stifled it. "And you're writing it?"

He nodded and grinned, pleased with himself. "But I thought I'd have the budget to do it properly. Unc—Mr. Morrissey promised me I'd be in charge."

Tom was in no mood to coddle him. "Artistically, you are. But I'm responsible for the budget. We'll be able to use the mill for the outside of the mall, too. I think we can afford a quick paint job. Of course, we'll only be able to paint one side of it, but the camera can only see one side, right?"

"Oh."

Their coffee came. Everyone braced themselves to see the look on his face when he tasted it.

He sipped. "This is delicious. It tastes like McDonald's."

Maggie drank a bit of hers, then put it aside. "Out of curiosity, Eric, what's your own favorite movie?"

"Well, *Freddy Vs. Jason* would have to rank pretty high."

"Not *Citizen Kane*? Or *Psycho*?"

"Nah. None of that old stuff. *Psycho*'s a good idea for a movie, but they didn't have CGI or anything else that could have let them make it properly." He wrinkled his nose in distaste. "Chocolate syrup for blood."

Tom couldn't resist. "I hate to tell you, but we don't have the budget for CGI either. You'll have to make do with mechanical effects. And simple ones, at that." He added with emphasis, "The old-fashioned way."

Disappointment registered. Then he turned thoughtful. "Well, if I keep it visually interesting, no one will notice. When will the crane for the crane shots get here?"

"No crane shots, Eric. No money for them."

"But—"

"Sorry. Anyway, I've asked Maggie here to stay on for the production. Just to keep an eye on things, safety-wise."

The waitress brought their lunches. Eric took a long swallow of his coffee, then forced himself to smile. "Well, I guess we'll have to make do. Francis Ford Coppola started with *Dementia 13*, after all."

"You know who Coppola is?"

"Sure. He used to be a director."

Ruth took a mouthful of pot roast and grimaced. "So anyway, Eric, as we were telling you, there are a lot of interesting sites in town. You may have an easy time giving your film visual interest."

"I promised Nicole crane shots."

"Nicole?"

"Nicole Kammerfleischer. She's our star." It was clear from his voice he was a bit in love with her, or at least in lust. "You must have seen her. She was in *Pumpkinhead 7*."

Maggie lit a cigarette. "Damn, I think I missed that."

Tom was deadpan. "Cast of promising newcomers."

They ate their lunch without much more conversation. Eric was silent and, to appearances, thoughtful. He seemed to like his burger. After a few minutes he brightened up and said, "Yeah, we can use the town for locations."

Tom put on a big smile. "Good thinking."

"And maybe we can use some of the residents for extras."

"That's the attitude. We'll get this film made despite what the front office did to the budget." He wanted Eric to realize that Uncle Phil might not be his best friend.

Eric turned to Ruth. "So when can you show me the town?"

"This afternoon, as soon as we're all finished eating."

"Great. I can start rewriting the script for the new locations."

Ruth found herself starting to like Eric. She avoided

Tom's eye. "Anything the Town of Steadbridge can do to help, just let us know."

"My production designer will be here next week or the week after. Will you show her around too? She's good. She'll know just what to do with these old places."

"Good for her." Tom drained his cup.

"And I think we should have this place do our catering. The food here's terrific. Will you talk to them about it, Tom?"

He kept his face blank. "Anything you like, C.B."

"Speaking for the town, that's what we like to hear." Ruth was feeling more and more friendly toward Eric. "Pump as much money as you can into the economy here. We need it."

MCKINLEY SQUARE. ERIC LOOKED AROUND, squinting at things and sighting along his thumb, hoping he looked professional. Tom left him to Ruth; Maggie headed out to the mill; Tom made a beeline for Hank's bar.

"Afternoon, Tom. Bourbon?" Tony smiled and set up a glass. Tom was becoming a regular. There was jazz playing on the radio.

"Hi, Tony. Make it a double, will you? I have to get the taste of Walchek's pot roast out of my mouth."

"You'll never get it out of your memory. I hear the movie people are starting to arrive."

"Well, one of them's here. For what it's worth."

"You never mentioned what this movie's about."

"No, I didn't. It's a crummy horror thing. We're calling it *The Colors of Hell*."

He poured Tom's drink. "No good, huh?"

"If the truth in advertising laws had any teeth, we'd have to call it *Andy Hardy Directs a Movie*."

"I don't get it."

"You're better off that way, believe me."

From the back of the room someone called Tom's name.

It was Bill. He had the last booth. "Come on back here and sit with me."

Tom took his drink and joined him. He was in his clerical collar, and he had a ham sandwich and a bottle of beer. "Afternoon, Father. You here looking for sinners to save? I'm your boy."

"No, just getting a quick lunch. The sandwiches here aren't great, but they beat Walchek's."

"I just left a gourmet who loved the place."

"You're kidding. Sit down for a minute."

Tom slid into the booth. "Does His Eminence know you hang out in dives like this?"

Bill raised his glass in a toast. "His Eminence can kiss my ass." He took a long swallow.

"That's not your first beer, is it?"

"Not even my second."

"Look," he lowered his voice. "You're the priest in this town. You can't let people see you like this."

"They can line right up behind the bishop."

"Bill." He tried to sound firm, but with Bill it wasn't easy.

"I was hungry. And thirsty."

"Drinking alone, in the rectory, that's one thing. But you can't make a public display of it."

Bill stared at him. "Why not?"

The question caught him off guard. "Look . . . look, I don't want to see you go down in flames, that's all."

"They can't fire me. There's a priest shortage."

"If they knew the things you get up to, that wouldn't matter."

Bill started to take another drink, then caught himself. He put the bottle down. "Take me home."

"Sure. Just let me settle my tab, okay?"

Tom went back to the bar. Tony was pouring a drink for himself.

"Should you be doing that? What if Hank catches you?"

"Hank couldn't catch Jack the Ripper if he was standing on his foot."

"Listen," he lowered his voice and nodded in the direction of Bill's booth. "Has he been in here a lot?"

"More and more, the last couple of weeks."

"That's not good."

Tony glanced back at the booth. "And he's been drinking more and more. Last night I don't know how he made it home."

"Home's just across the square."

"Yeah."

"Oh." He whispered even lower. "From now on, if he has too much, give me a call, will you? He's an old friend, and this isn't good."

Tony paused, not certain it was quite proper. Then, "Sure, Tom."

"Thanks."

"About that job on the movie . . . ?"

"You've got it. I don't know yet what I can give you, but as soon as we need someone, you're it, okay?"

Tony beamed. "Thanks. Boss."

"Don't let Hank hear you say that."

He got back to the booth and helped Bill to his feet. "Come on, padre."

Without saying another word, they left the bar and crossed the square. Outside the church they stopped.

"Have you had anyone check out the structural damage yet?"

Bill shook his head. "I don't care enough."

"We don't want the place to fall down on you. Tell you what, I'll have my engineer Maggie come over and check the place out first thing tomorrow, okay?"

"If you want."

"I'll put it in our budget. It'll say we're checking out St. Dympna's as a possible location or something."

"Maybe you could blow it up instead of the mill."

"Get inside and get some sleep. What do you tell Mrs. Charnocki when you're like this?"

"Fuck her."

"Yes, father."

He got Bill to the rectory door and started to say goodbye.

"Come in for a while."

"Can't. Ruth's showing our director around town. I have to get home and check on Alex."

"Stay away from him, Tom."

"He doesn't pitch rocks at me any more. We're pals now. He's a good kid."

"Stay away from him."

"Look, Bill, go and sleep this off, okay? Some of your parishioners might need you."

"Come on in. You never stop by any more."

"I guess I don't." He felt bad. "Believe me, it's not deliberate. I've been so busy, that's all. Why don't I come by tonight?"

"Dinner?"

"I'd rather wait till the old lady's gone."

"Eight o'clock, then."

"And I won't let you get too drunk."

"Some friend."

ALEX WAS IN HIS ROOM, SKETCHING. HE SMILED when he saw Tom. "Where's mom?"

"She showing that director guy around Steadbridge."

"Oh. Eric."

"Yeah, Eric. Have you had lunch?"

"No. Can we get pizza?"

"Is there a pizza place left here?" He hadn't seen one.

Alex nodded. "Out in the country, on one of the big roads."

Tom got his car and they headed out of town. There were a few farms. Crops were withering from the recent lack of rainfall. Scattered houses needed paint. Here and there were herds of underfed cows.

They found the pizzeria easily enough. It was a small place, not much more than a tiny storefront with a counter where one of the front windows had been. Tom wasn't hungry again; Alex asked for two slices with anchovies. Tom found himself thinking that Bill might be right about the boy; anchovies had to be a sign of a bad character.

Back in town, they both felt restless and decided to take a walk.

"Why don't we head up to Number Five? You mom may be there with the Boy Wonder."

"Okay."

For a while they walked without saying much. They were enjoying each other's company, and Tom was glad of it. "So, Alex, do you think you'd like to see New York City?"

"I don't know."

"I thought maybe I could take you and your mom for a weekend sometime, just so you can see it."

"I don't know if mom wants to go."

"We can talk her into it."

"I don't know if I can leave."

Odd comment. "There's a lot to see and do there."

"I keep busy here, Tom. You know that. There's so much I have to draw, so many things I have to get into my art before—" He caught himself, as if he was saying something he shouldn't.

"Before what?"

"Nothing."

The mill was in sight; Ruth and Eric weren't. Tom went to the back entrance and shouted their names, but there was no answer. He looked at Alex and shrugged. "Maybe she dropped him off at day school."

"You don't like him, do you?"

"Well, let's just say working with him is going to be a challenge."

"Why?"

"What do you see when you look at him, Alex?"

"Nothing."

"That's the answer to your question."

"Oh." He turned thoughtful.

"I know what. Let's cross the bridge to the island. I've never been out there."

"Okay." He had that doubtful tone kids use when an adult has an idea that isn't very good.

Tom stepped onto the bridge. As it had before, it vibrated and creaked under his weight. But he wanted to get across. He quickly grabbed the handrail, waited for it to steady itself and took another step. Then another. The bridge's ancient steel let out a groan and swayed like it was ready to collapse.

Alex had stayed fixedly on shore. "Come back, Tom."

Instead of subsiding, the bridge's sway was getting worse, and its groaning was like a roar. Tom suddenly found himself terrified. He jumped as hard as he could and landed on his side, back on the riverbank beside Alex. The bridge kept oscillating, almost as if it was alive.

"Jesus."

"Are you okay, Tom?"

"Yeah, I think so."

"You shouldn't go out there again."

"Believe me, I won't." He stood up, still shaken, and dusted himself off. "I'll have to have that closed off as soon as I can. Enough people have died here already."

"More will."

Tom froze. He had not gotten used to these pronouncements by Alex, and he still didn't know what to think about them.

"Didn't you ever hear about Long John Pulaski, Tom?"

"No, I don't think so."

They strolled along the river, as they had done earlier that day.

"Long John Pulaski was the first man to die here. Way back when Number Five first opened, in the 1800s."

This was news to Tom, but he had never been one for the local legends.

"When the mill first opened, the steelmen used to swim

out to the island on their lunch breaks. It was a way for them to cool off in the middle of the day. And they used to find Indian arrowheads they could sell for a few extra cents. Long John was the biggest, strongest and bravest of them all."

The boy was reciting. He must have heard this story a hundred times. From Ruth? Or Mrs. McKibben?

"One night there was a storm and the next day the river was running really fast. The other men were afraid of the current. But Long John laughed at them and stripped and jumped in. And in no time he was caught in the current and drowned while all his friends stood and watched. They couldn't do anything to help him.

"And then he began to take them with him. One by one for days afterwards, as the men swam out to Washington Island, Long John would pull them under until they drowned. The men wanted the company to build a bridge for them because they were afraid to swim out there anymore. But the company said no.

"Then one day one of the owners brought his wife and two little children to see the mill. His wife wanted to see the island; she said she wanted to have a picnic there. So they got a rowboat and started to row out to the island. But Long John was in the water, and he wanted them. He capsized their boat, and the wife and children were pulled under and drowned. That's when the owners of the mill decided to build the Pulaski Bridge. Not for the steelmen but for themselves, if they ever wanted to use the island for a picnic or anything."

Narrating this seemed to give Alex pleasure. Tom listened attentively. It was so much like all the local myths he remembered, most but not all about the workers at Number Five.

"That's a good story, Alex."

"It's true. Grandma Kibben said so."

"I'm sure it is. Listen, why don't we head home and see if your mom's back yet?"

"Okay."

She wasn't. The house was empty.

"Tom? I made a sketch of Long John once. Do you want to see it?"

"Sure."

Alex headed up to his room. In a moment he was back, holding the sketch out to Tom.

He recognized the man in the picture at once. It was the steelworker he had met and talked to in the mill when he was a boy. The one who had vanished. Tom froze. It was the man, down to the last detail. For an instant his mind flashed back to that day, the fire, the blackness around it, talking with the man, seeing his father's death.

His phone rang. It was Ruth. "I just wanted to let you know, Hank just found Ben's car, abandoned about a quarter of a mile from the mill. We're thinking those other remains in the mill, the ones that were torn apart . . ."

Life in Steadbridge, life with Ruth and Alex, had become so routine he had almost forgotten how strange the boy and the town were.

THAT NIGHT HE WENT TO VISIT BILL AT THE REC-
tory, as he had promised. Mrs. Charnocki opened the door and glared at him, as usual.

"Good evening, Mrs. C."

"Father Bill's not here."

"Are you ever going to be anything but rude to me?"

"He's not here, I said."

"Where is he then? He made me promise to stop by tonight."

She looked suspicious. "He's in the church. Leave him alone there."

"He spends too much time there."

"Leave him alone there. It's what he needs. It's what Steadbridge needs." She closed the door on him.

He glanced at the church windows. They were black.

Charnocki was lying. Nonplussed, he decided to look inside anyway.

The front door was unlocked but stuck; the crack in the facade had made it tight. He pulled it open, wondering how the old women ever dealt with it.

Inside it was pitch black except for one small candle burning on the altar. Yes, Bill was there, apparently hunched down or kneeling. Tom stood at the back of the church and watched for a moment, then walked slowly up the aisle, trying to make as little noise as he could.

On the altar beside Bill stood a vodka bottle, nearly empty. Bill was on his knees, facing the altar, praying and bowing his head repeatedly. His prayer was spoken aloud but softly; Tom couldn't make out the words. He moved nearer.

And he realized that Bill was not merely bowing. He was beating his head against the edge of the altar, pounding it like a man half mad. "The link must be severed," he prayed. "The link must be severed. The link must be severed. The link must be severed."

"Bill." His voice was not much higher than a whisper.

Bill went on with his prayer.

A step closer, a bit louder. "Bill."

Bill turned to face him. His eyes were wide open, like the eyes of a demon, and the skin on his forehead was broken. Blood cascaded down his face. "The link must be severed. The link must be severed."

"Bill, for the love of God, what are you doing?"

He stopped short and looked up at Tom. There was desperation in his eyes. "Help me, Tom. Help me cut the link."

Tom put an arm around him. "Here. Get up."

Slowly, with Tom's help, Bill got to his feet. Tom saw that the blood running down his face was mixed with tears. "What have you done to yourself?"

"I'm the only one who can do it, Tom. I'm the only one who understands."

Tom shouted, "Mrs. Charnocki!" His voice echoed in

the cavernous church. "Mrs. Charnocki!" He put his other arm around Bill. "Come on, we've got to get you to the rectory. There has to be a first aid kit there." He steered Bill toward the connecting passageway. Again he shouted, "Mrs. Charnocki!"

After a moment the housekeeper appeared. "Father Bill!"

"Help me get him to the rectory."

Between them they managed. They sat him in an over-stuffed chair and turned a lamp on him. Tom checked the wound. "It's not as bad as it looks. It's not too deep, just bloody. Get some clean cloths and some bandages."

She hurried off to get them.

Bill looked up at Tom. He seemed completely lost. "Tom, I'm the only one who can do it."

"What you need to do is get better."

"No."

"We're going to get you cleaned up and bandaged, and we're going to put you to bed."

"I need a drink."

"No. No more tonight."

"I need a drink."

Mrs. Charnocki was back with warm water, towels and bandages. She brushed the wound tenderly with disinfectant, then helped Tom wrap the bandage. Before long they had Bill in bed, asleep.

Tom wasn't sure what to do; he felt suddenly useless. "I . . . I guess I should go. Will you call me if he does anything else?"

"I should go home myself. I only work till eight."

"Oh. Well, maybe . . . maybe I can stay with him to-night. Is there someplace I can sleep?"

"There's a guest room on the second floor. I'll get it ready for you. Then I have to go."

He called Ruth and told her where he'd be, told her Bill had had an accident but didn't give details. "Is our little director settled in?"

"I guess. It's hard to tell when they're that young. Is Bill all right?"

"He'll be fine in the morning."

Mrs. Charnocki left. Tom tried reading but couldn't concentrate. When he got to bed he slept fitfully. There were dreams, none of them pleasant.

9

"**I** LOVE THIS TOWN."

Isabel Montgomery climbed up the statue of McKinley to get a better look around. Tom watched her, a bit bewildered. Steadbridge wasn't the kind of place people fell in love with at first sight. "Watch out for the pigeon droppings."

"I don't mind. I'm not afraid of soap and water."

Eric stood a few feet apart from them fiddling with the viewfinder on one of his cameras. She called out to him. "Eric, why didn't you tell me this was such a fantastic town? This movie's going to look terrific."

He kept his attention focused on his camera. "I hate this place."

"You may hate it, but you're going to make a really striking film here."

"I don't think so. The place is a dump."

"Just leave it to me." She jumped down again, beaming.

"Tom, do you think we could get permission to shoot from the church tower?"

"I'm not sure. There's some structural damage."

Over the last three weeks, several more film people had arrived in town: Eric's assistant, a boy even younger and greener than he was; a production secretary named Rachel who kept whining about being out of New York; and a driver, complete with a Lincoln Town Car. Tom tried to send him back. "This town is too small for us to need any drivers."

Phil wouldn't listen. "It's a matter of perks for the right people."

As near as Tom could see, there were no right people. And he said so.

"Tom, you are the right people. You've been promoted, remember? Overbrook takes care of its executives."

"Oh." So he'd keep the driver. He could always have the guy do something else; there was sure to be plenty of work. "Do me a favor, though, will you? Don't give Eric a car."

"My precious little brat of a nephew? He'll be lucky to get a pair of roller skates. If my wife hadn't—never mind. I'm sending some experienced production people to guide this thing. If there's a conflict with Eric, you're to back them up, understand?"

"With pleasure."

"He doesn't know it yet, but he's getting a cinematographer. Don't tell him, okay? I want it to be an unpleasant surprise."

"Sure, Phil."

Isabel was the production designer and costumer; she was the first of them who actually seemed to know or care what she was doing, and the first to express any real enthusiasm for the project. A blonde woman in her early thirties, she dressed in jeans and a t-shirt, didn't wear much makeup; there was no pretense and no nonsense about her. She seemed to baffle Eric, which instantly endeared her to Tom.

She stared up at St. Dympna's tower. "If we could get a camera up there . . . I'll bet the square looks fantastic from that angle."

Eric finished whatever he was doing and put his camera in his bag. "I'm sure Tom can arrange it. He and the priest are good friends." He said this in a tone that suggested there might be more between them than met the eye.

Isabel ignored it. "Can we get a look at that old theater over there? If the interior's preserved . . . some of those old places are just gorgeous."

Eric sniffed. "It's a ruin."

"This is a horror movie. What don't you get?"

Game, set and match. Tom put on a big smile. No sense telling them about the broken side door he and Bill had used. "I'll have to get the keys to the place. Why don't we get you settled into your house? We can have lunch with Ruth Fawcett. She's our liaison with the town. I think you'll find her anxious to help you."

Isabel looked up at the church again. "Can I at least get up there and get a look? It might give me a few more ideas."

"I'll talk to Father Vicosz."

"Can you show me the river?"

"Sure. It's just down here."

The weather had moderated. It was a gorgeous early summer day, bright, sunny, deep blue sky pocked with pillowy clouds. When Isabel saw the river she broke into a huge smile. "This is terrific. The valley's so pretty, and the contrast between all those trees up there and the old town . . . Oh, Eric, why did you tell me there was nothing here worth putting on film?"

He snorted.

Tom was warming to her more and more. "If you like, we can take you upriver later on. There are some nice places, even some little streams with waterfalls."

"Really?"

He grinned and nodded. "And there's a dam about two

miles up. Just a small one, for flood control, but you might
be able to use it."

"Great. Eric, I want the latest draft of the script right
away. I can't wait to start making notes on all this."

"Sure."

Tom got the impression Eric was expecting an ally in
his hatred of Steadbridge. Tough luck.

TOM FOUND BILL AT THE ALTAR IN ST. DYMPNA'S,
head bowed, praying. For a moment he was afraid this was
a repeat of that terrible night, but Bill was quite still.

Grinning, he walked up behind him. "Bless me, father,
for I have sinned."

Bill looked up. He had been lost in his prayers, or his
thoughts. "Tom."

Tom put a hand on his shoulder. Bill had been sober
since that night. "How about some lunch, padre?"

"Sure. You don't have to confess to me, anyway. I
already know all your sins."

"I committed most of them with you."

"See? We priests do have influence on our flocks."

"Baa."

They headed to Walchek's. Tom's first impulse had been
to go to Hank's, but he didn't want Bill to get tempted.
They ordered the meatloaf special. There was a lot of small
talk; Tom kept looking for signs to reassure him that Bill
was all right now. Things seemed fine.

"Our production designer hit town. She thinks we
should shoot from St. Dympna's tower."

Bill turned thoughtful. "How much could you pay us for
the use of it?"

"You really are a priest, aren't you?" Tom laughed at him.

"We're a poor parish. Looking out for things like that is
part of my job."

"We'll take care of you."

"Are you sure?"

"I control the budget."

Their lunch came. It was as bad as usual. Tom tasted his and made a sour face. "Ruth should open a restaurant. Edible food is a virgin market here."

"Ruth missed the boat on that one years ago."

"Father Vicosz, you are a world-class bitch."

Bill laughed. "You should meet the pope. Are you and Ruth still . . . ?"

"More or less. Not actually living together, though. Have to keep up appearances." He washed down a mouthful of tough meat with some bad coffee.

"Are you falling in love with her all over again?"

Tom shrugged. "I keep trying to figure out what I'm feeling. But it's such a tangle of emotions. My home, and I hate it. My old girl, and I . . . I don't know."

"Emotions can be like that. There are times when I envy insects. If I could get rid of half the things I feel . . ."

"You'd be a better priest?"

"I'd be a happier man."

The waitress came and asked if everything was okay. Tom put on a sarcastic smile and told her it was no worse than usual. This seemed an acceptable response.

"Alex says you're been acting strange around him, Bill. I think he's a bit afraid of you."

Bill fell silent; he pretended to be focusing on his food.

"Look, he can't help the way he is, Bill. You can't blame him for it."

"Just because he can't help it doesn't mean it isn't wrong." He was tense. Tom decided to change the subject.

"I never saw the report Maggie did for you. How bad is the church?"

"Mostly it's cosmetic damage. She says the structure should hold up for another few years, at least. If nothing else happens."

"What could happen to a church?"

"Now who's being a bitch?"

Ruth and Maggie came in, with Alex tailing behind. They

had become friends. Ruth kissed Tom and Bill hello, they moved some tables together and everyone started to chatter about nothing much. Tom noticed that Alex sat as far away from Bill as he could.

Tom was surprised to see them. "I thought you'd be showing Isabel around."

"She's unpacking. How's the meatloaf?"

"Like last year's support stockings."

"As usual." She ordered burgers for herself and Alex.

Maggie decided to brave out the special. "And bring me some hot tea."

The waitress looked doubtful. "There's fresh-brewed coffee."

"I'm not that gutsy."

Ruth asked Bill how he'd been. "I haven't seen you much since your accident."

Bill glanced at Tom, who kept his expression carefully neutral. He had told everyone Bill stumbled accidentally and hit his head on the edge of the altar.

"I've been okay, Ruth. Really busy. The bishop asked me to take on some extra duties for the diocese. He says it'll help justify keeping St. Dympna's open."

If this was true, it was the first Tom had heard of it.

"Well, that's good. We don't want to have to commute to church. A lot of the older people don't even have cars."

"I took pains to point that out to him. But he can't ignore the economics."

Tom spoke up, decisively. "Overbook will be paying the church a good sum to use it as a location."

As soon as he said it, he regretted it. Not for his budget's sake. But why was he helping prolong the life and vitality of Steadbridge? He should want it to die quickly rather than slowly. Eric's facile dislike of the place annoyed him more than he wanted to admit. Still, if Overbrook was going to build a permanent facility here . . .

Everyone at the table seemed happy to hear it.

"It's such a gorgeous old building, Tom." Maggie

dipped her teabag into a cup of lukewarm water, hoping for the best. "They don't build them like that any more."

He was mordant. "It's too bad they ever did."

"Tom!" Ruth acted shocked. "You are the most bipolar creature I've ever known. In a split second."

"Tom?" He played it deadpan. "My name isn't Tom. I'm Mr. Hyde."

"Right. Anyway, Isabel seems to have some great ideas for the movie. If she can get Eric to go along with them."

"Isabel has more authority than you might think."

She let this go. "He'll have to rewrite his script again."

"Good. Have you seen it?" *Doubly good,* he thought. *If I can keep him writing by night and directing by day, that'll pretty much keep him out of my hair.*

Alex had been eating his burger, not saying anything. "Are you still going to let me work on the movie, Tom?"

Ruth looked from one of them to the other, not sure what she thought about this news.

"I thought we might use him to run errands now and then." He tried to sound reassuring. "Just part-time."

She still looked dubious.

"We'll pay him very well."

"I'll have to think about this. You know I don't like him hanging around the mill."

"I'll be there to keep an eye on him. So will you, for that matter."

"And so will I." Maggie smiled at the kid.

"And you won't have to pay for a sitter. There you are, Ruthie. It's settled."

"Please, mom? I want to learn how movies are made."

"Well . . . let me think about it, okay?"

Maggie tasted her tea. She grimaced and set it aside. "I think Alex will make a good mascot for Overbrook."

"Yes." Bill was finished with his lunch. He stood up and put his napkin on the table. "Mascot for a horror film. Alex, I think you've found your calling."

"Bill!"

"Father Vicosz!"

The women seemed genuinely upset to hear him say this. Tom looked from Bill to Alex. The boy's face was a blank. So was the priest's. Suddenly Tom's appetite was gone. He put it down to the food.

On the cracked sidewalk outside the café Tom caught up with Bill. "Listen, to answer your earlier question, yes, I think things between Ruth and me may be getting serious. Alex may be my kid someday. So I want you to lay off him."

"It isn't like you to be so naïve, Tom."

"If you want that production money, you'll behave yourself."

Bill's face turned to stone.

"In every way. Understand, Bill?"

"Yes, Mister Producer. But let me ask you one thing."

"Hm?"

"What if I'm right about him?"

"You're a priest. Are you right about the Virgin Birth? About the pope being infallible?"

Bill took a step away from him. "There's just no way to make you see it, is there?"

"Probably not."

They parted, heading in separate directions.

OVER THE NEXT WEEKS MORE OF THE CREW arrived, carpenters, technicians, plus some of the cast. The front end of the mill and the side facing the river got painted, under Isabel's supervision. It could easily pass for a downscale shopping mall. Inside, she oversaw the building of sets. Maggie supervised another crew to reinforce parts of the building that might not be quite sound. Tom had the power company run in heavy-duty lines, and the lights were installed. And he got permission to rent the old highschool as a kind of production headquarters for making props and costumes, editing, and even a small private projection room. The crew got the place cleaned out and refurbished in fairly short order.

Nicole Kammerfleischer arrived with an entourage, which consisted of her mother and a makeup man. She struck Tom as being focused on her career, or at least on her image, not the type to make trouble or generate nonsense. She spent a lot of time hanging out with Isabel; they were old friends, it seemed, and Tom suspected they might be a bit more than that. Eric stayed in his house, writing and rewriting. Tom had the impression he was overwhelmed by the number of people and the size of the production. As the new crew members arrived, Tom got them settled into their quarters and had a good talk with them, explaining who was really in charge. He ended each speech with, "This is *not* an auteur film."

The leading man was still being cast. Tom hoped he'd be like Nicole, not Eric.

The one extraordinary rule he established was a daylight-only work rule. No one, absolutely no one, was to work at the mill after dark. Everyone found it odd, and it might work hell with their schedule, but there was no way to explain it. He felt uneasy enough about shooting in the mill at all. Why hadn't Maggie told them not to shoot there?

Eric was petulant. "We have night scenes to shoot."

"You can shoot day-for-night, can't you?"

"No one does that anymore."

"All it takes is a filter. We can afford one. Shooting at night would make our expenditures for power and lights skyrocket."

The cinematographer arrived, Barry Nash. He was in his late fifties and like Nicole he seemed to have a no-nonsense attitude. Tom was grateful.

Eric was not. "I was supposed to shoot this myself."

"Not any more, Eric."

"But I'm the director."

"And Barry's the D.P." Tom tried not to make it too

apparent how much he was enjoying this. "You tell him what you want, and he and the editor will work together to shoot it."

"I'm going to call my uncle."

"Good. Then he can explain his decision to you himself."

Eric sniffed. "I took a film history course. I read about how all the front office men used to meddle in the work of directors. But I thought those days were past."

"This," he said with a big smile, "is not an auteur picture. Overbrook does not make auteur pictures."

Maggie and Isabel and their crews worked closely together, making sure the mill was safe, that nothing would fall from the roof and kill anyone, and that everything they built met Somerset County's fairly lax construction codes. Working with Barry, they planned to shoot from the top of Number Five's smokestack and St. Dympna's bell tower; they built a platform to get high-angle shots up the river valley; they lit the sets. Eric was more and more glum.

"They're not even letting me do the casting." He ran into Ruth in Walchek's one day at lunchtime and complained to her.

"Why should they? It's their money and their picture."

"The opening credit is to read, 'A Film by Eric Charles Benson.' It's in my contract."

"Giving you a credit and letting you spend their money are two different things. Even a Steadbridge hick like me knows that."

"I hate this."

"Look, Eric, this is a shlock horror movie, not *The Birth of a Nation*. It's not worth getting upset about. Your next project will be better."

He was wide-eyed. "Shlock!?"

"Shlock." She said it as firmly as she could manage without laughing. "Why don't you take a walk around town and cool off, okay? Maybe you'll get some ideas."

Eric clearly thought there was no one who understood him. He finished his burger and walked.

The square. President William McKinley stared down at him. He picked up a pebble and threw it at a pigeon.

Hank's Bar. He thought about getting drunk. But that would give them all the ammunition they needed to replace him.

St. Dympna's. That was it. He could check out the church, plan how he wanted to shoot here. Isabel had been dictating camera angles to him. It was time to assert himself.

He pulled open the front door. It was heavier than he expected, more solid. Inside, the building was quiet and dark. A pair of old women sat in the last pew, working their rosaries.

He noticed that a few of the stained-glass windows had panels missing and were filled in with cardboard. How much would it cost to replace them? They'd look so much cooler. He'd better not ask.

Everything was so old. It all looked shopworn. How could he film it in an interesting way?

"Can I help you?"

He turned. It was the priest. Eric introduced himself.

"The director? I thought you had to be one of the film people. No one else would come to Steadbridge."

"You're telling me."

"I'm Father Vicosz." The priest frowned. "You are still planning to film here, aren't you? I mean . . . well, to be honest, the parish needs the money you'll be paying us."

"I imagine so. I don't really seem to have a lot to say about it."

"Didn't you say you're the director?"

"No, my uncle said it. He's never liked me."

This wasn't at all what Bill expected to hear. "Are you Catholic?"

"No. Jewish."

"Good. How'd you like to come over to the rectory for a drink?"

"I shouldn't. I'm supposed to be in charge. At least in theory."

"Then you need a dose of confidence."

"Can I see the bell tower, please? We're supposed to do some filming up there."

"Sure, if you like." He led Eric to the winding staircase and they began climbing. Halfway up he reached under his cassock and produced a hip flask. "Scotch."

"No thanks."

"A joint?"

Eric hesitated. "Sure."

Bill lit up, inhaled and passed it to Eric.

"Where do you score herbs in a town like this?"

"Are you kidding? It's all over the place. Try Tony Kowlaski, the bartender at Hank's."

"He have anything harder?"

"I've never asked. Probably."

Eric had a thought and smiled. "This is just like *Vertigo*."

"Minus the killing." Under his breath he added, "I hope."

Two huge bells hung in the tower; ropes went down to a lower floor, where the bell ringer worked.

"Who rings them?"

"I do. There's no one else. I do everything but the janitorial work." They finished the joint. "You want another one?"

"Maybe later."

"I read someplace that Richard Burton was so stoned when he shot *Where Eagles Dare*, he didn't even remember making it."

"Who's Richard Burton?"

"Never mind."

The town and the Mon River Valley opened out below

them. The sunlight was brilliant. Despite himself, Eric found it rather beautiful. "Wow, Isabel was right."

"About . . . ?"

"She said we could get some stunning shots from up here."

"This is the house of the Lord, after all."

Eric looked at him. He wanted to ask if he really believed that, but something made him stop.

"Come on, let's go back down. I promised you a drink."

"No, thanks. I'd rather stay up here for a bit and study the view. Shots in movies have to be planned very carefully if things are to come out right, you know."

"So do shots of Scotch too. They'll help your creative juices to flow.

"Another time, thanks."

"Will you be okay up here by yourself?"

"Sure."

They shook hands and Bill went back down to the church.

Eric shaded his eyes and looked the valley up and down. The mill loomed large; he could get some good exteriors of it from here. When they imploded it, it would look terrific from this viewpoint. Then he looked more closely. There seemed to be people ascending and descending the smokestack stairs. A great many of them. And he could swear he saw wisps of smoke ascending from the chimney. What could be happening?

He squinted to get a better look. There was no one there after all. Trick of the light. *If only I could get special effects that good,* he thought.

FOR THE FIRST TIME IN YEARS, STEADBRIDGE WAS becoming an active place. Money was being pumped into the local economy. Two catering businesses opened, with fourteen employees between them. Other townspeople were hired as housekeepers, clerical help, extra labor on the construction crews, security . . . And it would only get better. Tom, despite himself, was beginning to find the place a bit congenial.

His secretary, Rachel Goodson, seemed good at keeping track of the budget. She gave him daily reports. Every dime was being accounted for, and he could justify every expenditure. His production assistant, a nineteen-year-old film student named Jeremy Fitts, was attending to all the routine details as the production geared up.

"All you have to do," Ruth told him, "is walk around acting important." She was around constantly. Her stipend as an advisor to the production enabled her to quit her bakery job and take a leave of absence from the police department.

"Then I'll expect a bit more respect, Mrs. Fawcett."

"See if you get it."

"Listen, why don't we get out of here for a few hours?" It was another hot day. He was watching some touch-up painting on Number Five.

"I know a good Italian place in Johnstown, if you're up for it."

"Sure."

He told Jeremy where he'd be going, got the car and Ruth, and they headed up the valley. The road paralleled the river.

"You know, this really is lovely country, Ruth. In between all the dying towns, that is. The county should hire a PR firm and get the word out. People would flock here if they knew. This could rival the Hudson River Valley. I'll bet in autumn, when the trees turn—"

"And where would they stay? At the Steadbridge Hilton?"

"Point taken."

"You're fonder of this region than you like to let on."

"Like the man said, there's no use asking if the air's good when there's nothing else to breathe."

Every few miles there was a flood-control dam. White water churned and frothed below them. "Do these really do any good?"

"Nobody knows, actually." She shrugged. "They've never really been tested."

"Oh."

"Here's hoping they never are."

They stayed to watch a barge pass through one of the locks, then moved on.

Compared to Steadbridge, Johnstown seemed a thriving metropolis. It sat in a magnificent valley where the Mon converged with the Conemaugh River. Tom drove around the town for a few minutes and Ruth pointed out various landmarks, parks, city hall, the hockey arena. "Over there is the house where they shot that Tom Cruise movie."

"And I didn't think there was anything of historic value here."

The restaurant was called Catania. The booths were plush, the upholstery red, the atmosphere more than a bit gaudy; canned Italian mandolin music played. But it was a breath of fresh air after Steadbridge. Tom ordered eggplant parmesan. "I had forgotten there was such food. It may take my taste buds a few minutes to wake up."

"Don't worry. Your tongue hasn't failed you yet." Ruth had lasagna.

"Where's Alex today?"

"Off with Maggie again. They're nuts about each other."

"Good. She can keep him away from Bill."

She smiled sardonically. "Our priest."

The waiter brought wine, a good Chianti. Tom was pleased with the place. "What's this place called again?"

She told him.

He drank a bit more and turned thoughtful. "I'm worried about Bill, Ruth. About what he might do."

"He's a priest. What could he do, spout maledictions or something?"

"Do to himself. He's drinking again."

"Sacramental wine?"

"I thought you liked him."

"I like my son more."

Their food came. Half expecting it to be like Walchek's, Tom sampled his carefully. Then he broke into a smile. "This is wonderful."

"Glad you like it."

"By the way, what do you think of Eric's latest script?"

She looked puzzled. "You know I haven't seen it."

"Good gosh, that's right!" His tone, like his smile, was exaggerated. "There. We've discussed business. This lunch is a legitimate expense for Overbrook."

"Keep that up, you'll need Bill for confession."

"Don't be morbid."

"Anyway, if Alex starts getting in the way, I want you to let me know."

"So far he's been a delight, Ruth. Everyone but Eric seems to love him. And he really has been useful running errands for me."

"That's good. Lord knows he can be difficult."

"Not with us." He drank a bit more of his Chianti. "All the activity seems to fascinate him. I think he genuinely wants to learn about movies. I mean, little things, like why we're only bothering to paint two sides of the mill. He can't get enough of that stuff."

"He's . . . I've never really told you about him, Tom."

"This salad dressing's wonderful, too." He sipped his wine. "What about him, then?"

"Why he is the way he is. Why he . . . It's all so strange."

"Tell me. You know how attached we've become."

"Alex was born dead."

Tom stayed silent.

"The day Pat died. I was pregnant. I don't remember what I was doing, probably getting dinner ready or something. The shop steward, Jack Kowalski—he was Tony's father—came to the house. I could tell right away, from the way he was acting, that something was wrong. He told me about Pat's accident. In the blink of an eye I stopped being a happily domestic housewife and became a widow seven months pregnant.

"I became hysterical, Tom. I started crying, screaming, I went around the house tearing things up. Then I passed out.

"Jack rushed me to the hospital. When they managed to revive me, they told me I had miscarried. My husband was dead, my baby was dead. I wanted to be dead, too."

Tom took her hand. "Ruth."

"An emergency team tried to revive Alex. Finally they did. But not until . . . not until the brain damage had happened. Tom, I was shattered. I had no idea—how do you take care of a brain-damaged child? I was . . . I was . . ."

She was becoming agitated. He stroked her hand, hoping it might calm her down a bit.

"It wasn't obvious till later how the brain damage had affected him. From the first time he picked up a box of crayons it was clear he had a wonderful artistic gift. Then all the . . . all the deficiencies became apparent. He'll never read."

"He's a sweet boy, Ruth. You've done the best possible job raising him."

"He's still part dead, Tom. Part of him is still with his father. From the time he was old enough to talk, he made it clear. He sees his father. He sees his father's world, wherever it is. He sees all the dead from Number Five, he talks with them, they show him their world. He's linked with them somehow. You've seen his drawings and paintings." She looked into Tom's eyes then quickly away.

"Yes, I've seen his paintings." This was all more upsetting to him than he wanted to admit. "He has imagination, that's all."

"He knows what his father looked like, Tom. He even knows what your father looked like."

Tom went cold. He needed to make this all seem rational, for Ruth, for himself. "Boys have imagination.

Gifted boys have more, and it's more vivid with them. That's what makes them gifted."

She started to say something but caught herself and stopped. After an indecisive pause she went back to eating. "I know how it sounds. But it's true. Ask Bill."

"Bill's a fool."

"So am I, Tom. So are you. Look at us."

For a moment they both fell silent. The waiter hovered, refilled their glasses, asked if everything was all right. Tom waved him away.

"If this is true, Ruth, it's one more reason why you should get Alex away from Steadbridge."

"Do you think I haven't thought about that? I'm afraid what would happen. I'm afraid if I take him away from here, he'll die. More than he already has."

"That can't be."

"No, Tom. None of it can be. Let's eat up and get out of here."

"Look, I'm not . . . I don't disbelieve you. I've seen so much . . . I'm not sure there's any other way to explain it. Listen to me, rational Tom Kruvener. But Ruth, there has to be something we can do to save Alex from this."

"Save him from his father?"

"His dead father, yes."

Her eyes began to tear up. "Oh, Tom. I'm so scared, so confused. I wish I knew what to do."

"No one ever really knows what to do, Ruth. We just muddle through as best we can."

"I can't muddle, can't you see that? Not where my boy is concerned. Not my Alex. He's all I have."

"You have me, if you want me."

"No, I mean he's all I have of his father."

For a while, neither of them said much besides occasional small talk, the food, the day. On the drive back the sky began to cloud up. There was a stiff wind. The river was steel grey beneath a darkening sky. The water at the dams seemed especially turbulent.

"I'm sending out résumés, Ruth. I can't keep working for Overbrook. Not if it means staying here. Promise me you'll come to New York with me, even if it's only for a while. To see how Alex takes to it."

"I don't know if I can do that."

"Please."

"Not now. I can't promise that now. Maybe in time, but I don't know."

"AFTERNOON." TONY KOWALSKI PUT ON HIS BEST bartender's smile. "What can I get you?"

Eric looked around and sniffed, not quite sure he wanted to be in Hank's. "Whiskey and ginger ale."

Tony set it up. "You must be one of the kids working on this movie."

"Oh, I'm one of the kids, all right. I'm the director."

"Oh. Sorry. I didn't mean to—"

"It's okay. You're probably closer to the truth than I want to admit."

Eric sipped his drink; Tony went off to tend to a couple of other customers. He switched on the radio and tuned it to a jazz channel. When he came back, Eric's glass was already empty. "You movie people sure know how to put it away."

"We do?"

He nodded. "Tom Kruvener's in here all the time."

"Huh. What's he have to drink about?"

"Same as anybody else, I guess."

"I don't know much about anybody else."

Tony raised an eyebrow, but said nothing. A good bartender knows how to angle for tips.

"Listen." Eric lowered his voice to a confidential whisper.

"Hm?"

"I hear you might, er, you might be able to get me something better than this."

Tony looked around. "Herbs?"

"If there's no coke in town."

"I'll tell you what." Tony poured Eric another drink. "You know where the mill is, right?"

"Sure."

"I'm working security there, nights. Why don't you come out and see me tonight, say around ten. I'll have something then."

"Good stuff?"

"As good as any in the Mon Valley."

"That's not what I wanted to hear."

"Well, it's all I can tell you. Tonight, okay?"

"Okay."

Eric finished his drink, put some cash on the bar and left.

McKinley Square opened out in front of him. Every time he saw it, the sight depressed him. The church, the park, the statue of McKinley . . .

For some reason he found himself looking at the Hippodrome, or rather its ruins. It seemed a fit symbol for his career. Maybe he should go back and have another drink. Or maybe . . .

Mrs. Charnocki opened the rectory door. "Yes?"

"Is Father Vicosz here?"

"Father Bill? Who are you?"

"Eric Charles Benson. I'm the director."

"Of what?"

"*The Colors of Hell.* He said when I was in the neighborhood I should stop in."

She frowned. "He's not here."

"Oh. Will he be back soon?"

"I don't know."

"Sorry to bother you."

She closed the door.

Four o'clock. Six hours. He looked out across the square again. Nothing. The empty, ruined movie theater seemed to be laughing at him.

·   ·   ·

JUST AS TOM AND RUTH WERE PULLING BACK INTO
town his phone rang. It was Overbrook.

"Hi, Phil." He said it loudly, so Ruth would know who
it was.

"How's everything going?"

"So far, fine. Construction's a day or two ahead of
schedule. Everyone's happy but our director."

"Screw the little jerk. We've found a leading man. Stage
actor, he was running around naked in some damnfool off-
Broadway thing. Italian kid. I'll fax you his résumé."

"When will he be here?"

"Day after tomorrow."

"Good. If everything holds together, we should be able
to start shooting sometime next week." Still talking to Phil,
he stopped in front of Ruth's house, kissed her and let her
out. Then he parked and went into his own place.

"Listen, Tom, the board's having second thoughts about
this whole movie thing."

"Second thoughts?"

"Building a studio and all. We've pretty much decided
to dump this thing straight to video, then get out of the
business."

Oh. So much for being Head of Production. It was one
more reason to find another job, but fast. "I'm not sure how
Eric will feel about his film being treated that way."

"Eric isn't on the board."

"Point taken."

"We don't want this to get around, though, okay. This is
strictly confidential. It might affect morale, otherwise."

"Don't worry, I won't tell a soul."

So much, he thought, for *The Colors of Hell*. And so
much for the prospect of having to stay in Steadbridge a
minute longer than necessary. If only he could convince
Ruth that leaving was possible.

. . .

LATE NIGHT. RUTH AND TOM SAT IN HER KITCHEN, drinking. He was tempted to tell her about Overbrook's decision, but there didn't seem any point.

"For an Executive in Charge of Production, you've been in a mighty restless mood."

"Yeah."

"Still got the Steadbridge Blues?"

"That's only part of it. This town . . ." He got up and refilled his glass. "Things have been going too smoothly. I've been expecting more trouble."

"Three dead. Two missing. That's pretty smooth, all right, Mr. Kruvener."

"It could be worse. Every instinct I have tells me it will be."

"You always were the optimist."

He got up and walked to the kitchen window. "The mill's quiet tonight. Dark and calm."

"Count your blessings."

"The cops aren't looking for little Bob or Ben or whoever he was."

"Ben. Really?" She drained her glass. "Why not?"

"It seems when he was a kid he ran away a couple of times. Even when he was in college, he disappeared between his junior and senior years. They're putting this down to another one of his larks."

"But we found his car here."

"Yeah, but there are other ways out of here. Maybe he walked. Maybe he hitchhiked."

"And maybe that was him, shredded and scattered around the mill."

"You echo my sentiments, Mrs. Fawcett."

"Another drink?" She got up and poured one for herself, then one for him. "Do you love bourbon as much as you love me?"

"More. Bourbon doesn't make wisecracks."

"Want to take a walk, Tom?"

"No, I'm too tired tonight."

"Good. So am I. What's the word on your two missing colleagues?"

"Oh." Again he took a deep drink. "Nobody's looking. Actually, nobody much cares what happened to them, that I can see. Apparently their affair was common knowledge. Mike's wife has pretty much convinced the police they ran off together. Melissa's husband's already got a live-in girlfriend. And I thought I was the only one who wouldn't miss them."

"Again, their car was here."

He shrugged. "Is Hank doing anything about it?"

"Be serious."

He finished has drink and kissed her. "I've got to get some sleep tonight. See you tomorrow."

"When's our leading man get here?"

"Tomorrow. I'm sending Jeremy to meet him at the airport in Pittsburgh. His name's Angelo Capella. 'Starring Angelo Capella and Nicole Kammerfleischer.' How's that for box office?"

"It'll knock 'em dead."

"I think Nicole and Isabel are lovers, by the way."

"More power to them."

"Eric has the hots for Nic." He laughed, kissed Ruth good night and went next door to his own place. She locked the doors, turned out the lights and went upstairs to bed.

LATER, IN THE MIDDLE OF THE NIGHT, WHEN THE house was perfectly quiet, Alex crept out of his room. He paused outside Ruth's door to make sure she was asleep. There wasn't a sound. Then he headed down to the kitchen, to the cabinet where she kept the liquor.

So many bottles. He didn't like vodka; the night he tried it he got sick. Scotch didn't make him sick but he hated the taste. Gin was better, but only if he sipped it. Tonight he decided to try wine again. There was a half-bottle of something red. He pulled the cork out and smelled it. Nice. He poured some into a glass and tasted it. It was good, a bit bitter but good. He poured more and drank.

Even the ones he didn't like did something good for him. When he drank he could see more.

NEXT DOOR, IN HIS BEDROOM, TOM GOT UNDRESSED and stood at the window, staring at what he could see of Steadbridge. Dark, quiet town. He had gotten used to so much. The shadowy streets with only half the streetlights on at night, or fewer. The ghostly figures in the streets after dark. The fires at the mill night after night. Tonight there were none. Hiring security had been the right thing.

He loved Ruth; there was no doubt in his mind anymore. He even loved Alex, strange as the boy was. There had to be some way to help the kid, some way to rid him of whatever demons were haunting him.

Demons? He had a vision of Bill conducting an exorcism. Bell, book and candle, Latin prayers and formulae . . . It was too absurd. Besides, whatever demons there might be were haunting the town, not Alex. Alex was simply the one who could see them best.

Tom had updated his résumé and spent some time online, doing a job search. There seemed to be a number of promising openings. He found himself wishing he'd had another drink. Then he yawned, deeply.

Bed felt good. It would feel better when he was in New York City. With Ruth. With Alex. Somewhat to his astonishment he found himself thinking of them as his family.

He was drunk, or he felt drunk. And he slept. Heavily.

There were dreams. He and his new family on a picnic. He and his family on the roller coaster at Coney Island. He and his family . . .

There was light in the room, bright and yellow. Groggily he opened his eyes and realized the room was ablaze with it. It couldn't be sunrise yet. He rubbed his eyes.

Fire. There was fire in a corner of his bedroom. A column of it, seeming to rise up out of the floor and nearly touch the ceiling.

He jumped out of bed. His house was on fire. He looked around frantically for something he could use to extinguish it. Then he snatched the sheet off his bed and began to beat the fire with it. He had to be able to put it out.

It was blindingly hot. It seemed hotter than anything he'd ever felt. He beat it and beat it, but to no effect. It burned, but it didn't spread.

It was not spreading. That was not possible. A fire this bright and hot . . . He ran to the door.

There was a whisper, faint, just at the edge of his hearing. "Tom."

He gazed at the flames. There was something in them. A face, a hand, a body . . . "Tom," the fire whispered.

It was his father. His father was there, in the flames. Tom stared in terror.

"Tom."

His father's features were twisted with pain. He was burning, and all Tom could do was watch.

"Tom."

He had to do something. Without thinking, he crossed the room to the column of fire and reached in. He had to pull his father out, he had to save him.

"Tom." This time it was not a whisper, it was a loud, agonized groan.

He tried to grasp his father and pull. His hands burned. He screamed. And the fire was gone.

He screamed with pain.

Someone was knocking on his door. Aching with fear, feeling the fire in his arms he made his way downstairs and somehow got the door opened.

Ruth was there. "Tom, I heard you screaming, and . . ." She saw his hands. "Oh my God!"

"Ruth, my father was here. I saw my father." Tears were cascading down his face.

"For God's sake, Tom, get into the kitchen." She held his hands under the tap and ran cold water on them. It seemed to ease the pain a bit. "Wait here. I'll get my car and get you to the emergency room."

"No. I'll be all right. My father—"

"This is no time for macho heroics."

He stared at her. The horror of what happened was only beginning to dawn on him.

"GOOD MORNING, EVERYONE."

Tom had assembled the entire company in a conference room in the highschool, which had been cleaned out and fixed up very nicely. Actors, technicians, secretaries and Eric Charles Benson sat at old, battered school desks. Some of them seemed eager for word that production was finally starting; others seemed bored. There was coffee from Walchek's and pastry from McCormick's. Hank, Ruth and Alex were at the back of the room. Rachel prepared to take notes.

Tom's hands and lower arms were bandaged. "For those of you who haven't heard, I had a little accident." Holding up his hands he went on, "Nothing really serious, despite how these look. A small mishap with my kitchen stove." He was still terribly shaken by what had happened. Only Ruth knew the truth.

For two days he had relied on his secretary Rachel, who seemed delighted to be kept busy for once. She, Jeremy and several other staffers had fussed nonstop over Tom, writing his reports and memos from dictation, getting him coffee, doing all sorts of things both major and minor. He was feeling like an executive. One with second-degree burns, but an executive.

"For anyone who may not have met him yet, I wanted to introduce Angelo Capella, who's playing Josh in *Colors*."

A young man stood up and smiled at the assembled crew. "Hi, everyone. Great to be working with you." Dark features, large brown eyes, killer smile. He looked to be in his early twenties, though Tom knew he was near thirty. He had "gay boytoy" written all over him, but Tom knew better than to ask or tell.

Tom went on. "I know a lot of you have been anxious to get into production, and we're finally ready. We start shooting tomorrow."

There was a general murmur; to Tom's ear it sounded mostly positive.

"You all know we're on a tight budget and an even tighter schedule. Two months—we have to have everything finished by the Fourth of July. For a small film, that's a generous schedule, and there's some extra time built into it, so we should be fine. We're scheduled to implode the mill the day after the Fourth. Once that's done, obviously, we've shot our bolt as well as our film."

Tom's secretary spoke up. "Will we all be able to stay and see the implosion?"

"No, I'm afraid not. Only essential people will still be here for that. We'll need Angelo and Nic, since the script calls for them to be making love in front of the mall when it goes. The rest of the cast and as much of the crew as we can spare will be sent home. This is mostly a health concern. These implosions tend to send out enormous clouds of dust and debris. The county health department's concerned about how it may affect people's health." He did not add that they were also concerned that the dust and debris might be toxic.

Then a carpenter raised his hand, one of the younger crew members. "Tom, some of us are finding this town really weird. People won't talk to us, nobody's friendly. We see people in the streets at night, and when we try to talk to them they leave."

He wished it hadn't come up. "Maybe we could have Ruth or Hank say a word about that."

Hank and Ruth looked at each other, and Ruth took a step forward. She put on a big PR smile. "I think you're just running into a case of small-town-itis." Mild laughter around the room. "Steadbridge has been so dead, or rather dying, for so many years, having you all here takes a bit of adjustment. Even for me and Hank." A bit more laughter. "And you have to remember, a lot of our residents are elderly. They may not be able to see or hear you well without a bit of effort.

"People will get used to you. Having you here means so much to the town. All the money that comes with you, it's like a transfusion of nice, red blood."

The carpenter laughed at this. "So this is a town full of vampires?"

This was a bit too close to the edge for Tom. He decided to cut off that line of discussion. "Now, I think Eric wants to say a word or two."

Eric had been sitting silently. There hadn't even been a smile. He got slowly up and started what he obviously hoped was a pep talk. Almost at once, people's attention began to stray. Tom hoped he'd have the sense to keep his remarks short, but he showed no sign of brevity.

Tom picked up his coffee cup, slowly, painfully. His burns were more painful than anything he'd ever felt. He sipped. The extra money in Steadbridge's economy hadn't helped the taste of Walchek's coffee. He was surprised no one had complained; maybe they were all like Eric.

Eric droned on. Film is art, we are at the forefront of American culture, and on and on. Tom guessed it was a string of recycled film-school platitudes. No one showed the least sign of taking any of it seriously. Tom ambled to the back of the room and stood beside Ruth.

"Morning." He whispered it.

"Hello, Mr. Thalberg."

"Does that make you Norma Shearer?"

She struck a vampish pose. "I see myself more as the Mae West type."

"Dream on."

Eric was saying something about the Free Cinema movement and somehow confusing it with Dogme. People were doodling.

Tom carefully picked up a cherry Danish from a tray nearby. "Mm, McCormick's has gotten better since you quit."

"Just so you don't think it's because I quit."

"Are they going to start making their jelly donuts again?"

She shrugged.

Eric was lecturing on Hitchcock. It had gone on long enough. Tom waited for a suitable pause, then interrupted him. "Well, I'm sure we all appreciate hearing your viewpoint, Eric. We all know how important you are to this project. Now I think we've all got a full day's work ahead of us."

Glumly, realizing his erudition had been in vain, Eric sat down.

Tom asked if there were any more questions. Everyone looked around, waiting for someone else to speak up. Someone complained about the coffee. Tom promised to talk to the caterer about it, or find a better one. Ruth spoke out. "Be careful what you say about Walchek's coffee. It's been terrible since before any of us were born. It's been served to presidents, foreign dignitaries, even a visiting pope. President Kennedy drank Walchek's coffee and complained about it. So you're part of a long, treasured American tradition."

Isabel raised her hand. "So this is what really killed Kennedy?"

General laughter.

"Listen, what I'm trying to tell you is that this is an old town. There are traditions, goofy as some of them are. The past haunts us. You'll find this a more pleasant place if you're willing to meet people halfway."

Isabel said, "It's fine for the past to haunt the town,

Ruth, but do we have to have it in our coffee? This stuff tastes like runoff from the steel mill."

Tom was more pleased than not with this. If they kept grumbling about small things like the coffee, they might not notice the things they should really be concerned about. "You're right. I'll have a word with Gary Walchek," he told them firmly. "If he's too wedded to the family recipe, we'll just find another place to get our coffee."

There was loud, exaggerated applause.

"Anything else?"

Again everyone looked around.

No one seemed to have anything more on his or her mind. Tom was just about to let them go when a loud voice came from the back of the room. It was Alex.

"Tom, do you really have to b-blow up the m-mill?"

Silence. Everyone seemed surprised the boy had spoken and even more surprised at the force he voiced his question with.

"Alex." Tom's demeanor turned serious. "Yes, I think we have to."

"Don't." His voice registered a bit lower.

"Well, it's the big finale of the movie, Alex. And even the county wants it to come down, so they can develop the land for something else."

"Don't, Tom. They don't want it to happen."

Tom wasn't at all sure how to deal with this. It was the last thing he wanted discussed in front of the cast and crew.

"They've been quiet, Tom. They won't be. They'll be out of the mill, everywhere in town. They'll do terrible things." His voice was growing deeper and deeper, sounding like an adult's. Tom heard something familiar in it, but he couldn't be certain what.

He wanted Ruth to quiet Alex, but she looked mildly panicked, as if she didn't know what to do.

"Tom!" Alex's voice thundered. It was now fully deep and mature.

And Tom recognized it. It was his father's voice.

"Leave the mill alone! Leave it standing!"

Suddenly Alex fell to the floor, convulsing. Rigid limbs flailed wildly; he foamed at the mouth.

Someone quickly put the corner of a wallet into his mouth.

Amid much confusion Tom dismissed the meeting. Some people left. Others crowded around Alex, concerned about him. After a few moments the seizure stopped and he fell asleep. Jeremy lifted him carefully onto the conference table, trying not to wake him. Tom asked everyone else to leave.

"You never told me he was epileptic, Ruth."

"He isn't. The seizures are related to his brain damage." She touched her boy's cheek; there were tears in her eyes. "He hasn't had one for years, not since he was three. The doctors said it was safe to take him off his medication."

Tom put an arm around her. "It must be all this excitement."

"It's my fault. I should never have permitted him to hang around here."

"No, it's not. There was no way you could know this would happen."

"I had every reason to think something would happen, Tom." She leaned against him. "And you know why. Now . . . I don't know what to do."

"Let's get him home. You can call his doctor. We'll get him there as soon as we can."

"You have work to do here."

"It'll keep."

Suddenly Alex opened his eyes. He looked around, confused. "What happened?" His voice was his own.

Ruth tried to explain to him about his seizure.

He looked at Tom. "You can't blow up the mill."

"Let's talk about that later, okay? Right now we have to make sure you're okay."

"I'm okay."

Ruth straightened out his clothes for him. "Well, we want to be sure. Okay?"

"I guess."

They got him home and into bed. Ruth sat with him till she was sure he was sleeping. Then she joined Tom downstairs. "I'll call the doctor now. Are you going back to the shoot?"

"I pretty much have to. Let me know what the doctor says."

"I will."

He kissed her and started to go.

"Tom?"

"Hm?"

"Maybe you should listen to him. Maybe this is too dangerous."

"I don't know what I can do. I can't simply close down the production. Even if I tried, Phil would have another exec here tomorrow. At least I know what to expect. Someone else . . ." He spread his bandaged hands apart to show how helpless he felt.

"I'm worried, Tom."

"So am I."

"I never thought Alex would be one of the people they'd hurt."

It took him a moment to digest this. "Neither did I. No, I thought it would be me." He held out his bandaged hands.

"It may still be."

"I know."

THERE WAS A HUGE FULL MOON THAT NIGHT. AT eleven P.M., it was high overhead. Steadbridge was bathed in ghostly light. The trees around town and along the river were a dark green–black. There was no wind.

Eric walked up the road to Number Five, carrying, absurdly, a battery-powered lantern. He had spent the afternoon polishing his script. The production secretaries saw that it was copied and distributed to Tom, the cast and the appropriate tech people. He had slept for a while. Then he went to Hank's looking for Tony. But another bartender was on duty. "Try the mill, when you want him after dark."

Every evening for a week he had bought stuff from Tony. First marijuana, then crystal, then powder. When he was high, the pressure he felt went away. When he came back down, Steadbridge looked uglier than ever. Two months. How could he make it through two months?

A small shack had been built at the mill entrance, headquarters for the night guards. He looked inside. Empty. Tony was out checking the grounds. He'd be back soon enough; there wasn't that much to guard.

Sounds from the river came to him clearly, the gentle rippling of the current, the occasional splash of fish jumping. Suddenly there was a light in the mill. Orange-yellow light. Fire.

"Tony!"

He looked around. There was no one in sight.

"Tony?"

Nothing, no one.

One of the sets must be on fire. He ran past the security checkpoint and headed for the mill. The fire burned brighter.

Around the back of the building to the entrance. He pushed open the heavy door.

The inside of the mill was black. No fire, no flame, no smoke, no anything.

"Eric? That you?"

Tony was sitting on the smokestack stairs, smoking something. He got up slowly and joined Eric at the main entrance.

"Tony. I thought I saw lights, fire."

"Nah, everything's cool here."

"I know what I saw."

"I'm the one who's smoking. You want a hit?"

Eric switched off his lantern and put it on the ground. Then he took the joint and smoked. "Good stuff. I know I saw the light of a fire in there."

"Trick of the moonlight reflecting off the river."

"But I—"

"Do you see any fire? Smell any smoke?"

He took another drag. "No. What do you have for me?"

Tony took a small vial out of his pocket and held it up. Moonlight glistened on it. "Best in the Mon Valley."

"Heroin?"

He smiled and nodded.

Eric took it eagerly and paid him.

"Be careful, Eric. It's really pure."

"Don't worry. I know what I'm doing. I went to NYU."

"Sure." Tony looked around warily.

"Cops?"

"No. I just thought I heard something. It was nothing."

"Why do I feel paranoid?"

"Because that's what you are, Eric. I'll see you later." He disappeared inside the mill.

Eric stood alone for a moment, looking around. There had been a fire. He had seen it. It must have burned itself out. There was no smell of smoke, but that didn't mean that—He decided he didn't care, picked up his lantern, switched it on and began to walk.

All the Overbrook houses but one were dark. Tom was up. Eric started to wonder what he was doing, then decided he didn't care and kept walking. In what seemed no time he was at the square, regarding it with his usual contempt. The bench where he sat was cool against his body. President McKinley. Rot. Carefully he sprinkled some of the H onto the back of his fist and sniffed.

Sweet, very sweet.

He sniffed more, then closed his eyes and tried to forget where he was. This wasn't rural Pennsylvania, it was Chelsea; no, it was the East Village; no, it was a dingy sex club in the meat-packing district, and he'd find someone cute to lay.

There was a sound, he wasn't sure what. He opened his eyes. No one, nothing.

His eyes drifted to the Hippodrome. Hell, they don't even have movies in this godforsaken town.

There had been some talk of renovating the place and holding the premiere of *The Colors of Hell* there. But there was no money for it. Why spend the money to refurbish the dump when it would be shuttered again right after the premiere? He had asked Tom repeatedly where the film actually would open, but Tom always brushed the question aside.

He got up and crossed the square to the theater. One side of the marquee was hanging a bit lower than the other; it was only a matter of time before it would fall down. He hoped, when it did, it would kill somebody. And that he'd be here to see it.

With nothing else to do, he thought he'd look inside. It took a bit of work but he managed to pry one of the doors open. Then before he went inside he stopped and sniffed some more of his heroin. The light from his lantern was nowhere near bright enough to illuminate the huge space.

There was someone inside the lobby. Tall, muscular, handsome. There seemed to be a spotlight on him though Eric couldn't tell where it was coming from. The man smiled, and Eric took a step toward him. The man erupted into flames and vanished.

Eric stood gaping. Goddamn Tony, he must have cut the H with something else. There shouldn't be hallucinations like that. . . .

There were sounds coming from the auditorium. He walked to the top of the lobby, his lantern swinging at his side. The doors to the auditorium were stuck too, but he managed to force one open fairly quickly. Inside, everything was dark and quiet. Shafts of moonlight broke the blackness, pouring in through cracks in the roof. He switched off his lantern to get the effect. Would this photograph? It would look terrific on film. He'd have to get his people to work on replicating it. This was too good not to use, the kind of thing every horror film needs to make it distinctive.

Studying the effect, he sat down in one of the old theater seats. The upholstery was heavy with dust but he didn't mind. A spooky old movie theater. Terrific idea. If he couldn't work the idea into this film he could use it in his next one. He took another sniff.

There were people around him, an audience, staring at the dark, blank, torn screen. He looked into their faces. They were dead. Mutilated, decaying. Through the heroin high he realized this wasn't right. There was something else in the drug.

The projector flickered on. The shaft of light from it cut through the dusty air and made the screen blaze. Phantom images of long-dead actors flickered and vanished, to be replaced by more. This wasn't possible. Eric's paranoia, if that's what it was, returned, and he felt a wild urge to get out of the theater. The hands of the people around him forced him back into his seat and held him there.

A shower of dust and debris came from the ceiling. Something was moving up there.

More images filled the screen, vaguely familiar faces, he couldn't be certain who or what. One of them, he realized, was himself. They must be screening one of the student films he had acted in.

The theater's dead surrounded him. He felt hands on his throat, choking him. These people, these things, weren't real, it was the drugs, it was the town, it was . . . When the truth became inescapable he screamed.

From somewhere came a shout. "Who's in there?"

Everything went dark and silent. Eric was hunched up in his seat, clutching absurdly his lantern.

"Who's there?"

Eric whimpered.

Whoever it was stepped into the auditorium. "Hello?"

Eric turned and looked. He held up his lantern and could just barely make out that it was Father Vicosz.

"Eric?" The priest rushed to him. "For God's sake, what are you doing here?"

Eric sniffled. "I wanted to see the theater."

"Hasn't Tom warned you? This isn't a friendly town after dark."

"I'm not afraid."

"Don't be foolish." He helped Eric to his feet and brushed off his clothes. "Are you all right?"

"I think so. I don't know."

"What happened in here? What did they do to you?"

"Nothing. They tried to . . ." He fell silent.

"Come with me."

Eric didn't have the strength to resist. The priest put an arm around him and led him out of the auditorium, through the lobby and out into the square. Eric covered his eyes. The brilliant moonlight was hurting them.

"Come on over to my place. You can spend the night, if you'd like."

"Your housekeeper doesn't like me."

"She doesn't like anyone. Come on."

Supporting Eric, Bill crossed the square to St. Dympna's. The sanctuary was almost pitch-black; the only light was moonlight, filtered through stained glass. They walked through the church to the rectory.

"You're still trembling."

Eric seemed to be getting his grip back. For the first time he looked Bill in the face. "Why were you there?"

"I often go walking late at night. Steadbridge feels right to me then."

"Oh."

"Do you want a drink?"

He shook his head; that was the last thing he needed. The drugs were beginning to wear off, and he was glad of it.

"Let's get you undressed and into bed, then."

They slept side by side. Late into the night Eric woke and remembered everything that had happened. In the dark room he reached out and put his arm across the priest's chest. "Thank you."

But Bill was deep asleep.

10

FIRST DAY OF SHOOTING. RAIN.
   Second day. More rain.
   Forecasts were for a solid week of it. Eric was unhappy, seeming to find nature disrespectful of his importance as director. He had let Isabel persuade him to write a good number of outdoor scenes into the film, so they could take advantage of what she called the uniquely decaying architecture all over Steadbridge. Everyone else simply moved inside the mill, where a number of sets had been built and lit, with no fuss or grumbling. Angelo and Nicole did their nude love scene; neither of them seemed to find it pleasant, but they covered well enough. The electrical crew brought in generators, on the off-chance the power company—which was at the far end of the county—might not be able to meet their needs.
   Walchek's agreed to use *The Joy of Cooking*'s recipes for the meals they provided to the cast and crew. So people were eating and feeling better.

A hotshot kid named Justin Smithton was brought up from Pittsburgh to do "special makeup effects," which of course meant gore. In an unprofessional but irresistible moment Tom changed the sign on Justin's workroom to read SCHOOLBOY NASTINESS DEPT.

All in all, things were going smoothly. Tom went to see the rushes, which he learned were really called "dailies," each afternoon. It was hard for him to imagine them as parts of a finished film, but at least the individual bits looked okay.

He was learning to cope with his bandaged hands, doing at least simple tasks without too much trouble. Better yet, each day the pain seemed to lessen.

Alex seemed to have recovered from his seizure with no lasting effects. His doctor gave Ruth some pills to keep the boy calm and some anti-seizure medication, which he told her not to use unless there was another episode. Alex watched the production, seeming to find it all fascinating, apparently memorizing every detail. And he was on his best behavior, no running off, no rock throwing, no talk about the dead.

He tended to hang around Tom, which was okay, since he never got in the way. His fascination with everything fascinated Tom in turn. "So, do you think you might want to be a director some day?"

Alex glanced at Eric, who was working on the next set. "No thanks. I want to be a p-producer, like you. You're the one with the real power around here. Everyone says so." He smiled. "This is your movie."

"What about Eric?"

"He's the n-nephew."

He didn't mention the implosion again, and Tom was glad of it. The one time Alex overheard a couple of grips talking about it, he let it slide. He laughed and said it might not happen after all; Tom was happy to leave him with that belief.

Ruth was busy working with Isabel, getting clearances

for all the locations they wanted to use. They stopped by the mill once or twice a day to eat and keep Tom posted on developments. As expected, everyone in town was anxious for their share of the money the production was spending.

Phil called with the suggestion that Eric write in a lesbian love scene for Nicole and one of the bit players. "It'll help sell the picture. People love that stuff."

She refused to do it. "I have to think of my image."

Tom was tempted to ask, what image? But he was a prudent enough executive to keep quiet.

Angelo tried insisting he only be photographed from the right side. "That's my best profile."

"I'm not sure that's practical, Angelo."

"Claudette Colbert was only shot from the left side."

Tom tried to be patient. "And you see yourself as the new Colbert?"

"I have to think of my image." He was insistent.

"Well, okay then." Tom put on an indulgent smile. "But if we can only use half of your face, we're only paying half of your salary."

Angelo went back to work and didn't raise the issue again.

On the third afternoon Phil called again. Tom started to assure him everything was going smoothly. But Phil had something else on his mind.

"What the fuck is SPOSH?"

"I don't know what you're talking about, Phil."

"Apparently it stands for Somerseters for the Preservation of Our Steel Heritage. Who are they?"

It caught Tom off guard. "I've never heard of them. How should I know?"

"Because you'll be meeting them in court. They've gotten a district magistrate to issue an injunction to keep us from blowing up the mill. They're trying to get it declared a historic landmark."

It was the first Tom had heard of it. "Swell."

"We were served with the injunction this morning. You don't know anything about these people?"

"Nope. But let me get on it. I'll find out who's involved. I know the county wants the mill brought down."

"Good. Didn't you say there's some toxic waste there or something?"

"Well, yeah, Phil, but we don't want to bring that up. We got our permits for the shoot on the understanding that the site's safe. We don't want any attention from OSHA."

"Hell. Who'd think a bunch of goddamned hicks would have the nerve to—"

"Relax, Phil. This shouldn't be too hard to kill."

"I hope so. We've done some market research. The town's ripe for redevelopment. We want to put up a mall on that ground."

"After making a movie about a mall where bloody murders take place?"

"Why not?"

"Overbrook has balls, I'll say that much. You sending lawyers down here?"

"Not if we don't have to. Use that guy from Somerset who handled all the permits. Just get that injection quashed."

"Yes, sir."

"I mean it."

"So do I. If worse comes to worst, I can't imagine local judges cost too much."

"I like the way you think, Tom."

ON THE FOURTH DAY THE SUN CAME OUT. BUT IT was uncomfortably cool and damp. Eric was happy. Nearly everyone else wanted to stay indoors.

Maggie approached Tom that morning. He was looking over still another revised script. "Thanks for interrupting."

She put on a grin. "You owe me one."

"Have you read this thing? Any of the drafts at all?"

"No, I'm leaving camp to Angelo."

"Smart engineer. What's up?"

"Well . . . I don't know if it's my place to mention it, but . . ."

Trouble. He knew it. "Go ahead. Please."

"Well, last night, late, I had some thoughts about one of the sets. The one for the interior of the convenience store. I went over to Eric's to discuss it with him."

He tossed his script aside. "Yes?"

"The set was built in the back corner of the mill, where those offices used to be."

"Uh-huh."

"Well, on reflection I'm not sure how safe it is back there. The stairs and those upper-level offices . . . I warned everyone not to build anything too close to them. I thought we'd be okay, but now I'm not sure."

"You should have come to me, not Eric."

"You were at Ruth's."

"Oh." He looked slightly abashed. "Thanks."

"And Isabel was at Nic's. That pretty much left Hitchcock Junior."

Tom let out a good laugh. "I wonder if it's usual for directors to get so little respect."

"I wonder if it's usual for directors to be pompous juveniles."

"These days, probably yes. Anyway . . . ?"

"I happened to see in through his front window before I knocked." She hesitated.

"Come on, Mag, spill it."

"He was on the sofa, snorting something."

"Fine. Splendid." Just what he needed.

"He wasn't alone."

"Who . . . ?"

"That priest."

"Oh, Jesus."

"No, Tom, just the priest. You didn't hear it from me, okay?"

"Sure."

"Now about that set."

He riffled through a stack of budget estimates. "Tell you what, why don't you find Isabel and check it over. No sense taking chances."

"Will do."

"If it looks bad, how easy would it be to move it?"

"It's pretty cumbersome—it weighs a ton."

He looked at the script he had thrown on the floor. "Well, if it's a problem, we'll just have to shoot around it. The weather's breaking. We can shoot exteriors."

"Yes, boss." She turned and headed back to the mill. Tom started to read his script again, then decided it wasn't worth it. Another two days, Eric would have still another revision. Whatever he was sniffing must be giving him lots of pep. Tom scanned some of the dialog and thought, if only it was sharpening his mind, too.

THE COUNTY SUPERVISOR CALLED AND ASKED IF Tom knew about the lawsuit. "Yeah, we've got our local counsel on it."

"I just want you to know we're behind you on this. That mill's an eyesore. A dangerous one."

Tom found himself thinking, on that basis, half the towns in the Mon Valley should be imploded. But instead he asked if the county would be joining Overbrook in fighting the suit. The supervisor assured him that, yes, they would. "These preservationists are a pain in the county's ass. Every time somebody wants to put a new coat of paint on an old drug store, they start squawking and protesting."

"Any idea who the judge will be, or where he'll stand?"

"Ray McClellan. He owns an old drug store."

Good. The suit wouldn't be much more than a nuisance.

He hoped. There were headaches enough for him to deal with.

"Tom?" It was Angelo. He was wearing a costume soaked with unnaturally red stage blood. An artificial eye hung down the side of his face. "I need you to talk to my leading lady."

"What now, Angelo?"

"Every time we have to kiss in a scene, she eats garlic."

Tom let out a long sigh. "I'll have a word with her."

"She's pissed I don't want to sleep with her."

He couldn't hide his surprise. "I thought she was with Isabel."

"She is. She wants me, too."

"Damn whoever invented sex."

"Huh? What's wrong with sex?"

"You're too young to understand."

"No I'm not."

Tom looked him up and down. He wasn't much younger than Tom himself, though he looked like a kid. "When the Greek playwright Sophocles reached an age when he was past sexual desire, he cried out triumphantly, 'I am free of a cruel and insane master!' "

Angelo looked at him like he might be dangerous. "I don't get it."

"That's probably just as well for you. I'll talk to Nic, okay?"

"Thanks." Looking more than slightly puzzled, he walked away.

An instant later Ruth came in.

"What do you want?"

She scowled an exaggerated scowl. "My loving boyfriend."

"Sorry, Ruth. It's just been one headache after another today, that's all. I didn't mean to—"

"I know. Relax."

"Do you suppose the old movie moguls had headaches like these?"

"You ever hear about Jack Warner and Bette Davis? It sounds to me like you've got it easy."

"Thanks for the support."

"Come on, I'm taking you to lunch."

They ambled from his office to the mill, where Walchek's had set up lunch tables for cast and crew. People were eating, chatting, smiling. A harmonious set. Why did Tom want to mow them all down?

"TOM?"

"Hm?"

"Why are people afraid to d-die?"

It was nearly dinner time; production had shut down for the day. Tom and Alex were taking a walk along the river-bank; it was turning into a daily ritual for them.

"You do ask the damndest questions."

"I want to know."

"I like it better when you ask me about the movie."

They strolled on. Tom hoped Alex's mood would pass, but after a few moment he repeated his question.

"I don't know, Alex. Are you ever afraid of the dark at night?"

"Sometimes. But that's not the same."

"I think it is, in a way. You're scared of the dark because you don't know what might be hiding in it. People are afraid of dying because they don't know what's waiting for them after they die."

"I could tell them."

Tom stopped and got down on a knee. "I think you probably could. At least a bit. But I'm not sure they'd believe you."

"Why not?" He seemed genuinely puzzled.

"Because ... well, because there are other people telling them other things. Father Bill, for instance."

"He doesn't know."

"He doesn't know much, that's for sure."

"Then why don't they—"

"They just don't, that's all, Alex. People don't make a lot of sense. Look around." He got up and they went on walking.

"They should."

This was nothing Tom wanted to be talking about. "Did you learn anything interesting today?"

"Yeah. I think Angelo's c-crazy."

"I'll second that."

"Huh?"

"I mean I think so too."

"And Nicole is not crazy, except when Angelo's around."

"That makes sense."

"And Eric's going to die."

Tom froze. "Why do you think that?"

"He wants to die. He's the only one who's not afraid."

"Are you sure about his?"

Alex nodded. "They're waiting for him."

"Will you promise me not to talk about this with anyone else?"

"Um, I guess so."

"Thanks, Alex."

MRS. CHARNOCKI OPENED THE RECTORY DOOR AND, as usual, glared.

"Good evening." Tom put on the phoniest smile he could manage. "I need to see Bill. Now." He leaned on the last word forcefully.

Her frown got deeper. "*Father* Bill is—"

"I'm not in the mood for your nonsense, Mrs. Charnocki. I have to talk to him and I'm going to."

"You never did have proper respect."

"Are you going to get him, or do I have to push my way past you?"

"I'll call the police."

"You can call God himself, if you want to, but I'm here to see Bill, and that's what I'm going to do."

Glumly, realizing her usual demeanor wasn't working, she went off to get him. Tom sat in a plush chair and waited, wishing he was anyplace but in a church. After a few minutes she came back and told him, "Father Bill doesn't want to talk to you."

"Goddamn it." He got up and stormed into Bill's den, leaving her to protest his rude behavior.

Bill was on the sofa, asleep. Tom shook him. It became quickly apparent that he wasn't simply asleep but passed out. God knew from what.

Mrs. Charnocki followed him into the room. Tom rounded on her. "You are a lying old fool. He's in no condition to tell you anything, about me or anything else."

"He's sick."

"He's stoned out of his goddamned head, and you know it. You're not doing him a favor by covering this up. Make some coffee."

"I don't think I—"

"Make some coffee, dammit!" He barked as loudly as he could. Startled, plainly unhappy, she went off to the kitchen.

Tom slapped the priest's face. "Bill."

Again. "Bill, wake up."

Groggily Bill opened his eyes. "Eric?"

"No, Father." He leaned on the word sarcastically. "It's me, Tom."

"Where's Eric?"

"I don't know or give a damn." He slapped him again, not as hard. "Come on, Bill, snap out of it."

"That hurt."

"Good."

Tom sat in a char and watched as Bill tried to sit up. It was a struggle. After three tries he managed to right himself. Rubbing his eyes, he gaped at Tom. "What are you doing here?"

"Can't an old friend drop by for a visit?" Again he didn't try to hide his sarcasm.

"I think you broke my jaw."

"Don't be an idiot."

Mrs. Charnocki was back with a pot of coffee and two mugs. "I don't want to hear you talking to Father like that again."

"Put the coffee down on that table and go home, Mrs. Charnocki."

"I work till eight."

"It's close enough."

"What are you going to do?"

"Something you should have done a long time ago."

"I don't think you should—"

He bellowed, "Will you get the fuck out of here?! Your priest and I have to get some things straight between us."

Horror showed in her face. But she turned and, slowly, resentfully, left.

Hands shaking, Bill poured himself a cup of coffee. "I guess I should be grateful." He sipped. "But I'm not. I was having a lovely vision."

"Like St. Theresa of the Little Flower." Tom had bellowed enough. He lowered his voice. "What are you doing to yourself?"

"Exactly what I've always wanted to do. This priest thing was a detour, that's all."

"You're giving drugs to my director."

Bill drained his cup in one swallow and poured another one. "Boy, have you got it backward."

"You mean he's the one who—"

"Got it in one. You should be a detective."

"But—how can he be? Who could be his connection here?"

Bill put on a big smile. "It's a small town after all."

"Shit."

"Yeah, and good shit, at that."

Tom got up and poured himself some coffee. "Are you sleeping with him?"

"Not yet, no."

Not knowing whether to believe this, Tom stared suspiciously. "Really?"

"Not yet. But I have Catholic tradition to uphold."

"Leave him alone, will you? He's a kid."

"He went to NYU."

Suddenly Eric walked into the room. "And graduated with honors." Slowly, deliberately, watching Tom from the corner of his eye, he bent down and kissed Bill, long and hard.

Tom yawned. "I hope that wasn't meant to shock me."

Eric stiffened. "You think you know everything, don't you?"

He shrugged.

"Well, I know a thing or two, Tom. I know what you're doing to me, undermining my authority with my crew, cutting the budget for my film."

Tom was about to drink more coffee but he decided on whiskey instead. He got up, opened a bottle, and poured himself a glass. "One: they are not your crew, they are Overbrook's. Two: I haven't cut a dime out of the budget. This was conceived as a low-rent horror film. That's what you were hired to direct, if you haven't figured it out. And it's my job to see it stays that. Do you understand?"

"What about my artistic vision?"

"What about it?"

"I have a right to my vision."

"And when you produce your own movies, you can exercise that right. On this film you're doing work for hire. Understand?"

Eric glared. There was hatred in it. "You can't fire me. There's no one else who can direct this film."

"Well." Tom was breezy. "Now you know why we brought in a cinematographer. Promoting him will be no problem, if we need to. Uncle Phil really has you pegged, Eric."

During this exchange Bill had buried his face in his hands. He got up and took the bottle from Tom. "Give me that."

Tom snatched it back.

"I want that."

"No you don't. Bill, stop doing this to yourself."

"I'll do any damn thing I want to myself."

"And so will I!" Eric screamed it. "You can't stop me."

Tom sighed, long and deep. "Eric, will you please go back to your place and get a good night's sleep? We can talk in the morning. Right now I—"

"I don't have to talk to you at all. I'm the director!" He crossed to Bill, pressed something into his hand and rushed out of the room.

Tom watched him go, mildly startled. Then he looked at Bill and put on a wide grin. "My director. He needed to hear all that."

"I wouldn't push him too far, Tom. He's . . . hell, I don't know what he is."

"Back in the 60s some avant-garde artist used to build machines that were designed to destroy themselves when they were switched on. I'll bet you they looked at lot like Eric." Tom sat down again and took a long drink.

"Or like me?"

"It's not impossible."

"I hate myself, Tom." Bill got up, paced a few steps, then seemed to think better of it and sat down again. "I'm stuck here, and I feel nothing but contempt for the place. I had forgotten. I had made myself forget. But having you here has . . ."

"Give me that stuff."

Bill opened his hand. There was a small bag of white powder. Looking a bit lost, he handed it to Tom. "I remember when we were kids, how we used to talk about getting out of here. You did it. I never had the nerve. When you left, I . . ."

"Come on, let me get you to bed."

"No, I'll be all right. Get me another cup of coffee, will you?"

Tom took his cup and refilled it. "Here. You sure you'll be okay?"

"I think so, yeah."

"Good. I have to go ask a lesbian actress why a gay actor thinks she's sexually harassing him."

Bill looked wide-eyed. "Now that has sobered me up."

"Good."

"Are you serious about it?"

"Unfortunately, yes."

"Wow."

"Will you promise me not to see Eric any more?"

"I guess. Are you jealous?"

"You've been a priest too long. You're not in love with him, are you?"

Bill nodded slightly, as if it embarrassed him. "A bit."

"He's a wasted kid. Even sober, he's empty."

"I know it. He's the best I've been able to come up with."

"Then you're right, it's time to get out of Steadbridge." He started to take another swallow but changed his mind and put the glass down. "Play sick. Blackmail the bishop. You must have plenty of dirt on him."

"When we were kids, Tom, when we . . ." He looked away. "I've never stopped being . . . a bit . . ."

"I know, Bill." Without realizing it he took a step away from him. "I was a kid. I was horny. I would have fooled around with anybody." He tried to smile. "No love here. Not that kind."

"I can't help it."

"Don't waste your love on me. I'm a movie producer."

Bill had to steady himself against the couch to stand up.

"I'll be okay. I should never have said it. I'm going to bed now. I feel like a damned fool."

"Don't. Everybody knows I'm irresistible."

"Well, now, hold it. I said I was a bit in love, not schizophrenic."

They both laughed. Tom was glad to see Bill's mood improve, however fleetingly.

"Why don't you stop by the mill tomorrow, around lunch time? We're shooting some murders."

"I'll do it. I can give the last rites."

"See you then. Sure you'll be okay?"

Bill nodded. Tom said good night and left, hoping Bill really would be all right.

THE NEXT MORNING, RAIN WAS THREATENING again. Tom was dreading the day. He'd have to have a long chat with Eric, be firm with him but nice enough to keep him working. He stopped by the office. Rachel was typing something long. Tom got the largest mug off the hook and poured himself some coffee. "What's up?"

Rachel showed him what she was working on. It was the latest version of the script. Eric had written in a suicide scene. The character, who hadn't appeared in any of the earlier drafts, was named Eric.

"You've been pushing him awfully hard, Tom."

"He needs it. Hell, he deserves it."

"You want him suicidal?"

"I'll talk to him. I'll hold his hand till he's better, okay?"

He checked for voice messages and faxes. There was nothing that needed his attention.

"I'm going over to the mill. I'll check in before lunch, okay?"

"You better have another cup of coffee before you go. You're going to need it."

"What's wrong now?"

She smiled a coy little smile. "That would be telling."

He headed for the door. "Tom?"

"Yeah?"

"Go easy on Eric, okay?"

"You don't actually feel sorry for the little jerk, do you?"

"Not that, no. But he's a kid, and he's seeing his dreams crumble. That's never easy, for anyone. They may be silly dreams, but still . . ."

He made himself stop and think for a moment. "You're probably right." He didn't add that there seemed to be a lot of dreams crumbling around Steadbridge. And he was at the center of it.

When he got to the mill, there were half a dozen protesters picketing. He stopped in his tracks and gaped at them. "What the—?"

All but one seemed to be middle-aged or older. Their signs read things like PRESERVE OUR STEEL HERITAGE. So this was SPOSH. It was the last thing Tom needed. Damn Rachel for not telling him to expect this.

Three of them were chanting "Hey, hey! Ho, ho! Overbrook Media's got to go!" The film crew mostly seemed to be going about their business, ignoring them.

Ruth was there. She waved and crossed to him, smiling enormously. "Good morning, Mr. Production Executive."

He kissed her on the cheek. "Morning. How long have they been here?"

"About an hour."

"You know," he said wistfully, "I thought about becoming a college teacher. The business world seemed so much more rewarding."

Ruth followed him as he put on a big, professional smile like a bartender and approached the man who seemed to be in charge. He was old, tall, heavy. Tom wondered if he might have been a steelworker once himself. The man had a placard that read PROGRESS SHOULD NOT FORGET THE

PAST. Tom was grateful there were only six of them. A sizable demonstration might actually have attracted the media, from Johnstown and Altoona if not from Pittsburgh.

Tom smiled and extended a hand. "Good morning. I'm Tom Kruvener, the executive in charge of production."

The man scowled. "Jack Sharp. SPOSH." He shook Tom's hand grudgingly, with ill grace.

Tom was tempted to make a joke—"SPOSH you, too"—but it didn't seem like quite the thing. "What exactly can I do for you, Mr. Sharp?"

"You're going to destroy Number Five." He gestured at the mill, as if Tom might not know what he meant. The other protesters went on with their chant. "This," said Sharp, "was the last working steel mill in this region."

Tom glanced at the other picketers and wondered why anyone thought simple-minded rhymes might be an effective form of social activism. "We're planning to bring it down, yes. We'll be imploding it later this summer."

"You can't."

"Er . . . could you ask your colleagues to stop that chanting? It makes conversation kind of hard."

Sharp started chanting with them, loudly. Swell.

"Mr. Sharp?" Tom raised his voice.

Sharp went on shouting.

"Mr. Sharp?" Tom shouted too, to be heard above them. "There really isn't much point to this. We have every reason to think the court is going to quash your injunction."

"Hey, hey! Ho, ho!"

"Mr. Sharp, this ground is contaminated with toxic waste. If we need to, we'll get the EPA to come in and knock the mill down for us, so they can start a clean-up."

Sharp stopped. "Toxic?"

"Toxic, yes. Do you really want the kids growing up here to be exposed to it? Do you want it seeping into the river? How many communities are being poisoned, or might be?"

"We didn't know about that. Still, our heritage . . ." He glanced at the mill uncertainly.

Ruth had been listening to the exchange from a few feet away. For the first time she spoke up. "Mr. Sharp, I'm Ruth Fawcett. I work for the town of Steadbridge."

He looked suspicious. "Good morning."

"I want you to know the town is behind Overbrook one hundred percent. And so am I. I have a ten-year-old boy." She pointed across the yard to Alex, who was carrying a length of coiled rope for one of the grips. "That's him there. I want him to grow up in a healthy place. And I have to tell you that I resent you trying to prevent that from happening."

Uncertain what to do, he quickly rejoined his colleagues. "Hey, hey! Ho, ho!"

There was no use talking to him any more. Tom and Ruth left him to his singsong and walked off.

"Thanks for backing me up on that."

"My pleasure. Will the EPA really be coming here?"

"No, but it sounded good, didn't it?"

She laughed. "Bluffs like that have a way of backfiring. What if he calls them to check on what you said?"

"He doesn't have any facts. You think the EPA is going to take anything he tells them seriously? The county will kill their damned injunction, and that will be that. I need more coffee."

They headed to the catering wagon. Tom asked for an extra large cup of coffee; Ruth got herself a Danish and some tea. Then he took her off to one side. "How's Eric this morning?"

"He seems fine. I mean, he's his usual self. Why?"

He gave her an abridged version of the previous night's scene, and the suicide he wrote into the script for himself. "I don't know whether to be worried about him."

"I don't have a lot to do now. All the clearances and permits are done." She took a big bite of her pastry. "You want me to keep an eye on him?"

"You already have one problem child to worry about."

"I can handle both of them, believe me. Tom?"

"Hm?"

"Is this ground really toxic?"

"I don't know. The county seems to think it might be." A passing electrician jostled him and he spilled his coffee. He went back to the wagon for another cup, then rejoined her.

"I'm wondering if . . . I mean, Alex always plays here. Even though I tell him not to. He's here a lot. If there's toxic waste . . ."

"Then it's another reason for you to come to Manhattan with me."

"You're a monomaniac, do you know that?"

"I'm a movie producer. It's in my job description."

They found Eric. He was overseeing some last minute additions to a set for a book store. Isabel was standing and watching him, seeming to enjoy herself. Tom went over to him and tapped him on the shoulder. "Do you have a minute to talk?"

"Not now. I'm not happy with this."

Tom took in the set. It seemed fine to his eye. "What's wrong with it?"

"Too many books."

"Oh!" Tom was deadpan. "I would never have thought of that."

"And we're putting in some TV monitors."

"No book store is complete without them."

"We'll talk later."

Tom scowled. "Yes, sir."

An hour later Bill showed up. He seemed to be in a fine mood; there were no apparent aftereffects from his bender. Alex and Ruth both avoided him quite pointedly. Tom got him some coffee, and they walked around the site chatting.

Bill noticed the protesters. "What's that all about?"

Tom explained.

"They actually want you to keep this place up?"

"Yeah. Weird, isn't it?"

"Would it help at all if I talked to them?"

"Why would it?"

"Well, I mean, a priest . . . It might make them . . . I don't know. But it might."

"Go ahead and try, if you want to."

He watched as Bill strode over to them and started to say something. Almost at once they upped the volume of their chant. When he came back he looked crestfallen. "No one has any respect anymore."

"Bill? Will you promise me there won't be any more repeats of last night?

"Well," he stammered, "I'm not planning on any."

Tom looked around to make sure no one could hear. "Except for you and Ruth, I'm pretty much alone here. I don't want things between us to . . . to . . ."

"Don't worry. It won't happen again."

Tom's phone rang. It was Rachel. "Good news, boss. The judge has thrown out SPOSH's suit. Apparently they don't have standing."

"Can they appeal?"

"Sure. But they still won't have standing."

"Great. Now if we could only get rid of the SPOSHers themselves. They're giving me a headache."

"Have you forgotten, Tom? We own everything for a thousand yards around the mill."

"That's right! Do you want a raise?"

"No, Tom, just your love."

"Smartass."

He hung up, explained to Bill what had happened and went off to round up his security men. "Take their sorry asses off our property. We're going ahead as planned."

Bill was sober, Eric was working busily and apparently happily, Ruth and Alex were closer to Tom than ever. The weather moderated.

To all appearances, everything was fine.

THAT EVENING TOM TOOK THE SENIOR CREATIVE people and Ruth to dinner at Catania as a celebration. Eric drank a bit too much wine but seemed to be in a good mood.

Later Tom, Ruth and Alex took one of their evening walks. There seemed to be a million stars in the sky. The moon lit the valley, the river, the mill. Tom took Ruth's hand as they walked.

"I had forgotten how beautiful the sky at night can be."

"Explain to me again, Thomas, how you are not a romantic."

"All I need for perfect happiness is a genuine McCarthy's McKinley jelly donut."

"Then you'll have to stay imperfectly happy. They're still buying from a chain."

"Don't I know it."

They stopped at Number Five, mostly for lack of any-where else to go. Tony Kowalski was manning the front gate. "Evening."

"Hi, Tony. How's everything?"

"Dead calm."

"I'm not sure I like that turn of phrase."

Alex peered through the chain-link fence. "Is every-thing really quiet?"

"Sure, Alex." Tony seemed a bit puzzled by the ques-tion. "Quiet as a grave."

"The g-graves here don't stay quiet. You know that." He was still staring at the mill. Tom had the impression he was looking for something specific. But everything was dark and quiet.

"Sorry," Tony was breezy, "but there's nothing whatever to report."

Ruth put her arms around herself. "I'm starting to feel a bit chilly, Tom. Do you mind if we head home?"

"Sure, let's go." He said good night to Tony and they walked back toward town.

Behind them, ever so faintly, fires began to glow inside the mill. Alex, looking back over his shoulder, was the only one to see.

"T-t-tom?" The boy's stutter was getting more pronounced. Tom hoped Ruth hadn't noticed, though he was sure she must have.

"Hm?"

"They've been q-q-quiet so far."

The word *they* was not one he wanted to hear. *They* might be the dead Alex saw, or seemed to; they might be the hoboes Tom was still certain hung out in Steadbridge now and then; they could be anyone. "Yes, they have."

"They w-won't stay quiet. N-not for long."

Ruth sensed Alex's mood. "Maybe we should walk a bit more after all." To Tom she mouthed the words *tire him out.*

"Sure. Let's." Tom tried to act hearty. "What do you say, Alex?"

"Let's w-walk."

In a short while they reached the square. Someone was sitting on a bench at the feet of the statue. Slumped there.

"Tom." Ruth caught his arm. At the same instant Alex took hold of his other hand.

It was Eric. His throat and wrists were slit. Blood had poured all over him. The bench and the ground were soaked with it. In his right hand, held limply, was a straight razor.

"Oh God, Tom."

Tom felt Alex's grip tighten. "Tom, look!"

Around them the square was filled with people. In its heyday it had never been busier. Ghostly white figures came and went in the moonlight, moving in slow motion. Dozens of them, ghosts. They were surrounded.

Eric opened his eyes. He stared directly at Tom. And began to laugh.

The square was empty again except for the four of them.

Eric stood up, laughing, laughing hard. "I never thought you'd be the ones to find me. This is too good." He passed the razor over his forearm. It was rubber.

A wave of anger hit Tom at once. "What the hell is this?"

"I had Justin Smithton make me up like this. I wanted to see how you'd react when you heard I was dead. I never thought you'd be the one to actually find me." He found it hilarious.

"You dumb son of a bitch. I ought to kick your damn-fool ass from here to Johnstown and back. This is the kind of thing I'd expect from a highschool kid."

"What's the matter, can't you take a joke?"

"You pull something like this again, you'll find out."

Alex, sensing Tom's extreme anger, stepped behind Ruth.

For the first time Ruth spoke up. "This is an awful thing to do, Eric. Just awful."

He laughed at her and started to walk off in the direction of the Overbrook houses. "What a couple of geeks you are. It was nothing but a joke."

Tom caught him by the shoulder. "Well, I think we can safely lay to rest the proposition that you're a responsible professional who deserves professional treatment."

"Since I haven't been getting that anyway, what difference does it make?"

"Go home and get good and stoned, Eric. You're off the picture."

For the first time he fell silent; the smirk left his face. "You can't do that."

"The hell I can't."

"I have a contract. I'll sue."

"Get right in line behind the SPOSH people."

"I'll sue you and my uncle and everyone else."

It was Tom's turn to laugh. "Docket Number 54548. Eric Charles Benson v. Everybody."

Eric looked around, not seeming to know what to say or do. "Justin? Where are you?" Not getting an answer, he said, "He was hiding someplace around here."

"If he has an ounce of brains more than you do, he won't show his face."

"Justin! Justin! Tell them it was just a joke!"

The square was silent.

"Now get the hell out of here, Eric." Tom was the boss and sounded like it. "I'll have Rachel order your plane ticket back to New York first thing in the morning."

"You can't."

"Wait ten hours and see." He turned to Ruth and Alex. "Come on, let's get home." He took each of them by the hand and they left.

ERIC WATCHED THEM GO. THEN HE SAT BACK DOWN on the bench and stared at the stage blood on his wrists and arms. The statue of McKinley looked out over his head impassively. He buried his face in his hands and started to cry, not loudly, but he couldn't make himself stop.

When he looked up again the square was full of ghosts. They walked without seeing him. Men, mostly, and a few women and children. They came and went, some of them a few feet from him, and didn't see him.

He had not done any drugs that night. Well, weed, but that was all. There must have been something else in it.

Still crying he said loudly, "Notice me."

They went on and on, and ignored him.

"Please."

No response. The dead were as indifferent to him as the living, or so he thought. He stood up, then sat down again. There had to be a way to . . . It took him a while to convince himself that they wanted him, and that they were showing him as much love as they could.

RUTH GOT ALEX TO BED AND JOINED TOM IN THE living room. "Well. So much for C.B. DeMille, huh?"

Tom was still tense from the encounter in the square. "A twenty-three-year-old man with the mind and personality of a junior highschool kid."

"Are you really firing him?"

"What do you think? A stupid stunt like that. Suppose one of the elderly people around here had found him. Jesus."

"You want a drink?"

He looked at his watch. "No, I ought to get over to Barry's and give him the news."

She hesitated. "Just one?"

"Well . . . okay."

She got him his usual bourbon and made a highball for herself. "Maybe you should give him another chance."

"His entire stay here has been a second chance as far as I'm concerned."

"His uncle—"

"Will back me up. I don't get the impression they're a close, loving family."

She saluted him with her glass. "Most aren't. Now what about the ghosts in the square with him? Can you fire them? Cheers."

"They're there anyway, Ruth. Besides, the sooner he joins them, the happier I'll be."

"You can't mean that."

Tom took a long drink. "No, I guess not. But what a goddamned pain he's been."

They suddenly realized Alex was on the stairs, listening to them.

Ruth got up and took a few steps toward him. "Is everything all right?"

"I guess so."

"Then you should be in bed. You know that."

"They're everywhere tonight. They're all over town." His voice turned low and unnatural: the voice of Tom's father. "You will not destroy our home."

Ruth looked from one of them to the other. Tom seemed hardly to have noticed. He was sipping his drink.

Alex, still in that voice not his own, bellowed, "We will not let you destroy our home. We will not be forgotten."

Quietly Tom put his drink down and said, "No. Of course not."

Slowly, whatever had taken hold of Alex let him go. He looked at his mother, who was looking at him. Without saying anything she climbed the steps with him and put him back to bed.

When she came down Tom still hadn't finished his drink. He looked up at her as she crossed the room to him. "I think I'm going to die here, Ruth."

"No."

"Maybe I should have died here twenty years ago. Maybe I should have overdosed when I was a punk kid."

"You're talking nonsense, Tom. You just let the scene with Eric get to you, that's all."

He stood up. "Yeah, that's all."

"Come on upstairs. Let me give you a good back rub."

"No, I have to see Barry."

"See him in the morning." She touched his cheek. "Come on, Mr. Producer. I've got something for you."

He followed her upstairs.

ERIC POUNDED ON THE RECTORY DOOR. AFTER A minute or two Bill came and opened it. Eric stood there, covered in blood, the fake razor still in his hand.

"Jesus."

"It's all right. It's just makeup."

Bill looked up and down the street, then pulled Eric inside. "Isn't it a bit early for trick or treat?"

Eric smiled sheepishly.

"Let's go to my study and have a drink. What on earth is wrong?"

They went to the den and Eric sat down. "It's too late for me, Bill."

Bill poured drinks for them. "Here. It's never too late."

"Yes, Father."

"What's wrong? What happened? Why are you—?"

"Joke. A little joke I played on Mr. Thomas Kruvener."

"I hope he found it funnier than I did."

"No. He fired me."

"Oh."

They both fell silent.

Eric looked at the glass in his hand, apparently surprised it was there. He put it down without drinking. "I want death, Bill. I want to be dead."

"You have it. You are. We all are."

"I mean it."

"So do I."

"I've fucked up my life so badly."

"Everyone does."

"Stop patronizing me!" He shouted it.

The priest let silence come between them for a moment, then said, "Do you think I don't know anything about death? Do you think I don't understand this town and what happens to people here?"

"I was fucked before I ever came here."

Bill stopped and took a drink. "Probably."

"I want to be dead, Bill."

"Stop saying that. You don't know a thing about death. You don't have a clue what death is."

"It's the opposite of life, that's what it is. And it's what I want. I'll show them. I will."

There was a thick book lying open on Bill's usual chair. He tossed it aside and sat down. "People talk about death all the time and never know what it is. Everyone says what you just did, that death is the opposite of life."

"It is."

"Then what's life, Eric?"

The question startled him. "Everyone knows what life is. Energy, vitality, creativity, love. Fucking. Doping. I don't have any of that, not any more."

"That," Bill said heavily, "is all rubbish. Love, energy and all that, that's what people think life is. But it isn't."

Not liking what he was hearing, Eric picked up his glass and drank.

"Look at people's lives, Eric. Look at your own, or

mine. Life is pain and deprivation, life is loneliness, emptiness, life is failure and defeat. Whatever those things you
listed are, they aren't life. Life is the opposite of them.
Death is only a footnote."

Eric let out a quick derisive laugh. "Is this supposed to
make me feel better?"

"No." Bill said it calmly. "It's supposed to make you
feel more real. More like the rest of us."

"If that's what life is, I don't want it."

"It's all there is, Eric."

"You're a priest, goddammit. You're supposed to be
telling me positive things, God loves you, your life matters,
there's a special providence in the fall of a sparrow."

"There isn't. I love you too much to lie to you."

Eric got to his feet. "I came here because I wanted you
to hold me. To help me, comfort me, make me feel better."

"I wish I could."

"You can. Hold me, Bill."

There were tears welling up in Bill's eyes. "My life is
empty too. I've wasted it. We all do."

"No. I can't hear that."

"It's the truth."

"Then fuck the truth, and fuck you."

Eric turned and left the room, slowly, deliberately.
When he was on the street strange people surrounded him.
Dozens of them. He walked through them, or past them
and tried to remember, is Tony working at the mill or at
Hank's tonight? There was an easy enough way to stop
feeling what he was feeling.

Bill watched him from the rectory window. And he
cried. When Eric had gone out of sight, he found himself
wondering if he was crying for the boy or himself.

IN THE MORNING THERE WAS HEAVY RAIN, LIGHT-
ning, thunder, severe wind. Tom got up early and asked
Ruth to get out a quick memo to everyone, calling a nine

o'clock meeting at the school. "Tell the caterer we'll need coffee and breakfast there."

"It's short notice for them."

"They'll cope."

"Something up?"

He nodded. "I fired Eric last night."

"What happened?"

"I'll tell you about it later. I have to get over to Barry's and let him know. He's our director now. Then I'll have to call Uncle Phil and give him the news."

"Will he care?"

"I doubt it."

Rain was running through the streets in torrents. The wind almost turned Tom's umbrella inside out. Barry was still asleep when Tom knocked at his door. Tom apologized for waking him and explained what had happened. "You will take over the filming, won't you?"

"Sure. I've been director in all but name anyway. Eric talks to me about art, about chiaroscuro, about mise-en-scène, then I put the camera where I think it'll do the most good and shoot."

"Thanks, Barry. I'll be calling New York now. As of this morning, you're drawing a director's salary."

"Can I keep shooting it myself?"

"Sure."

He smiled. "The camera's the only thing I love."

Tom headed to the school. The storm was getting worse. Phil's number at Overbrook wasn't answering. He left a detailed massage, explaining what had happened and why he had fired Eric and promoted Barry. Waiting for the crew to assemble, he paced. He decided it would be a mistake to make more than a simple announcement. Where was Phil?

Slowly the crew began to filter in. The weather seemed to be getting to everybody. No one was smiling or even talking much. Maggie nodded at Tom, smiled faintly and yawned. Ruth stood at the back of the room by a window, watching the storm. Rachel came in and sat down at Tom's side, ready to take notes. Walchek's finally arrived with coffee and Danish. Not many people ate.

When everyone seemed to be there, Tom started the meeting. He explained briefly that Eric had been removed from the film. There wasn't much reaction, certainly not much surprise. A few people even let out what sounded like relieved sighs.

A blindingly bright flash of lightning lit up the sky, followed by thunder so loud everyone jumped and the windows rattled.

Tom glanced at his watch. "This is supposed to go on all morning. So I guess we're shooting interiors again." He waited for questions. There were none. "Well, I guess that's it then."

Slowly everyone got up. There was some quiet talk among them. Some of them got coffee or pastry. In small groups they began to filter out. Tom joined Ruth at the window and watched as rows of umbrellas moved up the street.

"Where's Alex?"

"In bed, not feeling well."

"Nothing serious . . . ?"

"No. I don't think so."

Everyone else was gone but Rachel. Tom asked her to get back to the office and try Overbrook again. "It's my first real executive decision. I'm kind of proud of it."

Rachel held her tongue and left.

"Come on, Ruth. Let's go. Are you coming to the mill later?"

"That's where the food is."

Almost at once his phone rang.

"Tom, this is Mag. You better get over here right away."

"Why? What's wrong?"

She hesitated. "Eric."

They left quickly. The storm seemed to be easing off. The wind died down a bit, the rain seemed less heavy. Even so, making quick progress through the flooded streets was difficult. They walked side by side, arms around each other's waists, their umbrellas touching.

"I don't remember this kind of thing happening here. The streets never used to overflow like this when we were kids."

"Yes, they did. You're showing your age."

"Thanks."

Then they were at Number Five. Everyone seemed to be standing outside the river-side entrance, all under umbrellas. Why would they be out in this?

Maggie saw them approaching and rushed to join them. "Thank God you got here. We've been trying to reach Hank but there's no answer. We've called the county police."

"What on earth is wrong? Why aren't people inside?"

"Look." She pointed upward.

Through the rain it was just possible to see a figure at the top of the smokestack.

Ruth tightened her grip around Tom's waist. "Good God, Tom."

Tom told Maggie to keep trying Hank, then rushed away from them, to the base of the staircase, and started to climb. A chain with a DANGER—KEEP OFF sign lay coiled on the ground. Looking up he shouted, "Eric! Eric, for God's sake, come down here."

Whether Eric didn't hear him or simply didn't want to answer, it was impossible to tell.

Tom climbed a few more steps. Maggie rushed up behind him. "Tom, don't. That staircase isn't safe."

Eric began to shout something. They couldn't make out what.

"Someone's got to go up there, Mag. I can't leave him there." He took another step.

Maggie caught at his sleeve. "Tom, it's too dangerous!"

Suddenly the rain all but stopped. It was so abrupt it startled everyone. The wind kept up. Tom and Maggie looked up at Eric again.

They could see him clearly now. He stood perched on the top of the smokestack. He was still shouting. The wind made it impossible to hear more than every third or fourth word. ". . . dead . . . death . . ."

Tom looked at Maggie. "Someone has to get him down. It's my responsibility. I can't leave him up there like that."

She let go of his sleeve. "Be careful, then."

"I will."

He started up the staircase, holding the railing loosely with his bandaged hands. The steps creaked, groaned, swayed. They were worse than he'd expected. When the wind blew they swayed even more. Seeing what he was doing, Ruth ran to the foot of the steps. "Tom, come back down here!"

He looked down at her. "I can't, Ruth. This is my responsibility."

"Tom, please!"

He kept climbing.

Halfway up, fifty feet off the ground. He looked up and saw that Eric was watching him. Suddenly the wind stopped, as the rain had. The stillness was eerie.

"Eric?"

Eric watched him and said nothing. He climbed.

"Eric, will you please come down?" His tone made it an order, not a request.

Eric walked back and forth across the lip of the smokestack, not taking his eyes off Tom.

"Eric, I'm coming to get you, okay?"

For the first time Eric responded. "Fuck you, Kruvener. Fuck your movie."

Good, he was talking. As long as he kept talking he wouldn't . . .

"No one wants you to do this, Eric."

"Fuck you all."

There was the sound of sirens. Tom looked down and saw Hank's car pull up, followed by a county EMS crew. He took another step. The stairs swayed wildly under his weight and he nearly lost his balance. He caught the handrail with his left hand and it exploded with pain. He steadied himself against the rail with his wrists and forearms. But he kept climbing.

"I want to die," Eric shouted. "All I've ever wanted is to be dead." He was glaring, eyes wide open, at Tom.

"No one else wants you to die, Eric."

"No one else gives a fuck about me. I want to die."

Tom was making steady progress upward. He was three fourths of the way up to Eric, still steadying himself with his arms and wrists. The staircase trembled and shuddered with every step, but he knew he couldn't let anything happen to the young man. He'd never be able to live with it.

"Eric. Come on down. We'll talk."

From below came the sound of someone on a bullhorn. "Come down, both of you."

He looked down at them, saw that it was Hank, then kept climbing.

"Come down! Mr. Kruvener, you're putting yourself in danger."

"Do you think," he shouted, "I don't know that?"

He looked up at Eric again. "Come down, Eric. Please. You're throwing away your life for nothing."

Bitterly Eric mimicked him. "Do you think I don't know that?" He stepped to the very lip of the smokestack. His feet were four inches over the lip. "I want to die, and I'm going to die. Death is the only act of creation left to me."

He held his arms out wide. Tom froze. And everyone on the ground froze. Eric was going to jump.

Suddenly there was a violent gust of wind. The stairs swayed wildly. Tom caught the railing and gripped it as tightly as he could, hoping the stairs wouldn't collapse under him. He slipped down half a dozen steps before he managed to catch hold, wrapping his arms through he railing.

Eric nearly lost his balance. Tom held his breath.

From the sky came a terrific bolt of lightning. It struck the smokestack. And Eric was gone.

Everything shook violently. Some of the bolts that held the stairs to the brick chimney tore loose. It swayed; it undulated in the wind. Tom was sure it would collapse. He closed his eyes and held as tightly as he could.

There was more wind, then it died down. The rain began again. Tom was left on the stairs, gaping upward. There seemed to be smoke where Eric had been. The wind dissipated it quickly.

"Tom!" It was Hank on his bullhorn again. Tom looked cautiously down at him. It seemed his least movement set up awful sympathetic vibrations in the steps. He began to inch downward. Slowly, carefully. His hands were completely useless, the bandages soaked with blood and some other fluid, yellowish, Tom didn't know what.

"Tom, don't move!" It was Ruth's voice. He forced himself to ignore it and kept inching down.

"Mr. Kruvener!" It was another voice, one he didn't recognize. "We've got a hook-and-ladder on the way from Johnstown. Try not to move."

"I have to," he shouted. "This won't hold."

"It's more dangerous for you to keep climbing down than to stay where you are."

"I'm not willing to take that chance." The steps shuddered. He crept slowly down. It seemed to take forever. When he looked at the crowd it seemed he had made no progress at all. He was a million feet in the air, he would never reach the ground.

They kept talking to him, kept urging him to stop and stay where he was. He ignored them and continued downward. Every now and then the entire staircase would vibrate, like an extended spring. When the wind kicked up it was worse.

Finally he was thirty feet above the ground. "I'm going to jump."

The EMS crew held a net. He leaped into it, bounced, fell off and hit the ground. Everyone crowded around. A medic gave him a quick once-over and said there were bruises and contusions, nothing too bad. But he'd better get the emergency room and get a more thorough checkup.

"No, I'm okay." He sat up.

"Thomas Kruvener." Ruth planted herself directly in front of him. "You will get in the ambulance, you will ride to the hospital, you will let the ER crew change your bandages and check you over, and you will drop this macho foolishness. Do you understand that?"

Suddenly, unexpectedly, he did feel like a fool. Quietly he said "Yes, ma'am."

The medics got him onto a stretcher and strapped him to it.

"This is silly. I don't need—"

"That's enough, Tom. Just stop it. And it's not even ten in the morning. I have to get home and check on Alex."

He looked around. Everyone seemed to be in mild shock, or worse. First the storm, the lightning, Eric's death, then his ordeal on the staircase. He asked Rachel to tell everyone production was shutting down for the day. Then he let the EMS team lift him into the ambulance. As the doors were being closed Ruth told him, "I'll pick you up at the hospital later."

Inside the ambulance it was dark, cool and quiet. Tom closed his eyes and went to sleep almost at once.

EVERYONE DISPERSED, SLOWLY, TO THEIR HOUSES or to find themselves food or drink. Ruth checked to find out where Tom was being taken, then stood and watched the ambulance drive off. The rain was starting again, slowly, but the drops were large and heavy. There was distant lightning followed by low, ominous thunder from downriver. What they had seen was only the beginning of the storm.

After what seemed only a short moment she found herself alone outside the mill. She had hoped Maggie would hang around and keep her company, but there was no sign of her. Alex would be waking up soon, if he hadn't already. She had to get home.

Slowly, almost imperceptibly the rain got heavier and the wind kicked up again. Her umbrella wasn't doing her much good. Fire ignited in the mill, the hot fire of steel-making. She watched for a moment. They knew. The decision to explode the mill had been taken, and it was final now, nothing could stop it. They would not rest; they would fight. They had taken Eric. Everything she knew told her so. She had to get home to Alex.

There was no one else in sight. Where could they all have gone so quickly? She started walking.

Rainwater cascaded through empty streets. Lights burned brightly in windows. She was glad people had someplace warm and dry to go to, out of this terrible storm. Then she realized: these were the empty houses, the abandoned ones, the ones in such poor shape they couldn't be renovated. Lights burned in every window, bright and hot.

When lighting flashed she could see figures in the streets. They ignored her; they stared straight ahead of themselves, impassive, dead. They walked. In lightning they glowed; then they were shadows. Ruth moved faster and faster. The lights in the Overbook houses, the occupied ones, were not as bright as the lights in the empty ones.

Finally she got home. Inside she quickly put down her umbrella and called out to Alex.

The house was still, silent.

"Alex?"

No reply.

She rushed up the stairs to his bedroom.

He was sitting at the window, watching Number Five. The fire burned brighter than either of them had ever seen it.

Slowly the boy turned to face her. "Eric d-d-d-di-d-d—"

He had never stammered so badly. She didn't move and couldn't speak.

"Eric d-d-d-died."

"Yes," she whispered. "Yes, Alex."

"F-f-f-fell."

"Did he fall?"

Alex nodded.

"We all saw the lighting hit him. We thought he had been . . . I don't know, vaporized or something."

"F-f-fell. He's at the b-bottom of the chimney."

Ruth took a step toward him. "Are you all right?"

"I'm s-s-scared."

She went to him and put her arms around him. "We're all scared, Alex."

"You too?"

"Yes, me too."

"And T-t-t-t-tom?"

She kissed the side of his face. "Yes, darling, Tom too."

"We're g-going to d-d-d-die. All of us. St-st-st-steadbridge."

Tightly she held him. "No, Alex."

"Grandma Kibben saw d-d-death when T-tom came."

She ran her fingers though his hair. "Oh, Alex, I wish I knew what I could tell you."

"They won't ever rest now."

"I know."

"It's terrible to try and forget them."

"I know, Alex. But everyone forgets. All the time. It's part of what makes us human."

For a long time she sat holding him, and neither of them spoke. Finally, very softly, Alex repeated, "I'm afraid."

TOM WAS DISMISSED FROM THE HOSPITAL, COVERED with bandages, that afternoon. Ruth was waiting for him. They kissed, and he winced in pain from one of the sore spots she had touched.

"First my burned hands, now all this. I'm starting to look like Karloff in *The Mummy*."

"You're not tall enough."

"I'd slap you, if it wouldn't hurt me more than you."

She smiled. "Do it, then."

"Come on, Mrs. Fawcett."

Production resumed the next day under Barry's direction. He worked slowly, steadily, methodically, planning his shots, taking pains to light them the way he wanted. Tom found himself feeling a bit impatient for Eric's more slapdash style.

Alex showed up for work early each day. He seemed to have lost his boyish enthusiasm for the film; now he worked seriously and with no playing around at all. Everyone noticed how badly he was stammering.

That afternoon they were shooting an exterior in the square. Bill came out of St. Dympna's and watched. He stood and peered intently at everything and everyone. Tom made a point of greeting him.

"It's a good day for outdoor shooting," he explained. "It's slightly overcast. Barry says that helps diffuse the light. The things you learn, huh?"

After a long silence Bill said, "I miss Eric."

"So do I. So does the whole crew, Bill. We never wanted—"

"You don't miss him the way I do."

Tom was going to disagree, but there didn't seem any point. "You want to have dinner tonight?"

"No thank you."

"Oh. Bill, I—"

"You should never have come here, you and your movie company. Eric won't be the last, but none of the rest will hurt like that."

"Bill, I'm sorry, but he—"

"I have to put a stop to this."

Tom took a step away from him. "There's not really much you can do about it."

"There is." He said it softly, turned his back and went back inside the church.

The dailies looked wonderful. Angelo, Nicole and the

other actors were ecstatic at the way Barry was making them look. Angelo found a boyfriend among the bit players. "Like Gary Cooper and Andy Lawler," he told Tom cheerfully.

As they were leaving the projection room Tom button-holed Barry. "Will we be able to stay on schedule?"

"If the weather holds, sure. Maybe even if it doesn't. It would help it we could start shooting nights."

"No!"

Barry was a bit startled at his firmness. "Whatever you say, Tom."

"Sorry, I don't mean to be so vehement. But . . . the cost of lighting the mill would be prohibitive. I have to keep my eye on the budget."

"Sure."

Tom, Ruth and Alex had a quiet dinner at Walchek's that evening. No one else from the crew was there; they had been in town long enough to have found other places, or to have started cooking for themselves. Alex was very quiet. He was having so much trouble speaking; silence seemed preferable. Tom and Ruth made small talk, both of them carefully avoiding anything too unpleasant.

Later at Ruth's, after Alex went to bed, they sat on the sofa and held each other. No talk, just quiet affection. They fell asleep that way. Tom awoke first and realized it was midnight. He tried to slip away without waking her, but it was no use. She rubbed her eyes and yawned.

"Are you sure you want to go?"

"I think I need to be alone, Ruth. This is all so . . ." He spread his hands in a helpless gesture.

"You knew it would be."

"That doesn't help."

"Tom, I don't want to be alone tonight. For some reason I—"

"I know. Me too, I guess. It isn't easy for me to admit it."

"Men."

"Let's go upstairs."

Suddenly there was a shriek, a loud piercing shriek. It came from upstairs. It was Alex.

Tom bolted for the steps with Ruth right behind him. There were more screams, hysterical ones. They raced to the boy's room.

The window was wide open and Bill was there. He was holding Alex by the hair. He held a large bread knife to his throat. Alex struggled. His eyes were wide with terror.

"Bill!" Tom and Ruth shouted his name simultaneously.

The priest looked at them. "Get out of here. I have to do this."

"Bill, stop." Tom tried to make his voice calm and reassuring. "He's only a boy. He's not responsible for any of this. If you want to blame someone for Eric's death, blame me."

"I do." He gave a tug on Alex's hair, causing the boy's head to jerk violently. The tip of the knife pressed into his throat. "But you're not the link, Tom."

"There is no link. Think what you're doing, Bill, for God's sake."

"It is for God's sake that I'm doing it."

Ruth tried to rush at him but Tom caught her and held her back. She was crying, almost hysterical. Seeing her, Alex began to cry too, long wailing shrieks. She struggled to get free of Tom's grip. "Bill, please. He's my son. You're my friend."

"Not any more. Not since you joined yourself with him." He gestured at Tom. "You're both permitting this. They'll take vengeance on us all now."

Suddenly Tom snatched a sheaf of drawings from Alex's desk and flung them at Bill's face. Then he rushed him. Bill slashed at Tom's hands; blood flowed. Finally Tom caught hold of the knife and pulled Alex free. Alex darted to his mother.

Tom and Bill fought. Furniture was knocked over, the bedroom window shattered. Bill tried and tried to get his knife back. It plunged into his cheek; blood flowed; but he got it back.

His back was to Ruth and Alex. He was going to kill Tom if he could, it was clear. Then would come Alex and Ruth. Ruth took her phone out of her pocket, pushed the emergency number, then pushed it into Alex's hand had shoved him out into the hallway. "Tell them what's happening."

Tom and Bill stood facing each other, neither of them moving. Blood poured from Tom's hands.

Bill lunged, Tom ducked to one side. Again and again. A standoff. Ruth picked up the lamp from the nightstand and quietly stepped up behind Bill. She waited till he was recovering his balance after a lunge, then smashed it over his head. He turned and gaped at her, startled. His eyes rolled up in his head and he collapsed.

Tom's bandages were soaked with blood again. It was all too much for him. He sat down on the floor and began to cry uncontrollably. Ruth and Alex got down beside him and they all held each other until the county police arrived.

11

"THERE. ALL BANDAGED UP." THE ER NURSE frowned at Tom. "You really have to take better care if these are to heal properly."

"No kidding." He was on an exam table, naked but for a hospital gown. Bandages covered cuts on several parts of his body.

Ruth stood to one side, watching with a faint smile. "You'll have to excuse Mr. Kruvener, nurse. He thinks he's macho."

The nurse didn't seem to know if she was kidding. "These men. Only ten stitches—nowhere near as bad as it looked."

Tom got to his feet. "If you two are finished with your male-bashing, I'd like to get out of here."

The nurse gently pushed him back onto the table. "The doctor wants to see you before you leave. Wait here." She left, with a quick smile at Ruth.

Tom lay back on the table and stared at the ceiling.

"Nurses in movies are always young and beautiful and selflessly devoted to their patients."

"Just your luck to run into the real world."

"Well," he glanced at her then looked quickly away, "at least I didn't run into it as hard as poor Eric."

"So all of a sudden it's 'poor Eric,' hm? Two days ago you couldn't stand him."

"Two days ago he wasn't dead."

"Nostalgic for the past." She pulled up a chair for herself. "You know, you look cute dressed like that. Men should wear those things all the time."

"All men? Would you like to see Hank like this?"

She laughed. "No thanks. He wants to talk to you when we get back to town, by the way. He needs a statement about what happened tonight."

"He already knows what happened. Bill admitted it."

"Even so. He's at my place, watching Alex. It'll be his last official duty."

He sat up and looked at her. "He's retiring?"

"Nope. Believe it or not, he's been hired as a field investigator by the FBI."

"If you're counting on the pain killers to have made me gullible . . ."

"No, I'm perfectly serious. They like the way he does his paperwork. They say he must be a good investigator."

"You do his paperwork."

"Don't I know it."

After a moment's pause to digest this, Tom laughed long and hard. "Hank, at the FBI."

"Bizarre, isn't it?"

He shifted uncomfortably. "I wish the damned doctor would get here. My ass is freezing."

"I'd offer to warm it up, but—"

There was a quick knock and the doctor came in. He smiled at Ruth and asked her to leave the room for a moment.

"I'm not going to miss the prostate exam, am I?"

"Please, miss."

She made a little wave in Tom's direction and left, closing the door behind her. The waiting room was stacked with ladies' magazines. Scowling, she sat down and started thumbing through them.

A few minutes later the doctor came out, followed shortly by Tom. The doctor started to shake Tom's hand, then realized what he was doing. He smiled an embarrassed smile. Tom tried clumsily to tuck in his shirt with his bandaged hands; after an awkward moment the doctor started to help him.

Ruth put on her smile again. "Are you two boys having fun together?"

The doctor blushed and left the room quickly.

"Stop being a smartass, Mrs. Fawcett, and help me get dressed."

"Yes, junior."

Ten minutes later they were in her car heading back to Steadbridge. It was four in the morning, pitch dark under a heavy canopy of clouds. The day's storms had been heavier than any in memory. Large, deep puddles still dotted the roads. Tree branches, leaves and less identifiable debris were scattered everywhere. Ruth drove slowly.

Tom still seemed a bit shell-shocked. "He gave me a tube of this new cream he says should help kill the pain. I've got it here in my pants pocket."

"And I thought you were just glad to see me."

He decided to ignore this. "Ruth, I'm worried."

"About . . . ?"

"What are we going to do without Hank?"

"Probably the same thing we've been doing with him. Why?"

"He's our only real connection to the outside authorities. If things start getting bad . . ." He looked at her. ". . . or, rather, worse . . ."

"We can always call the county police, Tom."

"They're half an hour away. And even if they come . . . how do we explain to them what's happening?"

"Do you think Hank could?"

"Good point." The thought made him glum.

"I'm guessing he'll be glad as hell to get out of town, if only for that reason."

A rabbit ran frightened into their path and Ruth swerved to avoid it. Tom braced himself against the door with his right hand, then cried out in pain.

"Sorry, Tom."

"It's okay. I'll have to get used to it, that's all."

"Did the doctor say how long it'll be before they heal?"

He shook his head. "He told me to use them as little as possible for the next week. If I heal quickly the stitches can come out then. The cuts on top of the burns have him worried about infection, though. The bandages have to be changed twice a day."

"I can do that for you."

"Or Rachel can, if you're not around. Or that damned assistant director, Jeremy. Lord knows he has little enough else to do. I asked the doctor if they'll be scarred and he dodged the question. So I guess they will."

"They can do grafts."

"I guess. We'll see. I only hope I'll still have the full use of them." He hesitated. "I'm really worried what we'll do without Hank, Ruth. I mean, yes, he's Barney Fife, but at least he's a real law enforcement official. The town will be even more cut off without him."

"We're posting the job next week. We'll find someone."

"It could take forever. Longer than we have."

"How long do we have, Tom?"

"God knows."

They were nearly back to town. Suddenly the clouds parted and a bright shaft of moonlight lit the road. A man was standing by the side of it. Ruth slowed down. He was scarred, disfigured. He stared at them menacingly. Then the clouds closed up again, the light vanished, and so did he.

Neither Tom nor Ruth said a word.

As they approached the mill, they could see fire. A plume of flame spiraled up from the smokestack. The mill's windows were lit bright yellow.

In the streets of Steadbridge dozens of them came and went, glowing when there was moonlight, becoming fugitive shadows when there wasn't. Some of them seemed to be on fire.

When they reached her house, she parked and they went quickly inside.

Hank was waiting for them. As Ruth had said, he needed statements from them about what had happened with Bill. The sight of Tom's hands wrapped in thick gauze bandages seemed to make him uneasy.

Alex was asleep on the couch, with the TV playing softly. Ruth got him up to bed, than headed for the kitchen to make coffee.

Hank sat where Alex had been. "Are you okay, Tom?"

"I'm not sure." He couldn't find anything comfortable to do with his hands; after fidgeting he finally just let them lie in his lap. "The cuts aren't as bad as they looked. But I won't be able to use these for a while."

"Too bad." He got out a notebook and turned official. "Tell me what happened."

Tom described the events of the night, Bill's attempt to kill Alex, Ruth and himself.

"Did he say why?"

Uncomfortable question. Tom played dumb and answered no. Keep it simple for Hank's report.

Hank made notes. "I've known Father Vicosz since I moved here. I never would have thought . . ." He made a little shrug.

"He's been drinking a lot." Tom felt like a heel saying it. Ratting on a friend. But a friend who had stabbed him. "And doing drugs."

Ruth rejoined them with hot coffee. "Decaf."

Hank asked her the same question: Why had Bill done

it? Without thinking she said, "He thinks Alex is the link to the ghosts. The one who makes it possible for them to—"

"There are," Hank said firmly, "no ghosts." Of course not. Not with the FBI reading his paperwork.

"It's what he said, Hank."

"If he believes in ghosts, then we can safely assume that . . . that . . ." His voice faltered. "It must have been the drugs, I guess."

Tom tried to pick up a cup; it took him a moment to balance it lightly between both hands. "This is going to be so pleasant."

Ruth started to take a cup for herself, then seemed to think better of it. "Where is Bill now?"

"I've got him locked up at the jail. Tomorrow I'll have him moved to the state hospital for psychiatric evaluation. Believe it or not, I've already had a call from a lawyer for the diocese, trying to persuade me it was temporary insanity."

"How on earth could they know what happened?"

"Bad news travels fast, Ruth. Someone must have called them. Probably that Charnocki woman."

They had pretty much covered everything they could. Hank quickly downed his decaf and got up to go. "I'll probably have a few more questions in the morning, after the shrinks examine him. You'll both be around?"

They nodded and Ruth showed him to the door. He seemed to have something on his mind he was reluctant to say. Ruth pushed for him to open up.

He hesitated. "If you need any help with Alex, let me know, okay? The county police have a counselor for situations like this. For victims, I mean. I can call them in the morning."

"Thanks. I hope he'll be okay. I'll be keeping an eye on him, and I'll take him for that counseling, but—"

"Ruth, this business about him being a link to someone or something. While he was asleep on the couch, he was muttering something to someone, asking them not to kill."

Tom stood up and joined them at the door. With false heartiness he said, "A nightmare about Bill. What else could it have been?"

Hank liked the sound of it. "Yeah, that's it. What else could it have been?"

He left. There were shadow figures in the street as he walked to his car. He was determined not to notice them. His town was coming unstuck but he would not see.

Tom and Ruth put out the lights and headed up to the bedroom. Ruth helped him undo the fastenings on his clothes. Soon they were lying in bed, in the dark, neither one saying anything. Tom was the first to fall asleep.

From the next room Ruth heard Alex talking to someone, very softly. She listened for a moment, unsure what to do. Should she waken Alex from whatever dreams he was having? Finally she got up and put on a robe. As she was passing the window she noticed a bright yellow-red glow and glanced out.

"Tom?"

He muttered something and rolled over.

"Tom, wake up!"

He opened his eye and stared at her. "What's the matter?"

"Hank's car is still in the street. It's on fire."

She quickly called 911 for the county police and fire department, then the two of them ran down to the street. Hank's police cruiser was completely engulfed in fire; the flames were jumping ten, twelve feet into the air, licking a nearby telephone pole, almost touching the power lines. The paint had blistered and peeled off the car. Inside they could see his burned corpse.

The flames burned higher. Ruth looked around helplessly. "What can we do?"

"Wait. And keep away from it. If the gas tank's full . . ." Tom tried to put an arm around her, then remembered his hands and pulled back. They moved back to what he guessed would be a safe distance. "They'll be here as fast as they can."

A few other neighbors, awakened by the bright fire, came out into the street. Maggie, pulling on a robe, joined them. "What on earth happened?" She saw how Ruth was shaking and put an arm around her.

"We don't know, Mag." She looked up and down the street, as if concentrating could bring the police sooner. "I looked out my window and saw it."

"How are your hands. Tom?"

He held them up to show her. "I get to wear mittens. I'm a kid again."

Overhead, one of the power lines crackled and snapped. Amid a shower of sparks it fell to the street, snaking about like something alive. After a moment a second one did the same thing. It hit the burning police car. After a moment it exploded. A fireball billowed into the sky. Lights up and down the street went out. Windows were shattered.

Tom quickly took charge, herding everyone onto the opposite sidewalk and away from the downed lines. The car fire ran its course and began dying down. Everyone stood there uselessly watching the sparks and the diminishing flames. After what seemed hours Ruth turned to Tom and told him she wanted to check on Alex; she went back into the house.

Almost at once a county police car rounded the corner and approached them, red lights spinning. Its headlights caught the small crowd of people. It was heading directly for the power lines. Tom tried to wave it to a stop but it kept coming. When it hit the lines, there was another explosion of electric sparks. The car spun out of control and plowed into a pole, which fell, bringing all the remaining lines with it. The car burst into flames.

Everyone screamed and moved quickly back another five yards or so. Tom started toward the car but Maggie stopped him. "No. Let the pros do it when they get here."

Ruth came running out of the house. "Tom! Alex is gone!"

From a distance came the sound of a siren. Everyone looked in that direction. Shortly a fire engine rounded the corner. This time Tom planted himself squarely in the middle of the street, hands in the air, so there wouldn't be a repeat of what had happened to the police. The truck coasted to a halt.

Ruth and Maggie watched as a firefighter got out of the truck and had a quick exchange with him. Ruth pulled free of her. "I have to find Alex."

"He could be anywhere, Ruth. Wait a few minutes and we'll be able to help you."

"No, I think I know where he must be."

She headed off in the direction of Number Five. Maggie looked helplessly at Tom and the fire captain, having their discussion. The other firefighters were getting out, putting on protective gear. She looked after Ruth. "Wait, I'm coming with you."

She ran and caught up with her quickly. It was obvious where they were headed. "Why would he be at the mill?"

"You can't understand."

"I can. Just try me."

"The mill is at the root of all this. Haven't you figured that out yet?"

"I haven't even figured out what 'all this' is yet, Ruth. I've never been in a place like this before."

"You should have gotten out when you could."

They walked briskly. Figures like dark ghosts surrounded them now and then, then parted to make way. Maggie was aware of them but didn't know how to make sense of their presence. The sky was beginning to lighten. It would be dawn soon.

"Ben and I talked about an earthquake fault under the town, maybe."

"They've taken Ben. Surely you know that."

"Who are they?"

"I can't concentrate now. I have to find my boy. I'll tell you about it tomorrow, if we find him. It won't make sense."

The mill was in sight. Brilliant fire glowed in the windows. Flame and smoke arced out of the smokestack.

Maggie kept up with Ruth's pace but couldn't stop gaping at the mill. "Ruth, this isn't possible. There must be an explanation."

"Like what? Surely you've seen this before now."

"Yes, but I thought . . . Gas. Methane, maybe."

"No."

They were at the entrance. The ground was rumbling. The air was filled with the roar of barking dogs. Ruth started to run.

"Ruth! We can't go in there. It's dangerous."

"I'm going in. I'm going to find my boy."

Anxious, confused, Maggie followed her.

On the river side the door was wide open and the ground was lit brightly by the fire inside. Ruth stopped. In an instant Maggie was beside her.

All signs of the film—cameras, sets, lights—were gone. But the mill was alive. Blast furnaces bellowed; molten steel flowed. The building was filled with machinery, all of it functioning. Conveyor belts moved huge fragments of steel, jackhammers roared, electric winches shuttled overhead. And there was no one operating any of it.

In the center of the building, in a wide open area, stood Alex. He looked impossibly small amid the fire and the machines. A furnace tilted, its gate opened and a river of molten metal poured into a flume.

"Alex!" Ruth screamed.

The boy stood quite still, watching the furnace and the melt. He gave no sign of hearing her.

She ran inside. A shower of sparks covered her, but she kept going till she reached him. She got down on one knee and threw her arms around him. "Oh, Alex!"

The boy seemed to be in a trance. He stared ahead, not seeing or hearing her.

"Alex!" She shook him. "Alex, it's me!"

Maggie joined them. "Come on, let's get him out of here."

Each of them took one of his hands and they began walking toward the entry way. He resisted. The furnace roared. Voices, men shouting to one another, dogs barking, came out of the air, from no one visible. Ruth tightened her grip on Alex's hand and walked faster.

Then they were outside.

It was almost dawn. In a few minutes the sun would climb above the horizon. Behind them the mill went dark and quiet. The ground stopped its rumbling. Steadbridge was as it had always been, quiet and passive. The river lapped serenely against its banks, the clouds passed overhead. Inside the mill, in the dim morning light, cameras stood on their tripods, sets waited silently for the actors and crew who would use them. The steel inferno might never have been.

It seemed like forever before either of them spoke. Maggie exhaled deeply, let go of Alex's hand and put an arm around him. "Are you both all right?"

Alex stared straight ahead. Softly he said to her, "T-terrible things are going to happen here, terrible things."

Ruth got down on her knees again, hugged him and kissed his cheek. "Terrible things are already happening, Alex."

"W-w-worse ones will."

"What? What do you see?"

"Hell. Hell everywhere."

Maggie, clearly shaken, hugged the two of them. "I think we should leave here."

A voice came from the darkened mill, calling softly Alex's name. It was a woman's voice.

For the first time Alex reacted. His eyes widened and he stared into the dark interior.

"Little Alex," the voice whispered.

He pulled free of the women, took a step toward the entrance, then stopped.

"Alex, darlin'."

He answered. "Grandma Kibben."

The sun notched the horizon.

"Alex, I'm here." The voice faded to no more than a whisper, soft rasping like the rustle of a dry leaf. "Alex." And it was gone.

Suddenly Tom rounded the corner of the mill, followed by a county policeman. "Ruth! Alex! Maggie!"

"We're here, Tom," Ruth called.

Maggie was spent; she couldn't find her voice. When Tom got to them she hugged him but stayed silent.

Alex looked at Ruth. "Did you hear her?"

Ruth couldn't make herself answer.

"Grandma Kibben's in the mill. She wants me."

Tom took hold of the boy's arm. "Stay here, Alex. Your mom and I want you, too. And Maggie, too. Don't you, Mag?"

She nodded.

"And we need you, more than she does. Grandma Kibben doesn't need anyone where she is."

Slowly, so as not to frighten Alex, Tom bent down and picked him up, carefully, using his arms not his hands. "Come on. I think we should all get home and get to bed."

Alex put his arms around Tom's neck and let himself be lifted. The policeman, puzzled, followed them. "You told me there would be trouble here."

Maggie told him, "There was. There is."

"What trouble?"

"Nothing any of us could explain."

The sun had climbed a few degrees into the sky, and there was every sign this would be a beautiful day. Deep, transparent blue sky; wispy white clouds.

When they got home there were tow trucks jacking up

the two burned vehicles, preparing to haul them away. A repair crew was working on the downed lines.

Ruth took it all in. "Home sweet home."

Maggie said she had to get some sleep. Tom yawned and seconded her. There were kisses all around, too tired to be quite affectionate. Alex asked if he could stay outside and watch the trucks and Ruth told him firmly no.

Maggie headed home. Tom decided to sleep in his own place. "I'm apt to be restless. I'll have to call Rachel and let her know I'll be late."

"You're going to let them work at the mill today?"

"Why not? In daylight it's fine."

"The devil never sleeps.

He got out his cell phone, but it was dead. "Damn. I must have forgotten to recharge it."

"I'll call her and leave a message for you."

"Thanks."

Alex fussed. "I want to watch the tow trucks."

"Come on." Ruth took hold of his hand. "You didn't have your medicine last night. It's time to take it."

Unhappily he followed her into the house.

Tom stood and surveyed the street for a moment, then went to his own place. There had been no sleep all night. He yawned. First Bill, then the crashes and the fires, then Alex at the mill . . . When he got into the bed he slept deeply and peacefully, not restlessly.

SOMEONE WAS POUNDING ON HIS FRONT DOOR. Groggily he reached for his watch on the table beside the bed. Noon. Maybe they'd go away.

The knocking grew louder and more insistent. Irritably he climbed into some clothes and went downstairs to the door.

It was Rachel. "Tom. We've all been wondering where you were."

"Right here in Dreamland. Ruth was supposed to call you and tell you I'd be late."

"Oh. She couldn't. All the phones are dead."

"She has a cell phone."

"They're not working either."

He yawned. "That's not possible. You heard about last night's accidents. That's why the phones are dead. They must not have got all the lines repaired yet." He looked out into the street, expecting to see phone company workers; there were none. All the lines seemed to be up and reconnected. "That wouldn't affect cell phones, though."

"We don't have any power, either."

"Damn." He looked out into the street again. Where were the repair workers?

"The crew's hooking up the backup generators now. They think we should have power by one o'clock or so. But you're such a stickler for the budget and the schedule, I thought—"

"Thanks. But don't worry about it. Tell everybody to get as much work done as they can today. But they are absolutely to be out of the mill before sunset. Do you understand?"

"Sure, Tom, but—" She noticed his hands. "Is it my imagination, or have those bandages gotten bigger?"

"I'll tell you about it later. Has anyone called the electric company?"

"The phones are down."

"Well, then, call the—never mind. We'll have to send Jeremy into Somerset to tell the companies."

She hesitated. Tom was awake enough to realize she was a bit frightened. "Tom, none of the cars will start."

He tried to hide what he was feeling. "That isn't possible."

"I wish you'd stop saying that. It's happening."

"Shit. I'll . . . I'll get dressed and come right down. Do you know how to change a dressing?"

"Sure."

"Then help me with these. I feel like I need a shave."

"Don't you use an electric?"

"Shit."

"Oh, and by the way . . ."

"God, what else?"

She hesitated. "SPOSH is back. Those protesters are outside the mill again.

"Wonderful."

Twenty minutes later, unshaved but with freshly bandaged hands, Tom went out into Steadbridge. By the time he got to the mill, the generators were working and production had resumed. He pushed his way past the SPOSH pickets. Their leader caught his sleeve and he pulled free. "Not now, Mr. Sharp. I've got more important things on my mind."

He called a quick meeting to tell everyone about the accidents of the previous night, suggesting in the vaguest way that the problems with the phones and power were due to them. Fortunately no one asked any difficult questions. He made a point of not telling them about the incident with Bill.

"Now I'm going to take a good long walk and see how far these outages go."

They didn't go far, as it turned out. The parts of Steadbridge that had been taken over by Overbrook were out. The rest of the town—the businesses on the square, the outlying residential areas—seemed fine. The old high school, production headquarters, was on the far side of the square. Power should be on there.

It wasn't. There were a few people there, who said they'd been waiting to hear from Tom. Everyone else had gone to lunch, hoping the phones and power would be on by the time they got back.

Tom headed back to the square. Walchek's had phones. He called the power and telephone companies, both of which insisted all the needed repairs had been made and everything should be functioning normally.

"They're not," he told the power company's service rep.

"They must be."

A moment later he repeated the call almost word for word with a woman at the phone company. It didn't sound as if there was much they could do.

Then he headed back to Number Five.

TOM CONSCRIPTED JEREMY, THE YOUNG ASSISTANT director, to be his personal aide. "You're going to be my hands. Do you know how to change dressings?"

The prospect didn't seem to please him. "Can't you have one of the women do it?"

"The women all have work to do. What have you done to justify the salary we're paying you?"

Jeremy looked away.

"You've been an errand boy. When Eric was the director, you weren't even that."

"He thought I wanted his job."

"Did you?"

He seemed surprised by the question. "Well, yes."

"You'll report to me first thing every morning and stay by my side till we knock off for the day."

"Yes, sir."

"Call me Tom."

Mid-afternoon the phones and electricity came back on. Both companies had insisted they hadn't done anything. Tom thought there must be loose junctions somewhere, but the companies refused to do anything more than they had.

"Tom?"

"Yes, Jeremy?"

"Uh . . . you can go to the bathroom by yourself, can't you?"

He wanted to laugh. "Don't you know? That's what assistant directors do."

"But I—I—"

"Relax. I should be able to handle my own elimination." He couldn't resist adding, "I hope."

His top priority was security. He called together the guards. "No one," he told them emphatically, "absolutely no one is to be on the mill grounds after dark. Do you all understand that?"

Tony Kowalski spoke up. "Not even Barry?"

"No one. I mean it. Half an hour before sunset you're to comb the entire area, including every part of the mill, and get everyone out."

Jeremy took notes on the meeting. They seemed a bit baffled but were prepared to enforce it.

Rachel tracked him down. "The company cars are running again."

"Good."

"We were able to get them started at around the same time the phones and power came back on."

"The batteries must be low. Have the mechanic check them over."

Her expression showed that she didn't believe it. "Yes, boss. But what mechanic do you have in mind?"

"Don't we have one on retainer?"

"Not the last time I checked, no."

He sighed. "Find one. Ask Ruth who's reliable."

Jeremy offered to take care of it.

Next came a conference with the heads of the various departments, including Maggie and Isabel. He wanted a reliable estimate of whether the film could wrap by the Fourth of July, as scheduled. The sooner they could all get out of Steadbridge, the better, though of course he didn't say so. There were various guesses; each of them wanted her or his own department's needs front and center, which led to a lot of bickering. After an unproductive half hour, he told them, "I want a firm estimate from each of you. You

know your departments' needs and responsibilities. Lay
them all out. And I want everything on my desk by tomorrow morning."

There was some grumbling; they left, all but Isabel and
Maggie.

Isabel cornered him. "Tom, I've been watching horror
movies all my life, and I've designed six. There's something wrong here, and I want to know what."

"You've seen too many of the damned things."

"Tom, I want to—"

"There is nothing wrong. I told you all, the accidents
last night caused the power outages."

"And the people in the streets at night? The ones who
aren't there in the daytime because this is practically a
ghost town? What causes them?"

"You should write screenplays, Is."

She left, obviously upset with him. Maggie stayed
behind. "Do you think you can keep bluffing everybody
forever?"

He shrugged, looking a bit helpless. "What else can I
do?"

"You can tell them the truth."

"What truth? Until last night, you wouldn't have
believed it yourself."

"Point taken. But, Tom, if there's something dangerous
going on here . . ."

"I don't know what I can do, Mag. I've dropped hints to
the brass at Overbrook, but they shrug it off. If I tried to
explain it to them outright, Christ knows what they'd
think."

"Can't you come up with some pretext for closing down
and getting everyone out of here?"

"I can't think what. Besides . . ."

"Yes?"

"I'm not sure they'll let us leave."

On that note Maggie left, looking more than a bit concerned and unhappy.

Jeremy had been in the corner, taking more notes. "Should we be scared, Mr. Kruvener?"

"Tom." He had forgotten the boy was there. "No. I'd appreciate it if you'd forget that conversation. And destroy any notes you made on it."

"Everyone on the shoot's been talking about all the shadow people in the streets at night. Half of us are afraid to go out."

Tom smiled ironically. "Overbrook morale."

"People just stay in their places, getting drunk or stoned and fucking. If they have anyone to fuck."

Tom sat down. "You know this is my hometown?"

"I had heard, yeah."

"Well, I haven't had a good night's sleep since I got back here last spring. How's that for a homecoming?"

"It's the way I always feel in my parents' house."

"Me too, Jeremy."

"They say that priest's been taken away to the nut house."

"Believe me, he's better off that way. And so are we."

"It's funny. Here we are, shooting a movie about a mad slasher. And right there in front of us is this crazy priest."

It was the first time Tom had ever talked to Jeremy. He was beginning to warm up to him. "Would you be surprised if I told you the crazy priest was one of my oldest friends?"

"Yeah, I guess so. There has been some gossip about the two of you, though. Something about the way he looks at you."

"Well, there's nothing to that."

"Good. It's bad enough with Angelo. He keeps hitting on me."

"I thought he had a boyfriend."

"He does." He shrugged. "Does that mean anything?"

"I guess not. Listen, will you keep me posted on what people are saying? About the town, I mean? About what's happening here?"

The suggestion seemed to make him uncomfortable. "I don't know."

"If things get too bad, Jer, I'll just have to shut down production and get everyone the hell out of here, Overbrook be damned."

Jeremy thought about this. "I guess so."

"I can't know what people are thinking unless someone tells me." Jeremy still looked uncertain. "It's for all our good."

Doubtfully he said, "Okay. I guess so."

Next Tom stopped by the set. Barry was shooting a night scene. "I'm glad you thought of shooting day-for-night," he told Tom. "It eliminates so many technical problems."

Nicole approached him nervously and asked if the production was in trouble. Ten minutes later Angelo did the same. He assured them both everything was on track.

Maggie had been eavesdropping. "Do you really believe that?"

"I don't know. I'm terrified what will happen after dark."

AROUND DINNER TIME RUTH ARRIVED WITH ALEX IN tow. She kept a firm grip on his hand. "I'm quitting, Tom. I have to. And so is Alex. I don't want him around here."

He told her he understood, and he did. "How about one last meal on Overbrook?"

"Sure."

They got plates and waited in line at the catering wagon. Alex was restless. "Can I go inside?"

"Absolutely not."

"But—"

"Alex, you are not to go into the mill."

"But—"

"That's final."

He sulked. When Maggie showed up for dinner she took him off Ruth's hands for a while.

Tom and Ruth strolled by the river, eating and talking. "Ruth, I'm scared. I mean really scared. I don't know how to deal with this."

"How could you?"

He was having trouble managing his food. "Let's sit down."

Ruth spread some newspaper and they sat on the rusting railroad tracks. "Maybe they'll leave us alone if we do the same, Tom."

"I wish I could believe there was a chance of that." He balanced his plate on his knee and ate slowly, carefully. Bending his fingers hurt. "If they were confined to the mill . . . but they're all over town at night. What they did to Hank, they can . . ." He spread his hands apart helplessly. His plate began to slip off his knee and he grabbed it and winced in pain.

"Are you okay?"

He nodded, then glanced at the sun. "We've got, what, about two hours left? We'll know then."

"If I were them, I'd lay off for a while. They've given us ample warning what they can do. Now they should wait and see if it has any effect. You need to stop the demolition."

"I can't, Ruth. Not without scrapping the whole film. And I don't have the authority."

She ate without saying much more. Tom wanted to bring up the subject of the three of them moving to New York together, for the umpteenth time. But the atmosphere wasn't right. There were more immediate things to be thought about.

Finally they saw Maggie and Alex coming toward them. Alex seemed in a better mood. Maggie was clearly upset.

"Alex has been telling me about the mill. About . . . I feel so damned silly saying it . . . about ghosts."

"You've seen them." Ruth unfolded another sheet of newspaper for her, and she sat down. "You've seen them in the streets at night. You saw the mill come alive last night."

"Seeing isn't believing, Ruth. Not to an engineer. There has to be a sane explanation. Scary, maybe, but rational."

Tom stood up and brushed off his trousers, getting his bandages dirty in the process. "And if there isn't?"

"Then there has to be a sane way out of this, Tom." She sounded confident. Both Tom and Ruth wondered if she really was. "There has to be."

A county police car pulled up. The officer who got out seemed too old and too fat to be much use in crime fighting. He approached Tom. "Mr. Kruvener?"

He nodded.

"They told me to look for a guy with bandaged hands."

"You've found him. What can I do for you?"

"We wanted you to know. Father William Vicosz escaped. We were taking him to his arraignment and he bolted."

Ruth spoke up. "Bolted? How could you let that happen? He tried to kill my son."

"I guess none of us thought a priest would—you Mrs. Fawcett?"

"Yes."

"Good. They told me to give you the message, too."

Tom caught him by the arm. "Look this man is dangerous. What are you doing to find him?"

"Everything we can, sir." He smiled a professional smile, got in his car, and left.

12

SUNDOWN APPROACHED. TOM, RUTH AND ALEX had a quiet dinner. Nothing they could have said seemed quite necessary. Alex was agitated but nearly silent. His stammer was getting worse and worse, and he seemed horribly self-conscious about it. When they finished eating he said he wanted to go to his room and do some sketches.

Ruth did not want to seem too concerned. "Maybe you should work down here tonight."

"I w-work better in my room."

"Well . . . all right." She caught Tom's eye. She'd have to check on him every few minutes without seeming to hover. Alex headed upstairs.

The early evening sky was unnaturally bright and orange. Shadows were long, deep. Tom turned on a few lamps, then helped Ruth clear the table. "I'm going to climb up on the roof. I want to watch as night falls."

"Be careful."

"I think Maggie was right. I think they'll leave us alone for a while."

"I mean be careful you don't fall and break your neck."

"I'll be all right."

"Correct me if I'm wrong, but don't most veteran climbers use their hands?"

He slid them behind his back. "I'll be okay."

"I should call Maggie. I should have asked her to dinner."

"Go ahead."

He headed toward the stairs as Ruth picked up the phone.

"Tom, it's dead."

It was not what he wanted to hear. He got out his cell phone. Dead. A moment later the lights flickered and went out. It was still twilight. There was enough light in the room for each to see the expression on other's face.

Ruth made a show of changing the tablecloth. "Do you think they'll do this every night?"

"It's their town."

She looked around as if there might be some visible explanation. "I'll go down to her place and ask her over."

Alex was in his room, drawing intently. Tom tried to catch a glimpse of the sketch without making it obvious he was checking on the boy, but the angle wasn't right. He headed up to the attic and unlatched the trapdoor to the roof. The ladder was old and shaky; he steadied himself against the rails with his wrists.

The sky was a deep transparent blue. A few bright stars were just appearing. The mill was dark, so far.

Up and down the street windows were dark. One by one, lights appeared in them. He had sent Jeremy to buy a supply of candles and hurricane lamps. People were using them. He had told the cast and crew the power company was having trouble with its lines and there might be blackouts after dark. They had grumbled, comments about hick towns and such; but it seemed that they'd cope, at least in the short run. Tomorrow he'd have more generators delivered, enough to power the Overbrook streets. Fortunately, no one had made an issue of the fact that none of the company cars would run; for that, he could have no convenient excuse.

Then he realized that the main part of Steadbridge was dark too. The ghosts were extending their sway.

He noticed lights in the church. The sanctuary was lit brightly, the stained glass windows beamed.

Could it be Mrs. Charnocki? Why would she light the entire building? And how?

As he was climbing down, the ladder shifted slightly. He quickly grabbed at the side rails, then screamed at what he'd done to his hands.

Alex was still sketching busily. If the priest was back, the boy didn't know it, yet. Ruth was in the kitchen washing dishes. He didn't want to tell her about the church. The prospect that Bill had returned would be . . . "I'm going out for a walk."

"Wait, I'll come with you." I want to stop at Maggie's. She reached for a towel.

"No, you'd better stay and keep an eye on Alex."

She found his manner odd but she knew he was right. "Do me a favor then. Stop at Mag's and ask her if she wants to come up here for a few hours."

"Sure."

It was nearly dark. Deep blue sky, bright stars. He glanced toward the mill. No fire, no light. Maggie seemed grateful for Ruth's invitation. She quickly grabbed a sweater and headed down the street.

Tom paused for a moment in front of his parents' house. It was still dark, still empty and unused. He had kept it so quite deliberately. The thought of going in made him physically ill. He headed off quickly.

McKinley Square was deserted. There was not one light except in the windows of St. Dympna's. He heard faintly the sound of hymns. There were no birds; there was not even a breath of wind.

Slowly, careful of his hands, he pulled open the heavy church door. Inside scores of candles blazed everywhere. The altar was so brightly lit there seemed to be spotlights focused on it. The strains of church music faded in the air and fell silent. The building was empty except for two figures, one at the altar, the other in the front pew.

The one on the altar was wearing full priestly vestments, blood red, and saying Mass. To a near-empty house.

Tom moved down the center aisle, watching him. The priest was completely immersed in his priestliness, seeming to see and hear nothing but what was directly in front of him. The man in the front pew was in early middle-age, dressed in a dark grey business suit. Tom had never seen either of them before.

When he reached the altar rail he stopped and watched for a moment. Empty church, solitary worshiper, oblivious priest. It seemed so absurd. There seemed no point letting it go on. "Excuse me."

The priest froze, then slowly turned to face him. He was a young man, still in his twenties, short and plump.

The man in the front row stood up. "You should not interrupt a solemn Mass."

"I'm sorry." He felt a bit foolish. "I thought . . ."

The man opened a briefcase and leafed through a fistful of papers. "You are Thomas Kruvener of Overbrook Productions."

"Overbrook Media. And you are—?"

"Jonathan Seymour, of McCracken, Philips and Seymour, Pittsburgh." He held out a business card. A lawyer.

For the first time the priest spoke up. "I'm Father McEntee. Mark McEntee." He extended a hand. Tom shrugged and held up his bandaged hands. "The diocese posted me here to tend St. Dympna's till Father Vicosz returns. I just graduated from seminary." He seemed pleased to announce it. "Mr. Seymour will be tending to the church's legal interests."

"Father Vicosz is going to return?"

Seymour spoke up. "I am here to see that he does. The charges against him reek of anti-Catholic bigotry."

Tom couldn't quite believe what he was hearing. "You do know that Father Vicosz escaped from the police late yesterday, don't you?"

They looked at each other, startled. They clearly hadn't been told.

But Seymour forged on. "If you attempt to sue the church, you will be excommunicated."

"That would be a bit redundant."

McEntee put a hand on his shoulder. "You have fallen away from the church?"

"No, Father McEntee, I jumped."

"Oh."

Seymour picked up a briefcase and pulled out a sheaf of papers. "We'll require your signature on these." He pushed them into Tom's bandaged hands.

"You can't possibly think I'm green enough to sign these without having a lawyer look them over."

"The Diocese of Pittsburgh is prepared to offer you a settlement of—"

"Settlement? We haven't even discussed what we're settling."

"I shall be requiring Mrs. . . . ." He referred to his notes, ". . . Ruth Fawcett's signature on an identical set."

"That's fair, isn't it?" McEntee beamed.

Tom had trouble believing all this was happening. "Mr. Seymour, Father McEntee, there have been some very disturbing things going on in this town. Not least, Father Vicosz's attempt to murder me, Mrs. Fawcett and her son. But the two of you take the cake."

"The church must look out for its corporate interests." The lawyer was smug.

"Well, you listen to me. I'm not signing a damned thing.

Until just now, I hadn't given a thought to legal action, but you've given me a swell idea. And you can consider that as coming from Ruth Fawcett, too. Why don't the two of you go back to Mass?"

McEntee and Seymour glanced at each other. Seymour paused, then seemed to decide to try another tack. "Look, Mr. Kruvener, we don't want to turn this into an adversarial action."

"I thought you already had."

"We have become aware of some . . . irregularities in Overbrook's relations with county officials."

Suddenly, quite loudly, the church bells rang. They pealed once, deafeningly loudly. Dust and debris shook loose from the ceiling and from the crack in the church's front wall.

McEntee's eyes widened. "There shouldn't be anyone up there."

"It must be the wind." Seymour sounded uncertain.

"Could the wind have rung it that loud, and just once, Jonathan?"

Tom was pleased. "Perhaps you could threaten the wind with legal action, too, Mr. Seymour." The priest and the lawyer ignored him and stared at the rear of the church, in the direction of the belfry. From nowhere came a gust of wind; all the candles in the church flickered in it. Tom raised his voice a bit. "I would advise you to leave Mrs. Fawcett and her son alone, Mr. Seymour. They've both been through something terrible, and the boy's badly traumatized. Harassing them wouldn't be good for business. I have a very efficient public relations machine at my disposal. Believe me, irregular relationships with county officials will look like nothing compared to threatening a widow and her developmentally challenged son." He turned and headed up the aisle toward the entrance.

"You'll have to deal with us sooner or later, Mr. Kruvener."

"And you'll have to deal with me. You belong in this town."

"There's no need to be insulting."

"Mr. Seymour, you don't know the half of it."

Tom walked briskly up the center aisle. Overbrook's lawyers could dispose of this nonsense quickly enough. He'd have to call them in the morning. Or whenever the phones came back up. Just as he reached the door the bells rang again. Once. And were silent. He glanced at the stairs leading up to the tower and was almost tempted to climb up and see who or what was there.

Over his shoulder he called, "The two of you should go up there and see who's trespassing. You might find the Holy Ghost, or at least one of his less holy relatives. The Ghost of Steadbridge Past, maybe."

Seymour and McEntee were huddled by the altar rail. They looked at him. "Is that supposed to frighten us?" Seymour was still playing attorney.

"No, not exactly."

"I don't frighten easily, Kruvener, not after the judges I've faced."

"Good. Then you won't be around very long, making foolish threats."

He left.

OUTSIDE, IN THE SQUARE, EVERYTHING WAS QUITE still. Tom paused to take a deep breath and let his anger pass, at least a bit. He'd have to warn Ruth, of course. A suit against the Catholic diocese could leave her and Alex set for life.

Something caught his eye, he wasn't sure what, some slight movement somewhere in the square. He looked up at the bell tower. It was perfectly dark. Obviously the two men hadn't had the nerve to go up and investigate. But there seemed only one explanation for the bell. Then he realized the church too had gone dark. Without realizing it, he smiled. In the morning, he could . . .

Again something moved, the slightest flicker. He

scanned the square slowly. It was coming from the Hippodrome. Over his shoulder he could see that the mill was still dark. Every light in the church had gone out. But there was someone in the theater.

There was still absolutely no wind. Tom crossed the silent square, trying to ignore the flickering light in the Hippodrome. After Seymour and the priest, he wanted a drink. Without thinking he headed for Hank's. It was closed, boarded up, like most of the other buildings on McKinley Square.

There was another bar a few blocks away, past the old highschool. He was so used to Hank's, he had only been to the other place once. But now it was the only game in town.

Empty streets, still night air, footsteps echoing. The neon sign over the door, CHARLIE'S PLACE, was dark. Inside there were lights. He pulled open the door and stepped inside.

Half the tables were empty. People sat at the others in twos and threes, drinking, talking softly. A half dozen more stood at the bar. Hurricane lamps burned on the tables and every six feet or so along the bar. For a startled instant he found himself wondering if the patrons were real or if they might be phantoms.

"Evening, Tom." It was Tony Kowalksi. He was tending bar.

"Tony. Shouldn't you be on duty at Number Five?"

"I quit. We all did. What'll you have?"

The news came as a blow. "Quit? When?"

"The town's coming unstuck, Tom. We don't want to be in the line of fire."

"You reported to me. You should have come to me with your concerns."

"Most everybody thinks you're the cause of them. We told Rachel."

"Oh."

"So, what'll you have?"

Tom ordered a double bourbon, straight up. Tony smiled

at him. "We've all been wondering when it would really start getting to you."

Some of the other customers were watching him and whispering. He felt more an outsider than he had his first day back. All he'd had to deal with then was a small boy throwing rocks.

Tony poured his drink and set it on the bar. "I'd drink up and go if I were you. You movie people aren't real popular around here now."

A man got up from his table and crossed to them. He was old, big; Tom decided he must be one more retired steelworker. The man pointedly elbowed his way beside Tom at the bar. Tom obligingly moved. "Excuse me."

The man pushed. "Get away."

"I said excuse me. I—" He realized the man hadn't meant just out of the bar.

"Why you serving this piece of shit, Tony?"

Tony looked a bit scared. "His money's green."

"Yeah, but how's he earn it?"

This couldn't be allowed to continue. Tom pushed back, just slightly. "Look, you have to realize Steadbridge was dying before I ever came back."

"But you came back anyway, didn't you?"

"I thought some money in the local economy . . ." He knew how lame this must sound. But at least it was the truth.

"Money? Shit! We don't even have lights. Look at us, huddling around kerosene lamps."

"That's not Overbrook's fault. The power company—"

"We had power. You came. Now we don't. It's as simple as that. Why don't you get the fuck out of here? Take your cameras and your goddamned pansy actors and get the fuck out of our town." He reached up slowly and took hold of Tom's collar. "You understand?"

Another man got up from another table and joined them. "Now, now, Mike, that's no way to treat Mr. Kruvener. He's an executive, aren't you, Mr. Kruvener?"

"C-call me Tom."

"Oh, no, Mr. Executive Kruvener. We couldn't call you that. You're much more important than all us poor Stead-bridge people."

"I never said that. I—"

Mike tightened his grip on Tom's collar.

"You'll have to excuse Mike, Mr. Kruvener. It's just that he's a patriot. With the Fourth coming in little more than a week and the town like this, why, he can't help being upset."

Tom finally managed to pull free of the man's grip. "For Christ's sake. Look around you. You know what kind of place this is. You have fireworks here, Fourth of July or not. That's not our doing."

"No." The second man drew very close and abruptly, suddenly spit in Tom's face. "And that's not mine."

Tony came around the bar and got between them. "All right, boys, that's enough. Tom, I think maybe you better go home."

Wiping his face on his sleeve Tom muttered, "Yeah. Sure."

Tony saw the two men back to their tables. Tom downed the last of his drink. "It looks like I'll have to hire more security in the morning."

Tony opened the door and held it for him. "Good luck finding them."

Tom thanked him for intervening and stepped out onto the sidewalk.

The night was as it had been. Unnaturally dark and quiet. There was no one in the streets, there were no lights in the houses. For the first time in memory there were not even any ghosts to be seen, no fugitive shadows at the corner of his vision. Steadbridge might have been completely dead, at last. But he knew better than to believe that.

It was only a short walk back to the square. St. Dympna's was still dark. He was tempted to go inside again and go up to the bell tower, to see it . . . But not now, not in the night. That would be for the morning.

So he stood at McKinley's bronze feet, watching the theater. Again there were lights inside.

No power anywhere. Lanterns, or torches, or . . . ? Perhaps at long last he'd find those hoboes, way too late to believe in them.

He had to see.

The side door was still partially open, off one of its hinges now. He worked it open even further; its bottom scraped the cracked sidewalk. And he stepped inside. The place was dark again.

"Hello?"

No answer. Nothing.

"Hello?"

It must have been still another trick of the moonlight. He longed for the time when there would be no more.

Suddenly a light flickered in the old projection room. A shaft cut through the black theater and the screen lit up. The face of Lon Chaney Jr. stared down at him, thirty feet wide, scowling. He knew instantly what it was. The movie . . . he couldn't forget it if he wanted to. Terrible film. Steadbridge couldn't even conjure up an echo of a good horror movie, just a B-list piece of junk.

There were voices in the air, kids' voices. Shrieking with mock fright at the indestructible fiend on the screen. Maybe if he listened carefully enough he could hear his own voice among them, and Ruth's, and Bill's. This place, this building had meant something to him once. He could not remember what.

The image flickered, turned faint, disappeared. He was alone in the abandoned theater. And he felt terribly empty and had no idea why.

"THANK GOD YOU'RE BACK." RUTH THREW HER arms around him and kissed him.

"I should go out for more walks."

"Tom, the county police were here."

"What's wrong?"

"They still haven't found Bill. They wanted us to know."

"I don't suppose it occurred to them that they might stay and protect us."

She didn't have to answer. He needed another drink but didn't want one too strong; getting drunk would not be a good idea. She mixed drinks for them. "Bourbon and water, okay?" Then he sat heavily down on the couch. "I think there might have been someone in the church belfry, playing with the bell. That's where they should look." There was no sense telling her about the incident in the bar. And the ghost film at the Hip could hardly have surprised her.

She went into the kitchen. Over her shoulder she said, "We should tell them."

"The phone's out, remember?"

"Tom, I think I'm scared."

"So am I."

She came back with drinks for both of them. Tom made an ironic little toast with his glass. "Alex is in bed?"

She nodded. "Restless, though. He had trouble falling asleep."

"There's a new priest at the church, a kid. He's got a lawyer with him." He told her about the legal documents and warned her not to touch them. "If the bastard gets anywhere near you, refer him to me."

"And what will you tell him?"

"To call Overbrook's lawyers."

"Tom, I'm afraid." She hesitated. "What if he comes here?"

"He's only a lawyer."

"I mean Bill."

"Oh." He took a long swallow. "You're mixing these too strong. If it was the drugs that drove Bill to . . . to do what he did, then he must have come down by now."

"And if he hasn't? Or if it was something else? Alex is still having trouble sleeping. If he knows Bill is back . . ."

"We don't actually know that he is. I'm only guessing. It might have been the wind that rang the bell. Or maybe it's just that the damned church is shifting, starting to crumble. It looks like it's ready to. Bill could be any-where."

Ruth leaned against him. "I think we should get out of here. Tonight if we can."

"How? The cars won't run, the phones won't phone . . ." He kissed her forehead.

"As soon as we can, then. I think Alex should sleep with us for now. And you . . . you'll spend nights here?"

"I do anyway, don't I? When I sleep at my place, I see my father."

For a while they lapsed into silence.

Alex came down the stairs, carrying his sketch pad. He looked at them in one another's arms, smiled and went back up again, without either of them knowing he had been there.

But without him realizing it, a few of his sketches fell onto the steps. Later, when Tom and Ruth decided to head upstairs to bed, Tom found them. By the light of a match, held carefully in his bandaged fingers, he examined them They were portraits of hell, of fire and suffering. One was another image of his father, afire, blazing. One of them after another, after another, was a picture of hell.

ODDLY, UNEXPECTEDLY, TOM SLEPT WELL AND deeply, no dreams, no ghosts.

He woke early, before either Ruth or Alex, and managed to dress himself without making his hands hurt too badly.

He headed back to St. Dympna's. The whole town was asleep, it seemed, and it struck him as . . . not right. If something terrible was coming, some catastrophe about to happen, surely everyone should be . . . He didn't know. But a quiet Steadbridge was not what he should be seeing; every fiber told him so.

The door to the sanctuary was unlocked, and there was no one in sight. The air smelled of smoke from all the previous night's candles. He walked to the foot of the belfry stairs and craned his neck, trying to see up.

"Bill?" He called softly.

Except for a bit of dust dislodged by the sound of his voice, everything stayed quiet. Suddenly he felt foolish, in a naked way. If Bill was still psychotic, confronting him could be . . . He should have brought a weapon of some kind. But what? He didn't have a gun. The only thing he might have brought was a kitchen knife. But with his hands, he could hardly have used either.

Carefully, he climbed. It was foolish, he knew; if Bill really was there, anything could happen. But he had to be certain one way or the other.

At the top of the steps he could see all of Steadbridge below him. The bronze bell hung still and silent. There was no one there, and no sign anyone had been there. If Bill had come and gone, there was no way to know.

He climbed back down and went home to tell Ruth the news. She was just getting out of bed. "I slept so deeply. I feel almost as if I'd been drugged."

"I felt the same when I got up. Ruth, I went to the church. Bill's not there."

"I don't know whether that should comfort me or make me feel frightened. At least if we knew where he was . . ."

"I know."

"Do you want some breakfast?"

He shook his head. "I ought to get out to the mill."

Alex was still sleeping soundly. He had been restless all night; there had been nightmares. Now neither of them wanted to wake him.

When Tom got to Number Five Rachel was there, waiting for him outside the gate. "We have more trouble, Tom."

"God, what now?"

"That guy from SPOSH is back."

"Just what I need."

"He's dead."

So much for the seemingly quiet night. Without either of them saying anything, she led him inside. Sharp was hanging thirty feet above the floor, a cable coiled round his throat. His face was hideously discolored.

Tom stared up and the corpse. "How the hell did he get up there?"

"Maybe someone sprinkled him with fairy dust and he thought wonderful things."

"You've been hanging around me too much, Rachel."

"You're telling me."

He walked to a spot directly under the body.

"I'd be careful, Tom. He seems to have soiled himself."

"Lovely."

There was no rigging, no ladder, no way Sharp could have climbed so high in the building. Still, he said emphatically, "Why would he kill himself?"

She shrugged. "The ultimate protest?"

He did not for a moment believe Sharp had died a suicide. He had gone into the mill at night, at the time when it belonged to the dead, to do God knew what. But suicide had to be what they told everyone. That had to be the story, some weird kind of final protest or some such. "Are the phones working?

She shook her head and looked up at Sharp. "Poor dumb bastard."

"Aren't we all?" He walked in a wide circle, looking up at the dangling body. "There has to be some way to get him down. We can't have people showing up for work and seeing that."

"Why not? This is a horror movie. It might help the actors with their motivations."

He sighed, deeply. "We don't have any security. They all quit without even saying a word."

"I know. That's how he managed to get in here."

"Yeah." He looked around. "Go try the phones again, will you?"

Sharp's body was swaying overhead. Tom realized there was no wind. Yet something was moving it. It swung back and forth more and more quickly, more and more violently, until the cable snapped and it fell to the floor. It burst open. Fragments of Sharp splattered for yards around. Tom just barely managed to jump out of the way and stay clean.

13

STEADBRIDGE WAS DARK.
Steadbridge was still.

Steadbridge was quiet, and so were its inhabitants, both the temporary ones and the ones who had lived there all their lives and never thought about leaving. And so were the ones who had long since died.

By day everything was fine. Each night the power went off, and the telephones stopped working, and repeated requests to the electric company and the phone company accomplished nothing. Cell phones stopped functioning, quite inexplicably.

Cars would not run at all. A few members of the film crew tried to leave on foot. They found roads blocked, impassable. One technician tried to escape downriver in a canoe, but something pulled it under the water; he swam to shore and that was that. Tom wondered what Overbrook's corporate people made of the silence from their film location. But if they were concerned, they never sent anyone to investigate.

Work proceeded on *The Colors of Hell*; there was little more to shoot than a few location sequences. Isabel had long since scouted all the locations. Barry and his crew set up their cameras, rehearsed the actors quickly, and got most of the shots in one or two takes.

On a bright grey afternoon they took their cameras, mounts and lenses to the top of St. Dympna's bell tower. They shot panoramic views of the town and of Number Five, in its disguise as a shopping mall. Then Angelo and Nicole had a scene to perform up there. In costume and makeup they climbed the stairs and joined Barry and the camera crew. It was simple scene, only a shot of them leaning out and surveying the town. But as they were doing it, inexplicably the church bells began to ring. They were deafening, and nothing could stop them. Everyone ran quickly downstairs and stood in the apse, wondering what had caused it, wondering when it would stop. Even in the church the vibrations from the bells were overpowering.

As they stood there the floor shifted under them and the crack along the face of the church widened an inch or so. Dust from it filled the air and they had to cover their faces.

Father McEntee had been watching it all. Like everyone else he covered his mouth and nose. Barry approached him. "We were told this place was safe."

"It is."

"You call that safe? I don't know what's holding the place up."

McEntee was sanguine. "Maybe the weight of all that camera equipment is what caused it."

"Rot."

The bells finally went silent. There was some quick talk of going back up to get more footage, but Barry decided against it. "We'll have to hope what we've got is usable. We can always fix it in the editing room."

Attorney Seymour had visited Ruth and tried to get her to sign a set of waivers. She referred him to Tom but Seymour never approached him again. After his encounter with Ruth, no one saw him again. Tom wondered how he had gotten out of Steadbridge.

Ruth was wry. "Maybe he found a loophole."

Next were to come some scenes in McKinley Square. The set dressers spent a few hours polishing the statue of the overweight president. It didn't look new, exactly, but it wasn't covered with bird droppings either.

Tom supervised it all, more closely than he had before. Everyone wondered at his newfound interest in the minutiae of the production. It was compulsive with him. He could not stop himself wondering what would happen next, what would go wrong, who would die. Each day his hands hurt a bit less.

Of Bill Vicosz, no one had seen or heard a thing.

AT THE LUNCH BREAK TOM STOPPED BY RUTH'S TO see her and Alex. She was sitting in the kitchen, a stack of the boy's drawings on the table in front of her. Tom kissed her and sat down across from her. "I was hoping you wouldn't find those."

"I was cleaning his room. Straightening up, you know."

"Snooping. Everyone's mother does it. It's in the job description."

"He had them face down, but I couldn't resist looking. And . . ." She looked away from him.

"I found them last week. It seems to be all he's drawing. All he has on his mind."

She leafed through them. Images of the inferno, of souls in torment, tortured by flames, by fumes. Elizabeth McKibben burning. Long John Pulaski drowning a child in the midst of the inferno. "How much more awful would they be if he knew Bill was at large?"

Tom got up, filled the teakettle with water and put it on

the stove. "He's not the only one. Everyone here is tense. The townspeople have stopped interacting with us movie folks. And everyone on the crew is getting more and more nervous. It's finally sinking in that we're all trapped here. They come to me and complain, but what can I do?"

"Why bother finishing the movie? You'll never get the film out of here."

"Do you think I haven't thought of that? But if I call a halt to production, it will only be that much more obvious that there's no way for anyone to . . ." He let the thought trail off, unfinished. "There seem to be a lot of drugs around."

Ruth turned her attention back to the sketches. "For ten years—for all of Alex's life—I've wondered about these visions of his. Are they real, or does he just have a vivid imagination? Now I think I know. For certain. Tom, I think we should go to New York with you."

He sat down again, keeping his eyes on the kettle, not her. "If we can go. The dead have taken hold of us. I keep telling myself . . ." He caught himself in mid-sentence. "Oh, hell, what's the use, it's so foolish."

"What?"

"I keep telling myself a horror film made in this kind of atmosphere will be a masterpiece, as a matter of course. It's an idiotic thought."

"It makes as much sense as anything else, right now." The kettle started to whistle.

"Let me get it." He got up and poured hot water for tea for both of them. "It's idiotic to assume this film will ever be finished even. Much less edited and released."

She nodded. "Hand me the teabags."

He opened the pantry. "We're out."

"Damn. Instant coffee?"

He shook his head. "Too much caffeine. I'm too worked up as it is." He rummaged in the cabinet. "There are some decaf teabags."

"No thanks. Like drinking boiled straw."

He got one for himself and dunked it in one of the mugs. Then they both sat down and faced each other.

"I've been thinking about Bill, Ruth. I think we should tell Alex about him."

"No."

"He needs to know. He needs to be extra careful when he's out and about."

"No. Tom, he's barely over what happened with Bill. I'm too afraid what knowing this would do to him."

"Where is he now, by the way?"

"Upstairs sleeping. He's been restless, like everybody else. I gave him a pill to calm him down." Suddenly she jumped to her feet. "I need some of that tea after all. Maybe it'll calm my nerves." She refilled the kettle and put it on.

"Isabel's a complete wreck. She can't get in touch with her family. She's been having crying jags."

"I know. She was here a while ago. And Maggie's drinking nonstop."

"My happy little Overbrook family."

Alex was at the door, yawning. "I'm hungry."

Tom pulled a candy bar from his pocket. "Here. The last one in town, I think."

"Really?"

"You deserve it, Alex."

He eyed the stack of drawings on the table. "Those are my sketches."

Ruth scooped them up and handed them to him. "We just wanted to see what kind of progress you're making. You're getting better and better."

"Thanks. I wasn't supposed to let anyone see them."

"Oh." Tom made a quick apology for invading the boy's privacy. "We won't do it again. But you really are good."

Alex took the sketches and started to go. Then he paused in the doorway. "Tom?"

"Hm?"

"I don't want to go to New York. If I try to leave Steadbridge, I'll die." Before either of them could say anything he turned and went back upstairs.

Tom looked at Ruth. "Some sleeping pill."

"It was just a tranquilizer."

"Oh."

"If he really believes that . . . maybe we shouldn't try to take him out of here."

"We'll see."

There was a knock at the front door. It was Maggie. She was drunk. "I thought you ought to know, your pal the lawyer turned up."

"Where?"

From the kitchen Ruth called, "I'm putting on water for tea, Mag. You want some?"

"No thanks. I'll drink some vodka, though, if you still have any." She came in and sat down on the edge of the sofa. "Squire Seymour's body washed up on the north end of Washington Island."

"He must have gotten lost and fallen in."

"Yeah, right. His body was so bloated from being in the water, he was unrecognizable. And most of his ID was washed out or blurred. But his credit cards were still readable."

Ruth joined them, carrying a tumbler of vodka. She handed it to Maggie.

Maggie toasted the empty air. "Here's to dead barristers."

Tom laughed. "If that isn't redundant."

She raised her glass even higher. "Then here's to dead all of us."

Ruth shifted uneasily. "Mag, I wish you wouldn't talk like that. With an impressionable boy in the house . . ."

She took a long drink. "Sorry. I've never seen a drowned corpse before. You wouldn't think a body could swell up so much. And there were fish nibbling away at bits of it. Carp, I think."

"Give me some of that." Tom took her glass and drank.

"All his life, Seymour's been preying on higher life forms. Now it's the fishes' turn, that's all."

Maggie had a good laugh. "Have you seen the church, by the way? That crack in the facade is even wider. Somebody ought to condemn it."

He shrugged. "Who?"

"Good point."

"Besides, the diocese would only send another lawyer to fight the condemnation." He took another drink, then handed the glass back to her.

"That would be okay. Those fish looked mighty hungry."

Ruth sat down at the table again. "All my life, doing housework, even things like washing the dishes, has taken my mind off my problems. Now that only makes it worse. I find myself wondering how much longer I'll be alive to keep doing it."

From upstairs they heard Alex cry out. They rushed to his bedroom and found him soundly asleep. It had been a nightmare, nothing more.

GREY AFTERNOON. FILM CREW SHOOTING AT THE old highschool. Number Five abandoned but for a few workers beginning to knock down the sets.

Tom was in the office, going over budgets, trying to convince himself they mattered. Rachel was trying, for the fiftieth time, to contact Overbrook. When she tried to call long distance the lines stopped responding. E-mail failed. She had been at it so long it seemed like a normal part of her job.

"Keep trying," he told her. "Who knows, maybe one of them will get through. By accident or something."

There was a loud rumbling. It sounded like a fleet of trucks. He left the office to see.

They were coming down the main road, heading for the mill. Yes, trucks, a fleet of them, dark grey trucks of various kinds, minivans, panel trucks, flatbeds, all with the logo ULMER & FUEST, DEMOLITION EXPERTS. They pulled to a stop a quarter mile from the mill and a man got out of the lead van.

When Tom reached him he was checking a' map and having an animated talk with his driver. "This should be it. Where the hell is it?"

"Morning." Tom put on his best professional smile and tried to act as if all was right with the world. "Can I help you?"

"Hello." The man barely took his eyes off his map. "We're looking for United American Steel Mill Number Five."

It was there in plain sight. Then Tom realized they were seeing it disguised as a shopping mall. "I'm Tom Kruvener of Overbrook Media."

"You are." The man glared slightly. "Just why the hell haven't you been answering your phones?"

"Um . . . because they haven't been ringing?"

"Your bosses want your scalp. They've been trying to get in touch with you for weeks, and there's been no response."

"There's been some trouble with the phone lines." Tight, professional grin. "Who are you?"

"Frank Ulmer." The man held out a hand. "Ulmer & Fuest."

"So I see." Tom looked at the little convoy, nearly a dozen trucks. "And what can I help you with?"

Ulmer's face went blank. "We're here to bring down the mill." He said it as if it was the most obvious thing in the world.

"The—"

"Overbrook says according to your schedule you should finish shooting in the next day or two."

"They do."

He nodded. "We thought we'd get up here now, start planting our charges and get back down to Pittsburgh for the Fourth. We'll come back up after the holiday for the implosion."

Tom felt a mild panic. He looked at the mill. They knew; they had to know. "We're still shooting. You can't plant your explosives till we're done." Another stiff smile. "They'd show."

Ulmer reached into his van and got out a fistful of papers. "Orders from Overbrook. Signed by Phil Morrissey. We bring it down right after the holiday."

Tom took the stack of orders without looking at them. "The Fourth is just two days away. You can't get—"

"We can get most of the explosives planted. The rest won't take long to finish. We're supposed to meet with your director—Eric—" He referred to some notes. "Eric—"

"Barry Hall is directing. Eric's dead."

This was the first thing he said that seemed to catch Ulmer off guard. Clearly his orders didn't cover such a thing. "Well . . . I'll have to meet with Hall, then. So he can work out where to place his cameras to film the implosion."

"Of course." He handed the orders back to Ulmer, unread. They couldn't mean much less. "I'll have my people get some houses ready for you."

"We won't be staying."

Tom stopped himself from telling him they wouldn't be able to leave. "Just in case, then. You might decide you want to spend the night. How many of you are there?"

"Twelve. But—"

"You'll have to double up, maybe even triple. But the houses should be big enough for you."

"I told you we won't be staying."

Tom decided he didn't like Ulmer. He chuckled and said, "Just in case."

Ulmer shrugged. "Whatever. When can we get to work?"

Tom shrugged back at him. "The mill's right there."

Ulmer started to get back into his van.

"Mr. Ulmer?"

"Hm?"

"What exactly does 'getting to work' mean?"

"We've got a set of plans for the place, but Morrissey said he wasn't sure how accurate they are. We'll have to do a complete inspection, so we know where to place all the charges. It'll probably take half the day."

Smile. "Inspect all you like."

"We will. Then we'll plant the charges."

Tom smiled a big professional smile at him. "Fine. But do not work inside the building once the sun begins to set."

"Look, Mr. Kruvener, we have a job to do."

"You have a job to do for Overbrook, and I represent Overbrook here. None of your people are to be inside Number Five after dark. Do you understand?"

Ulmer was obviously a bit puzzled. "Sure, if you say so." He got in his van; his driver stepped on the gas and led the other trucks to the gate at the mill.

Tom watched them for a moment, then went quickly back to the office. "Rachel, get Overbrook."

"What do you think I've been trying to do?"

"I mean it. This is important. I have to get in touch with them. Drop everything else and keep trying."

"Sure thing, boss. Are your bandages okay?"

He looked at his hands. He was almost used to having them bandaged. "I guess. I'll be at Ruth's. Let me know when you get through."

"Sure thing. If."

He started to leave.

"Oh—Tom?"

"Yeah?"

"People are asking if we're going to be working on the Fourth."

He stopped in his tracks. He hadn't even thought about it. "That's two days from now. Barry's ahead of schedule."

He looked around the office, not sure what he was trying to find. "Tell them, no. We all deserve a day off."

"Good. I was hoping you'd say so."

"You need a day off that badly?"

"No. I'm just wildly curious to see what people do to celebrate."

Tom snorted.

"Don't be rude, Tom. It looks like the Fourth will be a washout anyway, huh?'

"What do you mean?"

"Haven't you heard the weather forecasts? The biggest hurricane in fifty years is off the Atlantic coast. It's moving inland, and they're all saying its track will put it right over us, day after tomorrow."

"So we will have fireworks."

"Go home, Tom. I'll let you know if I can get through, okay?"

HE HAD LUNCH WITH RUTH. THERE WASN'T MUCH talk. They both avoided the subject of the demolition. Alex stayed in his room.

"They say a hurricane's coming." Ruth warmed up some beef stew.

"Yeah. These clouds must be the front edge of it."

"Just what Steadbridge needs."

There still had been no sign of Bill. Someone had found a few boards torn off one of the storefronts on the square, and it looked as if someone had been staying there. But there was no sign of whoever it was. And Tom was still convinced that Bill had been in the bell tower.

"Have you been in any of the stores lately?"

Tom was preoccupied, thinking about Ulmer's crew. "Hm?"

"The stores."

"What do you mean?"

"We're eating the last can of beef stew in town, Tom.

Supplies are running low everywhere. No one's been making deliveries because none of the store owners can contact them with orders."

He sighed deeply. "That's swell. They won't have to slaughter us all. They can just wait till we starve to death."

"This isn't funny."

"Do I sound amused? I don't know what we're . . . I don't know what we can do."

She ladled out the stew.

"Is this my fault, Ruth? Would this all be happening if I had never come back to Steadbridge?"

"I'm guessing it would. You're not that important."

"Thanks."

"Sooner or later someone would have wanted to tear the damned thing down. It just happened to be you and Overbrook."

He ate. "I wish I could feel confident of that. I feel like . . . hell, I don't know what I feel like."

"Tom, we're fast approaching a time when there won't be an undeveloped square yard of land anywhere in the country. Up in Mercer County, they're building a mall in a strip mine, for God's sake. This would have happened, sooner or later."

"I guess you're right. But I still—"

"Stop feeling sorry for yourself. You're not in this any deeper than the rest of us."

"No. I guess not." The stew was good. "I wonder if Mercer County has to deal with the ghosts of dead miners, though."

When they were finished he offered to wash the dishes. Drying them and putting them away, he noticed that Ruth's supply of liquor was running low. "I never thought it would happen."

"We've been drinking a lot. And as I said, stocks are running low."

From upstairs, softly, came the sound of voices. They looked at each other, puzzled. Without saying a word Ruth walked out to the living room, to the foot of the stairs, to listen. Tom followed.

Alex's voice. And a man's.

Ruth ran up the steps, with Tom right behind her. When they got to Alex's room the window was wide open and the screen had been removed.

The boy looked at them. "F-father Bill was here."

Ruth gaped at the open window.

"He s-s-says he's s-sorry for what he did."

Tom got down on a knee beside him. "Are you all right?"

"Yeah, I guess so. I was scared at first. But he was crying. He s-s-seemed real scared."

"He's wanted by the police, Alex. We didn't want to tell you."

"I knew."

"Oh."

Ruth went to the window and looked out. There was no sign of him. She turned to Alex. "If he comes here again, I want you to call me right away."

"He's s-sorry."

"Alex." She made her voice firm. "If he comes again, you call me or Tom. Understand?"

Her seriousness seemed to unsettle him. "Okay."

She busied herself replacing the window screen. Tom asked Alex what Bill had said.

"He said he was sorry."

"And what else? Did he say where he's hiding?"

Alex shook his head.

"Then what else did he tell you?"

Alex looked from Tom to his mother and back, uncertain what they wanted to hear. Ruth got the screen back in place and turned to face the two of them.

"He told me . . ."

"Yes?"

"He told me he wants to be our priest again."

"If Father McEntee goes the way of his lawyer, he may get his wish."

"Huh?"

"Nothing, Alex. I'm just being a smartass."

"Oh." Alex reached for his sketch pad. "The usual. Mom, I'm s-s-scared."

"We're all scared. It doesn't sound like Father Bill wants to hurt you any more. Is that . . . is that his picture you're drawing?"

"It's not of him." He held up the sketch pad. There was a portrait of Ruth, Alex and Tom inside the mill's blast furnace, visible through the open gate. Their faces were twisted with pain and what looked like rage.

"Alex, I want you to stop drawing things like this."

"I c-c-can't help it. It's what I s-see."

Tom took the sketch from him and studied it. "Have you ever 'seen' anything like this and had it not turn out to be true?"

He nodded. "Sometimes."

"Well, this won't turn out to be true. Okay?"

The boy seemed uncertain. "Okay."

Downstairs again, Ruth cried. "Tom, I'm terrified. Bill's crazy. He could do anything."

"It doesn't sound like he wants to hurt Alex now."

"Now." She said it emphatically. "What about ten minutes from now, or tomorrow afternoon? Tom, he's crazy. And we don't have any way of keeping him out of here."

"So we'll go back to having Alex sleep with us."

"And then?" She was getting more and more anxious. She looked around the room nervously. "If he comes back then? Look at what he did to you the last time. Can you stop him with those?"

Tom looked at his bandaged hands. "They're getting better. I have a lot of the use of them back."

"Tom, for Christ's sake, stop humoring me! We're stuck here, helpless, no police, no phone to call them even if there were any, no food, a town fill of vicious ghosts, and now . . ." She broke down completely. Tom put his arms around her, but she was sobbing uncontrollably. "I wish it was your fault, Tom. I wish it was that simple. I wish it was that easy to comprehend."

He held her tightly and waited for it to pass. There seemed nothing else he could do.

There came a knock on the door. Ruth quickly pulled away from him and tried to make herself presentable, straightening her hair, wiping her eyes. Tom opened the door.

It was Frank Ulmer. "Your secretary told me you'd be here." He looked past Tom and into the room; it was obvious something was wrong. Ruth went out to the kitchen. "I'm sorry, I didn't mean to interrupt."

"It's all right. What do you need?"

"We need you. Your people at Number Five say they need your authorization before they'll let us get to work."

"Oh."

"Can you call down there and . . . ?"

"I told you, we've been having trouble with the phones."

"Oh. Right. Can you come down yourself, then?"

"Give me a minute." He looked to the kitchen. "Tell you what, give me five. I'll be down as soon as I can."

Ulmer turned to go, with obvious reluctance. "Um, make it as soon as you can, okay? We really want to get everything placed so we can get home for the Fourth."

Almost against his will, Tom started to laugh. "Yeah, that'll happen."

THE ULMER CREW FOUND ANOTHER PLACE BILL had apparently been hiding, the empty offices at the back of the mill. One of the men, called Jack, showed it to Tom. Empty food packages, a few shirts he knew were Bill's, and a Bible.

"Should anybody be in here like this?" The man was

asking though he was sure, from his tone, he knew the answer.

Tom shook his head. "Tramps. We get them crashing in here now and then."

"Religious ones." The man picked up Bill's Bible and riffled the pages.

"Everybody has to believe in something."

He decided to ask Ulmer if his men could provide security. Ulmer scowled at the suggestion. "Maybe when we get back up here. After the holiday."

It was only a thought. "At the very least, you'll have to do a thorough sweep of the place before you push the button. Tramps. We don't want anyone killed."

"We're professionals, Mr. Kruvener. We know what we're doing."

"Right."

OF COURSE THAT NIGHT THEIR TRUCKS WOULDN'T start. Ulmer seemed to hold Tom personally responsible for it. "Jack is an ace mechanic, and he can't figure out why they won't run."

"What can I do?"

"You can put us in touch with a mechanic, that's what."

"Trust me, Frank, no one in town will be able to get your trucks going. I've had a few houses made ready for you."

Ulmer fumed. "Look, what the fuck is this? We need to get out of here. Our families are waiting. Our homes. We can't even call them—our phones aren't working."

"I'm sorry. There's nothing I can do but show you which houses are yours."

Tom got them settled—or as settled as they were willing to get. They were in the farthest block of Overbrook row houses, at the town limits. Jack was still fiddling under the hood of one of the trucks when Tom headed back to Ruth's.

When he got back he decided to treat Ruth, Alex and Maggie to dinner. He collected the three of them and they headed for Walchek's. When they got there, they found a sign posted on the door: CLOSED. NO FOOD. That was that. They went back to Ruth's and she cooked pasta.

Tom had moved Alex's bed into Ruth's room. Ruth put Alex to bed there, then fixed drinks for herself, Tom and Maggie.

"Is Alex all right?" Tom took a long swallow.

"He doesn't seem especially anxious. For once. And I think he's tired. He'll sleep all right."

Maggie tasted hers and scowled. "You're watering these."

"Supplies are running low, Mag. We have to ration."

"It's like drinking Kool Aid."

They sat talking together till the evening got late, then Maggie headed for her place. Tom and Ruth went to bed. Alex was fast asleep and not, to appearances, having any upsetting dreams.

LATE, VERY LATE, THE HOUSES WHERE ULMER'S men were sleeping began to quake. Groggily they woke up, one by one, and wondered what was happening. Ulmer went to his front window and looked out to see if this was an earth tremor of some kind. He had never heard of such a thing in this region, but . . .

As he stood there a fissure opened in the floor behind him. Fumes began to seep from it. He didn't quite recognize the odor, but it didn't smell right. He went to open the door and get out into the street, but it was locked. He pulled and pounded at it frantically.

All along that row of houses the scene was repeated. Cracks opened in floors and walls, more and more of them. Toxic fumes, acidic fumes slowly filled the air. One by one the men began to suffocate. The corrosive fumes peeled paint off the walls, rotted the fabrics of their clothes and ate away the men's lungs. They vomited blood. Then they were still.

Ulmer struggled to escape. A spray of sulfuric acid covered him. Screaming, he felt his flesh dissolve. Then he was dead like the others.

Slowly the fumes stopped.

NEXT MORNING WHEN THE BODIES WERE DISCOVered, a pall fell over the town, a deeper one than had been there. No one seemed to know what to do about what had happened, or even what to do with the bodies.

Ruth took charge. "I was the sheriff for years, in fact if not in name. I know where the forms are to record all of this. Not that it'll matter. We can't very well report it to anyone, can we?"

Not knowing what else to do, everyone deferred to her. She announced that she was commandeering the high-school gym to use as a makeshift morgue. "Any problem with that, Tom?"

He shook his head. "All the scenery and props are built already. And even so . . ." He spread his hands apart, as if to emphasize the empty air between them.

A few crew members with not much to do volunteered to help carry the corpses to the school. Ruth supervised, arranging them to her satisfaction, then going through what was left of the houses to try and find ID for them. She found drivers licenses for some of them; the rest went unidentified.

Barry took his cast and crew back to the square for retakes. He was not happy. Heavy clouds were building up. At ten o'clock in the morning it looked like twilight, and it was getting darker.

NO ONE TALKED MUCH THAT MORNING. TOM STOOD at a corner of the square watching the shoot. Angelo was missing; they had to shoot around him. Ruth joined Tom there. He kissed her on the cheek. "I hope the day hasn't been too much for you."

"It's not over yet. I'm here on official business. It looks like we have too many bodies."

"I don't know for sure how many there were." He didn't want to think about it. "A dozen or so."

"According to the stuff we found in Ulmer's truck, he brought exactly twelve. We have fifteen bodies."

He looked at the set. "Angelo's missing. But he wasn't in the row of—"

"I think his boyfriend was."

"Oh."

In the distant east there was a faint flash of lightning. Ruth ignored it. "Tomorrow's the Fourth, Tom."

He nodded.

"Remember how this square used to be on the Fourth of July every year?"

"I keep trying to forget it all, Ruth, every last bit of it." He put an arm around her, but she took a step away from him. "But I can't. It's in my blood, in my bones. Christ, how I hate it."

She sat down on a nearby bench. "Parades, the school band marching, hot dogs, fireworks after dark."

"I think we'll be able to manage those, at least."

"What's happened to us? To bring us to this?"

"Nothing that hasn't happened anywhere else. The world's getting old faster than we are, Ruth. That's a fact."

She glanced at her watch. "I should get home and check on Alex. Want some lunch?"

"No, thanks. I think I'll stay here and keep an eye on things."

She got up and left.

A moment later there was a ferocious gust of wind. The statue of McKinley rocked slightly on its base. Nicole saw it and screamed. It took Barry a while to get her calmed down so they could get on with the filming.

Tom closed his eyes and tried to imagine this film, his film, *The Colors of Hell*, being screened for an audience of kids at the Hippodrome. It was impossible.

He told Barry about Angelo.

"Damn. We'll have to use his stand-in and do a lot of long shots, I guess." Barry glanced at the sky. "If we can get any more work done at all, that is. Poor kid."

"Eric, Angelo . . ." Tom didn't want to be thinking about it. "We were supposed to be done by the Fourth."

Barry shrugged. "What can I do? Given the way things have gone . . ."

"The home office won't be happy." The wind gusted, a cold, damp wind. Tom wrapped his arms around himself. "But they can fuck themselves."

LATE MORNING. RUTH ENTERED HER HOUSE, NOT expecting to find anything unusual. She found Alex sitting in front of the television, watching a weather bulletin. The storm was expected to be as strong as any on record.

She kissed him on the top of his head. "Hungry?"

"No, not really."

"I could make some burgers."

"Ask Father Bill."

She stopped dead. "What did you say?"

"He might be hungry. Go ask him."

Without hesitating she ran to the stairs and climbed to the second floor. Bill was there, in Alex's room, looking at his drawings. The window was wide open again, no screen. When he heard her he looked up and smiled a gentle smile. "Hell. He sees hell."

"What are you doing here?" She looked down the steps. She could make a dash for the kitchen and get a knife.

"Hello, Ruth." He smiled again. His voice sounded weary. She took a step backward, into the hall.

"Please don't be afraid. I'm better now."

Another step.

"Ruth, I'm sorry for what I did. I was . . . I don't know, I was out of my head or something. I never wanted to hurt you. Any of you."

"I want you to leave here, Bill." She found a bit of resolve. "Now."

He put the sketches aside. "Please can't you just tell me you forgive me? I'm truly sorry."

"Save your confession for God."

"You're my best friend. You and Tom. If you don't understand, how will anyone else?"

"That's not my problem. Will you go?" She backed further into the hall.

"Go and get your knife, if that's what you want."

"How did you know I—"

He leafed slowly, carefully through the drawings and held one up. It was a picture of him, dead or dying, blood all over him, a knife in his stomach.

It was more than she could handle. She turned and ran back down the steps. Alex saw her coming and jumped up. She caught him by the hand and pulled him out into the street. There was a wild wind kicking up, gusting; she could smell rain on it.

"Mom, it's okay."

"No. He's—he could do anything."

"No. He's going to die."

"Stop talking like that. Stop saying things like that! You don't know. The things you see aren't true."

"A lot of them are." He sounded hurt, or disappointed.

She saw Bill climb out the window and jump onto the roof of the next house. He disappeared over the roof.

Ruth put her arms around Alex and hugged him. He pulled away.

"He's going to die, mom. We should love him."

NOON. DESPITE THE COLD WIND THE TEMPERATURE began to rise. At the square Barry canceled the day's shoot.

At the Overbrook office Rachel found herself sweating. She opened all the windows, but wind tore through all the rooms, upsetting everything. She closed them again, quickly, wondering how such a chill wind could be sending the temperature up.

Maggie woke up in her bedroom with a hangover, to find her bed soaked with sweat. From the darkness outside she thought it must be evening. Then she glanced at the wristwatch on the nightstand and saw that it was early afternoon. She poured herself another tall drink, rolled over and went to sleep again.

At McKinley Square a blast of wind tipped over the statue. It fell to the ground with a loud crash, but there was no one to hear it.

The bells in St. Dympna's tower began to ring, driven by the wind this time. Father McEntee stood at the foot of the tower stairs and stared up, wondering what he could do. He was hot, the interior of the church was intolerably hot, and he loosened his collar. Mrs. Charnocki joined him with glasses of lemonade. She drank hers quickly and covered her ears with her hands. "Make them stop, father."

"How? I can't."

The bells could be heard all over town. The film crew at Number Five and the ones at the highschool wondered what was causing it, the wind, or . . .

The people at the mill were sweating. The men took their shirts off. It kept getting worse. Before too long the heat was intolerable, and they got out. They stood in the street, staring from one another to the mill wondering what to do. Finally someone said they should get to the highschool and find Tom.

Just as they were about to cross the square they met him. He was walking around Steadbridge, trying to keep an eye on everything, trying to understand what was happening. He asked them why they weren't at the mill, and they told him.

"It's that hot there?"

One of the men nodded.

"Wait at the school, then."

He decided to head for Number Five himself, to see. There was a gust of wind strong enough to knock two of the men over, then it subsided. The air was oven-hot despite it. A sudden squall of rain drenched everyone, then like the wind it passed.

The bells above them rang clamorously, deafeningly. Father McEntee and Mrs. Charnocki ran from the building into the square, covering their ears. McEntee crossed to Tom and caught him by his shirt. "What kind of a place is this?"

Tom pulled free of him. "You're the theologian. You tell me."

He left the square, heading for the mill. On the way he stopped at Ruth's. She looked frantic. "Alex is gone."

He poured her the last of the gin and hoped it would calm her down. "I'll see if I can find him. I think he must be at the mill again. Everything seems to be centered there."

"Tom, it's never been like this. I'm terrified."

He kissed her. "I know. I can see it."

"I'm coming with you."

They went to the mill as quickly as the hostile wind would let them. Tom noticed that the closer they got, the more unbearable the heat became. Even there they could hear the bells, ringing insanely.

The mill was afire. Inside, not out. The furnaces were blazing, and the building radiated with their heat more fiercely than it ever had. Fifty feet away the Ulmer & Fuest trucks were parked in a row.

Ruth took Tom's hand. "Even when it was alive it wasn't like this."

Lightning struck a mile away. Thunder shook the ground. There was another rapid rain squall, and it passed as quickly as the first.

"Tom, look at the river."

They walked to the bank. It was running more swiftly

than either of them could remember. And it was rising; it was within two feet of the bank.

"It must be raining heavily upriver. It'll be here soon."

"For God's sake, Tom, what can we do?"

"McEntee asked me the same thing."

At the river-side entrance to the mill they saw Alex. He was standing there, staring inside, his body outlined in bright yellow by the fires. He was wide-eyed and not moving. Tom went to him quickly and caught hold of his hand. "Come on, Alex. We have to go home."

"They're going to kill everyone, Tom."

"No. They're dead. They can't hurt us."

"They can."

"Come with me and your mom. We should be together."

Ruth joined them and they all started to go. More lightning, more thunder, more rain. The mill shook. The fires inside danced more brightly. Trying to steady herself against a blast of wind, Ruth touched the wall. In was so hot it burned her hand. Tom took off part of one of his bandages and wrapped it for her.

There were other people coming to the mill, crew members, townspeople. A small group of them stood outside the main gate. More were coming, winding through the streets to Number Five, as if they were going to a church or a shrine. Their clothes were soaked with sweat. Some of them were carrying umbrellas.

Tom addressed them, told them all to go home.

"No, Tom. It's too hot to be comfortable there. Or anywhere else. And the bells are driving us mad. What's happening is happening here."

He looked back over his shoulder at the mill. "I'll be at Ruth's. If anything happens, come get me. If it gets worse."

"How could it get worse?"

Without answering, he left.

ALL AFTERNOON PEOPLE KEPT COMING TO THE
mill, film people, townspeople. They came compulsively,
almost hypnotically, it seemed; they stood, stared, waited.
When the heat became too much, they would leave for a
while to rest and recover, as much as the bells would let
them, and then return. The building became hotter and hotter.

Rain squalls were more frequent and heavier. People
stood huddled under umbrellas, fighting the wind. When
the rain hit Number Five, it boiled into steam with a loud
hiss. At times it was so loud it drowned out the constant
clanging of the bells, off in McKinley Square.

At Ruth's house she gave Alex a pill then put him to bed
for a nap; then she and Tom both went to bed too. Alex
waited patiently in his room till they fell asleep, then went
into the kitchen and poured a glass of red wine. He drank it
in three swallows, then went up to his room and slept. His
dreams were troubled. He saw death everywhere in Steadbridge.

Bill Vicosz climbed in the bedroom window. He stood
looking at Alex silently for a moment, then went to the
master bedroom and watched Tom and Ruth. They were in
each other's arms.

The bells stopped. Bill looked to the window. He bent
down and touched Tom's cheek, then climbed out the window into the growing storm.

AT DINNER TIME THE RAIN BEGAN TO FALL
steadily, not in squalls. It was heavier than anyone could
remember, and it was driven by ferocious wind. There was
more lightning than anyone in town had ever seen. Despite
it they all stood and watched what was happening to Number Five. As the late afternoon light began to fade, they
could see it was glowing hot, a dull red.

Tom, Ruth and Alex woke at almost the same time,
roused by the sound of the driving wind and rain. They had

a quick meal. Then they had to see the mill again. By the time they got there nearly everyone in town was there, the children, the infirm and elderly, everyone.

Tom walked to the riverbank. The water was running even more swiftly. And it was only four inches from the bank. If the rain didn't stop there would be a flood.

"Tom!" Alex ran to him and took tight hold of his hand. The pain made Tom wince but he bore it; the boy was in a state of panic. "They're coming, Tom."

At that moment, with a roar, a pillar of fire sprang out of the mill. At first it climbed the smokestack; then a moment later it separated from it and took on a life of its own. It twisted, spiraled, climbed, grew. A hundred feet tall, taller than the smokestack, whirling and roaring like a cyclone. Everyone ran; they didn't know where to go, where might be safe, so they scattered in every direction. The column of flame grew taller.

Inside the mill the furnaces roared. Molten steel flowed. The ghosts of men dead and mutilated stoked the fires. The temperature was unbearable. If there was no other reason to flee the mill, the awful heat would have driven everyone away. The earth shook. Phantom locomotives crawled along long-unused tracks. They shuttled in and out of the mill, off into the driving, blinding rain, and disappeared, to be replaced by more. Fire and ash spewed from them, adding to the hellish scene.

The mill still glowed, brighter red than before. The cold wind and rain were doing nothing to cool it. Lightning struck the smokestack. In the column of fire were the faces of the dead, Mike and Melissa, Grandma McKibben, Eric, Angelo, Ulmer and hundreds more, generations of dead no one knew or remembered. Tom saw his father, Ruth her husband.

Tom, Ruth and Alex stood at the mill entrance, gaping at the scene. Alex pulled a sketch from his shirt: He had seen this and drawn it, he had known it was coming. Before he could show it to Ruth the rain blurred the ink. In only moments all he held was a large blank sheet of paper. The church bells began to ring again.

Maggie woke and saw the pillar from her window. The top of it swayed back and forth, as if the wind was affecting it. Nicole stood in the center of Laurel Street, staring at the blazing column and trembling. Isabel joined her and held her. Tony Kowalski had fallen asleep in an empty house, a needle still in his arm. He woke up and thought he was dreaming. Barry Hall found a camera and tried to film the pillar but the mechanism wouldn't work.

Gradually everyone gathered in the street outside the Overbrook office. Rachel ran to Tom's side, in a terror. "What do we do?"

"A pillar of fire." Maggie had to shout to be heard above the roar and the clanging of St. Dympna's bells. "It's like something from the Bible."

"No." Rachel could not take her eyes off it. "It's like a medieval vision of hell."

Tom stared at it. It was both beautiful and terrifying.

The temperature was still climbing.

Then the fire began to move. It swayed and shot out streamers of fire like tentacles. They extended into the air, they curved and arced over the mill, then disappeared back into the column.

A long streamer shot out of the pillar and hit a row of houses. In a moment they were engulfed in flames, so intense it took the rain long minutes to begin to put them out.

More streamers developed, then disappeared. One arced high overhead and seemed to strike McKinley Square. The glow of fire came from there, then like the first one subsided. Lightning struck all around, starting more fires.

A tongue of flame licked the Ulmer & Fuest trucks. They were still loaded with explosives. The roar of the blast shook the town more violently than anything had yet. A fireball rose into the sky and dissipated.

A moment later the river topped its banks. Water poured though the streets of Steadbridge. Tom cried out, "Everyone get up on the roofs! Get to the highest place you can!" Everyone rushed into the nearest houses and climbed.

But Alex, seeing the onrush, panicked and ran. Ruth and Tom bolted after him.

Streamers of fire leaped from the column at the mill and set fire to half the town. The rain fought down the flames, as if there was a contest to decide which element could be more destructive. The water in the streets rose, four inches, six. Thunder roared, lightning flashed, the church bells never stopped pealing.

Tom finally managed to catch Alex just as he was entering McKinley Square. Ruth caught up to them a moment later. The square was becoming a small lake. Tom pointed upward. "There! The bell tower!"

"No, Tom, it's too loud!" Ruth held onto Alex tightly. He clung to her.

"It's the highest place. We have to."

He pulled open the church door. The water was rising, climbing the church steps just behind them. Tom led them quickly to the tower steps and they climbed. The bells were louder than seemed possible.

In an instant they were at the top. Tom tried to catch the bells, to stop them, but they were swinging too violently. Ruth covered Alex's ears.

There was someone else there. Bill Vicosz. He stepped out of a dark corner. He shouted, "You shouldn't have come up here."

Ruth panicked when she saw him. She moved behind Tom, pulling Alex after her.

"It's all right, Ruth, I won't hurt you. God's doing that."

All around them Steadbridge was ablaze; the fires seemed to dance on the surface of the water. Below, they could see people and debris being carried off by the rushing flood. Lightning struck the bell tower and it trembled violently. The pillar of fire spiraled at the mill; everything around it was in flames.

Two miles upriver more lightning struck the dam. It

cracked, and in a moment the raging water breached it. Millions of gallons roared downstream.

In the tower, none of them spoke. The apocalyptic scene, fire and flood, horrified them all into silence.

Then the surge hit. Cars and buildings washed away. Trees rushed like missiles, careening into buildings, demolishing them. The Hippodrome collapsed into a pile of rubble and was washed away. The water was twelve, fourteen feet deep. People fought the raging current for their lives, uselessly. One by one they drowned or were dashed to pieces against trees, buildings, rocks.

The church shuddered. Below them they saw it start to crumble under the force of the flood. The crack in the facade widened, Large chunks fell into the raging water. The flood filled the sanctuary. Wooden pews and the altar were carried out and away. One by one the walls weakened and collapsed.

Ruth threw her arm around Tom, still holding Alex in the other one. "We're going to die. Alex was right. We're going to die." Above them the bells swung wildly, the bells roared almost as loudly as the flood.

"No." Bill took a step toward them. When he saw Ruth recoil, he stopped. "The tower is a separate structure from the church. It's more solid. We'll be safe."

Another lightning bolt struck it. Alex, terrified, pulled free of his mother and ran. He climbed up on the ledge and stared down, panicked by everything he saw.

Bill lunged for him and caught him.

Alex screamed. "Let me go! Let me go!" He struggled and pulled himself free. Scrambling to get a grip on him, Bill slipped and tumbled over the ledge.

Tom ran there. Bill was hanging by one hand above the torrent. Tom reached out and tried to help him. Bill gripped his hand, and it exploded with pain. Without thinking he pulled back, and Bill fell down into the raging water. In an instant he was gone.

Lightning struck all around them. The church crumbled

to nothing, but the tower stood. The roar of the bells shattered Alex's eardrums; blood cascaded from his ears. Then they stopped. The pillar of fire faded and was gone.

The three of them stood and watched the storm, the flood. All of Steadbridge was gone. Gradually the flood waters subsided and the rain slowed to a steady shower. They curled up in one another's arms and slept.

When the Fourth of July dawned, all that was left of Steadbridge was the bell tower and three people trying be a family, not knowing quite how.

Epilogue

ALEX WAS ASLEEP IN THE BACK SEAT OF THE CAR.
Tom drove slowly, carefully. Ruth, beside him in the
passenger seat, read a newspaper.

"It says here we're the guests of honor."

"Lucky us."

"The only survivors of what they're calling the Steadbridge tragedy."

"Lucky us again."

It was high summer. The Mon Valley was lush and
green and, to all appearances, healthy. They passed the
hotel where Tom had stayed when he first came back to
Steadbridge. The sign in front read NO VACANCY.

For two years they had lived together in New York. Tom
had found a large three-bedroom apartment in Queens that
wasn't too hideously expensive. And Overbrook had given
him a promotion and a raise. No one there ever really
understood what had happened. The flood had destroyed
everything, including their movie, giving them a plum of a

tax write-off; that was as much as they seemed to want to know, and Tom wasn't about to upset any apple carts. Ruth, despite his repeated proposals, refused to marry him.

Overbrook decided the wasteland that had been a town must be ripe for redevelopment. They wanted Tom to supervise the project, but he refused adamantly. He tended to other business and occasionally advised the Steadbridge crew, usually by telling them to leave the place alone. "The dead are happier dead and forgotten," he always told them. He made it sound like a joke.

Overbrook forged ahead with their plans. Insurance more than covered their losses from the film, and the courts had declared the flood an "act of God" so there was no liability. But Phil Morrissey and the others could not seem to let go of the idea of Steadbridge.

The ribbon-cutting for the new Steadbridge Mall—it had narrowly missed being called the Overbrook Mall—was to be the signal event in the area's rebirth. Tom's presence was required. It was made clear to him that he was to bring Ruth and Alex, "for the PR value."

He decided to drive. Everyone wanted them to fly, first-class as befit an Overbrook executive. But Tom had driven the last time he went home to Steadbridge; he wanted to drive again. He wanted to see how the valley had changed, close-to.

Alex had thrived in Manhattan. His art teachers all assured Ruth and Tom he was extraordinarily talented. After a time they even stopped trying to coax him away from the scenes of horror and the supernatural he liked to draw. The fact that St. Dympna's bells had made him deaf hardly seemed to matter to him. He mastered sign language quickly—much more so than either Tom or Ruth, so that he frequently had to teach them—and not having to speak any more, not have to struggle with his stammer, seemed a relief to him. In two years his talent had developed enormously.

He woke and looked out at the valley. There were small

towns, some so small there weren't even signs to tell their names. None of them seemed to be thriving or lively. It was all serene and beautiful, except for an occasional chemical refinery or cement works or coal processing facility. Many of them were abandoned, as empty as United American Number Five had been. He tapped Ruth on the shoulder and signed, "We're home."

She smiled and nodded. It did not occur to her to ask what that meant to him.

A sign proclaimed:

STEADBRIDGE MALL

OVERBROOK MEANS PROGRESS

GRAND OPENING CEREMONY 2 P.M.

FREE BEER (WITH VALID ID)

Tom pulled into a parking area designated for VIPs, half a block from the mall. They all got out and stretched.

The mall looked nothing like the artificial one from *The Colors of Hell.* It was not on the same site. But the architects had incorporated what was left of St. Dympna's bell tower into a corner of it. At a meeting they had insisted it would "add interest to the building" and "maintain the region's history." Tom asked why they thought that desirable, but they dismissed the question with the contempt of "artists" for businesspeople. Around it, new housing developments were beginning to go up, also owned by Overbrook.

Ruth paused to inspect the building. "That tower looks idiotic. The horrific old infecting the antiseptic new."

"Or vice versa." Tom looked around. Except for the tower, nothing was recognizable. McKinley Square might never have existed.

A crowd was gathering. Overbrook had advertised the event widely, and even flown in a few minor soap stars to help attract the public. News crews from Johnstown and

Altoona were covering the opening as if it actually meant something. The offer of free beer had even drawn students from a few state universities in the region. A knot of them stood together, drinking happily, acting rowdy.

When it was time for the ribbon-cutting, the beer was cut off. The students grumbled but were too drunk to do much else.

Phil was there, officiating. There were speeches by state and county officials, none very interesting, the usual political/PR stuff. Tom, Ruth and Alex were introduced and paraded before the cameras. Alex was quiet and well-behaved. Tom hated it all. "I feel like the prize hound at a dog show."

Ruth smirked. "What do you think you are?"

After what seemed forever the ribbon was cut and the mall opened for business. Phil conducted a tour, more PR. With pride he pointed out all the franchises and the food court, as if they were something novel.

AMONG THE COLLEGE STUDENTS WAS PAUL GORdon, a fraternity boy who had had eight beers in under an hour. He tapped his friend Tank Kowalski, no relation to the Steadbridge Kowalskis, on the shoulder. "Let's get the fuck out of here."

Tank was cruising a coed from another school. She was ignoring him. He told Paul, "Yeah. This sucks."

They stumbled out of the mall and reeled a few blocks, being more sterotypically loud and crude than they could have realized. Tank kept repeating, "I want to screw that bitch." Despite this resolve, he kept walking with Paul.

They reached the site where Number Five had stood. Overbrook's crews had leveled it quite thoroughly. There was a memorial plaque marking the spot, but neither Tank nor Paul bothered to read it.

Washington Island was lush and green. Pulaski Bridge had been washed away by the flood. There had been talk at

Overbrook of replacing it, but it was deemed to be not cost-effective. Paul looked at the island, then at Tank, and said, "Let's swim out there."

Tank looked at Paul, then at the island, and said, "Yeah."

They stripped. Tank was an athlete, a star baseball player. His body was beautiful. He dove in.

The water was colder than they expected. It sobered them up a bit. They began splashing each other playfully, grabbing at each other, each trying to duck the other one.

Then Tank felt hands touching him, not in a way he liked. Paul was ten feet away. Hands touched him, too. There were men under the water, strong men, men with muscles he could feel.

Struggling, they were pulled under the surface, and they drowned. Paul resigned himself to it quickly. Tank's face held a puzzled expression as his lungs filled with water.

Since there was nothing going on at the mill site, no one found their clothes for days, and no one even noticed they had left, except the coed Tank had been hitting on, who didn't mind at all that they were gone.

Three days later their bodies washed up on the river-bank near Pittsburgh, seventy miles downriver.

RUTH, ALEX AND TOM SPENT THE NIGHT AT A BED-and-breakfast near Altoona. None of them wanted to sleep in Steadbridge. Early the next morning they hit the road back to New York.

As they were getting into the car Tom said, "Well, that's that. The last of Number Five and its ghosts."

Ruth translated for Alex as he crawled into the back seat.

Alex signed, "No."

But neither Tom nor Ruth saw him.

The debut novel that's a
masterpiece of modern suspense—

THE STRAW MEN

by

MICHAEL MARSHALL

Three seemingly unrelated events are the
first signs of an unimaginable network of fear that
will lead one unlikely hero to a chilling
confrontation with The Straw Men.
No one knows what they want—or why they kill.
But they must be stopped.

YOU KNOW WHO THEY ARE...
IF YOU'VE EVER KNOWN FEAR.

0-515-13427-9

**Available wherever books are sold or at
www.penguin.com**